The Silent Final

Henk Vaessen

The Silent Final

Novel

Uitgeverij Aspekt 2009

The Silent Final

© Henk Vaessen
© 2009 Uitgeverij ASPEKt
Amersfoortsestraat 27, 3769 AD Soesterberg, the Netherlands
info@uitgeverijaspekt.nl - http://www.uitgeverijaspekt.nl

Translation from the original Dutch text: Marijcke Jongbloed
Translation and restyling poems: John Pac
Final editing: Johanna Ruizendaal and Jim Congleton

Photo front cover: Henk Vaessen
Foto back cover: Bram van de Biezen
Foto author: Klaas van de Streek

Jacket design: Aspekt Graphics
Typography: Uitgeverij Aspekt Graphics
Print: Krips b.v. Meppel

ISBN-10: 90-5911-839-1
ISBN-13: 978-90-5911-839-3
NUR: 300

All rights reserved. No part of this publication may be reproduced in any form or by any means without the written permission of the publisher.

for Robert Leonardus

We can only reconcile
ourselves with our future
when we accept the past

Harald Richter - Pastor in Ladelund

CONTENTS

Prologue … 9

Part 1 … 17

Part 2 … 119

Part 3 … 219

Glossary … 383

Explanation and accountability … 388

PROLOGUE

It was during the severe winter of 1962 that Jacob and Saar van Zuiden spent a week's vacation on the island of Texel, together with their young children, two sons and two daughters. On a fine, sunny afternoon Jacob asked who felt like taking a brisk walk. Only fourteen-year old Benjamin, the younger son, stepped forward. And so once again they left together, as they so often did. First from *De Cocksdorp* to the southwest; then via nature reserve *De Slufter* towards the North Sea and from there back again to the north along the beach.

As usual they said little. Their own thoughts sufficed and they shared them only very sparingly - about the beautiful, pristine nature around them and sometimes, as an exception, something about life. Then they retreated again into long silences that both treasured as a pleasant change from the noise and liveliness of the family which they would rejoin later.

The need to be together without any obligation to explain everything they felt was the essential and unspoken secret of their bond. Jacob recognized in Benjamin the old "Van-Zuiden-clan", whereas his elder son David did not give him this feeling.

Esther, their third child, also had the same quiet, introvert nature. However, with Benjamin he felt that in his own, quiet manner he had the need to share certain things with him.

When after hours of walking, they approached *Post 28* in the early dusk and Jacob was already preparing himself for the reunion with his family, something happened that he had not at all expected.

'Papa?' Benjamin said hesitantly.

Jacob looked at his son in anticipation.

'Yes, what is it?' he asked when Benjamin still hesitated.

The boy thought a bit longer and then asked with touching caution: 'Did you know Mengele... I mean, wasn't he also there in... you know... uh... there in *Auschwitz?*'

Obviously it had not escaped Benjamin, Jacob gathered, that recently it had been mentioned a few times in the news that the infamous camp doctor might have been spotted somewhere in South America, but even so the question surprised him. It was the first time that one of his children asked him about his wartime past. Their mother had undoubtedly impressed upon them that he did not want to talk about it and that was true. However, now for some reason he did not want to remain silent. There was something in their relationship – something exclusive – stemming from dominantly inherited factors that gave them a special bond. A wonderful unity that he also used to have with Brammie, his twin brother. That feeling had faded, however, when Bram had left for Israel. But what he had with his own son was an even more intense feeling to him.

David, with his obvious Jewish appearance, his commercial instinct and hyperactive life, might seem to be the one in which the "Van Zuiden clan" would manifest itself in the future, but he felt that it was Benjamin who was destined to be the keeper of their spiritual inheritance. Benjamin would guard it, carefully store it in the silent depths of his soul and would only bring it to light when it was really necessary and would pass it on to those for whom he thought it was destined.

He looked into the questioning eyes of his son, gave him a familiar pat on the shoulder and sighed: 'Oh yes, Mengele ... I knew him...'

Looking around he saw that they were about a hundred meters away from the old beach pavilion.

'Come,' he said, 'let's have a drink there and then I shall tell you about it...'

The owner was just throwing some sturdy logs into the large Franklin stove. An old leather sofa stood in front of it, on which they sat down. As he bent forward Benjamin looked with fascination at the flames that burned high. When the man closed the door of the stove again, the crackling and roaring of the fire in the steel chimney drowned out the voice of his father, who was ordering some drinks. Jacob smiled as he watched Benjamin curl his hands around the mug of hot chocolate, seeing how the heat returned the color to his cheeks.

He himself sipped from his glass of "Berenburg" and put it on the small table at his side.

He countered the surprised look of his son, who saw his father drink an alcoholic drink for the first time, with a mischievous smile: 'Listen, son, when Jews refrain from drinking alcohol they do this because it dulls the spirit. This first sip was to get warm and the last I'll save until just before we go home. Because telling about the war as well as knowing how your mother will react when we get home far too late, believe me – it will be very nice to be a little tipsy then…'

Attentively Benjamin listened to what his father then quietly told him…

Starting with their forefathers – the Jeda family – that fled Poland long ago and ended up in Holland via Germany and Belgium… That, due to the restrictions imposed on Jews even in Holland, Benjamin's grandmother Liese, one of the daughters of that family, had as a young girl spent a long time in the penal colony Veenhuizen accused of vagrancy and begging… How she met the peddler Samuel van Zuiden somewhere along the road and married him, after which they settled in Elburg.

'Until the war started, we had a good life, were a family just like any other, but then…'

Jacob fell silent and sighed deeply. Cautiously Benjamin looked at him. He saw how his father stared into the flames and prepared himself for the most difficult part of his story, the climax…

'It took three days and three nights by train from *Westerbork* to *Auschwitz*,' he said finally. He paused again. Then without interruption he continued his account that was so awe-inspiring to Benjamin...

'That trip was a nightmare, three days and nights without food or water... sitting and lying on the ground... It was freezing and the stench of the children and adults that had died of exhaustion and dysentery and had been put in a corner of the cattle car became more and more penetrating. In order to stay warm we huddled closer. My brothers and I rubbed our frostbite-threatened limbs. We did not say anything. We only looked at each other with eyes wide with fear and listened to the coughing and moaning of the weak ones.

Finally the train drew to a halt and the wire with which the door of the cattle car had been fastened was cut. The first sound was that of barking dogs and the worst thing is that I can never get rid of that. I mean, every time when I hear the sound of something being cut with a wire cutter or when I hear dogs barking, I dream of *Auschwitz* that night. I wished that it would be over by now but on the contrary, it seems to be getting worse. And that is the reason why I am often so quiet and especially so tired. Believe me, son, you get so tired, so terribly tired of all those memories that keep coming back... triggered again and again by the slightest image or sound...

The SS had opened the door, a whip or rubber club in one hand and big black dogs on a tight leash in the other. They chased us, cursing and ranting, out of the cattle car. As we hobbled to the end of the platform in single file, suddenly my twin brother Brammie was walking beside me. He had been in another car together with our parents and my sister. "It's pretty bad here", he said. I gave him a questioning look and he reacted: "Don't you see those piles of suitcases there...? Why do you think they have meters-high fences of barbed wire here and that smoke and the stench...?" He pointed at a dark column of smoke in front of us.

The end of the platform was also the end of the rails and there the people were divided into two groups. Young, strong men and women – and some children – had to go to the right and were put to work later or used for the experiments of doctor Mengele. Sick, old and weak people together with the remaining children had to turn left and follow the signs that said: *To the baths and inhalation center.*

Totally bewildered and anxious I stood watching all this and tried to understand in what kind of nightmare we had landed, when suddenly Brammie said cheerfully: "They play music here", and he pointed to an army truck on which half a dozen men in striped pyjamas were standing, each holding a musical instrument. "This is our chance!" He grabbed my shoulder and pushed me right in front of a group of officers. He pressed his head against mine and said with a huge grin, pointing first at himself and then at me: "We are performers, *Die Zwei Smousies* and we have a marvellous show!" He bowed deeply, performing an elegant sweep with his left arm while pressing his right hand on my shoulder so firmly that I also had to bow. One of the officers answered, laughing at his colleagues: "Dogs that make people laugh… that I have to see!" The man who said that… that was doctor Mengele!'

Jacob fell silent and Benjamin saw in his father's eyes a pained expression that he had seen before, and of which he suddenly understood the cause.

A few times Jacob nodded slowly and sighed: 'Yes, dogs they called us, but those animals were treated better than we were.'

He looked at Benjamin and told him: 'What happened after that I cannot tell you because it was worse, far worse than can ever be expressed in words. The mass murders…! The horrific experiments with children… and the… the…'

He stopped talking and stared into the fire, overwhelmed by emotions. Benjamin gazed at him and asked himself what his father was thinking about now and what he could not or would not put into words. He did not dare ask, because it was undoubtedly something that was even worse than what he had told already. Finally Jacob slowly shook his head, took a deep breath and added: 'When evil possesses a nation to such an extent, people become beasts and life becomes hell.'

When they walked home in the darkness that had fallen on the island, Jacob explained how through the evil in the world there will always be people who for some reason or another will despise others; and that, due to the terrible consequences of this, he must always be aware of it, and he must never look on passively or be silent whenever it threatens to happen.

'For,' he concluded, 'every person should have the same chances and everything that lives is holy.'

Then he fell silent and walking in the quiet of the dark night, he allowed the boy to think about all that he had heard. Just when they approached their holiday home Benjamin halted and asked hesitantly: 'But… uh… say, all those Germans, you know, who murdered so many people…? Should they not be punished for that…?'

Jacob said: 'It is written: *God punishes, man takes revenge.* Hitler also thought the Jews had to be punished and you have seen what the consequence was. When God punishes it is always based on love, on making you aware of the wrong you have done and… you always get a chance to better your life. When people punish, it is more often than not based on retribution and revenge. Often it ends in hatred and you cannot live in hatred. That destroys you and others as well. And therefore you should leave punishment to God.' He took hold of Benjamin's shoulder and said in a low voice: 'Now we have talked enough, don't you think? Come, let's go and see if they left us anything to eat.'

But the boy remained standing and asked: 'But isn't God almighty and uh… couldn't He have made sure that it… you know… that it did not happen at all…?'

In Jacob's head the question mingled with the memories of all the times he had asked himself that question. He still had not really found an answer to it, but the thought that could possibly lead to one he did not want to keep from Benjamin...

'OK,' he said, 'what I am going to say to you now is not going to be an answer to your question. At best it is a beginning of an answer, but still you should never forget it...

At the lowest point of the misery in *Auschwitz* I sometimes wished that the Eternal One – praised be His name – would have chosen another people than ours. Through the institutions that were handed down through the ages and followed meticulously, our thinking and acting has often been at odds with that of other peoples. At the same time those who founded new developments in all sorts of areas were very often Jews. I just want to say, because His mark is so clearly upon us, it was in a certain sense inevitable that we were overwhelmed by jealousy and discrimination.

When I myself nearly became the victim of this, there were two people that saved me. First there was your uncle Bram. Everyone may think that we are identical, but I alone know and have experienced where he differs from me and that is in his incredible optimism. He was the main reason why I did not lose the courage to continue living.

But the person through whom I regained the real will to live, that was Mordecai. As a messenger of the Highest he brought the joy and gratitude of being a Jew back to life in me again.

How that happened, I'll tell you another time, but the most important thing for you now is the message of Mordecai, because it also applies to you... "Until the Messiah comes, the Eternal One, whenever He wants to reveal Himself in my life and that of my children and grandchildren, He will do so on the day after Passover".'

Without understanding Benjamin looked at his father but felt that he should not ask him anything more now. Silently they walked the last stretch home and there, from the depths of Jacob's soul, the age-old testimony rose up and, in the silence that surrounded them, entered the heart of his son... *Shoma Israel, Adonai Elohenou Adonai Egad... hear Israel, the Eternal our God, the Eternal is One...*

PART 1

1

From the end of the 17th Century the Jewish community in Elburg had left its own colorful impression on the daily life of the old fishing town at the edge of the Zuiderzee. None of that remained. The Second World War put a sudden end to it. Those that had made such a unique contribution to the Elburg society were mercilessly snatched away. Almost all perished in the extermination camps of *Sobibor, Treblinka* and *Auschwitz*.

The families of De Lange and Israëls had left in time; they went into hiding in Nunspeet and after the war went to live somewhere else. Joop Cohen, the butcher, who had also found a hiding place in time, survived the war.

Jacob and his twin brother Abraham were the only Jewish inhabitants of Elburg who had together survived the concentration camp. They owed this purely to their musical talents. Jacob played the mandolin and Abraham the clarinet. Up until their liberation by the Russians they entertained German officers, as members of the camp orchestra, during their parties. In addition they created short acts that they performed together, a few at a time, alternating with the music.

Drawing on the rich well of Jewish humor, using their remarkable physical resemblance, they presented themselves with great success as the gangly pair *Die Zwei Smousies*. Thus they made themselves "useful" to the Germans and this allowed them, in contrast to all those others, to survive. Day after day they saw how the children of their people were murdered in large numbers, but in the evening they had to entertain the perpetrators with their music and their jokes.

Jacob was the one who minded this the most. And when it was almost certain that all their other family members had died in the gas chambers, he could not stand it any longer. Abraham tried to convince him of the necessity to continue.

'If we stop,' he said, 'we take away the only reason for the Germans to keep us alive. Look at what some women and girls have to suffer to stay alive, that is much worse and much more difficult. Remember that it says in the Talmud that whoever saves one life saves the world. Think of Saartje de Lange. She is waiting for you, she prays for you, and if you manage to save your life, you will marry and your children and grandchildren will guarantee that our people shall not become extinct… Only if you stay alive, will they live and fill the empty spaces…'

Jacob had looked at him with tired eyes and, raising his hands to heaven, had asked: "Am I by any chance one of the just of the *Lamed Vav*…? Have I performed any miracles…? Am I a prophet, maybe, or a judge whom the Eternal One – praised be His name – gave special talents and powers to fulfil such an inhuman task in this hell…? No Brammie, I am not! I am only Japie, son of Sammie van Zuiden, the peddler and haberdasher from Elburg and I can no longer bring myself to be the devil's jester. I would rather die, hoping for my Creator's mercy".

Then Abraham had reminded him of their mother, Liese Jeda. How as a child she had fled with her whole family from Poland and had later married their father, Samuel van Zuiden. How happy she had been with her children who would be able to grow up in a free country. And that the fulfilment of that wish was now in their hands only. But it was no good. Jacob could no longer play the clown in front of the murderers of his parents, his sisters and so many of his people. That went too far; something inside him had shattered.

A well of sadness, forever increasing in depth and darkness had developed below the surface of his existence. It made him suffer and be silent. Sometimes it rose to his lips and some of it trickled out as a murmured elegy. With swaying body he would then intone fragments of Yiddish words, sonorous and monotonous.

Invisibly, the immense and unspeakable sadness mingled with the smoke of burning bodies. And silently it rose up… from that desolate plain in Poland to the far away and invisible throne of God.

※

Mordecai, a Polish Jew who played in the "house orchestra" as a violinist, took Jacob's place. The Germans tolerated it. They accepted the "excuse" that Jacob suffered from attacks of migraine and they were happy with the way in which the violinist replaced him.

Just before the war Mordecai had taken over the bakery shop of his father, but a year after his wedding day a massive deportation put an abrupt end to all his dreams for the future. During a raid in the spring of 1941 he was brutally taken, with his wife and their newborn son, from their home in Bochnia. With rough force they were herded out of the street to a waiting army truck, together with a few other Jewish families. Just before they reached the end of the street Mordecai saw Anna, an older Roman-Catholic widow, standing in the door of her house. During their conversations in the street and in the bakery shop he had come to know her as a sweet person with a good character. Bewildered and full of compassion she stood there watching what was happening before her eyes. The instant he saw her, Mordecai had a sudden inspiration which seemed right to him. Excitedly he looked around, took his son from the arms of his wife and quickly pushed him, in the midst of the chaos of the moment, into the safe arms of Anna. After arriving in the camp he did not see his wife or anyone of his family again. But Mordecai had a deeply rooted religious conviction that gave something special to his strong personality. The Talmud had become a kind of life companion for him, a second nature. He could cite from it endlessly, and encourage, comfort and teach his fellow prisoners…

'Water is water, but it makes a big difference whether it comes from a spring or from a sewer,' he said and continued to expound on "good" and "evil" in man.

Such a "sermon" always showed a high degree of knowledge and insight that he knew to share with enthusiasm and often even with refined humor.

Sometimes his words went beyond the ordinary and his interpretations gained a prophetic quality. That was the reason for his nickname "the visionary".

That same evening – right after he had replaced Jacob successfully for the first time in *Die Zwei Smousies* – he came to him in his hut.

'Do you remember what day it is today?' he asked. Jacob shrugged his shoulders and stared in front of him. Then Mordecai took Jacob's face carefully between his hands, turned it towards him and said: 'Listen, brother, listen carefully! Today is the day after Passover and I have convinced the Germans that it is necessary to give you some rest and they have agreed to that. Maybe you won't ever need to play for them again, for lately I feel more and more strongly that the end of this terrible situation is near.'

He still held Jacob's face between his hands and saw to his satisfaction that something of the old light that had been extinguished slowly returned to his eyes.

'Listen…' he said even more enthusiastically, 'and listen very carefully now, for thus speaks the Eternal One, the God of the covenant that He closed with us, His children: "Just as I delivered you from the yoke of the Pharaoh in ancient times, thus I shall deliver you from the yoke of this oppressor. I will bring you back to the city of your birth. Amidst its inhabitants you and your children will dwell as a sign that I did not forget My people. Just as Passover is the day of My covenant with My people, so from now on the day after Passover shall be the day of My covenant with you and your descendants. I shall be with them so that their name shall not be blotted from Israel. I shall bless them all the days till the return of the Anointed, who will bring peace and justice for you and all the earth from My beloved city of Jerusalem…".'

In the silence that followed snatches of the words that had just been spoken echoed inside Jacob's head… *the day after Passover*… "back to Elburg, the city of his birth…"

He looked at the friendly face of Mordecai whose prophecies he had taken with a pinch of salt till now. But this time "the visionary" had stirred a sensitive chord in him. Never yet had he taken him so seriously.

Oh yes, he was secretly jealous of Mordecai's optimism and he could quietly enjoy his qualities of dreamer and artist. When through all of this the obsessed philosopher and prophet suddenly appeared, it made him a very special and beloved fellow man in Jacob's eyes. The special, intense warmth that his words had instilled in him in that moment had touched him so strongly that two big tears rolled down his cheeks spontaneously. Mordecai smiled and as he slowly let go of Jacob's face, he dried his cheeks with his thumbs at the same time. *Zog nisjt keinmal az du gejst dem letzten veg… Never say you are on your last journey…* he cited the first line of a well-known Yiddish song. He looked at him with serious and penetrating eyes and spoke the memorable words that would support Jacob for the rest of his life… "Everything is *bashert*". Then he picked up his violin and while playing the first chords of the *Song of Deliverance* he turned around and slowly left the hut.

As if in a trance Jacob watched him go and listened reverently to the vibrating, pure tones that filled the simple hut for a few moments with heavenly colour and warmth. Only when the sound had dissolved into absolute silence, he lay down on his thin pallet and murmured softly: 'God, I thank You that I belong to You and Your children… Praised be Your name that I am a Jew and not a Nazi…'

And so he fell into a deep and peaceful sleep – on that memorable evening of *the day after Passover*.

Shortly afterwards they were liberated and with a small group of survivors, including Simon Steinmetz from Epe, they were taken by an American army truck to Maastricht. There members of the National Guard took care of them. After they had managed to contact the family De Lange in Naarden, they arrived there two days later.

A year and a half later Jacob and Saartje married and in the following year, on *the day after Passover*, their first son David was born in Elburg.

The small drapery shop of Samuel van Zuiden that had deteriorated considerably in the intervening period was officially allocated by the notary to the two remaining heirs.

Abraham decided to go to university and they arranged that Jacob would pay him half of the inheritance in stages. With the organisational and financial help of his father-in-law, Isaac de Lange, Jacob managed to turn the small drapery shop in the Jufferenstraat into a renowned ladies' and gentlemen's fashion establishment.

In the third year of their marriage the second son Benjamin was born and afterwards they had two daughters, Esther and Leah, named after his two sisters that had died in *Auschwitz*.

When the property of his neighbor came up for sale, Jacob bought it. An extensive renovation more than doubled the sales space. The shop was downstairs, the office, storage space, the canteen for the personnel as well as the living spaces were upstairs.

As the years passed and his son David had also become involved in the shop, Jacob avoided the busy shop more and more. The partly covered roof terrace became the place where he spent most of his time.

In the daytime he took care of almost all his administration there, and in the evening, when Saar was reading or watching TV, he stared at the crowns of the old oaks that stood on the city walls. Sometimes, when on a beautiful evening the sun was setting round and red, he walked to the wall of the terrace and looked at the old city. Almost immediately he would recall how together with his friends he would ring the doorbell of Naatje Cohen's house and then run away. Her little house was now a snackbar, where teenagers hung around purposeless. Naatje was no longer there, just like the other women who, on evenings like this, would stand in the porches of their homes to talk and gossip to their hearts' content.

The absence of the Sabbath-celebration was the most painful and unreal thing. In his memory he saw the men with their black hats and long coats walk through the streets, busily talking. Cloaked in pious pride – on their way to the centre of their existence the synagogue.

The building is now deserted and within its walls the eternal silence of the dead is respectfully maintained. Looking down on that holy place he sees the images of their deportation. From that very place, where they went every Sabbath to meet their heavenly Father, they were all marched off. *Westerbork… Auschwitz…* He feels it, sees it, smells it… and he shivers. Again he experiences the moment when something inside of him shattered. A mental attack that seemed to paralyze him and change him inside. The vibrant life before the war, the music, the humor, the people around him, all had faded and eventually disappeared almost completely. The challenges of his youth… The adventures with his bosom friend Sal Hamburger… The titillations that his first love, Saartje de Lange, caused him… The pride that he – a Jewish boy – was selected for the local soccer club… His creative talent and ambitions… It seemed at times as if it had all taken place in the life of someone else. The only thing that seemed to have replaced it was that silent, gnawing feeling of guilt. Had he deserved to live more than his parents, brothers and sisters, the rabbi and the elders of the congregation and all those others…? Wasn't it a disgrace, an unforgivable sin that he had achieved that by appeasing the Germans and by exploiting their own precious Jewish humor…? Cracking jokes while all those others were being murdered and burned…?

Before his eyes, the images on the roof of the synagogue fade. He only sees a wisp of smoke rise above a wide plain. Then he closes his eyes, sighs deeply and feels the words of the "prayer for the dead" rise within him. He feels like raising his hands and shouting with all his might over the roofs of the old city. But he utters no more than a broken *Shema Israel...* then his voice falters and he swallows the lump in his throat.

Two big tears roll down his cheeks. One disappears into his beard and the other just misses it to fall on the ground. At that very moment a soft sunray strikes it. Only the Lord on High sees it glow and takes it for a pearl that has fallen on the dark soft soil next to his House.

When Jacob turns around he sees, between the Vischpoort and the mast of an old fishing boat, how the last light of the day's sun colors a broad swath of clouds reddish-orange. And the appearance of the face of Mordecai, "the visionary", is like an ointment on the wounds of his soul.

His prophecy has been fulfilled... The Eternal One has indeed delivered him and brought him back to the city of his birth. Oh yes, he knows it for certain, for *the day after Passover* – the sign of His covenant with him – has been a special day for him many times already. And the words of the old psalms of King David, which Mordecai recited so often at the end of his "sermons", finally fill him with deep comfort... *My wanderings You have recorded, put my tears in Your jar...*

Again he looks towards the softly swaying crowns of the old oaks and thinks of Mordecai.

'What a man...' he murmurs softly and he realises that he did him an injustice. The person that he never really took seriously, except on that very evening in *Auschwitz*, has turned out to be no less than a personal messenger from God. Still, a wry after taste remains when he thinks of the mystery that the Eternal One promised him life and a return to Elburg, while six million of His children were killed.

Sometimes – before going to bed – Saar would sit with him. Together they would drink a glass of wine and talk about the children, the business or about trivial matters. She did so on purpose, hoping that he would be able to fall asleep thinking of those things. She never spoke deliberately about the chasm that the war had caused between them. The difference in their experiences was too great, too poignant.

Accepted as a daughter of the family on a farm in the neighborhood of Nunspeet, Saar had barely noticed that there was a war. How bad it had been she had heard only later from Jacob. Once he had told her his story because he felt that she had a right to know. Briefly and without describing in detail the atrocities that he still could not understand, he told her about life in the camp. Only the most moving event, right after their arrival, he had told her in great detail. Just because he wanted to make clear that he as the only one of his family had witnessed it and therefore had had to carry the extra weight of that terrible memory all this time.

'The shock was so terrible that it seemed as if I was paralyzed. I felt very nauseous, my stomach turned over. My throat closed tightly and I could barely breathe and strangely enough I could also not cry. I remember very well how clear it was to me that I had just entered the door of Hell. I cannot lose the image of that *kapo* ever again; his ghost is always around me and causes me to see and experience it again and again.'

He stared into the distance, took a deep breath and concluded: 'I have never told Brammie… for his own good, you see… You and my good friend Gérard are the only ones who know it now…'

'And Simon…?' Saar had asked cautiously. She meant Simon Steinmetz, a cattle trader from Epe, who had also been in *Auschwitz* and with whom they still kept in touch.

Jacob shook his head. 'No,' he said, 'Simon is my only friend to whom I do not have to explain how horrible it was… He knows!'

Saar had listened in a daze and from then on she looked after him with continuous care, often observing him silently, and only once asked him very cautiously, if all that blessing life had given him had not worn the sharp edges off the past. He had remained silent for a long time shaking his head occasionally. Then he had taken her hand and covered it with his, looked at her with moist eyes and, with a tenderness that encompassed all his sadness, answered: 'Saartje de Lange... woman of my youth and woman of my life... I understand what you mean, but you have to accept from me that the joy of pleasure has been taken away from me. It has been burned, consumed... I cannot retrieve it, because it is no longer there. The continuing shadow of *Auschwitz* lies across the happiness and peace of my life... heavy and unending... Do understand me, I wish that it were not so and that I could banish it, but I cannot. On the contrary, even though with time the past retreats from me, every morning when I wake up it seems as if it all happened yesterday...'

That outpouring had made a strong impression on Saar and she never mentioned it to him again. She understood that the wound in Jacob's life was too deep to ever heal.

In the same year in which Jacob's eldest son David joined him in the business, his twin brother Abraham left for good to Israel. An interesting job at the university of Tel Aviv and a better climate for his wife Rosa, who suffered from rheumatism, were the reasons for their departure. Afterwards a kind of numbness seemed to creep into Jacob's life. A wall of silence surrounded him and there was nothing that seemed to really interest him. David was very surprised when his father did not put up any resistance when he told him cautiously that he could no longer avoid doing business with German manufacturers of ready-made clothes. And when he proposed – because of the increasing rush and competition – to be open for business on Saturdays also,

Jacob answered with a shrug of his shoulders and a bitter undertone: 'If the Eternal One takes away all those with whom I used to celebrate the Sabbath; if He allows that His Holy House is turned into a music hall for the local band and if He did not even save His servant the rabbi to take care of all these things...' He spread his arms and with impotence and submission on his face and in his voice, he concluded: 'How could He then punish me when I get lost in the world of the *goyim*...?'

After a painful silence in which neither David nor Saar reacted, he stood up and said, gesturing widely in the direction of the edge of the roof terrace: 'Don't you see that the city in which I used to play in freedom in the middle of my people has become a place where the water is foul and where I have been living in exile for years now?' Then he turned his face away from them and said with resignation: 'Nah... do whatever you want, my boy, just do it...!'

Slowly he walked to the edge of the terrace. Leaning on the wall with both hands he stood there, motionless, for a long time, deep in thought, staring into the distance.

Saar did not oppose him. Up to a point she could understand her husband's attitude, but still it saddened her. Even though there was nobody left to celebrate Sabbath with, she still considered it a grave sin to work on that holy day. The fact that they were the only Jews in Elburg had even stimulated her time and again to safeguard the uniqueness of their identity. Because of that she insisted that both her boys were circumcised on the eighth day and became Bar Mitzvah in their thirteenth year. She also took care, as much as she could, that her housekeeping was *kosher*.

She ordered chickens in Enschede as soon as she heard that there was still a *kosher* butcher there. A representative in ready-made clothing who lived there was ordered, at the pain of losing a good client, to find out how many chickens he should bring every time he came to Elburg. Jacob's protests had no effect. Shaking his head he accepted it and murmured sadly: '*Kosher* chickens from Enschede... girl, why in heaven's name do you care...?'

'What I care about...' Saar repeated fiercely, her hands raised to heaven, 'is preparing a perfect meal for my husband and children. And yes, it will be perfect. Not because I care that much, but because the instructions for this were given to us by the Eternal One Himself.'

'What *mazel*!' Jacob growled cynically, 'that body of mine was already so dirtied by the mange and the lice and all that *treif* that I had to eat in the camp in order to survive, that it will never be pure again and...'

'Pfff... what is it that will not be pure again,' Saar interrupted. 'To get lost through no fault of yours is not a sin and everything is allowed to stay alive. But when you returned from the camp you weighed barely 70 pounds and now you weigh more than 70 kilos. Did you ever wonder how come...?'

With faked indifference Jacob allowed his wife to have the last word. To the sales rep he apologized every time when he arrived with a box of frozen, *kosher* chickens besides his collection of clothes. The man made no objections. He even seemed to find it amusing.

'Sometimes I think,' Jacob lamented while handing him the usual tip, 'that of all that the war took from us, she mostly regrets the butchery of Joop Cohen that disappeared from the Beekstraat.'

But when he walked upstairs in the evening after closing and the smell of Saar's chicken soup met him, he was sorry about his remarks.

In his mind's eye he saw her satisfaction in fulfilling her holy task as minutely as possible. How in her domain she kept the pots, cutlery and crockery for dairy products carefully separated from those for meat products. She even kept two more beautiful sets of crockery separate especially for the Passover week.

And when he entered the kitchen and saw her walk busily from the sink to the dining table, a feeling of tenderness and gratefulness dispelled his depression for a while. Sometimes he embraced her briefly and said, seriously but in a teasing tone: 'Saartje de Lange, woman of my youth and woman of my life, I love you more than you love your pots and pans...!'

In those moments he realised how his Saar was pickled through and through in unblemished Judaism and how she did all she could to keep her husband and children there too.

When David started to go out with a Jewish girl, Saar had experienced this as a special blessing and had secretly considered it a crown on his education. He had met her during his period of training in Antwerp. Saar would never forget the moment when he called her and asked if it was alright for him to bring his girlfriend home to introduce her.

'You can rest assured, *meme*,' he had said cheerfully, 'she is Jewish. We'll celebrate Passover at her home and then we'll come directly to Elburg for a weeks' vacation.'

When she had recovered a bit, she had walked to the roof terrace and faced Jacob; had gripped his shoulders and given him a look of mild happiness.

'Why are you looking at me so strangely,' he had asked her abruptly and a bit annoyed, 'am I becoming *meshuga* or worse, leprous?'

She smiled in intense contentment and looked into her husband's questioning eyes: 'Japie van Zuiden, my dear old pessimist, listen... You may have your questions and doubts about how the Highest deals with our people, but He keeps the promise that He gave you, He remains faithful... Sunday next week your eldest son – may he stay healthy – is coming to introduce what could be his future wife: a Jewish girl from Antwerp...!'

Speechlessly, Jacob had looked at her and then left the house, his head full of contradicting thoughts. In front of the old house of Naatje Cohen a few children were playing in the dusk. And as he looked at them the words that his brother Abraham had spoken long ago flashed through his mind: "Your children and grandchildren will ensure that our people will not be made extinct. Only if you stay alive, they will live and fill the empty places again".

He stood still for a moment and looked at the little house that had been converted to an auto-buffet and at the children. He took some change from his pocket and gave it to one of them. 'Here,' he said, 'go and get something nice with that and… make sure to share!' After he patted the child's head, he walked on.

As he deeply inhaled the cool evening air, he started to become very aware of the meaning of Saar's announcement and slowly but surely he was filled with an indefinable feeling of gratitude.

David, his "firstborn" – the corner stone of his family and his life. Imagine him marrying that girl… he mused, would he really be able to experience yet again there behind him, in the shade of the old synagogue, Jewish children, his grandchildren no less, would play in freedom? When he arrived on top of the city wall he stared out over the grand landscape that lay in front of him. In the distance on the right the silhouettes of the old farms on the edge of Oosterwolde were just visible and to the left he saw the contours of the IJsselmeer coast. In between, as far as the eye could see, only meadows. Somewhere beyond, far over the horizon, was Poland. He thought of his ancestors who once left from there to attain a better life… and of the fact that their offspring had been returned there against their will and had died there after all.

But just when those terrible images threatened to overwhelm him once again, the dominating image of a kind man appeared instead. As if in trance he saw him standing before him… almost tangible: Mordecai! And with a shock he realised that the day on which he would be meeting his future Jewish daughter-in-law for the first time would be *the day after Passover…*

In the following years it became increasingly clear that there really was divine inspiration in that memorable prophecy of Mordecai.

Jacob realised this more and more, and it became the key-point of his life. The profound amazement about the fact that the Eternal One had looked after him – an insignificant and sinful human being – so personally kept him going and prevented him from pining away in isolation, beyond reach for the people around him.

Sometimes – when he was unable to repress the memories that kept rising inside him – he pulled himself up on Mordecai's prophecy, as it were.

And now and then that secret would bring a barely visible, reverent smile on his sad face.

David married Thera Hoffman, his love from Antwerp. They moved into the apartment above the shop and Jacob and Saar moved to a small, comfortable home on the Westerwalstraat. The street was really more a cobble-stoned alley. There were eight characteristic houses that fell under the auspices of the Ancient Monuments Department. Jacob and Saar lived in one of the most beautiful. The previous owners – a young couple for whom the house had become too small when their family increased – had beautifully renovated and modernised the interior in style. Glass French doors gave access to the terrace and a nicely landscaped garden with a lawn bordering on the western city wall that was partly covered with shrubs. Meanwhile, *Van Zuiden Mode* became ever better known far and wide around Elburg. In the heart of the city the handsome shop stood as a solid monument that mirrored the promise – once given by the Eternal One to Jacob – for ever.

Although Jacob recognised more and more the typical characteristics of his father-in-law Isaac de Lange in his son David, this filled him nevertheless with contentment. Taciturn and quietly, he enjoyed both the business acumen of his eldest son and the traditional way in which David's wife Thera raised their children. Each Sunday she took them to the *Jewish School* in Apeldoorn. In this school that was especially meant for children from places where the communities had disappeared after the war, they were educated and prepared for the rest of their Jewish life. More than David she focussed them on the uniqueness of their origin. Urged on by that age-old tradition she had developed into a real Yiddish *meme* who, in her own spontaneous manner, made her home a space that filled itself continuously with the *shecheyonu*. Watching this in silence influenced Jacob's life, just as the first peaceful morning light dispels the bad dreams of a dark night. It set ajar the door of his heavy heart and allowed something in that supported him. A relief that comforted and strengthened him and that caused him to hang on to the courage and desire to live in spite of everything. In addition, the positive developments in the life of David compensated partly the worries that he had been having for years about the very different life style of his son Benjamin.

The latter lived from one day to the next like a good-for-nothing, unfettered by any limitations of whatever principle. Failing any initiative of his own he went at Jacob's urging to the *School for Retail* in Zwolle. There was no question of reluctance. On the contrary, together with his friends he enjoyed a life of sports and evenings out and was actively occupied with all sorts of things except with his studies. He steadfastly repeated every class and when he failed his final exams for the second time he left the school without a diploma. The director was more embarrassed with the situation than Benjamin, because he had to announce the exam results in front of a crowded auditorium. He sympathized with Benjamin and with Henk Elskamp – who had failed also – and therefore he decided to tell the boys the disappointing result beforehand. That would at least save them from the bitter contrast with the joy of the rest of the pupils. But in the corridor on the way to his office, as he was trying to find the right words, he was surprised to hear Benjamin say cheerfully to his friend and partner: 'What do you think, Henkie… are we the only two that passed…?!'

Without any self recrimination Benjamin thoroughly enjoyed the hot summer that followed. In the daytime he was usually to be found on the beach of the *Randmeer* and in the evening he was always in one of the many bars that Elburg boasted. He knew he was a good soccer player and just like his father he was chosen into the A selection when he was eighteen. Going out on Fridays, the day before the game, was strictly forbidden. That was the reason that he usually participated in the festive meals that his mother always prepared for the Sabbath evening. This did not last long, for when the club became champion and started to play in the highest leagues, the requirements of training three times a week were too much for him and he stopped playing in the course of the season. That was a great disappointment for Jacob. Discipline was just what Benjamin needed and in addition he excelled in a sport that Jacob himself had done with such enjoyment. He followed everything via the media and had even gone to the sports complex for that important championship game.

He had a very bad memory of the last time that he had played there himself…

… One of the most popular post war summer activities was the traditional soccer game between the government employees and the traders of the community of Elburg.

From their earliest youth Jacob and Arie Westerink had been close friends. The fact that they knew each other implicitly was apparent in their cooperation on the soccer field. Each knew where the other was without even looking and they were known at the club as the best forward pair ever. Whenever they both participated there were always many people to watch the friendly match during the summer festivities. The combination of "old glory" players and overweight men that had rarely or never played soccer ensured that the event was highly entertaining.

But in the summer of 1958 this popular tradition came to an unexpected and permanent end… Towards the end of the first half Arie suffered a heat attack and died on the spot.

Upset, the people left the quiet park. For Jacob the familiar beauty of the green turf changed suddenly to a macabre dark field. Transfixed by the lifeless body of his friend, he felt himself become light-headed. And just like his blood seemed to leave his body, his pleasure in the soccer game disappeared forever… For a moment that memory threatened to prevent him to go and watch Benjamin's champion match. Still, the desire to see his son play was stronger. People often said that they resembled each other both physically and in the way they played the game.

As he approached the sports park, the memory of that particular afternoon in '58 became stronger, and at the entrance he was suddenly overwhelmed by a suffocating wave of images and sounds from a much worse period of his life. The relaxed buzz that reverberated through the long lines was transformed into a soft elegy and on the iron arch above the entrance the letters *Elburger Sport Club* changed into *Arbeit Macht Frei*… The very moment that he walked beneath the arch he felt the cold sweat on his forehead. His legs trembled and he was frightened he would lose his grip on reality. The people around him faded into ghosts who floated through one another and uttered only monotonous and unintelligible sounds.

The announcer welcomed everyone to the sports-park and then mentioned the composition of both teams. His voice crackled through Jacob's head like the orders of a camp commander. The buildings surrounded him like grey huts. In a panic he turned and looked around wildly. A wave of people seemed to wash over him and after a few steps against the flow he lost his balance and fell backwards. Two men who knew him, carefully helped him up and asked him what was the matter and whether they should call a doctor.

'No, no,' Jacob answered quickly, 'that is not necessary, I just got a little dizzy.'

The men looked around, and one of them remarked: 'Come, there is a bench on the second field, there you can sit down for a while.' And they walked there via a small path through the bushes.

'Shall I take you home?' asked one of the men.

'No,' said Jacob, 'I am alright again, I think.' At the same time he realised that he owed them some explanation.

'It's that damned war that sticks in my head all the time… that is the cause,' he added.

And so they sat staring across the field, deep in thought.

Then one of the men said: 'Listen, Van Zuiden, in case you still want to see the match… we both have a ticket for the stands… If you take mine and sit next to him, then you have a super place to see well.'

Pleasantly surprised, Jacob thanked him for his friendly offer.

A while later – on the stands – he tried to concentrate on Benjamin's game. But just like in the first moments after waking up from anaesthesia reality does not quite replace the dream, fragments of the bad memory that had befallen him kept going through his head. The yells and carrying-on of the Elburg supporters, when they fell behind with 1-0 after an unjustified penalty kick, and the euphoria after the equalizer, far into the second half, still held vague associations with an environment that he wanted so much to forget, but was unable to. When Benjamin, just before time, had a chance to score the winning goal, something went wrong. The referee gave a corner kick to the Elburg team and before that was taken there was the usual pushing and shoving in the penalty kick area. Benjamin was standing a little bit towards the back, about 15 meters from the goal. The player who took the corner saw it and aimed the ball high in front, a little bit away from the goal. A defender recognised the danger just in time and they jumped high to head the ball at the same moment. When one feared to lose and the other had a chance to win the championship, they paid more attention to the ball than to each other. As a result neither of them hit the ball with their powerful head movement, but their heads hit against each other with force. The dull thud that could be heard on the stands was so powerful that both players fell to the ground. After some moments the defender crawled up again and walked around dazed, rubbing his head.

Benjamin, however, lay on the ground, motionless. He was unconscious for a while and then he looked with wide empty eyes at the paramedic, who had squatted beside him. Opening his eyes was the only movement. His whole body was lying still as death on the chilly turf. The medic pinched his arms and legs, but when there was no reaction to that he quickly ordered a stretcher.

The sports park had become very quiet. Jacob stared as if in trance at the motionless body of his son. For just a moment, when Benjamin fell, an image of a fleeing boy that was shot down flashed before his eyes. But he forced himself not to surrender to it again. Someone prodded his arm and roused him from his reverie.

It was his neighbor who said: 'I'd go have a look, if I were you, Van Zuiden…'

Jacob nodded, got up and walked from the stands to the exit of the field, where he arrived at the very moment when four men carried Benjamin on a stretcher to the treatment room.

When he saw him lying there motionless on the massage table and saw how he answered the paramedic's question only by moving his eyelids or softly murmuring "yes" or "no", Jacob had a fearful premonition. The last time he was here he lost his friend Arie. It couldn't be that another disaster was about to happen, could it? And during this threatening silence – while they were waiting for the arrival of the doctor who had been called – he saw Benjamin's life pass before him.

Up until Benjamin's puberty Jacob had felt more kinship with him than with his eldest son David. Not that he loved the latter less, or was less proud of him, certainly not, but David had that specific "De Lange-character" from his mother and even more from his grandfather Isaac; always busy, always asking questions, always examining and experimenting, hyperactive until he fell asleep at night. In Benjamin, on the other hand, he recognised clearly his own "Van Zuiden- traces": to listen carefully, to observe closely, and to go his own way quietly. Grateful and with pleasure he had often recognised the life-motto of his father Samuel in this: "You become wiser by listening than by talking, for all that you say you already know and if you listen you might learn something". He saw himself sitting for hours with Benjamin at the lakeshore near their summer home in Belgium. Away from the activity of the family. For hours without speaking, just thinking and looking at the float that bobbed gently on the peacefully lapping water. In the fall the two of them would still go there for a weekend. On Saturday – at the end of the afternoon – they would first drive to Beveren or Mechelen to watch a soccer match, and then they would go to a competition of pike angling on Sunday.

After the long walk on that particular beautiful winter afternoon on the island of Texel, where he told him – as the only one of his children – about his war experiences, slowly but surely a distance had developed between them. During his development into adulthood, coupled with his natural need to become an independent personality, Benjamin had consciously maintained a distance from his parents. Saar had often expressed her worries about his reluctance to study, and about his hanging around with bad friends, that even led occasionally to some trouble with the police. But Jacob had managed to convince her that the passage to adulthood involved falling and getting up; and that if you did not sow your wild oats in your youth, you would pay for it later. Still, he had shared some of her worries and had been very happy when Benjamin chose for soccer. Not only because in that he recognised himself so clearly but even more because it introduced regularity and discipline into Benjamin's life…

He was startled from his reflection when the doctor entered, greeting him fleetingly. Quickly he pulled back his hand that had been resting on Benjamin's thick hair all this time. After a thorough examination and various tests the doctor determined that there was no serious or permanent damage. His diagnosis was: a mild shock due to the loss of consciousness, a concussion and sprains of the muscles of the neck and upper back. His orders were short and sweet: "No more soccer and training until after the vacation and once a week to the paramedic for a check-up and massage". He gathered his instruments and disappeared. Relieved that it was obviously much less serious than it had appeared to be initially, Jacob went outside where it was clearly noticeable that Elburg had become champions in the last minutes after all.

He moved calmly towards the exit, through the celebrating throng.

Here and there an acquaintance stopped him to ask about Benjamin's condition, but finally he was able to leave the sports park.

Only when he walked among the high oaks on the city wall, did it become less busy around him. But it was a peculiar silence, comparable to the silence that reigns after a heavy storm. Even though the damage that the inner storm had wreaked within him in the past few hours would be difficult to assess for some time, he felt sufficiently upset that he resolved never to go to a soccer match again.

Benjamin, as if he had noticed his father's unspoken decision, stopped playing soccer in the course of the new season. After he had played in the first rounds of the competition against most teams, he noticed very clearly that Elburg was still a rung below the top division. Also he felt within himself that he completely lacked the motivation and obsession that he noticed in his team mates. Sometimes this caused a feeling of disappointment. He eased his mind quickly by the reassuring thought that there was more to life than soccer. But in his other activities, too, he lacked the challenge to get completely involved. Once in a while he felt that subconsciously a faint voice asked him why this was so and even demanded at times that this should change. But instead of searching for the cause of his disquiet and insecurity, he wallowed in it more and more; he fled into genial indifference and in the noise and the benumbing life of pleasure-seeking young people. Still, even in that ambiance he was sometimes overwhelmed by his inner feelings. Then he either retreated quietly within himself, or filled up with beer. And even though the consequences of being drunk were not always pleasurable, it was this very condition that caused something to be revealed that frightened him but later also started him thinking.

The location of Elburg on the Randmeer that gave free access to the IJsselmeer made it a popular attraction for large numbers of water sports-tourists from Germany. When their expensive pleasure boats were moored in the yacht harbor, they regularly visited the many bars of the city. As soon as one of these groups of Germans sat down near Benjamin on a terrace or in a pub, he was overwhelmed by restlessness and a vague emotion. Then his friends saw him change before their eyes. He would observe such a group very intensely – looking at them askance with narrowed eyes. If his gaze crossed that of one of them, he would look him straight into the eyes for so long that that person, somewhat disturbed, averted his eyes.

However, if he saw a somewhat older man in such a group, he would first give himself Dutch courage and then he would walk over to him, semi-innocently, holding a glass of beer in his hand. Like a talented actor he would then say, in an enthusiastic tone of voice and in perfect German: 'Ah… see here, fellow countrymen…!' And with a wide sweep of his arm he would add: 'Nice place, here, isn't it…?' Then he would bend closer and conclude: 'If we had not been betrayed back then, we would definitely have won the war and then all this would have been ours also, or not…?' Most of the time such an encounter fizzled, but sometimes it became clear from the reaction that a veteran Nazi had been addressed and then he went berserk. Grabbing the man by his shirt or sweater with his free hand, he would twist his fist, pushing it as closely as possible towards the man's chin, and snarl: 'Ich bin, Gott sei dank, kein Deutscher…! Ich bin ein Jude, ein "Smous" und dass ich hier noch immer wohne und lebe kommt weil Sie vergessen haben meinen Vater umzubringen…!' Then he would throw the contents of his glass into the man's face and push him away with force. He would growl at the whole group, with blazing eyes, and point at the exit: 'Raus…! Raus mit Ihnen und mit den faulen Mörder…!' Most of the time, the group would leave the pub immediately in heavy silence. Benjamin would then sit down at the empty table, hold his head between his hands and burst into tears. Often his two best friends – Alex and Johan – would come to sit with him, calm him down a bit and, after cautious insistence, take him home together.

The last time it happened, he did not want their sympathy. Roughly, even violently, he pushed them away and walked by himself into the alley opposite the pub. Confused and with hanging head he made his way through the old streets, lost in his own city and in his own life. Instinctively he avoided going towards the centre, so that he ended up in the east part of town. He collapsed onto the first bench he saw on the city wall. With his elbows on his knees and his head in his hands he tried in vain to organize the tattered emotions and disconnected thoughts that flashed through his brain… "God punishes, man takes revenge…" "Don't allow hatred into your life for it destroys you…" As mild as these truths were when they were handed to him by his father long ago, when he was a young boy, they now seemed to have him in a threatening stranglehold.

Coming from far in the past, from somewhere behind the endless horizon, these truths washed through and over him, heavy and with an almost judgemental authority. And when it all mingled with the images of the totally surprised Germans, he understood that he had landed in the emptiness and loneliness of the loser. It occupied his mind to such an extent that he barely noticed the man who took the seat next to him on the bench. For quite a while the latter sat next to him, lost in thought, and then he cautiously put his hand on Benjamin's shoulder. Benjamin started, sat up straight immediately and looked with surprised, bloodshot eyes into those of his father…

'How, uh… how did you know I was here…?' he stammered.

Jacob said that Alex and Johan had come to him and had told him what had happened; that they had seen him leave by himself and were worried.

'I walked here more or less intuitively and it did not really surprise me that I found you here.'

Benjamin looked questioningly at this father and saw how his gaze swept slowly across the landscape.

'There,' he pointed to the left, 'there is the *shul*, once the ultimate point in Jewish life and now only a symbol of death. And there,' he gestured to the right, 'there is the Jewish cemetery, the *Beth Khayem*, or the *House of Life* and between these inverted truths we have to try to remain upright… That is why we are sitting here, I think… Between the only two tangible remains that remind us of the vanished people, from which we stem.'

He fell silent for a moment, sighed deeply and then asked in a friendly tone of voice, but with a certain concern: 'Tell me, son, what happened?'

Benjamin shrugged, reflected for a while and then said: 'I really don't want to do this kind of thing at all, because I know that it is not right, but it is as if a voice within me says that it has to happen and then forces me to do it… what or who it is I don't know, but I do know that in such a moment it is stronger than I am…'

Jacob saw how the contours of the landscape slowly faded into the dusk. From a distant horizon the image of Mordecai appeared before his eyes and he heard him speak again about good and bad in man. After some time he murmured softly and approvingly: 'Hm… yes… water is water…'

Benjamin looked up with surprise and then listened carefully to the content of Mordecai's message. Afterwards Jacob looked at him: 'I don't have to tell you that there is evil in every person, and that it can make even you into a beast if you do not control it. We have talked about this before and tonight you have experienced it yourself. Listen, you cannot help meeting Germans – and you will meet a lot of them yet in your life, especially here in Elburg. But what you do with that fact, that is up to you. If you keep acting like this, letting evil have a free hand, then it will eventually turn you into an unhappy person. You know, it is written: *The person who controls his spirit is stronger than the one who conquers a city.* That control you have to teach yourself, otherwise it will destroy you!'

They looked at each other, both with the same tired expression in their eyes. Benjamin reacted resentfully, hitting his right knee with his fist: 'I really do not understand you… I mean, how can you talk like this now after all that you have experienced…?'

Dejectedly he hung his head.

'Listen carefully,' said Jacob, 'what I told you I had to learn by bitter experience and it kept me from going insane. Because of all the misery I went through and survived, it often happens that people come to me to unburden their heart and entrust me with things that they would never tell anyone else. Because it has to do with what we are talking about now, I'll tell you something, but you have to promise me that you will keep your mouth shut about it…

Last Thursday evening we were sitting around after the rehearsal of the oratorio society. Pastor Janssen from 't Harde sat next to me and because of the train hijacking in Wijster we started talking about the Moluccas and the war in the East Indies. He told me that he had been an army preacher there at the time and that he had returned to Holland just in time. "Because", he mentioned, "I felt that the rapist in me emerged". Do you understand why I tell you this? Such a decent man and father, whom no one could find fault with – a pastor no less – and yet, when he landed in an environment where evil dominated so strongly, it threatened to turn him into a beast too…! That is how it works and therefore you cannot give in to it, but you have to try to rise above it.'

In the meantime, the glow of the moon had replaced the light of the dusk.

Without speaking they sat in the peaceful quiet of that beautiful late summer evening. Then Jacob got up and declared:

'Come, *shabbes* is over; I am going to have a cup of coffee at *De Bonte Os*. Are you coming?'

Benjamin nodded, stood up and together they walked beneath the softly rustling oaks into town. He saw how the moonlight cast faint shadows of the trees on his father's face. It struck him how the grey hairs on his head and in his beard toned down the formerly deep black and framed that face more mildly. And for the first time in his life a feeling of deep respect and admiration took hold of him. At that moment it released him from how he had always felt as the son of his father, and suddenly he looked at that strong person with different eyes. Jacob's somewhat tired but quiet eyes had taken in so many horrible things as if on film and had stored them indelibly. The strength to handle that in such a balanced way… To analyze evil like that and to control his emotions at the same time… It contrasted rather strongly with his own uncontrolled performance earlier that evening. Images of that flashed through him and filled him with an almost paralyzing feeling of weakness and shame.

When they left the city wall and walked through the alleys to the centre, Benjamin asked: 'How, uh… how was that again, what you said about what is written…?'

With a faint smile Jacob took hold of his son's shoulder and answered: 'Remember well, boy, and never, never forget it again: *The person who controls his spirit is stronger than the one who conquers a city.*'

2

On the square in front of *De Bonte Os* Tilla, a mentally handicapped single woman, was looking for cigarette ends. At home she cut a bit off both ends, removed the paper and made new cigarettes from the tobacco.

As a child she had lived near Jacob for a while and for a year she had been in his class at grade school. She looked up shyly when both men approached her, but when she recognized Jacob van Zuiden and his son, she raised her arm and called spontaneously: 'Shalom Japie!'

With a smile Jacob answered the greeting with: 'Shalom Tilla. You're having good weather for it... aren't you?'

'Terrific weather, friend, for it is no good with rain,' she said a bit curtly and continued searching with a vengeance.

Even though Benjamin had not been inside *De Bonte Os* for years, he immediately recognised it. The ambiance was exactly as before. Two men were playing billiards and five sat at the large table near the window. There was no loud music as in most pubs; but there was a heavy smell of cigar smoke. Gérard sat at his usual place, at the head of the table, with a cigar between his fingers and a bottle of wine in front of him. When he saw Jacob and Benjamin enter he stood up and walked over to them.

'Sit down, friends,' he said, pointing at a couple of empty chairs, 'what'll you have?' And while he also ordered another round for the other men, Jacob and Benjamin joined them at the table.

Gérard was a special person. A flamboyant personality who, with a few soul mates, lived in the midst of the boring regularity of his rather taciturn fellow citizens.

Without ever having mentioned it, Jacob and Gérard felt that the reason of their bond lay in the fact that, as far as their religion went, they were loners. In the whole town only one Jew and one Roman-catholic of their generation were left, respectively Jacob and Gérard, and that was what connected them. It protected them largely from the social control within that conservative society, with its church rules and traditional austerity. A Jew who consistently and on principle rejected Jesus as his personal saviour and a Roman-catholic who had learned in that "damned papal mass" that he could be saved through confession, good works and indulgence – they were beyond salvation.

Gérard had had a difficult youth in all respects, somewhere in the far south of the country. However, one saying of his father he had taken very seriously and he had acted accordingly: "There is nothing you can do about being born poor, but if you marry poor, then that is your own stupid fault". That was the main reason that he had married Liesbeth van Zweden. She was fifteen years older than he, plainly ugly, but the single heiress of very rich parents. And as these were already elderly, Gérard did not have to wait long for that fortune. First he bought a prosperous pub close to the harbour and then a few years later also *De Bonte Os* in the centre. Especially before the war, *De Bonte Os* was a popular port of call for peat-boatmen and also for farmers from the surrounding area. They first drove to the harbour to load peat and before they started on their way back they usually had a cup of coffee or a drink in *De Bonte Os*. On the outside wall of the building that bordered on the square there still were six semi-circular brackets to which the reins of the horses could be fastened.

Due to his vast knowledge of humankind, Gérard always had good staff, but in the long run it was he himself who determined the character of his business. He was always at the habitués' table and in this way developed relationships – with some more intensely than with others. His lively interest in people resulted in close ties with his customers. Now and then he participated in or financed a spot of lucrative trade with one or more of those, but his first love was the catering business. A few times a day he took a leisurely walk from one of his businesses to the other. Cigar in mouth… having a talk here or there on the street or a pavement café… all entirely in accord with his life's motto: "It is good for a person to be occupied but it should not deteriorate into work". Through his walks from his one pub to the other and back via one of the pavemnent cafés, that part of Elburg soon earned the name *The Lazy Triangle*. In fact, this was dead against the prevailing attitude which was based on the thesis that a person does not die from working hard. Gérard did not oppose that, but to be on the safe side he had decided not to run any risks.

A few times, however, when there was a temporary lack of staff or when it was extremely busy, he had to join in giving service. Once, a visitor – a salesman type – ordered fried eggs with roast beef and a glass of milk. After half an hour the man indicated that he wanted to pay and was told that the damage was fl. 9.95. Gérard thanked him for the tenner he received, wished his client 'a nice day' and quickly resumed serving and clearing tables. After a while he noticed that the sales rep was still at his table and he asked him kindly if there was something else he could do for him.

'You still owe me a nickel!' was the irritated answer.

Gérard curled his toes, clenched his teeth and nodded politely; 'I am sorry, sir… just a moment.'

Quickly he walked to the Gents' toilets, took a packet of rubbers from the dispenser, placed it, together with the owed nickel, on a saucer and handed it to the sales rep. After the latter had first pocketed the nickel, he picked up the packet of rubbers from the saucer, glanced at it quickly and looked questioningly at Gérard.

'What is this for?' he asked tersely.

'Ah,' Gérard replied laconically, 'that is to prevent more of your kind in the future… good afternoon!'

That special and original sense of humor characterized him and ran like a red thread through his life. He was not at all the type of person who "cracked jokes".

His sense of humor was really a creative way to handle daily life situations. That, too, was one of the resemblances between him and his friend Jacob van Zuiden.

One beautiful spring day they were walking in Zwolle on their way to a reception. An acquaintance from the catering business was celebrating his 40-year anniversary. Jacob carried a generous bunch of flowers and Gérard a box of first-class cigars. In a park through which they passed four municipal workers were hoeing.

Gérard walked up to one of them. 'Good afternoon, sir,' he said with a poker face and as friendly and solemnly as possible, 'we are from the provincial directorate of park services. Each month we choose, in cooperation with the communities, the "community employee of the month" and we are very pleased to tell you that you are the lucky one this month. Here is a bunch of flowers for your wife, a box of cigars for you and you can take the rest of the week off!'

Surprised the man took receipt of the congratulations and presents. Open-mouthed with astonishment the other three men watched while their colleague cycled home in high spirits – the box of cigars on the carrier, the bunch of flowers in his hand and looking forward to his days off. When Gérard arrived in the crowded reception hall of the elegant restaurant, he waited for a chance to put his hands on a new present. A chic lady – obviously by herself - put a large bouquet of flowers on a table before she went to the ladies'. It did not stay there for long. Casually Gérard picked it up, quickly removed the card with the congratulations and the name of the generous donor, and gave it a few moments later – also on behalf of Jacob – to the guest of honor.

Jacob enjoyed these sorts of events more than he let on. It worked like a healing ointment on his deep wounds. It lightened his own, almost unbearable problems and helped him to even forget them at times. But if after such a relaxed afternoon he once more encountered "De Schim" and was thrown back ruthlessly into that well of oppressing memories, Gérard was there for him too. He possessed a special antenna with which he received those kind of signals without fail and it was translated into a subtle but intense sympathy. His few, well-chosen words, his gaze and attitude indicated his attempt to identify himself with the emotions of his friend.

"The friendship with Gérard is one of the best things that happened to me in my life", Jacob once said. And his children received the sincere advice: "If you ever get into trouble and you do not want or are unable to come to me, then don't keep carrying it around, take it to Gérard".

Unfortunately Gérard's marriage remained childless. Liesbeth mainly moved in better circles and regularly travelled to friends and family around the country and abroad. Her boring life of luxury, where everything went smoothly, just as she wanted, ended in style. She died in her sleep when she was seventy, of a heart attack.

Gérard decided that, considering his position as a well-known hotelier, he should inform people in the usual manner. That evening he thought for a long time about the text of an advert. And suddenly, when he realised how in his wife's life everything always went like clockwork, he started to write. The following Friday, a day after the funeral, the remarkable death announcement appeared in the *Elburger Courant*, in the section family announcements:

> *Today*
> *Liesbeth van Zweden's*
> *clock*
> *stopped*
> *silently*
> *without obvious reason.*

A few years later Gérard had to sell both businesses because of severe cardiac complaints. The pub he sold to a Chinese, who made it into a restaurant, and *De Bonte Os* ended up with Willem van de Weg. Wib, as he was generally called, was a true publican. He knew how to listen and to every fiery argument or tall story by one of his guests, he invariably reacted with raised finger: "Imagine that, at any given moment!" If he ever participated spontaneously in a conversation or if someone asked his opinion, he demonstrated the art of "talk a lot and say little". Deeply concerned that it could cost him clients, he skipped around his own opinion by means of a fascinating discourse and a great presentation.

'Fancy that!' Gérard sighed once, 'I mean… I see and hear you talk, but when you are finished you have said nothing and we know as much as two corpses!' To which Wib replied laconically: 'Tcha, imagine that, at any given moment…!'

Benjamin stirred the sugar in his coffee, his head still full of all that had happened.

In the meantime, Wib was telling in great detail how "De Vlek" had once again caused plenty of hilarity at the last council meeting.

The man – a simple, ultraright orthodox farmer and councillor for the reformed party *SGP* – owed his nickname to the large strawberry mark on his left cheek. In that particular meeting they had to vote about placing a public toilet in the centre of town. "De Vlek" had said: "I have no objections as long as that thing does not play on Sundays!"

The whole story and the laughter of the men barely penetrated to Benjamin. It flowed like a stream of incoherent noises past him, until "Red Kobus", who sat across from him, startled him from his reflections.

He only knew Kobus from the stories that he had heard about him…

That he broke into the town hall when he was seventeen in order to acquire a call-up form for military service in the East

Indies... How after his return from the Indies he had roamed the world as a sailor in the ocean-going trade... That afterwards he had worked for a while with Eibert van Triest, one of the last *Zuiderzee* fishermen of Elburg and then had stopped working when he was around fifty... That his two marriages had remained childless but that he himself had often said – smiling mysteriously – that his children lived all over the world...

If any moralist thought he needed to point out to him that his attitude to life was, ethically and biblically, abominable, then Kobus always cited, in a serious tone of voice and with his usual roguish expression: "Listen friend; if a woman has no man, then consider this: you can give her no greater joy than a baby!"

The little world of the Elburgers was too small and narrow-minded for Kobus.

All those little rules and laws, mainly produced by that church environment that was too restrictive for him, always tended to make him naughty and rebellious.

At the time he lived in his first house, a semi-detached, in the centre of Elburg. The iron, waist-high garden gate seemed to be a symbol of solidarity in front of the two houses. But that soon turned out to be an illusion, for one day Kobus' neighbor decided to sell some of the plentiful harvest of eggs that he gathered each day in his chicken coop. He placed a sign on the gate with the announcement: *Eggs for sale – Not on Sundays*. Kobus made an identical sign, fastened it at the same level to his part of the gate with the text: *Eggs for sale – Only on Sundays.*

In his youth he was able to play around with those narrow-minded rules and mock them, but at a certain point he had enough of it and ventured out into the world.

'What are you thinking of, boy?' Kobus asked and added immediately: 'It damn well looks as if you spent your last penny!'

It was quiet for a moment and Benjamin looked into a pair of sparkling steel blue eyes in a brown face framed with long, reddish hair. Slowly Kobus' face creased into a mischievous smile and he asked: 'Did your love let you down? Listen, if that is the case… I tell you, those women are not worth five minutes of chagrin!'

'Hey, hey,' muttered "De Balg", 'man was not created to be alone!'

'That may be so,' said Kobus, 'but it is with women as with mushrooms, one looks even better and more appetizing than the other, but if you hit the wrong one it finishes you.'

"De Balg" owed his nickname to his huge bulk. He was the owner of the small shipyard *De Helling* and just like Gérard and "Red Kobus" a frequent visitor of *De Bonte Os*. In addition he was also a member of the oratorio society and every Thursday evening he went to rehearsal together with Jacob. He liked his drink, but knew how to pace himself. He wanted to prevent at all cost the humiliation of being taken home in a drunken stupor once again – after that had happened that one time.

It was heavy weather that particular night. A stormy north-western wind chased the rain across the flat expanse of the *Veluwemeer* into the harbour. Some of his friends took him to his home behind the shipyard. For many years he had the same ritual before going to bed. In the kitchen he would clean his dentures and put them on a shelf in the built-in cupboard. Then he would walk outside to take a pee near the large currant bush. That evening however, his excessive intake of alcohol had affected his coordination to such an extent that he threw his dentures under the currant bush and peed into the cupboard – with his nose exactly above a large piece of old cheese that his wife had bought that afternoon. On all fours he struggled up the stairs and fell completely clothed into bed. His wife, who was still awake due to the thunderstorm, asked him what it was like outside.

'Woman,' he answered, 'you can believe it or not, but the whole world smells of old cheese…!'

"De Balg" did not say much but when he did speak you usually had something to think about. He had been looking at Benjamin for a while now. It appeared that he knew about the fight earlier that evening. For when there was a lull for a moment he bent towards Benjamin: 'I'll tell you something, young man, that which you should think about… If that Kraut, that you slapped about a bit tonight, really is a Nazi bully, than don't think he is impressed by your action. Probably he won't even think it is worth filing a complaint about. That is because it is nothing compared to the memory of what is on his conscience. He thinks about that several times a day and – even worse – he dreams about it almost every night. It is well-known – I read it somewhere recently – that many of these men, especially now that they are growing old, slowly but surely become mad with the nightmares in which the ghosts appear of the countless innocent people that they have killed.'

While Benjamin listened attentively to "De Balg", they were suddenly interrupted by the sound of the door being slammed by Tilla.

'Hey, where are you going?' Wib called out to her, when she walked quickly with bent head in the direction of the toilets. 'I don't want that here any more, understood?'

She looked around shyly and muttered, with her hands on her stomach: 'And I also don't want it here any more; man, I have to pee like a heron,' after which she quickly disappeared behind the door of the toilet.

'Man, man, listen to that,' Kobus remarked after a few moments, 'she did not say a word too much, I think; it damn well sounds like the Niagara waterfalls!'

When she walked through the pub again to the exit, Kobus called after her: 'Hey Tilla, how is it now? You OK again?'

She raised an angry fist in the direction of the laughing guys and left the pub muttering unintelligibly.

Gérard replenished his glass, indicated to Wib to give the others another round and resumed the conversation.

' "De Balg" is right,' he said to Benjamin. 'A few weeks ago Dina, my housekeeper, went to see her mother after having been to the market. Near the synagogue a group of German holiday makers is talking together. A girl of about ten is standing there, bored, licking an ice cream. She tries to decipher what it says on the plaque on the wall and in the end she asks her mother. The mother tries to avoid the question at first, but when the child insists, she says something like: "People who where taken from here and killed during the war…" whereupon the girl spontaneously asks the eldest man in the group: "Opa, did you do that…?".'

'You see,' Gérard concluded, 'that is a blow that would hit that man much harder than yours would. I just want to say: evil has its own punishment, you don't have to do it.'

"Red Kobus", who thought that he should also contribute his bit, added after a short silence: 'Yes, Germans… I don't like them either, but… they are there, just like flies… only… flies you can kill!'

After that remark Jacob felt that Benjamin had been given enough to ponder. He finished his coffee and stood up.

"De Balg" looked at Benjamin who was quietly staring ahead. 'Yes, my boy,' he reflected, 'life is not simple and it is full of questions and uncertainties.'

'But…' Jacob reacted with raised finger, 'one thing is certain in any case!' While everyone looked at him questioningly he took a few steps to the top of the table, put his hand with familiarity on Gérard's shoulder and said: 'Before the Messiah comes, that bottle will be empty…' and patting him again on the shoulder, he concluded with a big smile: 'Thanks for the coffee, friend, and see you soon!' Accompanied by the men's chuckles, Jacob and Benjamin left the pub.

Outside Benjamin asked: 'Shouldn't we also have bought a round?'

Jacob smiled and admitted: Normally yes, but if Gérard is there you hardly ever succeed.'

'Oh…?' Benjamin asked surprised, 'why not…?'

Jacob remained silent. 'You know,' he said finally, 'I can tell you something about that; the reason lies in his youth. His early years were poor and fragmented in all respects… He told me once that when he was about ten years old he was invited, together with his sister, to celebrate Christmas with very rich people. I think that happened because the son of those people was in his class at school. Whatever…they had looked forward to it tremendously, especially because – until then – they had never really celebrated Christmas. Much impressed by the large house, they followed the servant girl through the long corridor to the salon. There they had to sit down on an antique seat, where they sat watching all evening how one nice present after another, even nicer, was unwrapped by the children. To their great disappointment Gérard and his sister only got a glass of lemonade and a piece of cake. They left at the end of the party with empty hands. Around the same time, too, his parents divorced and so he grew up lonely and bitter. All that injustice in his early life led him to develop a strong involvement with less affluent people. Because he felt a relationship with them, he later – when his finances had improved – shared much, very much of his riches with them and spent it on their well-being. On the other hand the experiences of his youth have caused him to become obsessed with giving. He still has a lot of trouble accepting something from anyone just like that. That is the reason that he almost never accepts a drink from someone.

An event that also hit him very hard was the suicide of his best friend, when he was around twenty. For many years he managed to suppress al these things, but now that he is getting older, they surface more often. See, that is why it is so important that you do not suppress the bad experiences of your youth, but that you work through them and try to make peace with them. If you don't do that in your young, strong years, it later comes back twice as severely - when you are older and weaker.'

Benjamin looked at his father thoughtfully. In the meantime they had arrived home and sat down at the kitchen table. Jacob took off his jacket, hung it on a chair and poured himself a glass of wine that was left from the Sabbath evening.

'Much of the misery in your life you can handle on your own,' he continued, 'but sometimes you need help. In the Talmud it is written that a man should look earnestly for two people: a good friend and a good teacher.'

'And?' Benjamin asked, 'did you find those?'

Jacob nodded thoughtfully and answered: 'Yes, Gérard is such a special friend. He has helped me carry the stone, that lies on my heart, on those moments when I could barely lift it myself any more. And my teacher was the rabbi and of course later Mordecai. Although…' he mused, 'Mordecai really was both, friend and teacher. Tcha… what a man,' he sighed. 'He always retained some peace in the most terrible circumstances, in spite of his own intense grief… Inside of him there was a protected place where those bullies could not enter, whatever they did. For a while the two of us had to take corpses to the crematorium. I always wanted to return with the empty cart as soon as possible, but Mordecai kept holding me back. He would put his hand on my shoulder and say: "Come, first we say *kaddish*" and then he would pray and hum the prayer of the dying. I could not do that any more – was only thinking of myself – but at the same time I was jealous of the way in which he obviously could forget his own troubles and could honestly sympathize with the fate of his fellow prisoners. It seemed to raise him above the misery and hopelessness that surrounded us. And after such a prayer he seemed to have really worked through the largest part of his sorrow. "They are better off now than we and our bullies", he would observe as we pushed our empty cart back, "for they have gone straight to heaven where they are now being welcomed by Moses, Eliah and the Eternal One Himself".'

'Do you have any idea whether he is still alive?' Benjamin asked.

Jacob shrugged his shoulders. 'Ten years ago he was still alive,' he knew. 'Then Brammie returned to *Auschwitz* with a group of people from Israel and he met him there…'

'Really…? You never told me that,' Benjamin said. 'Didn't you want to go along at that time?'

As soon as he had posed the question he was sorry. He saw his father sink deeply into memories. For a moment a deep breath seemed to raise him above it, but that was an illusion. Benjamin felt uncomfortable and even a bit guilty. It was frightening how the quiet and peace that had still been on his father's face just now was suddenly transformed into an expression of tiredness and intense grief.

'Take it from me,' Jacob said, 'what I told you tonight, was sincerely meant. It has helped me to handle the misery in my life. But only that one... that...' He heaved a deep sigh, 'that "Schim", that ghastly "Schim"...'

In a flash Benjamin saw himself again, sitting with his father in the beach pavilion on the isle of Texel. There too the story came to a halt at the same unmentioned event. Now, however, he had added something – however briefly – with that one word "Schim". Something or someone causing that vexing memory to stay alive in him.

Jacob stared ahead with intensely sad eyes. After a tense silence, he took a few deep breaths and managed to stammer: 'I am sorry, my boy, but... we'd better not talk about it any more, for I... I can't stand it any longer...' When he felt the tears rolling down his cheeks he took a handkerchief from his pocket, hid his face in it and sobbed.

Upset, Benjamin focussed on the blue number that was tattooed on his father's lower arm and he felt how this moment was fixed in his memory for ever.

Already the next weekend Benjamin underwent the test that would show the extent to which his father's lessons for life had influenced his thoughts and acts.

On Saturday evening a performance of *Cuby & the Blizzards* would take place in the large hall of *De Stad Elburg*. Music was an important part of his life. From deep within it brought all sorts of emotions to the surface. And this applied to the most diverse kinds of music. A while ago they had attended an anniversary performance of the oratorio society with the whole family. At that time he had noticed in his father the same emotional experience of music. It was as if he saw his soul trembling on his lips and mirrored in those dark, shining eyes when he sang certain parts.

Cuby in "the blues", however, expressed feelings of injustice, insecurity and loneliness in a way that Benjamin not only enjoyed tremendously, but with which he also identified completely. As if what occupied him – and what was still lying unprocessed on the bottom of his soul – was being transformed there on the stage into the correct words and framed with the correct sounds.

In the intermission he walked to the bar, still full of the music and lost in thought. When he finally managed to obtain a beer, he pushed through the crowd around the bar and took his time looking around the hall. Unexpectedly he caught the eyes of a girl that he had noticed before. Her name was Nant and she came from nearby Oldebroek. That was all he knew about her. She smiled with a disarming trace of shyness when Benjamin walked towards her purposefully.

'Would you also like to have something to drink?' he asked.

'Yes, but uh… they are already getting me something,' she replied.

'I have seen you here before,' Benjamin remarked, 'but every time I wanted to talk to you, you were already gone again.'

'Yes,' she admitted. 'that's because usually we do the rounds of the town on Saturday evenings and then we never stay long in one place!'

'Would you like to do the rounds with me tonight, after the concert?' Benjamin proposed. Again she smiled a bit shyly, but nodded with conviction: 'Yes, that is fine…'

At that very moment Benjamin noticed with all his being a reaction that he had never felt before in connection with girls. Although it was the first time he heard her talk, it was as if he had known that voice for years. And the tranquility in her eyes made him feel he was coming home after a long journey.

While, flushed with excitement, they were still searching for the right words, they were rudely interrupted by an uncouth youth who bumped into him and then gave Nant a glass of cola.

'What does he want of you?' he asked gruffly.

Nant declared tersely that she had decided not to go into town with the rest of the group that evening. She would stay at the concert with Benjamin and he would take her home later. In the meantime another two boys and a girl had joined them.

The boy who had talked to Nant consulted briefly with the other two, whereupon he motioned with his head to the exit and told Benjamin in a threatening tone of voice: 'You there, come with me a minute!'

Benjamin did not have a choice, for as the lad walked towards the exit, his two friends pushed against his back, one after the other, and forced him to follow.

In the foyer the boy turned towards Benjamin and snapped at him: 'I don't know who you think you are, but you should know one thing… Nant belongs to us and Nant is mine, do you understand?'

Benjamin straightened his back and realizing that a discussion was definitely useless, he looked his opponent into the eyes as confidently as possible and waited calmly…

'Why are you standing there looking stupid… don't you understand me… get lost… take a hike!' the boy shouted impatiently, pointing resolutely towards the exit.

For a moment Benjamin gave the impression that he really wanted to leave, but then he turned around as quick as thought. One of the boys saw it coming and jumped in front of him, which led to a brawl. On his own he had no chance against those three and he was knocked to the ground. A fist hit him straight in the face and reverberated through his head. For a few seconds he saw everything double and unfocussed, and he felt blood pouring slowly and warm onto his lips.

When he pushed himself up with his back against the wall he saw and heard how Nant tried to calm the boys down. Still dizzy, he tried to reach her, walking between them, but they tripped him up so that he fell forward. For a moment he lay there, dazed, then he got up again and walked purposefully towards the person who had tripped him up. The other two immediately joined in and with the three of them they pressed Benjamin against the wall with their bodies.

Then one of them snapped at him: 'Dirty Jew… you keep your dirty paws off our girls, or else…' With their faces close to his all three made a continuous hissing sound, whereupon one of them yelled at him: 'Heil Hitler!' It cut through Benjamin's soul and he felt how it suddenly took away all his strength. He fell to his knees and put his hands over his ears… "Control your mind…" echoed his father's voice through his head… "Control your mind…"

When he looked up again, the boys had gone, but Nant was kneeling in front of him. Carefully she wiped the blood from his face. Benjamin looked into her eyes, gently stroked her half-long, curling hair and slowly bent forward. Softly he kissed her forehead and said, getting up with difficulty: 'Come on, let's go, we've had it here.'

When they reached the city walls, Nant explained that she came from a large family; that they had a farm where she herself also worked and that her real name was Jannie… 'When I was a toddler I always pronounced that myself as "Nant",' she chatted cheerfully, 'well, and that just stayed.'

But Benjamin barely reacted. He walked next to her without paying attention. He still felt the blood pulsate in his head, the blows to his stomach seemed to have taken all the strength from his muscles.

With trembling knees he finally sat down on a bench and tried in vain to make sense of the chaos of thoughts, images and emotions. Bent forward - his elbows on his knees - he stared silently ahead. When he felt Nant's hand on his shoulder, he suddenly realised that he had sat here exactly like this a week earlier. Then with his father, also after a fight. But at that time it was he who had been delivering the blows. Now he had only defended himself. And with a sense of satisfaction he observed that he really had managed to control himself. Still, he did not feel like a victor…

'Hey… are you alright?' Nant asked with concern.

Benjamin shrugged, sat up straight and looked at her.

Somewhat astonished he blurted out: 'I really couldn't be any better… when I look at you like this and think of you… I mean, that special feeling that… I have never really experienced that, so I think that I love you… no, sorry… I am sure that I love you…!'

Nant's blushing face glowed with happiness. 'I too have been thinking of you for a long time already,' she whispered, 'but I thought all the time that something like this could never happen because I… because you, uh… well, you know…'

Benjamin looked at her with surprise. 'For Pete's sake, what do you mean…?'

'Well, that I am not Jewish, of course…' she answered.

'But my dear, that makes ab-so-lu-te-ly no difference to me,' said Benjamin, 'in fact I am very glad that you are not Jewish… Take these guys tonight… If they had called me names like "Elburger botbek", that I could have understood. But "dirty Jew" and that hissing, what does that have to do with anything…? Where does it come from… that hatred, even now? Take it from me, that frightens me. And the idea that through you I can distance myself a bit from being a Jew, that pleases me.'

'But what about your parents…?' asked Nant.

For a moment Benjamin thought about it, then he smiled and said: 'Oh, my mother won't like it at all and she will moan for days on end to me and everyone else that the seed of "the Eternal One" has been planted in me in vain and the shame of it will be her death one day. Oh yes, I can just imagine it and I can hear her say it… My father will agree with her now and then for the sake of peace, but in his heart he'll be very happy that I have found such a wonderful girl.'

He thought about his words for a while, then nodded with satisfaction and added very confidently: 'Yes… oh yes, I am sure of it!'

Again he paused and then he remarked: 'Anyway, what about your parents… what do they think about Jews…?'

'Well, you don't need to worry about that,' Nant answered with a laugh, 'they will roll out the red carpet to welcome you as a son of "the chosen people",' and then she told him about the feeling of solidarity of her parents and grandparents with the Jewish people…

That it had to do with their faith and that he should prepare himself for a real cross-examination, specifically by her grandmother.

They talked for a long time afterwards about the character of both their families and then Benjamin took Nant home on his old *Zündapp* moped.

When he drove back to Elburg through the clear night, after their farewell at the driveway to the farm in Oldebroek, he was so full of feelings of happiness that he decreased his speed without noticing. He even felt a strong impulse to stop and turn around. The bad images of the fight had covered him like a veil for a large part of the evening. But after that magic moment of their farewell, during which their embrace was full of tenderness, that veil had lifted slowly but surely and in time dissolved completely.

Everything inside him is now taken over by that beautiful, pure vision that is called "Nant"… Back in town he returns as a matter of course to the bench on the city wall where he sat with Nant an hour ago and a week earlier with his father. Two people who have brought about so much in him in such a short time.

When in his mind's eye he sees his father before him and thinks back to the off-hand way in which he reacted towards Nant about his Jewishness, he notices a vague feeling of uneasiness. To see her as a welcome excuse to distance himself from that, while he feels and knows at the same time that this is impossible. He knows too well: even if you change the exterior, the shape… inside you remain who you are.

Only then does he realise how hundreds of generations before him planted the indelible characteristics of that deeply rooted Jewish identity in him too. And he clearly feels that the cause of his uneasiness lies in the fact that he has indicated, as it were, that he is ready to free himself from that.

But then he also thinks about how the bottomless grief of all the ages is still mirrored in the faces of the Jewish men and women he knows. He shudders when he relives that moving moment when his father burst into tears… He sees again the expression on the face of that boy who called him a "dirty Jew"… and he recalls his tone of voice…

Once again that inexplicable sadness and that strange fear take possession of him as he thinks about the hissing noise that they made and in his imagination he sees poison gas coming from ceiling showerheads… and then the cry "Heil Hitler" hits him again as a blow in the face…

Leaning his elbows on his knees and hiding his face in his hand, he sighs deeply. Then he smoothes his hair down, straightens his back and looks at the land in front of him that is illuminated by clear moonlight and thousands of stars.

More and more clearly and in the end almost tangible, the shape of Nant appears before his eyes. And suddenly it is of no concern to him any more whether or not it is alright to go out with a non-Jewish girl. His mother can lament as much as she wants – and pray that God may prevent it – it will not affect him. He will tell her once and for all that to him Nant is a gift from heaven for him. That nothing and no one will be able to prevent him from sharing his life with her and that she'll just have to be content with the fact that her eldest son David has already sufficiently protected the "Van Zuiden dynasty" from assimilation. And thus "Ben" van Zuiden, the son of Jacob, permanently concludes a period that has been dominated for a long time by indifference and insecurity. With a clear conscience he renounces the name "Benjamin" that was synonymous with it.

3

From the day on which Ben visited Nant's home for the first time a completely new world opened up for him. Even though the distance between their parental homes was only five kilometres, he landed in a totally different world due to the great difference in lifestyle, opinions and the type of daily work. The time and energy that his father and David had always spent in the business turned out to be no less than that of Nant's father in his farm. But soon it became apparent to him that the rhythm in the activities on the farm was less chaotic. One thing seemed to follow the other as a matter of course and without effort. The only interruption in this natural rhythm, that was dependent on the weather, was the tension during the hay harvest. Grass that has been mown has to be dried thoroughly by sun and wind and should not get wet before it is harvested. If it does rain, that does not only have a bad effect on the quality; wet hay can start to heat which can cause fire with all the consequences.

During such a short, hectic period any extra help was welcome and Ben enjoyed taking part. Together with Nant's father, with horse and cart into the polder to the hay field... The loading and unloading of the pressed bales of hay and the satisfied feeling when everything was stored high and dry in the hayloft...

The role Nant played in all this was truly a revelation to him. Long days of work – starting early in the morning – did not seem to matter to her. On the contrary, he sensed a deep satisfaction and contentment in her as she was busy in nature.

Once, when a foal was about to be born she even slept in the stable. She had attached a rope to her wrist that was tied around the horse's body and thrown across a beam. Because a horse always lies down before the birth of her foal, in this way Nant was woken up at exactly the right moment. For the birth of piglets and calves she was also always on standby.

One afternoon when Ben did not find her at home and heard that she was weeding the beet field with her father, he bicycled down there. When he reached the extensive field, he stood watching the two people that were working on their knees, pulling weeds. From time to time they stopped a moment and straightened their backs. Then they talked a bit, laughed and continued, bent over the fertile land beneath the high dome of imposing clouds. At the end of the field they both turned to the next row and slowly worked their way back to the side where Ben was watching. Half way down the row Nant noticed him. She flashed a brilliant smile and swept some strands of her long, blond hair behind her ears. Ben heard her say to her father: 'Hey dad, look there, what a handsome guy…!'

Nant's father looked up and asked laconically: 'Are you sure it is not some tax man?'

Nant smiled: 'If that is the case, then we'll grab our rifle and put a few pellets into his ass!'

The innocence that emanated from her face and posture at such a remark, touched Ben time and again in a very special way. Her special brand of humor was very original. She did not have to think about it or search for it, for the simple reason that is was just part of her nature. It had become clear to him that she had definitely inherited that from her mother. The latter wore her heart upon her sleeve – even more so than Nant - and said literally anything that occurred to her, obviously without being aware how funny that was at times. The first time when Ben met her some sheep had broken out that morning. It cost her rather a lot of effort to reattach the barbed wire to the posts of the enclosure. And when Nant saw the blood and scratches on her mother's hands, she complained: 'Mom, you should stop that; let papa do that…' whereupon she answered: 'You are right, child… by now I am also sick and tired of messing around with that damned barbed wire…!'

Only at that moment did she notice that Nant was not alone. She regarded Ben with friendly eyes and said: 'Well, well, "the Jew from Elburg"… jeez kid, so you are one of the children of Japie, the son of Sammie van Zuiden, the peddler. Yes, that was what we used to call your grandpa, "the Jew from Elburg". Tcha, that good man came here often with his trunk on his back. I once asked him whether there was dressing in the material I wanted to buy off him. "Yes, what did you think, for that price", he said, "chicken soup maybe?" He earned a fortune from us and now his grandson has come to take away my best help.'

She shook her head, raised her hand and sighed: 'Well, well, I planned that really well…!'

She patted Ben's shoulder and concluded laughing: 'Anyway, I'm afraid I shan't be able to change any of that now. Come, let's go inside.' And without waiting for a reaction she walked with big strides past the dung heap and the haystack to the living quarters of the farm.

In the kitchen Nant's grandfather was sitting in an old smoking chair in front of the window. In his hand was a fly swatter with which he slapped around him from time to time – mostly to no avail. On the back of his head was his cap, so crooked that the peak was resting on his left ear.

Nant put her hand on his arm and said kindly: 'Opa, this is Ben van Zuiden from Elburg and he…'

She could not continue for her mother interrupted her curtly with: 'It's one of those of Japie, the son of Sammie the peddler, you know, "the Jew from Elburg"!'

Opa took Ben's outstretched hand silently and without interest, nodded somewhat vacuously and continued staring quietly in front of him. 'He has been feeling off-colour for a few days,' Nant's mother apologized for the absentminded attitude of her father-in-law and added: 'Yes, and then those damn haemorrhoids, they also bother him quite a lot. You've got to take into account, those little perishers receive a lot of wind and no sun, and that does not make for quick healing…!'

Opa did not react. Now and then he slapped around him with the fly swatter and spat with a forceful "psht…" some juice of his chewing tobacco in a straight squirt into the spittoon that stood beside him on the floor.

In the meantime Nant's father had also sat down at the kitchen table. In passing, his wife gave him a friendly pat on his back and proposed: 'Hey you, why don't you make us some coffee, for you do that so incredibly well…!' To Ben's utter amazement he got up – as if it was the most normal thing in the world – and, in his dirty overalls, went to the coffee pot that was standing on the sideboard. Nant's mother noticed Ben's amazement and with an impish grin she whispered in his ear: 'You have to give them praise, those men, then they'll do anything for you…!'

Ben enjoyed the ease with which things were said and done. Parents, who had taken care of their kids and were being taken care of by them later. Money and luxury were totally unimportant to them, at least as long as what the land and the cattle provided was enough to live on. And vacation was something exclusively for "city folk" who were stuck in their shops and offices all year. It was exactly the confrontation with this relaxed way of life that fixed Ben's mind more and more on the difference with his own life. The calm and contentment that surrounded Nant and her parents like a pleasant smell were in clear contrast with the latent depression that – as a part of the collective Jewish grief – lay at the base of his parents' life. And although this clearly had to do with events that had not involved him, strangely enough it did have an influence on his own state of mind. It could suddenly overwhelm him and take possession of him. Memories of a past unknown to him, wrapped in a veil of abstract images and unrecognisable fear, caused him to sink into a deep well of loneliness and melancholy.

In the beginning of their relationship Nant had asked him a few times for an explanation of the apathetic behaviour that accompanied it. But, although it had been he himself, who had proposed – almost demanded – to keep communicating with one another as much as possible, at those moments he felt completely impotent, unable to explain to her what went on and how it began. It seemed like a nightmare that continued after waking and that led him astray in a spiritual labyrinth. Neither the beginning nor the end could be found …neither the cause nor the solution. It was an elusive feeling that led him to ascribe it to the unfathomable inheritance from his ancestors. For just as he had inherited the external characteristics and the typical attributes of his people, so fragments of the unprocessed grief could have lodged themselves in him. Even though he had tried to distance himself from it intellectually and had trained himself to control his spirit, it did not mean that the remains of that immense injustice had been removed from his blood and genes.

And thus it appeared, that the initially comforting thought, that through his relationship with Nant he could distance himself from the negative aspects of being a Jew, was in fact erroneous. Nant realised also that she would never be really able to share these specific emotions with him, due to their different origin. Still, it did not cause any alienation between them. On the contrary. Quietly respectful she comforted him with subtle body language or sometimes with gentle words, disarming because of her specific, down-to-earth humor, that was always more or less noticeable.

Along with the firm resolve to share the rest of his life with Nant, Ben's need for more certainty in his daily work increased. Until then he had worked two or three days a week on average as a freelance window-dresser. Basically it was well-paid, but because of the limited number of hours he ended up with only a moderate income. One day his father told him that he had talked to a colleague in Putten who was looking for a salesman/window-dresser. Thanks to the long-standing relationship of both entrepreneurs and to his experience as a window-dresser

Ben got the job. From that moment on his life changed completely.

Five days a week he drove with his old *Volkswagen Beetle* from Elburg to Putten, but on days off and in the evenings he continued working freelance as a window-dresser. After a few years, an apartment above the store in Putten became available, and they decided to get married and live there. An obvious decision with possibly for Ben an additional pleasant circumstance. For although he felt at home in Elburg, and up to a point felt involved with the people there and of course with his family and friends, at the same time it was the place where the consequences of the enormous tragedy of his people could not be ignored. And although he still could not really explain it, it was clear to him that his depressive periods definitely had to do with that. In traditional, mainly Christian Putten he would be able to create more distance, for the simple reason that no Jewish community had ever existed there. Because he lacked the distinct Jewish profile and because of his rather common family name "Van Zuiden", no one had till now associated him with it. Also, to his relief, he had – during the years that he had worked there – not yet been confronted with German tourists.

One thing was certain: after a turbulent past he would end up in quieter waters there. Silently he cherished the prospect of leaving Elburg behind and being absorbed in this new phase of his life, together with Nant in a comfortable non-Jewish anonymity.

If for him the concept "future" had mostly been limited to the next day, and halfway through the week to the weekend at most, from the moment when the wedding date had been fixed, a new dimension was added. He thought a lot about the way in which that day would have to develop, taking into account their different religious backgrounds. In any case, it was certain that it would be a turning point in his life. It was the happiness that had been given to him in the person of Nant that was the key to that certainty. A pleasant additional circumstance was that both sets of parents got along well together. It was only Saar in whom something of a dormant displeasure was still noticeable... "Ich sol em nich zehn unter di chupah" she would moan in Yiddish, expressing the disappointment that she would not experience seeing her son underneath the *chupah* – the traditional Jewish wedding canopy. But fortunately she managed to keep her laments always between the walls of her own home: about the fact that her future daughter-in-law and – God forbid – her possible grandchildren would be gentiles - and would therefore not belong to the chosen people.

'Chosen people...' Jacob repeated once, shaking his head and, looking at her with sad eyes, he had asked: 'I only have one brother left – somewhere far away. That is all... my parents, brothers and sisters, all my uncles and aunts, nieces and nephews, they were all murdered for one reason only, namely that they belonged to the Jewish people. Explain to me then... why is it so special to be chosen?'

Ben started to get so sick of his mother's nagging about forms and traditions and about her failure as a "mother of Israel", that in the end it became counter-effective.

The attitude of his father, on the other hand – quiet and modest – caused him to think more and more about the possible consequences of a mixed marriage. They never talked about it together. Sometimes he felt the need for it, but whenever he saw how straightforward and respectful his father approached Nant and her parents, he desisted.

In this period it became clear to him that this different attitude of his parents was caused, above all, by the fact that his mother, in sharp contrast to his father, had never had any negative experiences with relation to her Jewishness.

It was likely that he himself – as a post-war child – was more bothered by it than she was. Obviously in their family he was the one who was genetically most predisposed to such specific feelings. He realised that his father had always been aware of this and he thought back to the special moments in his life, at which this became apparent... the walk on the island of Texel, ten years earlier... the conversations after the fight with the German tourists and then... the moving moment that evening at the kitchen table, when his father told him about his tormentor "De Schim", after which he had burst out crying...

In the preparation period for his wedding Ben van Zuiden realised stronger than ever before that he was forever a part of Jacob van Zuiden. Although according to the age-old laws of his people he was a Jew via his mother's line, deep in his heart he became more and more certain that emotionally that line ran to him from his father.

As their wedding day approached, his need to acknowledge his Jewish identity on that day grew. When one nice spring evening at Nant's home they were talking about everything that still had to be organized, Ben mentioned it.

'I am not really sure how exactly we should bridge the differences between the Jewish and the Christian faith,' he said tentatively, 'but I know that it is very meaningful to us both and therefore I would like it to be present on our wedding day. A service in the synagogue or in the church will not be possible, but maybe we can think of something else...'

Nant's parents promised to think about it seriously. And if Ben could talk it over with his parents, they would certainly find an acceptable solution in due time. Because of all the talks about their mutual religious backgrounds, Ben started to discern the differences better. However, he was surprised that there were more similarities than he had thought at first. As Nant had predicted it was her grandmother on her mother's side in particular who gave him a clearer insight.

When the wedding date was fixed Nant wanted to personally invite her grandparents to the wedding. At this very visit something happened that no one had foreseen...

One afternoon they cycled calmly via the Kerkpad – a narrow, dead straight gravel path that runs through the vast pastures between Oldebroek and Oosterwolde – to Nant's grandparents. Around them, screeching godwits and lapwings flew circles above the places where their nests with eggs lay; apart from that, there was only the sound of crunching gravel. The old farm – situated on a dwelling mound just outside the centre of Oosterwolde – mirrored unmistakably the frugality that was so typical of the local character.

At the same time the perfect state of maintenance, the high oaks that framed the well-tended orchard and horse pasture lent a modicum of modest dignity to it all. A brother of Nant's mother, uncle Evert – horse lover through and through – had taken over the farm from his parents on the condition that "the old folks" could remain living there till they died.

Once inside Ben felt, even stronger than at Nant's home, that he was immersed in another culture. Even though the special smell – a mixture of sweet furniture polish and bitter silage – was foreign to him, he thought it fitted that quiet, timeless space of "the hearth". In some way it belonged to the museum-like ambiance of the old living room, where everything seemed to stand and hang in exactly the same way it had been arranged many years ago. Characters from biblical scenes, embroidered on so-called "letter-cloths", regarded the Frisian grandfather clock on the opposite wall with a serious gaze.

The wide oak mantelpiece lay like a massive dark roof over the fireplace that was inlaid with antique picture tiles. Between two brightly polished copper cartridges of "Second World War projectiles" stood a long row of identical, old, silver-plated frames that held the pictures of children and grandchildren.

Opa was sitting next to the large coal stove in an old smoking chair that seemed to have been made to measure for him. His calm attitude and friendly facial expression clearly mirrored the contentment that Nant had mentioned to Ben earlier.

'A darling,' she had called him, short and to the point, and she had added right away: 'Has always lived in the shadow of grandma who keeps watch over her entire brood and is not afraid to interfere when something does not go the way she thinks it should.'

Opa put down the book he was reading on the small chest that stood between his chair and the stove, after which Nant greeted him with three kisses. Oma got only one kiss, with which she indicated – probably subconsciously but still very clearly – her distinct preference.

'So, what is this I hear, are you going to live on the other side of the brook….? Well, I hope you'll be able to get used to living between all those "Hollanders"…'

With a face full of surprise Nant looked at her grandfather and repeated slowly: 'Hollanders…? Other side of the brook…? What are you talking about…? Isn't Putten also still on the Veluwe…?'

'Yes, that may be,' responded opa, 'but the border between the old Saxons- and Franks-land runs along the Hierden brook. That is why that hamlet between Hierden and Harderwijk is called "Frankrijk"… that is where the "Realm of the Franks" starts. Up to there it is all more or less "our kind" of people, but on the other side of the brook… That is totally different folk!'

Laughing, Nant concluded: 'So you think that you live on the "right" side of the brook…?'

'Ah, what can I say,' said opa, 'it's not that it is better or worse there, but it is just different… they talk differently, they think differently, they live differently and you have to take that into account if you want to live there permanently…'

After some general talk back and forth oma very subtly steered the conversation gradually to that in which Ben was so different from his future in-laws. Maybe Ben knew by now how much knowledge she had – and how involved she was with "the chosen people", but he sensed something like resistance rather than involvement, now that she was confronted with the definite alliance of her granddaughter with one of them.

Right away when he shook her hand he sensed vaguely a kind of superiority in her attitude and gaze that he did not like. And strangely enough he knew immediately – even before a word was spoken – that what he represented would be deeply irreconcilable, in spite of all that knowledge and involvement, with her truth that had developed from her own tradition. Calmly and in a somewhat strained friendly manner, she explained why the God of the Jews was no stranger to her… That He was also her God… That this was so because Christianity had developed from what had been present for many centuries in Judaism… And that therefore – because it concerned the same God – there was no objection to marry in church…

Ben looked at her with consternation and asked: 'But if the God of the Christians is the same as the God of the Jews, how can it be that those who have harmed us so much were mainly Christians…?'

In the silence, during which oma thought about a careful but clear wording of her reaction, an uncomfortable feeling came over Ben. The word "us" in his question echoed through his head. He was taken aback when he realised how he had involved himself definitely with the victims of anti-semitism. Now he had indicated spontaneously a cause for the fears and depressions that were undefined till this moment and that always overwhelmed him so suddenly. For the first time he had voiced this loud and clear as a personal declaration. It hung heavily as an unintentional accusation in the silence of the room.

Oma obviously did not feel at ease. More tense than usual, she sought for similarities. She had to prevent that too much distance would develop between them.

'Dear boy,' she finally said in a tone that held a sense of impotence and resignation, 'I understand very well what you mean, but if the greatest wise men still have not been able to find an answer to this and if there has never been a theologian who could explain how God could have let this happen, then how could I do that…?'

The loud ticking of the Frisian grandfather clock measured the silence. In Ben's head chaos reigned. For a moment he even threatened to lose himself in images, in statements and texts that were thrust upon him irrationally and that all contained some of the great grief that lay like a dark cloud over his family and all his people. He shivered… At the same time he marvelled at how deep that enormous tragedy had burrowed into him and become a permanent part of his life. Often when there was talk about the war and now too, one passage from a book by Elie Wiesel - of all the stories he had heard and read - occurred to him. He shook his head, heaved a deep sigh and said, clearly emotional: 'Of the six million Jews that have been killed Nathan was one. He was just a little boy when he was caught stealing a piece of bread in *Auschwitz*. That same day he was hanged and all the children were forced to look on. But his small body was so emaciated by hunger that he did not have enough weight for the hangman's rope to choke him. When it finally dawned on the hangmen why he just hung there still alive, they shot him…'

All these events intruded upon him and something inside him now demanded, as it were, that he use them to disclose the ultimate injustice. For a moment he asked himself whether it was reasonable, honest and proper to confront these old people with such a tragedy, but the urge within him seemed to be stronger than his common sense.

With monotonous steadiness the short loud ticks of the clock fell – like the drops of a leaking faucet – into the silence of the room. Opa and Nant stared fixedly at the floor. Oma however kept looking Ben straight in the eyes – seemingly unmoved.

Meanwhile, for him her black costume had slowly but surely lost the lustre of regional folklore and he felt – also because of what he still wanted to add to his story – that he should beware that it would not appear to him to become a uniform.

'Do you know what was written on the buckles of the belts of the Nazi-bullies, and therefore also on those of the ones that shot innocent little Nathan…?' he asked as controlled as possible.

Silently and carefully oma shook her head, whereupon Ben said very slowly but with great emphasis: 'GOD – WITH – US…

and because those very men read the story of the birth of Jesus to their own children and sang Christmas songs together, while on the same premises they let Jewish parents and children die in an indescribable manner in the cold, unhygienic huts… therefore I cannot understand that that God of yours is the same as ours…!'

It remained quiet… Then oma also cast down her eyes…

On the way back they did not say a word. Contradictory feelings filled both their heads. Ben was amazed at the fanaticism that had suddenly overpowered him. The fact that it had taken him over completely and that he obviously no longer had control over it, alarmed him. What was it that he had achieved in causing this old woman – who seemed to be so happy with her granddaughter's choice of partner – such confusion, he asked himself. He shivered as the small stones and the gravel of the Kerkpad crunched softly under his bicycle tires. In front of him the wind played with Nant's blond tresses and around him the godwits and lapwings threw their song of spring and freedom across the wide plain. In his mind's eye he saw again the proverb in its old damaged frame on the kitchen wall of the farm in Oosterwolde: *God has not promised us a calm journey, but definitely a safe arrival.* Passages from the books of Anne Frank and Elie Wiesel ran through his mind, and he remembered how as a little boy he always thought that there was only one place in the world where it was really safe… Israel.

Meanwhile he knew better. Now that the Jews were settling again in masses in the old country, it was becoming forever easier for anti-semitic powers to oppose them.

It was late in the afternoon when they reached the yard of Nant's home. Ben did not go inside but cycled straight on to Elburg. In his mind's eye he saw the face of his father and a latent sense of shame came over him. Again he had not been able to control his spirit and he asked himself how it was possible that his father was better able to do so than he. It alarmed him and for the first time he began to doubt his "solution" to marry a non-Jewish girl and leave Elburg. Something inside him told him that more should happen, but what? And who would be able to help him with that? One thing was certain, he wanted to spare his father the pain about what had happened that afternoon.

Once he was home in his room he tried to put the things that went through his head in order. While Cuby's *Desolation Blues* accompanied his efforts, he suddenly remembered an advice from his father… Purposefully he left his room, convinced his mother that he really did not need to eat and found his way to *De Bonte Os*. He was lucky, for "De Balg" was just paying his bill with Wib at the bar and the only other visitor was Gérard, who was sitting in his usual place at the top of the habitués' table.

Ben hung his coat on a chair and when he had sat down, "De Balg" put a glass of beer in front of him. 'Well, men,' he announced, 'I am going home, for it is busy in the yard.' He put his hand on Ben's shoulder with familiarity: 'All the best to you, boy… and uh… don't drink too much, otherwise you lose sight of north…!'

Ben raised his glass, thanked him and as "De Balg" left, he repeated slowly: 'Lose sight of the north…?'

'That is an expression from shipping,' explained Gérard, 'if you are no longer able to see on your compass which way is north, you get lost. But… tell me, what's wrong?'

'Why…?' Ben reacted astonished, just as he realised that his state of mind obviously could be read from his face.

' "Why", he asks,' Gérard said, shaking his head. 'Dear boy, you look as if you are carrying the misery of the whole world…! Well, tell me, what has happened?'

'Well…' Ben sighed, 'what happened… that is not really what bothers me, but why it happened and that I… well… that I am no longer in control at such a time… that is the problem, you see…? I mean, we arrive at Nant's grandparents. Everything is peaceful, quiet and cosy. An hour later we leave and what do you think…? Nothing but tension and misery! And just because once again I could not keep my mouth shut. I really do not want this at all, but when that woman starts about Israel and says that the God of the Christians is the same as the God of the Jews, then a strange fear comes over me that dominates me completely. Well…you know, then I cannot control myself any more. Tell me… why is that…?' he asked almost desperately. With raised hands he continued: 'and what in the world can I do about it…?'

The echo of his question remained, mixed with wisps of cigar smoke, suspended above the table in an oppressive silence. Gérard was looking straight ahead, deeply immersed in thought. Then he slowly turned his head towards Ben and asked: 'Are you just thinking aloud or is it really a question that you are asking me…?'

'Of course it is a question!' answered Ben, again raising his hands. 'For you are the only person whom I can ask… I don't want to confront my father with this. He once told me that, if there ever was something that I could not or would not discuss with him, I should not keep silent about it, but I should go to you with it… well and that's why… that's why…'

The serious understanding expression in Gérard's eyes convinced him that he did not need to finish his sentence. Ben dropped his arms on the table in resignation and listened attentively to what he was told…

'You have two questions for which you need to find an answer,' Gérard determined. 'First: where does it comes from and second: how do I solve it, isn't that so?'

Ben nodded silently.

'Well, I think,' Gérard continued, 'that it mainly has to do with heredity. I am not a psychologist but as you know, I read a lot, think about it, spend time with your father regularly and one thing is clear to me: a person inherits more from his parents than just the colour of his eyes. The fracture that runs through your father's heart will never heal again. Until his death he'll remain caught in the memories of *Auschwitz*. When he was still young and strong, and developing the business as well as having a family occupied him, things went reasonably well. But lately, as he became older and worked less, the past has caught up with him again. Images and memories were the unavoidable components of continuous nightmares. And do you know what's the trouble with nightmares? All day long they buzz in your head and the next night they hit you again. Once in a while you have a good night, but in fact it never ends. Tcha, and however strong you are spiritually, it tires you out completely and eventually you become more and more depressed.

As far as you are concerned, the trouble is that in Holland, and certainly here on the Veluwe, they do not pay much attention to this. That is the "blessing" of our down-to-earth attitude, something like: "That happened, we don't talk about it any more… just be glad that you survived". But if you were living in America or Israel, you would have already attended one of those many "second-generation syndrome"- therapy groups long ago. There they found out that many children of holocaust survivors are anxious because they fear a repeat. That fear, they say, is not just a psychological inheritance but also a biological one. To be really afraid appears to change something in your brain and to a greater or lesser extent you pass on that change to your children. That aggression of yours towards Germans is in fact for a large part fear. And I have to say honestly, when I watch the growing influence of the neo-nazis in the present German and Austrian society, then that alarms me also at times. But anti-semitism has a much wider and deeper origin than just Hitler and his Nazi-regime. Anyway, quite apart from that – whether you like it or not, you carry parts of the history of you parents and grandparents with you. And all this has to do with the question of where it comes from…

But now the question about how to solve it… What you should do – according to me – is for the time being to stop paying attention to all those stories that you read in books and that you hear in your family. What you should do is to literally write down your own story. And with "literally" I mean: EVERYTHING! Everything that you are grateful for and everything that you fear. You'll find that if you concentrate on that and write everything down, just as you feel it, this will bring you great relief. Such a self-analysis will help you to see things in their true perspective. And the second thing, that I want to advise you very strongly, is to visit *Auschwitz*.'

At this last remark Ben lifted his head and stared at Gérard with wide eyes and open mouth.

'Yes, I know, kid,' said Gérard, 'it sounds contrary but just to be resigned or to flee is too passive. It is the most obvious but at the same time the easiest way but it will never provide a solution. However, a confrontation with the place where the problem originated and trying to deal with it there, that is active. Then you really have a chance to bring most of it to an end. A wise man once said: "The infallible way to alleviate your fate is to stretch your arms out to it". That's what it has to do with, you understand…?'

Ben stared fixedly at one point on the table. 'Hmm…' he murmured a few times. 'OK,' he finally admitted, 'you could be right. I'll think about it seriously, but I still have one more question…'

'Yes… what…?' Gérard asked.

For a moment Ben seemed to consider whether this was the right moment to pose the question, but then he did: 'Do you know who Ischie is… and… who "De Schim" is…?'

Gérard remained silent, tapped the ashes from his cigar and stared at the ashtray.

'I don't think,' he said, that this is the right moment for that. 'I'll tell you about it later. I just want to say this: the last time when I met your father he was in particularly good shape. I asked him how he was doing and said that he looked well. "Yes", he confirmed, obviously relieved, "I haven't seen any Nazis for days and not even "De Schim" '. Smiling, he added: "I think he is on vacation or maybe he has moved away, that would be a real mazel. But the greatest blessing is that I have slept well for a couple of nights… no sadistic kapos, no cold and hunger, no lice or typhoid or rats that gnaw on corpses. It has been just falling asleep, waking up and nothing in between, only rest".'

Gérard looked at Ben with satisfaction and asked: 'And, what do you think, kid, why is that so, all of a sudden?'

Ben shrugged and looked wonderingly at Gérard. 'No idea,' he said and his surprise increased when the answer was: 'That is thanks to you, in a way…! Or rather, to your choice of partner. You only notice that your father does not make any problems about the fact that Nant is not Jewish, but what you obviously do not notice at all is the great positive influence that she has on him. You have no idea how much your father enjoys and loves her and how he counts himself lucky with such a future daughter-in-law. The few nights that he slept well were after he went with Nant and her father to the annual horse market in Zuidlaren. The next day he told me: "Gérard… believe me, I have never been so close to a person who confronts anyone and anything with such an open mind and heart. Really, I was amazed and I enjoyed it enormously. She sees through people and situations almost immediately and then reacts in a very clear and especially original manner. A wonderful combination of an intelligent father and a similarly uncomplicated, spontaneous mother".

He could not stop talking about how she moved about so relaxed in that typical men's world. Did you hear about that proposal…?'

'What…? Who…? Did Nant get a proposal…?' Ben stammered dismayed.

'She sure did…!' Gérard laughed, 'and not from just anyone. But you can rest assured, that guy is not going to try a second time. Bertus had sold a horse that morning to one of those rich riding-school owners from the south. Your father had already noticed that the son of that man was more interested in Nant than in the horse. And yes, at a given moment he approached her and asked if she would like to go out to dinner with him some time.

"Well, kid", Nant had hinted laconically. "I think it would be better if we don't start that".

"Yes, but…" the guy reacted with a serious face, "nothing else will happen!"

"Oh, in that case", Nant said, feigning disappointment, "I don't want to come at all!" "You've go to come down hard on those types", she had said resolutely, "otherwise they are on your tail the whole time". Your father had teased her and said that it really was a very good-looking guy, who also seemed to be very well off. "Mr. van Zuiden", she had said curtly, "take it from me: the best-looking guys are either thrice divorced or gay, and that one there, that dead loss, excuse the expression, with him I just wipe my ass, for I happen to know that he is even married!".'

Ben smiled. In his mind's eye he saw it all happen.

'Well, you understand,' Gérard continued, 'that in all respects that is a totally different world for your father than the one from which he himself comes. It is a relief for him and I really think that he owes his restful nights to that. It takes his mind off things and lifts him up out of the maelstrom of the forever repeating memories.'

For some time already two men had been playing pool and a group of women had sat down at the table next to them. The items they had bought during shopping night stood in large bags between them on the floor. When "Red Kobus" with two of his friends also entered the bar, Gérard decided: 'Well, I think we'd better stop here. Take your time thinking about it and whenever something bothers you, do come.'

Ben got up, put on his coat, shook Gérard's hand and thanked him. Gérard nodded, murmured something unintelligible and, while still holding Ben's hand, asked: 'Do you know your father's name for Nant…?'

'No idea…' answered Ben. Gérard let go of his hand, leaned backwards and said, his face breaking into a broad smile: 'Our "Wittekop…!".'

Once outside Ben mingled with the shoppers and then entered *De Stronkenbar*. But the group of boys that usually was hanging out here on Thursdays around this time was not there. He did not feel like talking with those that were there, and when after fifteen minutes none of his friends had appeared, he decided to go home. On the way home he was absorbed with all sorts of thoughts about the past day. He saw the images of people and places in sharp detail and clearly heard the echo of both the hard and the friendly and wise words. Then everything slowly dissolved because of the image of Nant that developed out of nothing and in the end dominated all the rest…

Ben actually had noticed before that his father felt comfortable in the company of Nant's parents. However, the fact that the person of Nant herself appeared to have an even more positive influence on him filled him with a mixture of great satisfaction and deep gratitude. That the purity of all her actions – something which she was totally unaware of - had helped his father to forget his past in the camp and had consequently given him a few restful nights, touched Ben in a very special way. It stirred in him a deep longing for her, just now when he would not see her for a few days.

That is why Ben van Zuiden sat down at his desk with pen and paper that evening, for the first time in quite a while. There he quenched his longing with the search for words that tallied with his thoughts and that he put into sentences that expressed what lived in his heart…

WITTEKOP

Meaningless people in the bar,
faceless hordes in the street,
days ahead without a purpose.
Yet in my mind an image I see,
instilling the patience of Job,
quietly waiting for those eyes of blue,
like two rainbows, shining
under a white thatch.

4

'Bart "malary" died and Bertus went to help put him in the coffin…'

It had struck Ben several times already that, since it was decided that Nant and he were getting married soon, Nant's mother more and more often spoke about "Bertus" instead of "papa".

'He completely lost the elasticity from his lungs…' she continued as she poured him a cup of coffee, 'and in the end he turned all blue, the poor soul… nothing could be done for him any more!'

Without having asked for it, Ben was given all sorts of information about the remarkable neighbors thanks to this tragic event…

… That Bart and Kees were two unmarried brothers who still lived in their parental home, and that they had worked forever and a day in a small local painting business. Bart had earned his nickname after - during the war in the East Indies – a neighbor boy had died of malaria. Bart then told anyone who cared to listen that his mate had died of "malary". And now after so many years, it was his turn.

It was more than a month ago that he had last worked, and he had had his usual weekend drink one more time with the other guys of the workshop that Friday. Earlier than usual he had called it a day. "Are you going already?" one of his colleagues, "Rembrandt" had asked. "Yes", Bart had answered curtly, "I am going home, to lacquer the coffin!"

"Rembrandt" was a first class craftsman and a dutiful hard worker, in spite of the fact that he regularly drank a lot. Only once had he erred in his work because of that. Thoroughly drunk, he had fallen into bed, that particular Saturday night. He woke up the next morning with an urgent need for the bathroom. To his alarm he saw that it was already half past seven. Quickly he donned his painter's overalls and then he cycled as fast as he could with his bread tin under the binders to the workshop, against the flow of the churchgoers. When he found the door locked, he realized that he had met all those neatly dressed people on his way down. Only then did it dawn on him that it was Sunday.

During the detailed account Ben had already wanted to get up several times to help Nant with packing. Their future home above the shop had become available recently, and they had planned to pack some of Nant's stuff that evening, in order to take it to Putten the next day. He looked through the window at the van that he had borrowed for that purpose from his brother David, took his last swallow of coffee and got up.

'And that funeral, that is going to give a whole lot of trouble yet...' Nant's mother continued indefatigably, while she replenished Ben's empty cup, 'for... "Malary" insisted on being put next to his parents in the old graveyard. The municipality agreed as long as they would not have to do anything. The family therefore has to dig and close the grave themselves...'

At that moment the door behind Ben opened and Nant entered. She put her arms over his shoulders and kissed him: 'Look who we have here... the Jew from Elburg!' whereupon Nant's mother sighed as she pointed to the van: 'Yes, but this one does not deliver... he only picks up!'

Ben got up and indicated that he wanted to visit the bathroom, but Nant's mother said: 'That won't be possible, kid, for opa is using it and that can take a while. Just go behind the hay barn, then your "willie" gets some fresh air too, that'll do it good!'

Ben left smiling and after the rural sanitary ritual behind the hay barn he carried the empty boxes and clothes bags, that he had brought, up to Nant's room.

Some time later, just as he finished loading the full boxes, he saw his future father-in-law coming out of the house of "Malary" together with another man.

'Well… did you get it done, man…?' Nant's mother asked when they sat down at the kitchen table a bit later.

'Up to a point,' Bertus answered, 'but I'm afraid there is more to do.' With a smile he made a tilting movement with his wrist, as if to drink from the imaginary glass in his hand, and continued: 'They are still saying good-bye. One drink after the other, because that is the way Bart would have wanted it. After some time "Rembrandt" said: "I'm going home", but Kees insisted: "Drink up, man, Bart would have enjoyed that so much". "That may be", said "Rembrandt", "but Bart can lie up tomorrow and I have to get up early", and he left. I promised that I would help dig tomorrow after milking…'

Ben and Nant spent the rest of the evening with preparations for their wedding, and the following evening after dinner Ben and his father drove the van once more to the farm in Oldebroek to collect more of Nant's stuff.

A few kilometres before the village, opposite the *Old Graveyard* a man, carrying a large shopping bag on the handlebar of his bicycle, stood waiting to cross the road. Only in passing did Ben recognise him. 'Hey, that is "Rembrandt",' he said to his father, 'he is going to render the last respects to his mate Bart "malary"!'

He enjoyed the surprise that this remark caused his father and asked: 'Shall we go have a look…?' Without waiting for a reaction he braked, backed up carefully and parked behind the open lop-sided wrought-iron gates of the graveyard.

Together they walked along the main path, bordered on both sides by old weathered gravestones, half disappearing in clumps of grass and weeds. Jacob looked at the names that were still legible on some of the stones, but he had not known those people. He had often attended funerals in Oldebroek, but always at the new graveyard on the other side of the village. He had never been here. In the mean time "Rembrandt" had reached the end of the path. He put his bike against a tree and walked along a row of headstones with the bag in his hand. Shortly afterwards Ben and his father also reached the place where Bertus and Kees sat kneeling at the edge of an almost completed grave, each with a bottle of beer in their hand.

'Well, well… see there,' said Kees, 'more help… join us, guys and have a beer…!'

"Rembrandt" took two bottles from his nearly full bag. Ben sat down near the men but Jacob refused, shaking his head. Motionless and with his hands deep in his pockets, he took in the weird scene. This, too, belonged unmistakeably to that other world of Bertus and Nant, but this time it did not give him relaxation and diversion. On the contrary. A dizzy feeling in his head made him close his eyes for a moment. For him this very bizarre situation held a threat that was not visible but nevertheless very real for him. With difficulty he took a deep breath and walked slowly back to the main path. From there he walked between the high trees and the old gravestones to the car.

As it gradually dawned on Ben how this event, that in itself was rather ludicrous, had possibly resurrected really horrible images in his father, he felt guilty. Full of remorse he shook his head, put down the still half-full bottle and got up. In the grave were two shovels, and next to him the voices of the men died down. Without greeting he left the place that had become a bit bizarre to him too.

When he arrived at the car, his father was already inside. Ben sat down next to him, put his hands on the wheel and for a long time they both sat staring ahead without speaking. Finally Ben turned his head towards Jacob and observed: 'That was stupid of me… I should have… well, I should have thought about it first – I'm sorry.'

Jacob gazed out across the meadows to the sun that seemed to be just a few meters above the horizon. 'Ah, you know…' he said finally, 'no one ever took me intentionally to a place that has associations with the camp. You did not do that just now and therefore you don't have to apologize. Sometimes things go well for quite a while but then suddenly one thing blends into the other. Just now, when I sat here by myself, I saw a hare run through that meadow there.'

He pointed straight ahead and shook his head. 'Did you ever see what movements an animal like that makes when he is shot while trying to flee…?' he asked. Without waiting for an answer he continued: 'First he seems to jump up suddenly, then he drops and usually there are a few last convulsions before he remains motionless.' He fell silent and looked ahead with sad eyes. Ben also remained silent and tried to figure out what the relation between a shot hare and the grave of Bart "malary" could be.

Then he said gently: 'Does that have to do with what you just said about one thing blending into the other…?'

Jacob nodded slowly, took a deep breath and continued his story: 'One day Mordecai and I were assigned to a group of men who had to take the bodies from the huts and bring them to the crematorium. Every now and then you recognised somebody…'

'Family…?' Ben asked hesitantly.

Jacob nodded again, and Ben asked: 'Also… from your family…?'

'Oh yes…' said Jacob, 'and that was the worst… that… and the rats…'

Again silence fell. The sun was now only a fraction above the horizon. Jacob wondered whether it made good sense to continue his story. Experts in the area of trauma-processing advise to write down or tell others your experiences. What had kept him from doing that, was that he was sure he would never be able to explain to someone, who did not have the same experience, what hunger, cold, beatings and a continuous lack of sleep can do to you. And how the realisation that you were delivered into the hands of fickle camp brutes – causing your life to be continuously hanging by a thread – made you behave more like an animal than a human being. He considered whether he should confront Ben with this now, just at the time when he was busy with the last preparations before his wedding. On the other hand he was the only one of his children who was really interested. And that made Jacob decide to finish his story after all…

'Along both sides of the huts were wooden plank beds in three tiers. There were three of you on a plank bed and as soon as you discovered that one had died, mostly when you woke up in the morning, you were obliged to put him down on the floor. For those in the upper tier this was the most difficult. In general they just rolled a body over the edge, causing it to hit the ground with a thud. Two of us would push a large four-wheeled cart through the huts that had been assigned to us. First we had to chase away the rats that were gnawing at the bodies in masses. In the last year it was an uncontrollable plague. Then we lifted the corpses one after the other into the cart and took them to the crematorium. One time we came back with an empty cart for the last time that day, when we saw that something was happening in the area where the roll-call used to be held. A few SS-men were amusing themselves. They had thought of a game for a group of about fifteen children. These kids had to run to the opposite side of the field as fast as they could, on all fours, like rabbits. During the crossing the men shot unceasingly at the last ones in the group causing incredible fear and panic amongst the children. Eight did not reach the other side and lay dead on the field. Children… shot like young rabbits. It was one of the many demonstrations that in their eyes we were absolutely no more than beasts. We were told to take them to the crematorium in the cart, but when we arrived there they sent us to a far corner of the camp to bury them there. So you see, it is not unusual for me to have to dig a grave.'

Now Ben realised fully what the scene they had witnessed earlier had released in his father. What he had told him, even though it was terrible, was not entirely new to him. He recognised the atmosphere from books that he had read on the subject. But now that he heard his own father – whose kin he was – tell about his own experiences, the distance that had always remained when he read about it was suddenly gone. His father put him right in the middle of it, as it were. During the story about the children he had to think again of little Nathan.

Cautiously and with some diffidence, he asked: 'Was… was Ischie also one of those children?'

Overwhelmed by an almost tangible misery, Jacob stared ahead to the meadow in which he had just seen a hare run. For a moment it seemed as if he had not heard the question but then he answered: 'No… that fleeing little rabbit they shot immediately after arrival in the camp…!'

Ben sensed that he should not ask any more.

After a long silence he started the car and drove to the house of Nant's parents. There he loaded her last belongings while they discussed another few details about the wedding, which would be celebrated in and around the farm.

In the end and to the satisfaction of all an acceptable solution had been found that would provide for both religious convictions. But as they discussed this, Jacob did not pay any attention. The intangible, unceasing stream of associations that kept confronting him with a past, that he wanted so much to forget, cloaked him in an apathetic melancholy. And that evening even his "Wittekop" could not change that…

When Ben returned home from work the next evening, he noticed the invitation for the *Seder* in the *shul* of Apeldoorn. Thanks to the cooperation of the communities of Zutphen and Deventer it was still possible to celebrate the Jewish holidays in this region. For the *Seder*, the celebration on the day before Passover, you had to register beforehand, because of the amount of food and drink that was needed for that.

After his Bar Mitzvah Ben had still gone to the *shul* sometimes with his parents. Later, his desire to celebrate whatever service or holiday had gradually disappeared.

However, as their wedding day drew closer, he noticed that he had begun to attach more value to his identity. It seemed as if somewhere deep within him something revolted against his plan to withdraw into a non-Jewish anonymity. A natural correction, inspired by something that was stronger than his own will. Even though it was no longer a question of any religious experience, inside him there was a deeply-rooted awareness that he belonged to an old and special people.

That same evening he asked his father: 'Are you going to the *Seder*?'

Somewhat surprised at this unexpected question Jacob answered: 'Your mother and I had just more or less decided not to go, because David and Thera are going to celebrate Passover in Antwerp this year. And your mother thinks I should not drive late in the evening in the dark from Apeldoorn to Elburg.'

'Well,' Ben proposed, 'I'll drive and I'll ask Nant if she wants to come too. That will give her a chance to experience some of our atmosphere.'

Jacob accepted the unexpected proposal as a delightful surprise.

'I would really like that, son,' he said, as a pleasant satisfaction took hold of him. Sometime later he told Saar about it and concluded, convinced of his own right: 'I have told you all the time that things will be alright with our Benjamin!'

But Saar raised her hands to heaven and reacted disconsolately: 'What will be alright…? He's the *goy* of the family and one *Seder* evening will not change that, especially not if he now marries a *shikse*, a baptised person… God save us. Woe unto our souls… Shame and disgrace will be upon us!'

Jacob shook his head about this naiveté that he knew so well by now. Of course he also considered it an extra-ordinary blessing that their eldest son David had married a Jewish woman. But you could hardly blame your children that, in surroundings where there was no longer a Jewish community, they went out and became engaged to non-Jewish partners. He did not feel like discussing it with her for the umpteenth time. Instead he quietly looked forward to a Seder evening together with two people who were starting to occupy an increasingly special place in his heart: Ben and his "Wittekop".

However, during that particular *Seder* celebration an overwhelming feeling of sadness unexpectedly assailed Jacob. At that time he discovered to his own surprise that the sadness and disappointment of his wife were actually present in himself also… During the trip by car to Apeldoorn he still felt satisfied and content. The relaxed chatter of Nant sounded as if she had been part of the family for years and surrounded him like an agreeable perfume. It even caused an occasional smile in Saar and drew from her a few remarks in which none of her disquiet about the non-Jewish state of her future daughter-in-law was noticeable. At the synagogue, too, there was a cosy buzz. The strong, clearly present sense of belonging impressed Nant greatly. Stripped of her usual light-heartedness, she looked and listened with respect to the women who informed each other with barely contained pride about the development of their children.

She saw also that the men took their time shaking each others' hands and patting each others' shoulders. Gesticulating widely and talking all the while, they entered. She wondered at how as a matter of course they brought out their skull-caps and donned them before entering the building. It seemed a bit funny, but at the same time it was very impressive.

When Ben took out his skullcap, Nant wanted to remark that it really needed renewal. 'That used to belong to my grandfather,' Ben said, rubbing his thumbs carefully over the old cloth that the years had faded into greyish-black. 'After my Bar-Mitzvah my father gave it to me.' She noticed that he was attached to it and she was happy she had not said anything. Ben pressed the skullcap carefully on his thick black hair, and as she silently walked inside with him, Nant looked at the still partly visible embroidery on its edge.

In the hall they joined Ben's parents who were talking to another couple. The man looked intently at Ben and then said with surprise: 'Now I can see it, that's Benjamin!' He shook his hand and continued: 'Tcha, you really have changed since I saw you last.' He turned back to Jacob and explained: 'That kid just does not have the "Van-Zuiden"-*ponem* like his brother... that is why I did not recognize him right away.'

Nant stood watching this, a little lost, while Jacob explained smilingly, with his hand on Ben's shoulder, that Ben might be a "De Lange" on the outside, but he was a real "Van Zuiden" on the inside. Although she could not understand it, Nant sensed that Ben's mother was telling the female half of the couple in the meantime about the difficulty she had with the impending mixed marriage of her son. A feeling of loneliness took hold of her. For the first time since she was going with Ben she felt lonely in spite of his nearness, and it seemed as if - because of the great difference in the culture and background of both - something of a gulf between them had developed.

To the right at the end of the hall was the entry to the synagogue and to the left was a large room where long tables had been set for the *Seder*.

'That was Simon Steinmetz,' Ben informed Nant as they entered the room, 'he was in the camp with my father and was the only one in his family to survive.' He glanced around the room and then said, pointing straight ahead: 'Come, let's sit there. There are two places free on the opposite side for my parents, then we can be together.'

Shortly after they had sat down, Steinmetz and his wife passed by. Now they also shook Nant's hand and congratulated her with her coming wedding. With an admiring glance at Nant, Steinmetz said to Ben: 'There are only a few of such natural beauties on earth. How is it possible that it is you who has the *mazel* to find one?'

'Ah,' Ben answered laconically, 'love has to be mutual... and the *mazel* is that I don't have such a *nebbish* "Steinmetz- or Van Zuiden-*ponem*...!" '

In the mean time Jacob and Saar had joined them and Steinmetz stood aside to let them sit down. But before he left he put his hand on Jacob's shoulder and acknowledged: 'You are completely right, my friend!' and pointing at Ben, 'inside he is indeed a real Van Zuiden... just as sharp as his father!'

Nant's wide-eyed gaze followed the Steinmetz couple as they started searching for a place at one of the tables in a relaxed manner. Then she cast her eyes over the set tables. She saw the flat dishes with contents that were rather indeterminate to her and also the piles of what looked like thin pancakes. Just when she wanted to ask Ben for an explanation, he continued his story about Simon Steinmetz...

'He is a nice guy. For many years he was one of the most important cattle traders in this neighborhood. I have accompanied him a few times to the market, and what impressed me most was how they settled up afterwards in a pub. In the middle of the table would be a bottle of gin that did the rounds till it was empty, and then there were cigar boxes with a few barely legible notes on the back side and fat wallets, that were attached to the clothes of the owner by means of a chain. And then it starts... you are sitting at the table with those with whom you did business. One receives money from the other and that one pays someone else again. It goes on like that for a while – back and forth, this way and that – without anything on paper. They remember everything... what and from whom they bought and to whom they sold all morning... It is really unbelievable!'

Nant had not really paid attention, for at the same time she was watching the people who entered. Mostly older people, but also a few younger couples with children. All dressed simply and mainly in dark colours. She caught bits of conversation in which words and expressions could be heard that she did not know, but she assumed they belonged to a language that existed only in the culture of the Jews.

On the one hand, as far as exteriors went, it gave her associations with the orthodox protestant faithful on the Veluwe. On the other hand, differently from the protestants, it seemed that there was no question here of being oppressed by strict Biblical rules, that are meant to make people concentrate on their evil and lost status in the eyes of a righteous God. Here one noticed more an attitude of gratefulness, fed by an age-old pride about belonging to the chosen people, in spite of all the unfathomable misery that had been done to them. She noticed it in the tone in which people talked with one another and also with the rabbi, Mr. Noah, who had meanwhile started the celebration.

After a cordial welcome to everybody he said in a friendly tone: 'And which of the children is going to ask "The question" tonight?' In the middle of the long table that stood against the back wall perpendicular to the other tables a young boy stood on his chair and called out in a clear voice: 'Why is this evening different from all the other evenings?' Straight away the rabbi answered: 'Because we commemorate that we as a people were delivered from slavery in Egypt.'

Ben bent towards Nant and explained in a low voice: 'In this way everywhere, in the whole world, *Seder* is started. Whether you celebrate it at home or in the shul, always a small child asks this question and the same answer is given.' In the meantime he had taken one of the booklets that lay on the tables and said: 'This is the *Haggadah*, the original story of the flight from Egypt; the most important event in the history of the Jews. From that time on we became for the first time an independent people. To remember the deliverance from slavery we eat unleavened bread,' he pointed at the pile of matses and continued telling, indicating the bowl with ingredients, 'and bitter herbs, a piece of meat that has been fried on the bone which symbolises the Easter lamb; and a bowl with salt water that depicts the tears that the Jews wept during their slavery; a hard boiled egg and a radish that we first dip in the salt water…'

'And that egg, what does that signify?' whispered Nant,

'It has to do with the sacrifices that were made long ago in the temple at Passover,' said Ben, 'but I have also heard that it symbolises the immortality of the Jewish people. Everything you boil either becomes soft or it melts and loses its original form, except an egg, that stays as it is and only becomes harder.'

The rabbi had started to declaim the story, half-singing and half-speaking in Hebrew, and Ben pointed out to Nant that she could read the Dutch text which was also printed in the *Haggadah*. However, she had difficulty concentrating on the story. The strange sounds in that monotonous, sing-song presentation… The expression in the eyes of some of the people present, especially Ben's mother, that only confirmed her feeling of "being a stranger here"… All of it put her in a trance, in a kind of twilight between dream and reality.

At a certain moment everyone present sang along with a certain passage. She looked at Ben and was surprised at how he enthusiastically joined in the singing of the cheerful-sounding Hebrew song, and how he clapped his hands at the right moments. As he sat there, with that old skullcap of his opa on his head and celebrating the feast of deliverance from slavery full of conviction, he suddenly seemed a different person from the one that she had thought to know till now. She noticed within herself a duality that she did not quite understand. On the one hand there were the depressive periods in his life that he himself always ascribed to his Jewish origin, and that he wanted to fight very consciously by creating as much distance as possible. On the other hand here it showed how indissolubly he was connected and interwoven with it. During the evening she realised more and more how impossible it would be for him to free himself from Judaism. More than anything else in his existence that was his basis and whether he wanted to or not, he would be forever anchored in it. She herself could, for instance, change her status as a Christian from one day to the next to that of an atheist. You become a Christian; you make a choice. But you are a Jew and you remain a Jew. There is no choice involved.

For the first time Nant felt something like guilt about the fact that, by linking herself totally to Ben in the near future, she would thereby loosen the ties that bound him to an age-old culture. Even though their children would be called Van Zuiden, they would be the first and only ones in the family that were not Jewish. With pain in her heart she saw the sad staring eyes of her father-in-law that were continuously fixed on his son. Nant felt that he had the same thoughts as she. Strangely enough she was almost certain about it and she was right. On that very same moment, when Ben sang along and clapped his hands, Jacob had suddenly seen his mirror image in that boy with the old skullcap of his father. Images from his own youth floated past him. Loose, unconnected fragments of an impoverished but nevertheless valuable time… The Sabbath meals on Friday evening, the celebrations in the *shul*; playing in the city and on the walls and later falling in love with the pretty Saartje de Lange; it all used to be so pleasantly normal, so wonderfully matter-of-course. Until – God knows why – they were thrown out of the Paradise that was Elburg to end in the Hell of *Auschwitz*. Even though he had survived, he never was really liberated. The experiences in the camp had evaporated his happiness and caused an irreparable fracture in his life. Indelible memories that, as he grew older, only became stronger instead of fading lay as barbed wire around his soul. Those memories kept him imprisoned in a camp that no one saw but he. His friend and fellow-sufferer Simon Steinmetz was in fact the only one in his neighborhood with whom he could share that feeling of "being a prisoner in a free land". A feeling that he could never explain to others…

Years ago, when Simon heard that Bram had left for Israel, he had visited Jacob several times. During his first visit they had eaten some new herrings at the stall on the market and had a drink with the men in *De Bonte Os*. 'Good people,' Simon had concluded contentedly when they left the city an hour or so later.

'Don't let Saar hear that,' said Jacob, 'she has nothing good to say about that *falderappes*!'

They strolled along the walls around the city and sat down on the bench at the north side, next to the two rusted old rampart canons. Until then they had talked about their wives and children, their activities, the world situation and the vulnerable position of Israel, about everything except that which connected them deep inside. There on that bench, looking out across part of the harbour and the Veluwemeer they remained silent for a long time. At a certain moment Simon took out a large red handkerchief, bent forward and blew his nose thoroughly. Then he wiped the tears from his cheeks. In silence Jacob put his hand on the broad shoulder of his friend. He felt the power of the massive body that hid such a strong personality. Simon Steinmetz was a man who commanded a lot of respect in the world of the cattle trade, but also in his family. But when this strong man turned his head and Jacob looked in the moist, dead eyes, he was taken aback by the vulnerability and the pain he saw mirrored there. The outburst that followed upset him even more…

Simon covered his face with his hands and wept. After a while he calmed down and heaved a deep sigh. He sniffed loudly and finally spoke, greatly relieved: 'Man, it is great that I don't have to be ashamed with you… really, I can't tell you how good it feels to know that you understand…'

Jacob nodded for a long time and said, troubled: 'Those terrible images… I hoped for so long that they would disappear as I grew older but it is only getting worse. I am afraid we'll have to live with them till we die.'

'I am sure of it,' Simon agreed. 'It was too much and too bad to be dealt with in one lifetime.'

That remark stayed with Jacob. He thought about it for a while and then wondered aloud: 'Would that be the reason that it continues in one way or another in your children… because it, say… because it is too much for just you? Take Benjamin for instance… I mean… I never talk with the others about the camp, the war or the Germans, only with him. With him I sometimes feel the need to speak about it and I feel that he has a very similar need to hear about it. I also feel that it is involvement rather than curiosity and now that you say this... that it was all too much and too terrible to deal with in one lifetime... tcha... Could it be that he is part of it in a certain way... that he takes on my burden from time to time... as a kind of lightning rod...? After all, you inherit more from your parents than just their brown eyes...'

'Or their crooked nose,' added Simon and continued: 'it could be... I don't know. But I do know that it won't happen to me a second time.' From inside his shirt he brought out a small, silvery tube, attached to a small chain. Jacob understood; he knew that Simon was not the only one who always carried poison just in case he would ever be arrested again...

Several nudges against his arm startled Jacob from his thoughts.

'What are you thinking of?' Saar whispered and pointed at the glass of wine that stood in front of him. Dazed he looked around for a moment and lifted the glass.

Mr. Noah had just explained that before one is allowed to take a sip from the first of the four glasses of wine that are drunk during the Seder, one should raise the glass while listening to a short passage from the *Haggadah* and then put it down again, without drinking from it.

When everyone had put his glass back onto the table and the lecture continued, Ben bent towards his father and whispered with a smile: 'Now I suddenly understand why you never bring Gérard along to the *Seder*. To be allowed finally after a few hours to pick up a glass of wine and then put it back without drinking from it would be beyond him!'

Some time later, about halfway through the evening, the rabbi interrupted the lecture and announced the meal. Large bowls with various salads and vegetables were put on the tables and soon the room was filled with a cosy buzz. Here and there people changed places and at a certain moment Ben walked over to a boy of his own age that he knew. His chair was not empty for long, for shortly afterwards Simon Steinmetz sat down next to Nant.

'Well...?' he asked her, 'can you manage between these *meshugenes?*' She did not know the word but sensed, coupled as it was with the mild irony in both his gaze and his tone of voice, that it was a rather mocking and toned-down description of the people around her and of the reason that had brought them all together this evening. Although she felt that it was clearly a matter of a certain involvement of an initiate towards a lay person, at the same time she noticed some kind of indifference.

'Oh, yes,' Nant answered spontaneously, 'I find it very interesting. I never knew that you have such an important celebration of the flight from Egypt. I always though it was an exciting story... of Moses, the ten plagues and the flight through the Red Sea when all the soldiers of the pharaoh drowned and...'

She fell silent because Simon shook his head with compassion.

'That is how it was, wasn't it...?' Nant asked innocently, 'that is what it says in the Bible...?'

Simon shrugged and said in an resigned tone of voice: 'Ah... it may all be true, but I could not care less.'

Nant was taken aback and looked at the man with disbelief. 'But...' she stammered, 'don't you believe it...?'

'It has been a long time since I believed,' Simon informed her, 'I lost my faith in Poland...'

Nant looked at him silently and with wide, questioning eyes, at which Simon explained: 'A God who first frees us from oppression by the pharaoh and then has us butchered in masses by Hitler does not make any sense. I mean, a real father does not allow something like that to happen to his children...? He would interfere, wouldn't he...? No, dear girl, I only believe what I see. Seh'n musz ich, do you understand? Seh'n musz ich...'

The confusion now was plain on Nant's face. 'Then why are you here tonight?' she asked. And again the strange logic in the laconic answer that he gave surprised her: 'Because of the fellowship, dear girl… only because of the fellowship.' As his facial expression slowly changed into a relaxed smile, he added, gesturing widely towards Nant: 'And because of the pretty girls, of course…!'

He made a quarter turn, took a radish from one of the bowls and leaning on his elbows on the table, said to Jacob: 'Sometimes I think: the only blessing of getting older is… the older you get, the more pretty girls there are.'

That latter remark was the last straw for Saar who had been biting her tongue during the dialogue between Simon and Nant. She looked like the avenging justice and snapped at him: 'Simon Steinmetz, may your manhood wrinkle in eternal barrenness. Do you really have to spoil my *Seder*, yes? If I were you I would dip that radish properly into the salt water. Then you can rinse your mouth before we continue the *Seder*…heathen!'

Completely unaffected Simon got up, bent over and put his hands on Saar's shoulders. 'Saartje van Zuiden,' he said, grinning broadly, 'I love you and you are the only woman I know who becomes more handsome when she gets angry.'

Then he walked back to his own place, relaxed, with one hand in his pocket and patting a shoulder here and there with the other. Jacob winked at Nant and she saw how he had difficulty suppressing a smile.

The second part of the evening had only just started when Jacob's thoughts already strayed again. He looked at Nant and saw that she had problems concentrating after all that had engulfed her till now. He had never yet seen her so vulnerable and lost. He tried to imagine how the strange culture and expression of faith of this evening would affect her. At the same time he could well imagine that Simon had confused her. Not to believe and still attend Seder would be as unthinkable to her as not to believe and still go to church. He loved her and was grateful for the good influence she had on Ben. Still, there on that particular Seder evening a feeling of melancholy gradually began to overtake him.

He looked at Ben. In a few weeks Ben would, as the first in the old tradition of the "Van Zuidens" and the "De Langes", commit himself with body and soul to a non-Jewish life partner. For the first time it finally hit him. Until now he had only rejoiced how Nant had brought his son out of the spiral of aggression and depression. Now, however, he realised that at the same time she was separating him from his Jewish roots. True, completely beyond her doing, but still… She would take Ben to a future that would be different in all aspects from his past. And it was unavoidable that there, in that strictly Christian environment of Putten, full of dubitable ideas about Israel and the Jews, he would be estranged from the Yiddish *neshome*.

Ben of all people, with whom he had such a unique rapport and who in some strange way seemed to be part of his own soul and his own *sores*. Feelings, steeped in their special camaraderie, involuntarily caused memories to pop up in his consciousness… Their walk on the island of Texel, the talks in the beach pavilion and later on the walls of Elburg and at home at the kitchen table. Ben's aggression towards Germans, which Jacob disapproved of – but at the same time secretly experienced as inexplicable proof of an extra and very special dimension of their relationship.

"The keeper of their spiritual inheritance"; that was the function that he had often given him secretly, alone among his children. Secretly, because he knew and sensed that everyone, even his own wife, assumed that he would give that role to David. David who was his eldest son and the "ideal" successor… Through and through a Jew who continued the old tradition faultlessly both in business and in his private life.

Jacob was very grateful that he, together with David, always in good harmony, had been able to develop the paltry drapery shop into a reputable fashion business. David lived and worked entirely in line with his forebears and had even given him Jewish grandchildren. This did not preclude that Benjamin, as the only one of Jacob's children, had a character trait in his attitude and behaviour towards his father that alleviated Jacob's suffering. And that caused a very special bond between them.

And while all the others that evening saw the people of Israel set out for the "promised Land" – after their liberation from heathen Egypt – Jacob van Zuiden saw his son disentangle himself as it were from that people and return to the world of the *goyim*.

All in all it had occupied him so much that he had not even noticed that Mr. Noah had left the recitation of the last passages of the *Haggadah* to his son Danny. He saw father Noah look with appropriate pride and satisfaction at his son and that filled him with a feeling of sadness. But then….when he looked at the boy again, he suddenly saw something familiar… that expression… that posture and the passion with which he, slightly swaying his upper body, intoned the sentences, awoke more and more clearly the memory of Mordecai in him. The resemblance caused him to long silently for his dear friend. The solemnly spoken words from the *Haggadah* resounded around him but did not really penetrate to his heart. At that moment he could only hear the old Yiddish words - from a distant past –with which Mordecai told him that memorable promise about his own departure and deliverance… "As I delivered you from the yoke of the pharaoh in days gone by, so I shall deliver you from the yoke of this oppressor. I shall take you back to the city where you were born. In the midst of its inhabitants you and your children will live as a sign that I did not forget my people. Just as Passover is the day of my covenant with my people, so *the day after Passover* shall be from now on the day of my covenant with you and your descendants. I shall be with them and bless them so that their name shall not be blotted out from Israel…"

Those last words stayed with him…" so that their name shall not be blotted out…" It reverberated through his head. At a certain moment he had a strong suspicion that those words were more than just a memory and that they were given to him telepathically at that moment by Mordecai himself. The *Seder* was the beginning of Passover and it was certainly not impossible that his friend would be thinking of him around this time. Besides, he was a man with remarkable gifts… "So that their" – and that clearly referred to all his children – "name shall not be blotted out from Israel…" He heard Mordecai speak those words as if he was sitting next to him. And while his gaze rested on Ben, he was suddenly filled with a pleasant feeling of comfort and certainty. It was a certain fact that the woman with whom his son was getting married was not Jewish, but it was equally certain that in spite of that everything would be right with all his descendants. He could not explain it, but somehow that fact was a certainty for him.

Pensively Jacob walked outside with the crowd some time later. At the door stood Mr. Noah with his son and shook everyone's hand.

'Van Zuiden… dear friend, why are you looking so serious,' he said when he shook Jacob's hand, 'there'll be another day after Passover!' He turned towards his son: 'This is Mr. van Zuiden, owner of the largest fashion business on the Veluwe.'

The boy shook Jacob's hand and reacted alertly: 'I am Danny Noah, descendant of the biggest ship builder of all time!'

While Saar, Ben and Nant mingled outside with the people, who wished each other *mazel tov* and "*gut Pesach*", Jacob walked to the car, still in contemplation. "After Passover there will be another day", Noah had said, without having the slightest inkling about the special meaning *the day after Passover* had for Jacob. Gratefully he accepted that off-the cuff remark as a confirmation of the certainty that he had acquired that evening, that things would be alright also with Benjamin and his possible descendants.

Contrary to the trip that afternoon, on the way back it was rather quiet in the car. The darkness seemed to afford everyone the luxury to withdraw unhindered into his own thoughts. And instead of still musing about that spectacular beginning of the creation of "The Promised Land", which the Seder evening really signified, everyone had plenty of thoughts of their own. Jacob cherished the "meeting" with his friend Mordecai and wondered whether it had anything to do with a similar meeting that he had a few weeks ago in a very strange dream. Saar thought that her opinion was confirmed that the impending marriage between Ben and Nant could not be blessed. *Do not reject the teachings of your mother,* it said in the *Tenakh,* one of the women with whom she had spoken had assured her.

Nant's head was filled to capacity with all the impressions she had received and Ben felt an increasing ambiguity about their imminent marriage.

When they reached Elburg Ben first dropped his parents off at home and then drove to Oldebroek with Nant, without speaking a word. He parked the car next to the farm. The outside lamp was still on and cast a faint light into the car. After Ben had turned off the engine, it was perfectly quiet around them. The tension could be cut with a knife. He looked at Nant who sat staring ahead as if in trance. 'Shall we let it all sink in overnight…and then talk about it in the morning?' he asked.

She nodded slowly and said softly: 'Yes, that is fine.' Then she turned her head towards Ben and added: 'But… I do have one question now.'

He was concerned. She had not been so quiet and reticent all evening without reason. Like him she would undoubtedly have been thinking about the great difference between their mutual background and experience. And now she had a question that was obviously so urgent that it could not wait till the next day. That must have something to do with her doubts about their future.

While he prepared himself for the worst, she looked at him with an innocent expression and asked with almost child-like naiveté: 'Tell me, what is a "Van Zuiden-*ponem*…?" '

Ben smiled and felt enormous relief flow through his entire being. Carefully, he put his hands around her face and told her:

'My darling, the most beautiful *ponem* in the whole world is the one I am looking at now; that I am holding in my hands now… do you understand?'

'Yes,' Nant said, pondering, 'but why don't you just call it a face?'

'Usually I do,' answered Ben, 'but… when Jews get together, especially when they are of my parents' generation, they automatically revert to the use of Yiddish words and expressions. They have been raised with those and especially now that there are so few left of our people, it gives them a sense of belonging. My mother does it more than my father… especially when she is angry or upset about something. It belongs to us just like the Veluwe dialect and the typical farm customs and expressions belong to you. In essence this could make our relationship very interesting, but then we must accept and respect the big differences that there are, otherwise it'll be a failure. That farmer's life and all it entails… your religion… your family customs… I find it all very fascinating and interesting, but that is not the reason why I want to share the rest of my life with you. The only reason for that is because I really love you so deeply.'

He took out an envelope and gave it to her: 'Just in case you ask yourself how much you mean to me, you should read this when you are in bed later.'

She put the envelope in the pocket of her coat and then they said good-bye. When she entered the house all sorts of thoughts about her future together with Ben went through her head. Never before had she seen and realised so clearly how deeply connected he really was with the Jewish people, even more than he himself had realised. To create a distance, as he had intended by marrying her and living in Putten, would never succeed. Whether he wanted it or not, it was too much a part of his life. And she did not mind that. In the meantime it had become more than clear to her that Christianity was the sequel of Judaism, just like the New Testament in the Bible was a sequel to the Old Testament. But she did worry about the fact that the reverse was not true.

For Ben the Bible finished with the Old Testament. The New Testament for him was definitely not a sequel to it. He even had an aversion of everything that had to do with it, such as the part that the Jews had played in the death of Jesus. According to him Jesus was no more than a rabbi, one of many, who had caused so much unrest and commotion among the people at the time that he had been sentenced and executed by the Roman authorities. If there was one reason why he could never be the Messiah it was because of all the misery that had been caused to their people, often in his name. That went dead against the prophecy which was given in the Old Testament, namely that the Messiah would be someone who would bring peace and justice for the whole world.

She recalled again the intense altercation between Ben and her grandmother in Oosterwolde. The fierceness with which he contested her and in the end shut her up, alarmed her somewhat. This evening during the Seder she had been rather occupied by a feeling of guilt about the fact that her input in their marriage would loosen Ben's ties with Judaism. However, now she feared his dominance more. Up till now there had only been a first, fierce love between them. But, she asked herself, when that would cool down and would turn into a next, long-term phase, wouldn't his influence diminish or smother her own faith…? And their children… couldn't they get entangled in the course of the years in the different cultures of their parents? Couldn't they, as a result, choose the easiest way out and believe in nothing any more and practice nothing…?

When later Nant was lying in bed, tired of all the thinking and all the impressions, she opened the envelope, took the card out and read…

ALWAYS

Always you are with me,
in belief or unbelief
as a shadow that is seen
if only for a moment brief,
should I be filled with happiness
or sadness, even grief,
then let remorse and satisfaction
tears and loud laughter bequeath,
that silent shadow always here,
the strength that lies beneath.

She noted how these words gradually pushed all the earlier doomwatching to the background. She saw only the image of a handsome, unique young man who held her face in his hands with all the tenderness he possessed. She read the poem again, cherished the words… and fell into a deep sleep.

When Ben returned home that evening, his father was still up. That was nothing unusual. Jacob often did that after he had been out in the evening. To just sit a while and think about the evening. To postpone sleep a bit longer and keep the dreams at bay. This time, however, he did not sit as usual in his easy chair in the living room, but at the kitchen table. Ben felt that his father indicated thereby that he wanted to talk to him. It had become a kind of code, something he only realised now when he was almost leaving his parental home.

Gingerly he took his place opposite his father and both allowed the other time to meditate.

'It may well be the last time that we are sitting together like this,' said Ben.

Pensively, Jacob nodded. He looked in silence at the open book which he had been reading. Ben saw that it was a part from *Devarim*, the fifth and last book of the Torah.

'Did you find what you were looking for?' he asked, pointing at the book.

'Yes... I did,' Jacob confirmed. 'It is a sentence from the prophecy of Mordecai that I had to think of very strongly tonight during the *Seder*. It is in chapter 25.'

He put his glasses on and read controlled and emphatically, first in Hebrew and then in Dutch: ...*so that their name shall not be blotted from Israel.*

Those words, embedded in historical eloquence, hung in the air between them, as it were, and Ben repeated them in a low voice several times. Then he looked at his father and asked hesitantly: 'I know that you like Nant very much... That you love her... But still it bothers you that she is not Jewish, doesn't it?'

Jacob looked at his son with love and covered Ben's hand with his own: 'Listen my boy... Nant is a pearl that you have to keep and guard as the light of your eyes. She will enrich your life more than many a Jewish woman would. I am one hundred percent convinced of that. And... yes, it did bother me that she is not Jewish, but now it is alright with me. After tonight I am sure that all will be well.'

He tried to explain to Ben why that was. How Danny Noah had reminded him this evening of Mordecai and that he had again been pervaded with the content of his prophecy. Because it mentioned that the name of all his children would not be blotted from Israel... he explained to Ben that the children of David were Jewish and that any children his sisters might have would also be Jewish, because their mothers were Jewish.

'Yes... and...?' Ben wanted to know, 'and my children...?'

'That too will be alright,' Jacob assured, 'don't ask me how. The ways of the Eternal One are often difficult to understand, but I received a promise and I cling to that. And that promise is for me and my descendants... without exception... "I shall be with them and bless them so that their name shall not be blotted out from Israel".'

Ben looked at his father and felt how the respect that he had for him was increased even more by the generosity of his opinion of Nant, without making concessions to his own religious conviction. He wondered how it could be that his father, in contrast to Simon Steinmetz and so many other survivors of the holocaust, had kept his faith. At that moment he could not find any explanation other than that it must have been due for a large part to the role that Mordecai had played in Jacob's life. And again he imagined how special it would be if those two would meet one another once again, after so many years, and… how much he would like to witness that…

His father's voice roused him from his reveries.

'What were you thinking of?' he said.

'To be honest,' Ben answered, 'there is something I have wanted to talk over with you for a long time. I am aware that it is a sensitive matter, but because it may be the last time that we are sitting together like this, I am going to ask it anyway. But… uh… first I have to confess something. That is… that some time ago I made a mistake again and again I was unable to control my spirit.'

Succinctly he recounted the collision with Nant's grandmother and the conversation afterwards with Gérard…

'According to him the explanation of my behaviour is a subconscious fear that that terrible persecution and extinction of the Jews can take place again, just like that. I have been looking too much for an explanation for it in all the books that I read about it and he thought I should stop that. It would be better for me to put down my own thoughts and feelings on paper. Well, he may be right there, and I want to start doing that more, write poetry and stories etcetera… But the point now is… eh… that he also advised me to… to…'

'Go to *Auschwitz*,' Jacob completed the sentence.

'Yes!' Ben said, surprised, 'how do you know…? Did he tell you…?'

Jacob shook his head. 'No. But I know what he thinks about that… "the infallible way to alleviate your fate is to stretch out your arms towards it".'

'Yes… that's right, that's what he said,' Ben reacted.

'I am not saying that he is wrong,' Jacob had to admit, 'but it is not the same for you as it is for me. David has asked me once as well. In any case, why don't you go once together with him?'

Van Zuiden Mode was specifically known throughout the country for its extensive supply of pregnancy fashion. Especially for the target group of orthodox believers, both Jewish and Christian, David had an exclusive classical collection, produced in Poland every six months. For this he drove twice a year to a workshop in a small town within easy reach of Katowice.

Ben shook his head and looked at his father: 'I don't want to put pressure on you, but if you don't come… I am not going either.' For a long time Jacob said nothing and looked at the open Bible. Then he took a deep breath and confessed: 'You know… while I was alone here just now, thinking about the whole evening… I have to tell you that more than ever I longed to meet Mordecai once again. But why should I go back to a place of which I see images every day that I want to get rid of so sincerely. I would give anything to get rid of the memory of *Auschwitz*. If that is so, you don't go there. It would only get worse instead of better. I know that some people found it very beneficial. That by going back to the scene of the disaster they felt as if they regained control…and as if they could create distance. Brammie had that also after he had been back. He even called it a relief and assumed that from that moment on he could leave it behind for ever. Some time ago I read a report in the *NIW* by someone who had had the same experience. But every person is different and I am just scared that it won't be like that for me.'

It was quiet for a moment before he continued: 'Do you understand my dilemma…? On the one hand the intense longing for my friend and on the other hand the just as intense loathing of the place where I could meet him. And anyway, talking about dilemmas. There could be a completely different reason to go to Poland. As you know my mother was born and raised there. She came from a family who lived there for many generations. The

Jeda tribe was known for the many rabbis and Talmud scholars that it produced. Forebears, who put their lives in the service of studying and teaching the Holy Scripture. And the older I become the more often I notice the desire to find confirmation for that slumbering part of my identity and to experience it in those places and with the people there. But what keeps me from it is the horrible fact that Poland, besides the land of my forefathers, is also and most of all the graveyard of my family and my people…!'

Ben could understand this and decided to drop the matter now. 'OK,' he said, 'we won't mention it again.'

Jacob did not react. It seemed as if he had not even heard Ben's remark. Deep in thought he stared at the empty surface of the kitchen table. Slowly he raised his head, looked at Ben, and said: 'One thing I still want to tell you… but it has to remain between us… yes?'

Ben nodded and listened attentively to what his father then confided…

'You know that I dream a lot, almost always about the war… the camp, our family, "De Schim", you name it. But a few weeks ago I had a very special dream. It was Yom Kippur and I was in Tel Aviv looking for the house of my brother Brammie, but I could not find it anywhere. Suddenly I heard someone sing the *Kol Nidre*. Even though I had never before heard it sung so beautifully and purely, I recognised the voice, but I still could not remember the right person. As I entered the synagogue from which the song came, an indescribable feeling of happiness and peace took hold of me. The bright light shone through the high windows onto the white prayer mantles of the men. In the middle, on the *bima*, Mordecai was singing. On either side of him stood my father and his old friend Moos Vecht, each holding a Torah roll. In the gallery my mother and my sisters were seated, they recognised me, but apparently thought it was completely normal that I was there also, as if we had never been separated. Only Mordecai did not seem to recognise me, so immediately after the service I went looking for him. It was very busy and I could not find him, but suddenly I saw him standing in a group of men. When I had almost reached him and wanted to talk to him, he walked towards the hall and put on his coat. Gingerly I put my hand on his shoulder. He turned around and looked at me with surprise. As if he saw me for the first time. "Mordecai…?" I asked hesitantly. Smiling, he shook his head. "I think that you must be mistaken, friend", he said, "my name is Joshua". He turned around and walked into the dark night with small irregular steps. At that moment I woke up and I did not sleep again that night. Early in the morning I walked to the bench near the two old canons. And since that time the thought that the son of Mordecai… Joshua… is still alive, does not leave me any more.'

Ben remembered that his father had once told him that Mordecai had a son. Cautiously he asked: 'But do you think it is possible that he is still alive? Weren't small children that came into the camp immediately…'

'Joshua never arrived in the camp,' Jacob explained, 'at least not at the same time as his parents. At the time when they were driven from their street, Mordecai managed to press him into the arms of an old non-Jewish neighbor, just before they were marched off. Whatever happened to him afterwards…' He shrugged his shoulders and sighed. 'When Brammie met Mordecai he asked him about it. Any attempts to find Joshua had been without result. And since he did not know where and how to search any more, he has been waiting for a miracle of reunion. You know, Joshua is not circumcised, because they were taken away one day before this was going to happen. At first Mordecai was sad about that, but later he realised that it may have been his salvation. For the Germans circumcision was, in case of doubt, the definite proof that someone of the male sex was a Jew. A week after the circumcision they had planned to see a specialist in Kraków. For Joshua was born with a club-foot and one of his legs was also thinner and shorter than the other.'

It was quiet for a while but then Jacob said with determination: 'And that is why I found that dream so remarkable, you see…? I can see him walking away from me with those irregular steps and other than that the very image of his father…'

Again he fell silent, and then continued pensively: 'What afterwards kept me occupied most was, that for the first time I had a war-related dream that was about the present… or maybe even the future. And that it happened just like that, without reason. I just want to say… that dream was not a subconscious remnant of something that had happened in the past. This was something entirely different. And… if it is confirmed… I mean, if it turns out to be really true that Joshua is still alive and those two would meet again after so many years… yes, then…'

He looked at Ben with his eyes filled with expectation, and concluded his sentence: 'then I want… then I have to share that happiness with him… then the positive reasons will dominate the negative ones… Yes… when that is true, then we'll go there together, I promise you!'

In the silence that followed both realised that soon – maybe even this evening already – there would be an end to all those meaningful moments at the kitchen table. Ben looked at the characteristic face of his father and at his eyes that, in spite of the fact that they had seen endlessly more sadness than his own, radiated such an inner tranquillity. And again this filled him with deep respect. He got up and said: 'Come… it is late, I should go to bed, for I have a long day tomorrow.'

Jacob nodded. 'Yes, it's been quite a day,' he agreed and got up too.

As he walked away from the table Ben said: 'Papa…one more thing.' Jacob turned around and looked expectantly at his son… 'I'll be leaving home shortly and uh… I don't know… well, let's say that I have not always been easy, but I want to tell you now that I have thought it was very remarkable how you always handled that, our talks together, here and in other places, they meant a lot to me. And… well, I just want you to know that I count myself lucky and proud to be your son…'

Jacob felt how with this remark – as the climax of an evening that had already been very special – a flood of gratitude ran through him. The sudden emotion that this caused in him made him clench his teeth for a moment. Outwardly calm, but with moist eyes, he walked towards his son. And there, during a short embrace, he exorcised the rebellion in Ben's life with the peace wish, stammered in their own language: … *'Shalom-aleychem,* boy, *shalom-aleychem.'*

PART 2

5

Nervously Saar was pacing through the house. Now and then she picked up something and put it back right away again.

'Hey… please, sit down for a while,' Jacob said, irritated.

'Yes, but… we have to be at the hairdresser's at nine o'clock,' she complained, 'and it is already five to nine… where are they?'

Ben was breakfasting at the kitchen table. He shook his head: 'Mamma… calm down.

We really won't start without you! And if they forget to pick you up, then you come along as you are… As far as I am concerned your hair is pretty enough!'

'Nah, at least you can't say that of your hair,' Saar answered bad-tempered. 'Much too long!'

Ben took another bite and looked at her with a smile. At that moment the door swung open and Thera entered, followed closely by Ben's sisters Esther and Leah.

'Where have you been…?' Saar cried. 'It is already past nine…!'

'Sorry, mam,' said Leah, 'but the train was delayed.'

'Yeah, yeah.' Saar complained. 'OK, but hurry now… we really should leave!'

Esther walked over to Ben first, kissed him and asked: 'How is my little brother…? Nervous?'

He shrugged. 'No more than usual for something like this, I think,' he reacted and continued his breakfast unruffled.

'In any case, you look terrific in that suit,' she said, sticking up her thumb as she left the kitchen.

'*Nebbish*,' grumbled Saar, 'such a light suit. He looks like an artist. People like us should wear a black suit with a white shirt at these occasions.'

'Hey mama, stop it,' said Esther, 'don't be so old-fashioned, that boy is not going to be confirmed as a rabbi today, he is getting married, right…?'

The sisters differed in age more than a year and had been living together in an apartment in Utrecht for the last three years. Esther worked as a nurse in the *Academic Hospital* and Leah attended the *College of Utrecht* where she studied journalism. She would finish the three-year theoretical part this coming year and was going to do a practical year in Israel after that. First a month of vacation while staying with uncle Bram and aunt Roza in Tel Aviv, then working for four weeks in a *kibbutz* and from November till March doing practice with a newspaper. She would do the obligatory part – four months of practice in Holland – immediately afterwards.

Uncle Bram, extremely happy with the coming family visit from Holland, had already written to her several times. Of his own accord he had organised all sorts of things for an interesting vacation, a *kosher kibbutz* and a practice position with a quality newspaper. In addition he had made suggestions to involve her in a project of the university where he worked, in order to give her practice report more content. He had even prepared his two children, Ruben and Els, to cooperate if necessary in the journalistic assignments of their cousin from Holland. Ruben was working – as became apparent only much later – for the *Mossad*, the Israeli secret service and Els had just finished her psychology studies. She now had a permanent position with the *Simon Wiesenthal House* in Tel Aviv, a treatment centre for traumatised survivors of the Shoah.

Leah was looking forward tremendously to the reunion with those dear people. She remembered their visit to Holland very well; she was about twelve at the time. Aunt Roza had thought it was great that Leah took violin lessons and had promised her that Leah could have her old violin later, because she herself could no longer play due to a rheumatic affliction. Aunt Roza had been given the violin by her mother and in this way it would stay in the family.

As long as the development of her children took place within the context of the traditions and rules of Judaism, Saar soon approved. Jacob however looked in a very different way at his children. He was more tolerant, especially because he was more conscious of the great blessing, that his children were able to develop themselves as they wished in a free world. All that did not have to prevent that in the end they would remain what they were from the beginning, that is, individuals with an age-old basic identity that could not be extinguished, deeply rooted in Judaism.

Ben and Esther were most alike; both were introverted and contemplative. They controlled the situation in which they landed and saw the people whom they had to deal with in perspective. Quietly they drew their conclusions and if they ever mentioned anything, it would be a terse, to-the-point and often cynical-humoristic remark.

Once, when Jacob casually linked threatening events in Israel with the possible coming of the Messiah, Ben, who was playing soccer in the A-youth league, asked if that could wait another couple of months.

'Of course I don't know that,' Jacob reacted, 'but why would it have to wait another couple of months?'

'Well,' Ben remarked dryly, 'then we could at least first become champions.'

David was the only extrovert person of the four. Asking questions about everything had characterised him from childhood. However, when someone put a question to him, he usually answered with a counter-question. In that, too, he was the spitting image of his grandfather Isaac de Lange, whose conduct was based primarily on the strong conviction that asking questions is the simplest way in which to become wiser and in addition it does not cost anything. "It is no accident that you have been given two ears and one mouth", he would say.

As a five-year old boy David had once seen his mother in the shower. The reaction only became apparent the next day in the supermarket. At first he was busy making neat piles of the purchases in the shopping-cart. Suddenly he noticed his mother's round backside, as she stood bent over to pick up something from a lower shelf and he called: 'Mam… mamma…?'

Saar looked around quickly and asked what was the matter.

'You have hair on your bum, don't you?' David called loud and clear.

Saar turned red and irritated by the amusement of the bystanders she reprimanded him harshly. When they had lined up at the cash register a little later, the woman in front of them had an enormous backside. Little David contemplated it with awe and called again: 'Mam, mamma…?'

Unsuspectingly, Saar answered: 'What is it?' Whereupon he asked with a penetrating voice: 'Does that lady also have hair on her bum…?'

Leah, the youngest of the four was distinctly lazy and indolent. The best example of this became apparent during a rather innocent dinner conversation about ideals for the future. After the oldest three children had mentioned and explained their favourite choice of profession there was a silence, 'And, Leah,' Jacob asked finally, 'do you have any idea what you want to be when you grow up?'

Laconically she shrugged her little shoulders and said with a deep sigh: 'I'd rather be nothing… I'd rather be dead… than I don't have to do anything any more…!'

Fortunately this rather destructive attitude to life turned out to be temporary. As she became older she developed a clear purposefulness. Whatever she set out to do, had to happen, at all costs.

Saar always took strict care that they all – as was proscribed – washed their hands before dinner. Going to the toilet during a meal was almost a mortal sin in her eyes. But Leah managed to do it, once…

'Really, mam,' she assured with both hands pressing her tummy and her face screwed up dramatically, 'I really can't hold it any more...!'

'Then you just press your *togus* more tightly to the chair!' Saar tried at first, but when she saw tears appear in those innocent little eyes, she relented and consented, a few minutes later everyone jumped at the scream from the toilet in the hall...

'Mamma... come quick!' Leah shouted at the top of her voice.

Alarmed, Saar ran to the accident site. Little Leah stood with a brilliant smile next to the toilet and, pointing at a long vertical brown turd with at the bottom a small horizontal bit, she said with childish pride: 'I made my letter...!'

After that it never happened again that any of the Van Zuidens got permission to go to the toilet during a meal.

After Leah's puberty she metamorphosed both physically and spiritually. Within a few years she changed from a tall and thin, shy girl with a pointed oval face into a pretty young adult with a mystical aura. She was tall and slim, with a characteristic face and thick hair that fell past her shoulders. She often wore it up, with an exotic band of thin cotton around her forehead. She had a wide interest in and a stronger link with the spiritual and social aspects of society than with the commercial and economic aspects. From early on she was convinced that she wanted to fight the injustice in the world. To travel a lot, to see a lot, but above all, to draw attention to that injustice and – wherever she saw a chance – contribute to changing it. In that sense she was also convinced of her choice of profession, also from a strong Jewish consciousness, fascinated by the prospect of being able to spend a longer period of time in Israel.

With increasing gratefulness Jacob followed the development of his children. Sometimes it overwhelmed him as an unexpected blessing that put the trauma in which he was caught in the shadow and even pushed it into the background. Four shafts of light that gradually pierced the wall that had been raised around him. They expelled, as it were, a part of the darkness from his life. It was a relief to notice how it increasingly returned some balance to his state of mind. The deep joy about his children and their assured future that lay anchored in the prophecy of Mordecai, often rose up in his heart to unfold into the invisible space of the heavens.

When the ladies returned from the hairdresser, the whole Van Zuiden family departed from Elburg in the direction of Oldebroek. Apart from the formalities at the town hall, the wedding ceremony and the festive reception would take place there.

At the beginning of the drive to the farm, Nant's oldest sister Antje stood waving and gesturing wildly when she spotted the cars of Ben and his family.

'Yoohoo… here it is!' she cried, waving enthusiastically.

Ben shook his head. 'Here it is…' he repeated, 'as if I wouldn't know…'

'I'll show you where you can park. Come along…' Antje called, gesturing busily.

With small quick steps she walked – still waving her arms – in front of the cars past the hay stack and the pig barn to the open gate of the pasture.

'Who is that *meshugene*?' Saar asked when they parked the car in the meadow.

'Mamma,' said Ben, 'don't ask me how it is possible… but it's a sister of Nant. It is really true… I don't understand it myself!'

'Oh…!' Antje called with a high voice, when the Van Zuiden family had alighted, 'you are all so beautiful…!' and walking back to the farm, she kept chattering about the nice weather and that it took quite a lot of effort to properly organize everything for a day like this.

The large square yard – enclosed by the farm, the cow stable and the hay stack – was decorated festively and full of tables and chairs. Even in the barn there were decorations. Along the newly white-washed walls stood high tables as well as low wicker tables and chairs, and a buffet for the snacks and drinks for the reception. In front of the open doors of the farm a provisional *chupah* had been built; four wooden poles with on top a piece of grey agricultural plastic, richly decorated with flowers. Underneath were two chairs for the bridal couple. A lectern had been put there also for Mr. van Dam and for Jacob, who would take care of respectively the Christian and the Jewish part of the religious ceremony.

While both families went to have a cup of coffee, Ben walked inside to pick up his bride. They came outside to loud applause. Nant shyly accepted the compliments of Ben's sisters, and when Jacob said – putting his hand softly on her shoulder – that she now was even more beautiful than usual, Nant kissed him spontaneously on his cheek. 'Thank you, Mr. Van Zuiden,' she said, 'that's very nice of you,' and bending towards him she added in a whisper: 'and it makes more of an impression on me than all those quacks and "ooohs" of those girls over there.' Jacob's contented look followed her as she then mingled cheerfully with the others.

Antje had been shifting restlessly on her chair for some time and looked at her watch continuously. Finally she jumped up, asked everyone's attention and started – again with busy movements and gestures – to explain in her own enthusiastic manner the program for the rest of the day... First a lunch and then together to the town hall. She explicitly asked people not to congratulate the bridal couple there, but to wait until after the ceremony, which would take place here immediately afterwards. Then there would be the reception – also here on the farm – and the party would continue and end in the restaurant in the harbour of Elburg. She stopped to take a breath and Ben remarked dryly: 'It boils down to the fact that we have to start lunch now!'

A long table had been set, taking up the full width of the large living room. Ben sat in the middle with on either side his parents, his brother and sisters and his grandparents on his mother's side, who had arrived in the meantime. Immediately across from him sat Nant and her family. While everyone chatted, waiting for Nant's mother who was still busy in the kitchen, Saar cast a critical eye over the richly laden table.

'Hmm...' she complained, 'half of it is *treif*...'

'But the other half is not...!' Ben snapped at her in a whisper. 'I would think that would be more than enough for you...'

At that moment Nant's mother entered with a large pan of steaming soup.

'There you are,' she said as she put the pan in the middle of the table, 'chicken soup, especially for the Van Zuiden family!'

Ben turned at Nant's younger brothers with a smile and said: 'Make sure you quickly get a large plate full, boys, before my mother eats half of it.'

Saar did not get a chance to react, for Nant's mother called out: 'Wait a moment ... first we fold our hands...!' and casting a severe look at her husband she continued in the same breath: 'Come on Bertus... pray!'

Obedient as always Bertus listened to the command of his wife and thanked the Lord for the beautiful weather...the fact that everyone was here and healthy and asked for a blessing for the meal and for the rest of the day. From force of habit he finished with: 'We ask this of You in the name of the Lo... uh...' Just in time he realised that – with regards to the company – he had better leave out the name of the Lord Jesus this time and finished haltingly: 'of the... of... uh... well, let's say, in grace amen... Enjoy your meal!'

Esther and Leah, who were at Nant's home for the first time, enjoyed the conversation and the cosy country atmosphere on the farm. At one point Jan, Nant's younger brother, called out: 'Mr. van Zuiden, please pass the *"nagelhout"*.'

Jacob looked at the boy in surprise and asked: 'The what...?'

'The *"nagelhout"*,' Jan repeated and pointed at a plate with cold cuts.

Jacob lifted the plate and looked at it carefully: 'But that is just smoked beef?'

'Yes, that's right!' Jan replied, ' *"nagelhout…!"* '

Laughing, Ben shook his head and said to his father: 'And then they think it is funny when we use Yiddish words… but this is much worse, don't you think?'

In good harmony all sorts of aspects from their so different cultures were highlighted back and forth during the meal. Saar was the only one who did not participate. To start a dialogue with *goyim* was not her priority at this moment. For the time being her attention was on enjoying the soup, richly filled with morsels of chicken breast, onions and celery, and the "nagelhout" sandwiches.

After the meal they left for the town hall where a large group of people – mutual family members and friends and also colleagues of Ben – was already waiting. Everyone followed the bridal couple and the family into the marriage hall. When the civil marriage had been officially solemnized and the whole company had arrived at the farm again, the bridal couple walked to the *chupah*. Nant sat down on one of the two chairs and Ben went over to the lectern that stood to the side.

Calmly he looked around and waited till it became quiet…

'Dear people,' he started, 'now that on this day… - the day of our life - our civil marriage has been solemnized, Nant and I also want to give expression to our faith. Aside from the party that we are going to celebrate in a while, that too is the reason that we have invited you here – our family and best friends. We really appreciate it that you want to witness this ceremony. We have found both my father and Mr. Van Dam, president of the youth society of the *Free Evangelical Congregation*, willing to take care of this. We are very grateful to them both that they have participated in our deliberations, sympathised with us from the beginning, and have agreed to do it in such a way that Nant and I can identify ourselves with it.

I was born on November 26th 1948 and eight days later my parents had me circumcised with the words: *This is my covenant that you shall keep between Me and you and your descendants.* Already at a young age I used to go to the *Jewish school* in the synagogue of Apeldoorn on Sundays together with my brother and later also with my sisters. When I was 13 years old I became Bar Mitzvah. From that day on you are adult as far as religion is concerned and you are considered a full member of the Jewish community. During that ceremony in the synagogue you had to read a part from the Torah – called a *parsha* – in Hebrew. You practised that text thoroughly, of course, and when you thought you knew it, you were allowed to read it. Our teacher would then tape it on a cassette. You were allowed to take it home to listen whether you made mistakes. I have that tape here now and there is a special reason why I want you to hear it today.'

Ben gave a signal to his friend Alex who sat near the sound system, after which everyone could listen for about five minutes to the clear young voice with which Benjamin van Zuiden, ten years ago, read his *parsha* – in Hebrew. And for the first time in history, age-old Biblical words in their original Hebrew sounded beneath the hard blue sky of this so distinctly orthodox-christian environment. And even though most of those present did not understand the content, still everyone seemed moved by the intonation of that pure young voice and by the authenticity of that old tradition.

When the tape had finished, Ben said: 'The most important reason why I had you listen to this is that in this part the same text occurred: *This is my covenant that you shall keep between Me and you and your descendants.* I want to let you know that I have thought a lot about those words recently. There was a time when they even caused me to doubt. Because, if I would marry a non-Jewish woman, then my descendants would, according to the law, also be non-Jewish. And I asked myself if I would not therefore be breaking that covenant. Nant and I talked about this a lot together and, in order to better understand each other, I have immersed myself rather a lot in the Christian faith lately. Even though a lot is still unclear and unintelligible to me, one thing is certain… and that is, that both of us – even if from a completely different approach and tradition – want to serve the same God.

That gives me a realistic hope that His covenant with our possible descendants will not be broken.

In this context the talks with my father have also meant a lot to me. On this day I want to mention that, papa… and to thank you for them. It has made a big impression on me how an important prophecy has sustained you during a large part of your life. It was through that prophecy that you were able to give me the certainty that it was alright to marry Nant. Finally Nant herself once pointed out a saying of the Jewish scholar Paul, who says in your Bible that of the three pillars in life – faith, hope and love – love is the most important. I have to confess that this suited me very well. I met Nant at the right moment and since that time my life has taken a turn for the better. From this day on I want nothing more than to share my life with her. She is the best thing that ever happened to me… she is always with me… she is my other half…

In the Talmud it says: *Man seeks a partner for life to find in her what he has lost.* In Johanna-Aleida – better known to you as Nant – I found what I had lost. Now I am happy to let Mr. van Dam speak and… Nant's father-in-law!'

While Ben sat down next to Nant, brother van Dam got up and walked to the lectern. Quickly he rifled through the large Bible that he held up in the palm of his left hand.

'Dear people… bride and groom…' he said, 'following on the words of the bridegroom, I would like to read a few words from the Old Testament with you, from the book of Ruth, chapter 4, verse 13 to 17. There we read: *So Boaz took Ruth and she became his wife. Then he went to her, and the LORD enabled her to conceive, and she gave birth to a son. And the women said to Naomi: "Praise be to the LORD, who this day has not left you without a kinsman-redeemer. May he become famous throughout Israel. And they named him Obed. He was the father of Jesse, the father of David".*'

When he had finished reading, he did not put the Bible down but lifted it higher and said with such enthusiasm as if he was about to reveal the greatest theological secret of all times: 'Do you know what is so beautiful in this story…? This story from the *Tenakh*, or as we call it… the Old Testament…?'

With a triumphant smile he looked around the throng, dropped his hand – with the open Bible – a bit and tapped his right index finger a few times with emphasis on the part he had read.

'This story,' he continued, 'tells us about a Jewish man who marries a non-Jewish woman. And… the Lord blessed it! Boaz did not have to be concerned that the Lord would break His covenant with him and his descendants because he married a non-Jewish woman. On the contrary… the descendants of Boaz and Ruth included – as we have just read – king David and… even more important: the lord Jesus!'

With the charisma and the fanaticism of an American evangelical preacher, he richly scattered his views over his audience – about deliverance, grace and love of God, for all people that know Him. Brother Van Dam seemed to own all wisdom and all truth. And his secret? The personal knowledge of the Lord Jesus, who had said of Himself: *I am the way, the truth and the life; no one comes to the Father than through Me.*

'Whatever evil and disaster can assail us from the ruins of the sinful, evil outside world,' he cried, gesturing wildly, 'and however our different views and traditions threaten to estrange us from one another, do not fear: for every problem… only Jesus!'

Saar's face was clearly showing irritation as she shifted restlessly in her chair and looked around her.

'Nah… what do you think,' she whispered to Jacob with chagrin, 'will that *chochem* ever finish with that nonsense…'

Jacob shushed her softly, with a calming gesture: 'Calm down… be quiet!'

Fortunately for Saar, the liberating, rather theatrically intoned "Aaa… men" of brother Van Dam was heard soon afterwards. Jacob put on his skull cap and walked to the front. For a minute he considered reacting to the speech of his predecessor. The latter had definitely not kept to their agreement. In the conversation beforehand with the bridal couple and both parents, they had agreed – in order to avoid unnecessary tension at such a festive occasion – to circumvent the differences in their convictions and to limit themselves to concurrences. Brother Van Dam would therefore speak of the remark of Ruth to her Jewish mother-in-law Naomi: *Your God is my God*. Clearly encouraged by Ben's remark about his initial doubt concerning a non-Jewish wife, he had obviously found it more fitting to highlight the relationship of Boaz and Ruth. Understandable maybe, but not very sensible, for by doing so he had landed logically at the Person that was so controversial in this gathering, namely Jesus. However, Jacob decided that it was better to not tackle that now, but to speak with him about it later in private.

He went into the stable and came back with a glass that was quarter filled with wine. Beneath the canopy he put it in front of him on the lectern. Then he took a small brown bag from the left pocket of his jacket and a glass jar from the right pocket, which he put on either side of the glass of wine. Taking his time and with a happy smile, he looked around the circle: 'Most likely you are now asking yourself what this funny exhibit is and what it has to do with a wedding. Well… you know… in our tradition symbolism plays an important role. We try to express the essence of what we commemorate or celebrate by visible or tangible objects so that it comes closer and reaches us more deeply.'

He picked up the glass and continued: 'How many glasses will break today … I don't know and neither do you, but this one will definitely bite the dust…

In a while, at the end of the official wedding ceremony, Nant and Ben will both have a sip of wine from this glass. Thereby they underline once again the promise that they gave each other at the town hall… namely, to share their joys and sorrows from now on. Then the bridegroom must make a declaration and step on the glass with his heel. The thought behind that is not, as has been said in fun at times, that the bridegroom is allowed "to put his foot down" for one last time. No… it has to do with the last of the seven blessings that are expressed during a wedding, namely the memory of Jerusalem. Even in moments of jubilant joy, a Jew should never forget the destruction of the Temple and the fall of Jerusalem. Also, the broken glass reminds us of the imperfection and draws our attention to the fractures in ourselves and in the world in which we live. And this…' he continued, as he picked up the bag and the glass jar at the same time and turned towards the bridal couple, 'these are bitter herbs and honey. This is based on a custom from long ago, at our home. Just like our children, I used to have a mother who prepared the meals with love and dedication. We used to look forward especially to the Sabbath meals on Friday evening and also those during feasts. We were not rich, but I'll never forget that my youngest sister remarked once during one of those festive meals: "Now it really seems as if we are rich also".'

The instant he mentioned this, he was alarmed at the emotion that it caused him. Calling up this sweet image from his youth confronted him, more violently than he had expected, with the bitter reality of that lost paradise. He clenched his teeth. With his head bowed and his eyes closed, he tried several times to swallow the choking lump in his throat. Ben and David, as well as Esther and Leah, sat motionless, breathless with fright – watching their father. For them it was the first time that they heard him tell spontaneously of a period in his life about which he had always been silent and about which they had never dared to ask him. Therefore it not only impressed them tremendously, but also Saar. In the oppressive silence the only sounds were of passing cars in the distance and the bleating of a sheep. No one of those present coughed or moved. Hopelessly lonely and lost, Jacob did his best to control the elegy that threatened to break loose from the very depth of his soul. Slowly he raised his head again. With moist eyes he looked at the breathlessly listening group of people in front of him. He was startled when in their midst suddenly someone stood up. But when he saw that it was his good friend Simon Steinmetz, who stretched out his hands to him in an inviting gesture, he noticed that the heavy feeling gradually streamed out of him to the open hands and the open heart of Simon.

After a deep sigh he excused himself for the interruption and continued with a somewhat broken voice: 'With *Rosh Hashanah* – that is our New Year – my mother always put out a bowl with pieces of sour apples for desert and next to it a bowl of honey. That meant to emphasize the wish that we would get enough sweetness in the new year to be able to cope with the bitterness. And in this way I want to wish you, too, from the bottom of my heart, that in the life that you are going to share together from today the sweetness will always be more than the bitterness. That's why this big pot of honey and this small bag of herbs. Whether the sweetness will dominate in your life… that I cannot guarantee. But I do know that it has a lot, if not all, to do with loving and serving the Highest and to live in accordance with His commandments. Therefore you are getting from your mother and me, just like David and Thera when they married, a *mezuza* to attach to the doorpost of your house in Putten.'

After he had handed the small metal tube to Ben, he said: 'On the parchment roll that is in there, the following words from the Torah are written: *Take heed to yourselves, that your heart be not deceived, and ye turn aside, and serve other gods, and worship them; And then the LORD's wrath be kindled against you, and he shut up the Heaven, that there be no rain, and that the land yield not her fruit; and lest ye perish quickly from off the good land which the LORD giveth you. Therefore shall ye lay up these my words in your heart and in your soul. And ye shall teach them your children, speaking of them when thou sittest in thine house, and when thou walkest by the way, when thou liest down, and when thou risest up; and thou shalt write them upon the door posts of thine house, and upon thy gates'*

After having pronounced the wish that both in the house and in the life of the bridal couple the joy in the law – that has been given to us by the Eternal One Himself – will be always present, he said after a short silence: 'Then I want to proceed now to pronounce the *Sheva Berakhot,* the seven blessings...'

Solemnly and with devotion he read each of the seven blessings, first in Hebrew and then in Dutch...

> *'Praised art Thou, O Lord our God, King of the Universe, Creator of the fruit of the vine.*
> *Praised art thou, O Lord our God, King of the Universe, Creator of man.*
> *Praised art Thou, O Lord our God, King of the Universe, Who created man and woman in Thy image, fashioning woman from man as his mate, that together they might perpetuate life.*
> *Praised are You, O Lord, Creator of man. May Zion rejoice as her children are restored to her in joy.*
> *Praised art Thou, O Lord, Who causes Zion to rejoice at her children's return.*
> *Grant perfect joy to these loving companions, as Thou did to the first man and woman in the Garden of Eden.*
> *Praised art Thou, O Lord, who grants the joy of bride and groom.*
> *Praised art Thou, O Lord our God, King of the Universe, who created joy and gladness, bride and groom, mirth and song, delight and rejoicing, love and harmony, peace and companionship. O Lord our God, may there ever be heard in the cities of Judah and in the streets of Jerusalem voices of joy and gladness, voices of bride and groom, the jubilant voices of those joined in marriage under the bridal canopy, the voices of young people feasting and singing.*
> *Praised are You, O Lord, Who causes the groom to rejoice with his bride.'*

Especially during the pronouncement of the Hebrew text all the guests were listening intently. Those words and sounds that were unknown to them, but still impressive, made them realise that they looked at and listened to a direct descendant from Abraham, Isaac and Jacob. A man whose life – they all knew – was marked by the most terrible and bizarre circumstances and who still radiated so sincerely, from the deepest part of his soul, a strong involvement with his Creator. It was visibly implied in the lightly swaying movements that accompanied the careful and attentive pronouncement of that age-old, original language with which he honoured and worshipped the God of his life… *Boruch Atoh Adonoi E-lo Heinu Melech Ha'olam… Praised art Thou, Oh Lord our God, King of the Universe…*

After Jacob had pronounced the last of the seven blessings David, Thera, Esther, Leah and Saar stepped forward. They stood between the guests and the *chupah* under which Ben and Nant were sill sitting. Then the old Hebrew words of Psalm 133, sung very purely – a capella and polyphone – spread themselves over the guests… *Hine matov u ma naim, shevet achiem cham jachad.* Then they sang it again, but now in Dutch and with violin accompaniment by Leah. *See how good, how wonderful it is that sons of the same house live together. One bond of love keeps them together. The blessing of God's exalted name falls on them full of sweet tenderness, like oil that the priest has dedicated.*

While the others remained standing, Jacob took the wineglass, walked towards the bridal couple and asked them to give each other the right hand, after which he said: 'In conclusion I ask of you, Benjamin van Zuiden, to make, in the presence of all these witnesses present, the statement based on which this union can be declared valid.'

Ben took the ring that he had put on Nant's finger at the town hall and said: 'See, by this ring you are holy to me according to the law of Moses and Israel. I shall work for you, honour you, support and sustain you in accordance with the custom of Jewish husbands who work for their wives, honour them, support and sustain them in all sincerity.'

Then Jacob gave the glass to Nant, who took a sip and passed it to Ben. When the latter had sipped the last of the wine, he cited the traditional word: *Shana haba a B'Yerushalayim.* Then he put the glass carefully on the floor and broke it to pieces with his left heel. While his family members clapped their hands enthusiastically and wished them *mazel tov*, Leah picked up her violin and with the notes of *Havah Nagilah Hava...* they sang and danced around the bridal couple.

Soon the other guests joined in the revelry and the bridal couple was congratulated extensively. Now that the official ceremony was finished, the merry-making crowd gradually increased to a varied party – family, friends, neighbors, colleagues from Putten and also from the companies where Ben worked as windowdresser. On the large lawn, parallel to the drive next to the farm, they sat down in the shade of the high oaks. Because everyone could pick up their snacks and drinks at the buffet in the decorated stable, soon all these people who were each so different were walking back and forth in a relaxed and informal manner talking now to this person, then to another.

Only Kees – the neighbor from across the road – and Nant's uncle Evert from Oosterwolde – the horse farmer – had a bottle of gin on their table. Such small glasses – Kees thought – that was too much effort. You would have to keep walking back and forth. After some time Jacob, Gérard and Simon Steinmetz joined them too.

'Well, Van Zuiden... congratulations,' said Kees, 'you have gained a beautiful daughter!'

'Yes... she is certainly beautiful,' Jacob agreed, 'and not only on the outside.'

'Look at her standing there, men!' said uncle Evert, inspired by his passion for horses. 'With beautiful straight legs and as white as silver.' He also observed approvingly Nant's girl friends with which she was talking some distance away at that moment. 'Such beautiful maids, eager to breed,' he mused. Because of his strong daily involvement with the natural course of things in the animal world, the other men did not really object to Evert's remark. In his case, they thought silently, this manner of qualification was even legitimate in a way. When Nant's closest friend Evelyn – also a farmer's daughter – walked over to Jacob to congratulate him, Evert even had an unexpected extra. With a frontal view of the girl's ample bosom that peeked voluptuously from the edge of her blouse, he said to Simon: 'Look at that… such udders!'

'Well, you know…' said Simon, who did not want Evert to be the only one with anatomical observations, 'for me they don't have to be big, but…' he continued with a poker face and raised finger, 'when I put my nose between them I don't want to hear anything any more!' It took a while for the joke to sink in but then Evert roared with laughter and he hit the table so hard that the gin glasses trembled.

Jacob shook his head, got up and put his hand with familiarity on Evelyn's shoulder. 'I congratulate you too, with your girl-friend,' he said and took her unobtrusively away from the table. Before they mingled with the other guests, Jacob confided in her, as he gestured with his head to the men behind them: 'It is probably due to the nice spring weather. Please take it as a compliment.'

She laughed disarmingly and said dryly: 'Oh, I am used to that sort of thing… typical horse folk, aren't they,' whereupon she joined her friends again.

Jacob then was congratulated by Fienus, the cobbler from Elburg. Fienus was also an uncle of Nant. He was married to the only sister of Bertus. For as long as Fienus had had his business in Elburg, Jacob had been his steady client.

'It's good that I see you,' said Jacob, 'I want to come to you this week with those shoes for which you made new soles the other day. They are already almost worn out, how could that happen so quickly?'

Fienus, who this afternoon clearly had other things in mind than hearing complaints about his work, raised his hands to heaven in a gesture of "force majeur". Hastily he escaped with the excuse: 'Tcha... I can't help that. Just figure, it is due to the fact that the earth is round... and your soles are flat!'

Smiling, Jacob shook his head and walked to the hay stack where Ben stood talking with a group of men.

'I just snared your son to give a talk,' Van Dam declared with satisfaction.

Jacob looked at him surprised and repeated slowly: 'A talk...? In your church...?'

'Yes, it is like this...' Van Dam explained, 'in the past winter season the theme of our youth meetings was *Church & Israel*. Soon we'll be having our last evening in which we also say goodbye to Nant. And well... because she was getting married to a Jewish boy, it seemed like a good idea to ask Ben to tell us a few things about that theme during the last evening. We do that from time to time... invite people that have a certain affinity with a specific topic. In the discussion afterwards we hope that our young people are encouraged to think more deeply about it.'

For a while Jacob remained silent and stared ahead. 'Hmmm... I understand your premise,' he said cautiously, 'and I uh... I also appreciate and respect your feeling towards Israel, but...'

He fell silent again and then slowly turned his head towards Ben. The men noticed the beginnings of a smile on the characteristic face of the man for whom they all had a certain respect.

'Be aware of what you start,' he warned, 'I know my son better than anyone...'

'Yes, and...?' Van Dam asked carefully, 'that means...?'

'That means...' Jacob answered, 'that he will not spare you!'

'Hey papa, come on!' Ben reacted, spontaneously raising both hands, 'I am not likely to spoil the good-bye meeting for Nant...!'

Jacob shrugged his shoulders in resignation, also raised his hands and concluded laconically: 'We'll see, kid... we'll see...' Then he took Van Dam's shoulder and gestured to him to walk along.

When Nant's mother saw them walk together past the hay stack to the meadow, she joined the group of men and said to Ben: 'Well, I hope that your father gives that Van Dam a good scolding and thrashes his pants off his behind. That shit talked about something entirely different than what we had agreed on.'

'Yes…' Ben agreed with her, 'I have to say that I was really disappointed in him.'

'So you see, kid,' she concluded, 'you can't trust any man and therefore…' she added encouragingly, 'trust the Lord, he never fools you!'

Uncle Evert, who had joined the group out of curiosity, had observed how Van Dam had smoothed his lank hair backwards a few times. Because of a low parting – just above his ear – a lock of hair always fell at an angle across his forehead when he moved his head.

'Tcha boys…' uncle Evert intoned with fitting seriousness, 'he's not a bad guy, really, but yes… you should always beware of someone with such a lop-sided blaze!'

Nant's mother left the men. She stopped Saar, who just passed by and remarked: 'We really have been lucky with the weather, haven't we? It is so cosy with all those people in the yard.' She pointed at the grandparents who sat together at a table, talking a mile a minute, and continued: 'Look at those old folks, all four of them sipping plum brandy and yacking. It'll be about Israel, I bet, looking at my mother. Still, it's great that they are still so well, because well… you have to take into account that once you reach that age… well, than you have eaten most of your bread!'

Ben saw that his mother tried to react a few times but hardly got a chance and secretly he enjoyed that. In the meantime Jacob was standing with Van Dam near the meadow. Leaning on their elbows on the large wooden gate, they looked out across the wide plain to the mill and the farms in the distance.

'Uh… you know, Van Dam,' said Jacob as his eyes raked the landscape that he had so often looked at from the eastern city wall, 'what I just meant with my remark that Ben will not spare you, if you ask him to come and give his opinion about *Church & Israel*, is the fact that for a long time already he cannot imagine that our God is the same as yours. Because of his relationship with Nant he has studied this problem lately, and he may have become a bit milder, but I have to say that in principle I share his lack of understanding. That we serve the same God... OK, but why can't you accept and respect that the Eternal One makes us follow a different road from yours?'

Without reflection Van Dam answered, with automatic self-evidence: 'Because Jesus has said that no one can come to the Father but through Him!'

'Jesus...' Jacob repeated with a sigh and looked silently across the meadows, 'Jesus is the God of the *goyim*, of the non-Jews. And I have to say that I am not very impressed by the behaviour of his followers throughout the ages. I mean, as a people we have experienced rather a lot of misery in his name. But OK, that is your responsibility. In principle it may be true what you say, that no one can come to the Father than through the Jew Yeshuah, but then that only applies to non-Jews.'

Brother Van Dam slowly shook his head: 'No, when Jesus says "no one" then that applies literally to everyone, without exception!'

'But, dear fellow,' Jacob said – with something of despondency in his voice for the first time – 'we already were children of the Father. Long before Jesus spoke those words, the Eternal One – praised be His name – had closed a covenant with us. You know the Bible, don't you...? Well, there it says, black on white, how He let us know, through Moses, our great prophet, that He had chosen us as His people for eternity.

And as I said, I don't understand that you do not want to accept and respect that. The *chassidic* Jews learn: "If people turn up at your door, you should receive them with open arms. But to pull them from their own path in order to push them into your house, that is not good". And that... – pulling Jews from their path and then to try and push them into Christianity… - that is something you cannot stop, can you? In your speech you did the same thing. And by the way, it is not even true that Boaz married a non-Jewish woman. Before Ruth married, she converted to the God of the Jewish people.'

In the meantime little Chaya, the daughter of David and Thera, had joined them. When silence fell, she asked: 'Opa, are you also coming to the party…?'

A warm feeling of tenderness took hold of Jacob. He took the girl on his arm and as he stroked her hair, he said: 'This little angel is an important part of the honey in my life.' He kissed her, took a few steps forward and peered at the horizon in the East. Somewhere far behind it he had once, at the deepest point of his misery, heard the voice of his heavenly Father say through the mouth of Mordecai that he would return to the city of his birth and would be allowed to rejoice in his children and grandchildren. Children of him… and… of the eternal Covenant… That certainty no one could ever take from him, and at that moment this truth filled him with indescribable gratitude. His look travelled along the hard blue, infinite skies high above him, and apart from the Highest, only Chaya heard him whisper with intense reverence: *'Boruch Atoh Adonoi E-lo Heinu Melech Ha'olam…'*

'Opa…?' suddenly the silence was broken. Jacob started from his reveries and looked into the large, questioning eyes of the little Chaya. 'Why are you crying…?' she asked, touchingly sweet.

Jacob smiled, kissed her again and explained: 'That is… because I am so happy with you, your papa and mamma, with oma and… and with everyone!'

He looked around and noticed that brother Van Dam had walked back already. Then he put the little girl down, took her hand and said gaily: 'Come… let's party!'

'Yeesss…!' Chaya shouted happily and skipped laughing along at Jacob's hand. 'When I grow up I am going to play the violin, just like aunty Leah,' she confided in him. Together they sang *Havah Nagilah Havah*, but soon that was drowned out by the applause and shouts of the guests. Surprised, Jacob looked around and suddenly he understood. "De Manke Van Essen" had arrived. He cycled straight towards him with his inseparable accordion on the front luggage carrier of his old transport bicycle. When he arrived at the hay stack he was almost standing still and he let himself fall sideways for convenience' sake. Jacob helped him get down at which "De Manke" took off his cap and bowed dramatically.

'Van Zuiden… man, thank you, and congratulations with the wedding of your son; another one taken care of, you've got to reckon, and that's great, for if they stay home, you're not happy either, are you…? Children are a blessing of the Lord but their appetite you can't afford!'

Meanwhile he had taken the old suitcase with his accordion from the luggage carrier and concluded: 'Well… let's first sing to the bride and groom before we take a few.' And he limped towards the lectern under the *chupah*…

… Even though the qualification "village idiot" would apply to "De Manke Van Essen", no one called him that. People liked him too much. His great passion was to sing and play the accordion. Most of the texts of his songs he wrote himself, mainly to existing melodies. With infinite patience he practised and practised until he could play such a tune on his "tummy organ" – as he always called his instrument. As soon as he found out that there was a jubilee or wedding somewhere in a village, he would turn up, true to tradition, and unasked he would then perform his "congratulations song". Almost everyone could join in the singing, for it had been the same tune for many years. In the cheerful text only the name of the person celebrating his jubilee or of the relevant bridal couple was changed. The last two sentences of the refrain were always sung by him in a lightly vibrating voice of due respect… "May the Lord's blessing fall on you, like a hammer on a horseshoe".

Aside from his solo-performances he was a fanatic member of the local men's choir *Praise the Lord*. That choir consisted mostly of members that had not passed the strict admission selection of the pretentious oratorio society. Every Wednesday evening they practised in the dancehall of the local pub, where they had a drink afterwards. Some men, "De Manke" among them, were known to sing louder on the way home than during practice.

Once a year *Praise the Lord* took part in a regional competition. None of the men had the illusion that they would ever win a first prize there. It was mainly a matter of a nice day out together which, with "De Manke" in their midst, was usually the case. Still, once it happened that the choir won a first prize. Of two participating choirs that had the best chances to win a large number of members were not present due to various circumstances. *Praise the Lord* grabbed its chance and gave a superb performance, with as a consequence a real first prize! Afterwards this unique success was celebrated exuberantly with the requisite drinks in the large tent where the competition was held. When finally everyone was sitting in the bus for the trip home and the driver counted heads, one passenger was missing: "De Manke Van Essen". Immediately two men went looking for him and found him in front of the entrance of the tent. Pleasantly tipsy, he danced around, limping, with a glass of beer in each hand and singing at the top of his voice: "Praise the Lord – two, three – will never die… praise the Lord – two, three – is champion!"

A nice circumstance was that that first prize was the reason to grant the choir's conductor, Mr. Van de Broek, a royal decoration. The marriage of this man had remained without issue and he compensated the lack of children with his many social and musical activities. During a heavily attended reception the chairman of *Praise the Lord* handed him an envelope with a gift of money. In addition "De Manke" gave Mrs. Van de Broek a large cake with the name of the choir in whipped cream. In his own characteristic way he spoke in a cheerful voice: "No namesake… still a cake!"

The love for music and poetry was expressed in the life of "De Manke" in accordance with his mental level, which was not particularly high. But the people loved him unconditionally. They cherished him because of his cheerful character and the original, spontaneous manner in which he – as their own village artist –brought colour into their daily lives.

Every year – during the village festival – he performed his entire repertoire in the evening in the music tent. A firm custom, that during all those years had been broken once – almost. For the celebration of a lustrum, the festival committee had decided to surprise the people with a "real", nationally known artist. In an expensive car he was driven right up to the music tent. He had made that condition, because he was afraid that – in view of his popularity – his enthusiastic fans would crush him. A group of farm boys were standing there, hands in pockets, looking sheepishly at that vainglorious fellow from Holland. It stayed that way when he started to sing. Whatever the man tried to do, he could not get the public going. Already at the third song people started to call for "De Manke", and as a result the expensive artist – for the first time in his career – gave up after half an hour and went home completely frustrated.

Accompanied by loud applause and shouts, "De Manke" then climbed the stage – together with his inseparable accordion – and then the party really started. Passionately they sang the songs from the hour-long repertoire, dancing and clapping hands. From *What a friend we have in Jesus* to *Blonde Gretchen from the polder* and from *Lammie with the mocha legs* to the dramatic final song *Fire in the bordello*. Then all set out in the direction of the beer tent, where the party continued till the early hours and "De Manke" accepted his rich rewards in kind from the people…

With a deep bow and a wide sweep of his arm "De Manke" received the loud applause for his "congratulations song" for Ben and Nant. Then he tied his old suitcase with the accordion tightly to his transport bicycle in order to mingle with the wedding guests. Apart from the incident of brother Van Dam's speech, it was a very successful afternoon. Anton van der Hoeven, one of Ben's colleagues from Putten, made a nice speech; there was music and singing, and a few family members and friends performed short plays.

Towards eight in the evening the last guests departed. Then the family went to Elburg, where the party was continued in a more intimate circle in the cosy restaurant at the harbour. Towards the end of the evening, when most of the guests had already left, Jacob saw how Nant's mother and Saar were talking together in a very relaxed manner. Unobtrusively he motioned to Ben: 'Look at that! It is probably due to the plum brandy but it does give you *nachas*, doesn't it?'

Ben nodded happily and together they moved a few steps closer, while talking, in order to catch a bit of the conversation.

'Let's hope they stay healthy and can live together in *shalom* and *menukha*,' Saar wished. She got up and concluded with: 'Well, till the next time and *mazel tov*!'

'Yes, exactly and uh… also something like that!' said Nant's mother, who had deduced from the tone and attitude of Saar that it all was meant well.

It was deep in the night before Ben and Nant, finally together in their apartment in Putten – tired but satisfied – looked back on a day that was long and moving but beautiful in all respects.

'I believe I am way beyond sleep,' said Nant when they went to bed.

'Well, so much the better,' Ben answered as he took her in his arms. And again, he counted himself lucky to be united with his whole being to this original "pure-nature woman".

'I can tell that your cartridges are far from being finished,' Nant chuckled some time later.

'What?' Ben reacted surprised.

'Oh…' Nant explained, 'my father asked uncle Evert the other day how his sex life was. "Bertus", he said, "don't even mention it. Dreadful… the pistol is still hanging there, but the cartridges are all finished".'

Smiling, Ben looked into those beautiful blue eyes from which both naughtiness and honesty radiated. He felt perfectly happy. And as he remembered his father's remark that Nant was a valuable pearl that he should guard and keep with all his might, Nant asked: 'What is it…? Don't you understand…? Or are you thinking of something else?'

'Yes,' Ben admitted and very tenderly took her face in his hands. 'I realise more than ever that you, my "Wittekop", are the most valuable thing I possess. A pearl that I shall guard and keep like the light of my eyes.'

'Jeez…' she said surprised, 'that is beautiful… it sounds like a line from a book…'

'No, no!' Ben denied immediately, 'that is not something out of any book, but from the deepest part of my heart…!'

She kissed him and nestled contentedly against him. After a long, deep yawn she whispered sleepily: 'Good night, Shake Spear.'

6

More than three weeks after their wedding Ben and Nant drove to Oldebroek one Sunday evening, to attend the last evening of the season of the *Free Evangelical Youth Society*. They were both so pre-occupied that they hardly said a word. As the day approached, Nant had become more and more anxious about it. She felt that it was going to be everything but an edifying and relaxed evening, and this had to do with two persons in particular…

The first was a boy who had tried for years to go out with her. His name was Jan-Willem van den Brink, but because of his imposing posture everyone called him "De Reus". He worked on the cutter of Van Triest from Elburg and therefore was at sea every week from Monday till Friday. During the Saturday evenings in Elburg and Sunday evenings at the youth society he had done his very best to link up with Nant. He was a handsome hunk and she knew plenty of girls that fell for him. She had gone out with him once, but the feeling she had when she met Ben, she had never experienced with "De Reus". Now that he had definitely lost his chance, he could use this last evening to vent his frustration on Ben. Knowing him, she would not be surprised if that happened.

The second person was Andries. He was the fiancé of the oldest daughter of brother Van Dam and studied theology. Being raised in a rightwing-reformed environment had made him into a convinced follower of the "replacement theology", that was widely accepted in those circles. It was a rather controversial theory, based on the self-proclaimed opinion that the Community of Christ had become the new Israel from the moment when the Jews had rejected Christ as the Son of God and as the promised Messiah.

Andries was the ideal son-in-law: you could not fault him. The fact that Nant called him a "tin-preacher" meant that there was something in him that she did not like. However controlled and considered – sometimes bordering on humility – he presented himself, she felt instinctively that all that knowledge and those arguments came from his head rather than his heart. She was certain that Ben was more a Jew than Andries was a Christian. However, Andries was a "theologian in the making" and therefore he would win the discussion this evening and he would try – probably very subtly – to belittle Ben.

Ben was thinking about the talk that he had to give. It had taken him a long time before he had found the right approach. A dry summation of the differences between Jews and Christians served no purpose, because they probably had better knowledge of that than he. No, he wanted to present them a mirror in which they could see that it had been specifically the Christians who had caused the lack of unity. In person-to-person conversations he could usually do this without problems, but this evening would be the first time that he had to talk to a large group of people.

Finding the proper form and arrangement had already caused him headaches, until some time ago he had met his friend Alex, after a visit to his parents, and on that occasion it had suddenly become clear. They had had a drink together in *De Stronkenbar*, and there Alex had told him about the problems with his half-brother. Ben was aware of the situation at his friend's home...

Alex's mother had died young. His father had remarried later and from that second marriage Peter was born. Alex told about the tensions and quarrels that – now that Peter was in his puberty – had become so violent, that he was afraid they would escalate one of these days. "On the one hand there is my father, who complains to me about his distress and unburdens himself", Alex sighed, "and on the other hand there is Peter, who vents all his frustrations on me".

That remark remained with Ben and became the starting point of his talk.

When they had arrived in the youth building behind the church, brother Van Dam welcomed everybody warmly. Especially Ben who, he explained again, had promised to come and tell - from his Jewish background - something about this season's theme: *The Church and Israel.*

After this announcement Ben walked to the lectern and arranged his papers containing all sorts of information which he might need in the discussion afterwards. Then he first looked around the hall, calmly and with self-confidence, and started: 'I thank you very much for the invitation. First of all, I want to make clear that all I have to say about this subject is my personal opinion. I am therefore speaking purely for my own account and not in the name of the Jewish community. Let that be clear above all.

OK... *The Church & Israel...* two brothers you could say. For they have the same Father... But to say that they form a unity, a family...? To attain such unity you have to first examine why it has not been achieved yet. I know that there is a large group of Christians – among them most of you – who feel a strong connection with Judaism. The reason why in general there is no question of unity that has to do, according to me, with the fact that you do not want to accept, that the Eternal One follows a different path with Israel than with the Church. That which – according to me – prevents our unity most, is not so much that we do not accept Jesus as the promised Messiah, but that you refuse to admit, and also confess, guilt for the unmentionable suffering that has been inflicted on us in His name.

As an introduction to what I want to say about that, first an example from practical life...

A mother died shortly after giving birth to her first child – a son. The father remarried some ten years later, and from that marriage another son was born. That boy developed into the typical spoiled and pedantic latecomer, irritating both the father and the eldest son.

The father loved both his boys, but he was acutely aware of the big differences between the two. In the eldest – the issue of his first love – he recognised much of himself; he was the calm point of his life. The other son often caused him worries. This boy appeared to have rather a lot of problems with his position within the family and vented his frustration about it on his elder brother. A few times in their lives this escalated to the point that it resulted in deep, incurable wounds in the life of the eldest son... In the Torah it says: *Thus speaks the Lord: Israel is my firstborn son*. In my opinion anti-semitism essentially stems from jealousy. Our heavenly Father has chosen and equipped his firstborn son – Israel – to bring salvation to the world. Aside from this spiritual task, he has endowed him with great intellect and many other talents, in order to be a blessing to the people of the world society. It has been proved, that almost all the developments - financial-economic, scientific, technological as well as cultural - that have led to our present civilisation and prosperity have been developed and started by Jews, in spite of the continual resistance of anti-semitic powers.

Many years after the birth of his first son Israel, the Father wanted to accept non-Jews also, as a second... younger son. He decided to do so through the fruit of his first love, his eldest son: the Jewish people.

In the first and crucial place through Jesus, of course. The religion about Him became Christianity; however, the religion of Him remained Judaism. In the second place through the apostles. All these Jewish men preached the Good News amongst the heathens and through them the guide for their life – the New Testament in the Bible – was created.

Thus, the second son – Christianity – was born years after the birth of the first son – Israel. While growing up, the second son noticed more and more clearly that the words of his father were entrusted to his big brother, and that he owed his salvation to his input. Instead of feeling grateful and proud to be allowed to also be a son of such a wonderful father, he felt he was second choice and vented his frustration about this on his big brother. A few times in their lives that escalated and led to deep, incurable wounds in the life of the eldest son...

The crusades, the inquisition and the holocaust have inflicted such awful and incurable wounds upon the Jewish people that a deep chasm has developed between them and everyone who calls himself a Christian. Let us limit ourselves to the most recent of those escalations…

Shortly after the rise of Hitler in 1933, the influential protestant theologian and Bible scientist Gerhard Kittel gave a public lecture in Tübingen with the title *The Jewish problem*. The solution that he presented for the Jewish problem was: extermination!

In the beginning of the forties Germany had an official institute for research into and elimination of Jewish influences in church life. In the statutes of that institute it said, amongst other things: *because in the course of historical developments a pernicious Jewish influence has also been active in Christianity, the elimination of Judaism from the church and Christianity has become the inescapable and decisive task of the church nowadays; it is a first requirement for the future of Christianity.*

Still worse were the opinions and advice concerning Jews, that Maarten Luther, who had a key position in the development of Protestantism, sent into the world. I quote: *Christian, remember that besides the devil, there is no more cruel, poisonous and violent enemy than a true Jew! For 1400 years they have given us pestilence, pain and misfortune. They really are devils, nothing less. What we should do with this depraved and condemned race is first of all: burn their synagogues. Secondly, their houses should be destroyed and annihilated. In the third place, we should take away their prayer books and Talmuds. In the fourth place, their rabbis should be forbidden to teach, on pain of death. In the fifth place, they should no longer be allowed to have passports and travel. In the sixth place, they should stop practising usury; that is to say, to ask a high interest on loans. In the seventh place, we should give young, strong Jews and Jewesses a flail, an axe, a pick, a spade, a distaff and a spinning-wheel; they should earn their keep in the sweat of their brow… These lazy chits should be eliminated from our society…Cast them out…*

Finally, you who have Jews in your midst, if my advice does not suit you, find a better one, so that you and I are freed from this unbearable devilish burden: the Jews! – unquote.

The result was that Christians started to assume, based on these pronouncements, the position of their elder brother Israel. However, the worst was that the attitude of mind of this church father – who is still very much loved in extended Christian circles – was the foundation for Hitler's program of propaganda and destruction. The *Protocols of the Wise Men of Zion*, an infamous anti-semitic document from the 19th century was part of the foundation of Hitler's *Mein Kampf: Whoever exterminates the Jews, executes a work of the Lord. Therefore, I invite all leaders and their colleagues to maintain meticulously the racial laws and the pitiless fight against the main poisoner of all peoples: international Judaism. Countless diseases are caused by one bacillus: the Jews, and only when we exterminate them once and for all shall we become healthy again.*

The Jewish author Elie Wiesel – survivor of several camps – once said: "I hope no one ever develops the idea to make a movie about the holocaust, for the massive and bestial butchery of fellow human beings cannot be understood, let alone be described, in words or images".'

After these quotes, Ben fell silent for a moment and then continued: 'That I am standing here, I owe to the fact that my father survived the extermination camp *Auschwitz*. Apart from his twin brother – my uncle Bram – all the rest of his family was murdered. Almost every night he experiences the terrors of the camp again and again in horrible dreams. He knows that it will never stop because – as he himself says – it was too much and too terrible to be dealt with in one single human life. And therefore he remains, despite the fact that the war has been over for so long, a camp prisoner for the rest of his life…'

In that instant something happened that Ben had not reckoned with. For the first time ever, he had spontaneously yielded up to a large group of people that he did not know part of what he had always treasured as something of value between him and his father. A sense of betrayal came over him and almost took his breath away. It was as if he had thrown the most intimate thing that had ever been entrusted to him – and that he had not even shared with Nant yet – out in the street. He fell silent, took a few sips of water and noticed that the lump in his throat slowly disappeared again. Because of the special connection with his father he sensed, as it were, that he would not mind, as long as he did not leave it at that. If he could only link it with the ending of his story, then the telling of it would be meaningful. Then it would serve its purpose. Amazed at the almost telepathically acquired certainty, and apologizing for the short interruption, he finished his story with obvious emotion...

'Those among you that are really interested in the question why Jews are so wary of Christians, who want to meddle in their lives and faith, I advise to visit *Auschwitz*. There you can hear and see, more clearly than in any other place, what the advice of your Christian church father Luther has unleashed. And if that then does not fill you with a paralyzing sense of shame and guilt, then the search for rapprochement between Church and Israel is – in my strong conviction – completely... really completely meaningless. You must realise that for many Jewish survivors of the concentration camps the memories of Christians consist mainly of Nazis who wore belts that had the words *God with us* on the buckles. Those men read the story of the birth of Jesus to their children and sang Christmas songs together, while their Jewish fellow humans died horribly in cold, unhygienic huts. In other words: how can you be so naïve to expect that Jews, based on the efforts of Christians, will accept Jesus as the Messiah, if such massive and indescribable suffering was inflicted on them, specifically in that name? When will you finally become adult, like that pedantic latecomer, and assume an attitude that is fitting, namely that of profession of guilt, humility and asking forgiveness...?'

After a short pause Ben concluded: 'Well... let's leave it at this for the time being.'

Calmly he left the lectern and sat down next to Nant.

As if the last judgement had just been passed on them, everyone sat completely still, staring ahead in dismay. Then brother Van Dam broke the silence and observed, after a few small coughs: Well, uh… I think that that was clear language, in any case. And…' he continued with a smile, 'I have to admit, Ben, that now I finally understand what your father meant when I told him that I asked you to give this talk. "Beware what you let yourself in for", he warned, "becasue he will not spare you". But OK… as I said, in any case it was clear. Whether we all agree with you, you'll find out in a while. I propose that we have a short break first and have a drink together.'

'Well, that was an unexpected blow, I think,' said Nant to Ben when they stood at the back of the hall having a drink a while later. Apart from a few young people, who talked with one another almost in a whisper and with cautious gestures, the majority of those present were visibly upset and stared ahead in silence. The only one who broke the oppressive silence was "De Reus". As if he were a guest at a cosy birthday party, he walked with big strides from one to the other. With a joke here and a shoulder tap there, he finally approached Ben and Nant resolutely. With one hand in the pocket of his jeans and holding the other out towards Ben, he observed: 'So that is the one who won the first prize…' and he continued in the same breath: 'Well… congratulations man, with your double election!'

Taken aback, Ben took the extended hand of "De Reus" and, while observing the tattoo of an anchor on the extended lower arm and the wide body behind it, he said: 'Sorry, but what are you talking about?'

Looking down on Ben "De Reus" answered with a broad grin on his face: 'Elected for "eternity" by the Creator of heaven and earth and elected for "the here and now" by the most beautiful girl of the village… yes…? Do you understand, kid…? Well… I wish you both happiness,' he concluded, turned around and walked away.

As Ben's gaze followed him, Nant observed: 'Well, obviously he finally understood that I did not have my milk skimmed by him.'

She smiled at the complete lack of understanding that now could be read on Ben's face. 'That is farmer-yiddish,' she declared, 'and it means that I am only satisfied with the very best.' She kissed his cheek: 'And the very best, that's you…!'

'Did he have the hots for you?' asked Ben

'Oh yes,' said Nant, 'he did, I didn't.'

Brother Van Dam was already standing at the lectern again and invited everyone to sit down, in order to start the second part of the evening. At his question whether anyone wanted to react to Ben's talk, a girl stood up and said: 'How can you say that the religion of Jesus was Judaism. I know that he was born a Jew, but I mean – if there ever was a Christian, then it must have been Him!'

She sat down again and Ben answered: 'As I said: his followers were Christians, but for us Jesus was only one of the many rabbis in the history of our people. Since I have known Nant, I have been studying Christianity a bit and in your Bible it says that the place where He preached was not a church or a hall, but a synagogue. He celebrated the Jewish feasts and up to his thirtieth year He developed into a formidable scholar of Torah and Tenakh. He also explained clearly to his followers that He had not come to dissolve the Torah, the law. This means that He, entirely in the spirit of Jewish teachings, attached enormous value to it and summoned people to obey the laws of God.'

At that moment he recalled a song of the American-Jewish country music singer Kinky Friedman. However, he decided that it would be better not to quote the title *They don't make Jews like Jesus any more*. Humor and self-mockery in relation to the Bible was rarely appreciated by Christians, that much was clear to him in the meantime.

The girl got up again and continued: 'But our eternal salvation does not depend on our obeying the law, but on the death and resurrection of Jesus.'

'That may be,' answered Ben, 'but if you know, in whatever way, that you are a creation, a child of God, then you would want to live as He thinks you should. He knows – as your Creator – better than you yourself what is good and what is bad for you. If you have such a Father, don't you – as His child – want to be like Him?

One of our religious feasts is *Simchat Torah*. That is the feast of the *Joy of the Law*. That joy is caused by the knowledge that the Creator did not put us on earth just like that, but that he has given us rules for living here. The better we follow those rules, the more we shall resemble Him. And that is not just good for us, but also for the people around us and for the earth on which we are allowed to live. At the occasion of *Simchat Torah* there is dancing in the synagogue and also for the children it is a celebration. We read the Torah to the end and then we start at the beginning again, signifying that we are never finished with studying the Law, but that we should strive to gain a deeper insight in how God wants us to live.

You know, someone once said: "The laws of God are written in the cells of your body". What I don't understand is that – although the Old Testament is considered to be a part of your Bible – you mostly ignore the rules for living that God Himself gave us via Moses.'

'Hey, hey, wait a minute friend… now you're going too far!' "De Reus" cried suddenly. His tall figure stood large and solid like a tower above the landscape of a plain full of timid listeners. 'Who says,' he continued in a dark and threatening voice, 'that I ignore the laws of God…?'

'Well, first,' said Ben, looking at him fixedly, 'if you really would not do that, then you would not have such a large tattoo on your arm!'

'Hey… what?' reacted "De Reus", rather taken aback, 'what does that have to do with it…?'

'Everything,' assured Ben, 'for if you knew the laws of God, you would know that He has forbidden to have signs pricked into your skin. It says so literally in the Torah, in your Bible! Also I take it, that you, as a fisherman, provide a large part of the need for eels that exists with your Christian clients.'

'Yes… and?' asked "De Reus", 'is that also forbidden?'

'Yes,' said Ben and just when he wanted to start explaining why it is forbidden to eat eels and other animals, "De Reus" raised both hands in a gesture of impotence and cried accusingly: 'Hey… Van Dam, what's this…? Why don't I know that…?'

For a moment there was a silence in which everyone looked expectantly at brother Van Dam. Clearly taken by surprise by that unexpected, direct question, he got up and answered: 'Well, look, uh… it's like this: We no longer live under the law, because Jesus has fulfilled it, but from grace. The Bible teaches us that we are not saved by the works of the law but by faith in the salvation work of Jesus.'

'But that does not mean that the law has become superfluous, does it?' Ben reacted. 'That does not mean that after the coming of Jesus pork is suddenly no longer impure and therefore no longer bad for you? Go to the doctor when you have skin- or intestinal complaints. The first thing he forbids you to eat is pork.

As far as I have understood, Jesus teaches that as long as we are here on earth not one title or iota of the law shall perish and that whoever disobeys just one of the smallest commands of the law and teaches people to do so, will be called very small in the Kingdom of Heaven. A bit further on it even says that only the person who obeys the will of God will enter the Kingdom of Heaven and that He wants nothing to do with people who ignore the laws of God; workers of lawlessness He calls them. And in spite of that you have no trouble at all to withhold the sacrifice of tithes of your harvest and income, to do away with the Sabbath and to eat without concern everything that God has forbidden.'

Now Van Dam gave Andries, who had stood up in the meantime, the opportunity to say something. Calmly and well-considered, he said: 'First of all I want to say that I am impressed with what you have said and that I understand, especially in view of your background, your emotion. Still I hope that you, in view of my background, can also understand that I found your approach of Luther rather subjective. That does not mean that I am saying that you told us untruths about him, but you have to see and judge that in the spirit of the time and of the circumstances in which he then lived. He really has had, apart from this negative influence, also an enormous positive influence on the growth and development of the protestant-christian faith.'

'That may be so,' Ben answered, 'but as far as I know there has never been an excuse from the side of the official Christian authorities for those particular statements. On the contrary, I think that they are still secretly cherished by the majority of you and I shall give you one example why I think so. In Wittenberg, the city of Luther, there is the *Saint Mary Church*. That is the first protestant church in which Luther himself used to preach. On the south side of that church a large stone relief was made in the wall during that time. It is the image of a prone pig. The piglets that suckle at the nipples of the pig all have the heads of rabbis. That extremely offending image of Jews in a very intimate relation with an unclean animal can still be seen on that church wall. It would not be a lot of trouble to remove it or cover it with mortar, but obviously up till now there has never been a Christian throughout the ages who cared. Buses full of "Luther-tourists" still stop at that church every week. That amongst them there has never been anybody who minded so much that he took action to have it removed… believe me, that frightens me!'

Andries got up again and without referring to what had just been said, he spoke without emotion: 'If I may, I would also still like to react to what you explained about the law. I believe that the true reason of your– in my eyes almost idolatrous – adoration of the law, has in fact a different background from what you said about it. But this as an aside. What concerns me now specifically, is that we have to realise that a large part of the commands and prohibitions as they are mentioned in the first five books of the Bible, applies especially to the Jews that lived in Israel at the time and are no longer relevant to us here, in the present-day modern West.

That does not mean that the Ten Commandments do not play a very important role in the Christian faith. It was Luther, especially, who taught us that through the law we become aware of our sins. The law works like a mirror in which we can see our shortcomings and by which we become aware of how much we need Jesus, who took the consequences of our sins upon Himself.'

'You know,' answered Ben, 'I think that specifically for people like you – people who think that the laws of God applied to another race, in another time – the Eternal One always added that they are "everlasting" decrees. And with regard to your remark about Luther, I'd rather not react. I can't do anything with that. Your mistake is that you have raised that man far above his position. The Eternal One has chosen a number of men to proclaim Him to us in His word, the Bible. That should suffice. What Luther said later, that is his personal opinion and that is worth no more and no less than that of thousands of other scholars throughout the ages. And by now you have – I hope – understood that I am not particularly impressed with his opinion. What does interest me is…what exactly you meant with your first remark, that our adoration of the law has a deeper background than that which I mentioned.'

Andries looked questioningly at Brother Van Dam for a moment, who in turn looked at his watch. Although he saw that there was still some time, he also feared that further discussion would not really improve the atmosphere. He knew his future son-in-law well enough by now to know that he would now bring matters to a head. He looked around the hall and observed: 'It appears that everybody is rather impressed by what has been said till now. I think you have received enough to think about. Therefore it seems better to leave it at this for tonight.'

'Yes…' Andries reacted with feigned indignation, 'but our guest speaker has asked us a question for the first time this evening. Then it is a matter of propriety to answer him, isn't it?'

Van Dam, who realised too well that Andries had provoked that question himself in a sly manner, sighed: 'Well, a short answer then to Ben's question and then we close.'

'OK,' Andries agreed. Then he continued confidently: 'The deeper background of your adoration of the law – according to me – is that you want to regain God's favour and thereby escape the punishment that the Jews incurred when they crucified Jesus, the Son of God.'

For a moment Ben looked intensely at Andries and was alarmed by the terrifying self-evidence in his attitude and by the complacent, cold look in his eyes. That touched him much more at that moment in this environment than the accusation itself, for he had become used to that by now. As a small boy he had experienced that physically in the school yard. A few boys from the top class were going get even with him and his brother David for having "killed the Lord Jesus". David had just managed to prevent a bad thrashing at that time. With believably feigned indignation he had managed to convince the boys that it was not they who had done that, but the Jews from Zwolle.

Ben had not really noticed the pleasure that David had experienced that time from the fact that those idiots really believed it. The nature of the event had moved him too much. And as he grew older it had struck him more and more that for many Christians this belief was a structural part of their faith. This had caused him even at a young age a vague sense of fear. Contrary to his brother he had never really had a close relationship with groups of children in school. With him there was always – deeply hidden – a kind of distrust and he was fearful of the anti-semitic feelings in the people around him. The only thing was, you never heard anyone voice those feelings, so that you never knew exactly who your enemies were. However, now he did know. Andries had stated his position clearly and opposed him directly, both literally and figuratively. Patiently and deliberately he had kept the final blow to the last and executed it with visible satisfaction. There he stood – complacent, proud and straight. Like a victor looking at his prey, waiting for the last twitch. But that did not come and it remained quiet for a long time... Icily quiet.

Motionless, – his fingers clamped around the edges of the lectern – Ben stared at his pages with notes. His head was in turmoil with thoughts and emotions that ran together, so that it was impossible to form rational sentences. Nant recognised better than anybody Ben's state of mind from his facial expression. This was what she had been afraid of all evening. To her relief, the attitude of "De Reus" had surprised her agreeably, but the performance of Andries had been exactly as she had feared. She looked at Ben and felt sorry for him. She recalled the derailed visit to her grandparents and suddenly she was overwhelmed by fear for a similar escalation. Resolutely she got up and walked towards Andries. When she stood right in front of him, she looked at him with contempt: 'Well Sjakie… did you finally get it together…? Are you sure that everyone, and certainly Ben, heard loud and clear that the Jews crucified Jesus…? Really… where do you get the idea! And you want to become a minister. Well, if I can give you some advice, I should first read exactly once more what it says in the Bible. Hopefully it will get through to you that it was the Romans who crucified Jesus. The only reason why He let that happen was not because the Jews demanded it, but to save us and you with that. Therefore, when you are brushing your teeth tonight, don't forget to look very carefully in the mirror. For there you'll see the person who is really guilty of the murder of Jesus!'

'OK… that's enough now,' brother Van Dam interfered soothingly. 'It seems to me unnecessary to convince each other here that Jesus was crucified due to our sins. I do assume that we all realise that very well.'

'Well, if I were you,' Nant said, 'I would make certain and explain this once more in detail to that nice son-in-law of yours. Otherwise it will be a disaster when he is a minister soon and preaches this kind of nonsense.'

Then she returned to her place and brother Van Dam concluded the evening. He thanked Ben extensively for all that he had given them as food for thought that evening. In his prayer of thanks he summarised the evening as follows: 'Father we thank You for this evening with which we concluded our winter season. Thank You for everything that You have given us to think about and help us to draw the correct conclusions when we think about the way that You deal with Your people Israel and with us as Church. We know from Your word that You have given Your only Son Jesus Christ to carry the sin of the world as the Lamb of God. We realise that we with our sins are in fact the ones who have crucified Jesus and we thank You that our debt with You has been paid. We realise the vanity with which we have put ourselves as Church often above Your people of Israel. This evening it has been made clear to us again what terrible consequences that has had and we ask of You in honesty: Forgive us. Be with each one of us in the coming days, especially with Nant who is leaving us and allow me, Lord, to bless her and her husband with the words that You Yourself have given Your people in the Torah… Nant and Ben, *The* LORD *bless you, and keep you; The* LORD *make His face shine upon you, and be gracious unto you; The* LORD *lift up His countenance upon you, and give you peace.* Amen.'

On the way back they also said little. Every now and then Nant looked at Ben and sensed that any remark she would make would be too much. She did not know the state of mind in which he was at that moment and she even asked herself whether Ben threatened to lose himself in it. They had talked about it from time to time, but he had never been able to give her a clear explanation about his behaviour, so that she would be able to understand it. This in fact was her greatest worry. That he could be beset so suddenly by a fear that was very real, but that he himself could not identify. And if you cannot even name it how could you fight it? It had become clear to Nant in the meantime that it had to do both with his being a Jew and with the war, but why didn't it bother David and his sisters – or at least much less? According to Esther, with whom she had once shared her concern, it was due to the fact that of the four children Ben was the most sensitive. The least commercial and most creative. During her medical studies Esther had done practice with the *Jewish Social Service*. There she had read a report of some research that had been done at the request of the *Ministry of Wellfare, Health and Culture* for the *Institute for Psychotrauma*. In that report it was mentioned that 53% of the Jews who were born between 1945 and 1962 has sought psychosocial help. That means that, on average, in each family at least one of the children has to pay the piper for the unprocessed traumatic events that have occurred in the life of the parents. And that affects mostly the most sensitive child. David for instance protected himself by surrounding himself with a wall of indifference and black humor. When he was asked whether he would not want to go to *Auschwitz*, he had answered laconically that he did not feel like paying a stack of money for such a trip, when in the war both the trip and the stay had been for free. Everyone had been aghast, but Jacob had said to Esther later that that, too, was a way of dealing with it, however macabre it had sounded.

When they arrived home, Ben walked via the kitchen to the terrace of their apartment. He sat down in a garden chair and peered at the silhouette of the wood's edge in the distance.

In his mind's eye he saw his father, years ago, when they as a family still lived above the shop, sit in the same manner on his roof terrace. A loner in Elburg then, just like he was now here in Putten. A loner, among people that professed to believe in the same God but secretly felt themselves far above "those that had crucified their Saviour". His father still had the bond with a woman from his own tradition – but which side would Nant choose, if push came to shove…?

He remembered his mother who warned him in all her pure simplicity not to deny his roots by marrying a *shikse*. But then the figure of his father appeared to him, almost tangible, as a solid image of his Jewish origin. The latter's deep sympathy for his "Wittekop" and his words which included so much reliability and wisdom were as silent and palpable as the wind that softly caressed him. And he noticed how that caused the melancholy to gradually disappear… Then two hands slid carefully across his shoulders. 'Hey, Van Zuiden, that was a very good sermon!' said Nant.

'Ah, you may think so,' Ben sighed, 'but what difference does it make? Words and sentences that will turn out to be no more than a drop in the ocean, especially if at the end of the evening such an anti-semitist gets a chance.'

'Don't get upset by that "tin preacher",' Nant said, 'that guy does not belong there! Anyway, that is not what I want to talk about,' she continued immediately as she sat on his lap, 'for I have to confess something…'

'Yes… what…?' Ben asked hesitantly.

'Well, you know,' Nant confided, 'until now I have only been in love with Ben van Zuiden, but recently – and certainly after tonight – there has been someone else…'

Surprised Ben looked at those beautiful blue eyes and at the tender smile that appeared on her face. He was sure that he did not need to worry. Still he had no idea what she was talking about.

'It really started during that *Seder* evening in Apeldoorn,' she told him, 'and after tonight I am sure that, besides being in love with you, I am also in love with "the Jew from Elburg…!" '

Ben sensed that that expression meant more than just a reference about how they used to talk about his grandfather at Nant's home. It was an expression of respect for that part of him that she had obviously not considered consciously before. He had always found it very pleasant that for Nant his Jewish identity had never been a hindrance in their relationship. But now that it seemed that it even added something to that, it filled him with a sense of happiness and enormous gratitude. He grabbed her shoulder, pulled her closely to him and said: 'Johanna-Aleida… woman of my youth and woman of my life… I love you.'

She sat up straight again, looked at him and said: 'That is again not from a book, I take it….?'

Ben shook his head in denial.

'Again from the depth of your heart…?' she asked.

Slowly Ben nodded. He thought of the man whose saying it was and confirmed: 'Yes, but this time… even deeper!'

7

During their courtship it had become more than clear to Ben that Nant's principles with regards to family planning were unalterable. That did not have to do so much with a church background or education, but rather with an inborn, strongly developed respect for the laws of nature. From a young age she had been involved in the natural process of sowing and harvesting, of fertilisation and birth, so that her farmer's soul rebelled at the thought of arbitrarily influencing this order of creation.

'I am not going to poison my own body with whatever chemical rubbish,' she said with holy indignation, 'or to fiddle with artificial stuff. No, dear,' she explained to Ben, 'if you cannot keep your bullets in your pocket, then you will have to calculate by yourself when you can shoot them properly.'

She meant that the only contraceptive method that was acceptable to her was periodic abstinence.

'But why would you deny yourself one of the most beautiful experiences that you can have together?' As Ben said it, he realised the senselessness of the argument, because it made no impression on Nant at all.

'You are right,' she admitted, 'it is indeed one of the most beautiful experiences you can get. Uncle Evert always said: "Even when they will invent something that is much better, I will just keep doing it". But what are you really talking about? A woman can get pregnant during ten out of the thirty days at the most. And abstinence does not mean that you cannot touch each other in those ten days. That is exactly a time to discover that sex is more than just the "deed". And if something happens anyway, well, in that case you can be sure that your children were procreated in love.'

'But… do you want children right away…?' Ben asked with some hesitation.

'Right away… right away…' Nant repeated, 'what right away…? You have to wait and see anyway. It is not quite such a matter of course!'

And in that she was right, for her first two pregnancies miscarried both after two months. The way in which she dealt with these disappointments, impressed Ben greatly. His respect for her simple, natural manner of dealing with the events in her life grew because of this. In spite of the fear he sometimes had that maybe she would not be able to have any children at all, he also experienced a sense of reassurance. However, that too – he knew only too well – had to do with Nant's attitude rather than with his own.

Secretly he envied her at times, both because of her enjoyment of the small, beautiful moments and because she accepted setbacks as a matter of course.

With him it was rather the opposite. For the slightest reason – and sometimes even without a directly demonstrable reason – a wave of depression could overwhelm him, just like that, and cause him to wihtdraw into an oppressive silence.

'Try to explain what bothers you,' Nant had said from time to time, hoping that talking about it would bring him relief.

'I really don't know it myself,' he used to say with resigned helplessness, 'my head is full of a kind of fear or threat, but I have no idea where it comes from.'

Usually she did not pursue the matter, but accepted Esther's explanation, namely that something like this is characteristic for the "second generation syndrome".

Esther had even noticed at a certain moment that Ben's state of mind was often parallel to that of his father, probably without them knowing it about each other.

To their great joy the third pregnancy went reasonably well. Because Nant had a rather high blood pressure by nature, there were some annoying complications in the last months, for which she had to take rest as much as possible. But in the fall of 1978 Nant delivered healthy twins: a boy and a girl. They were named after Ben's parents: Sjaak and Sarah.

It made a deeper impression on Ben than he had expected. More than ever before he realised how, because of his father's experiences in the camp, the family line had been hanging by a thread. It gave an extra dimension – a very important one to him – to the already so impressive event.

Late in the evening, when finally it was quiet in the house, he wrote the text for the birth announcement…

> *Unattainable far away*
> *in the silence of His seclusion*
> *God is creating life*
> *yet in that very moment*
> *I feel in silent wonder*
> *His hand moving*
> *in the depth of my being*
> *bringing the miracle*
> *of His love and forgiveness*
> *and perhaps*
> *the greatest mystery of all*
> *creating life in His image*
> *through me…*

In the week before the birth of the twins, Ben and Nant had received a notice of the municipality that a building lot had been assigned to them. Ben had registered for that at the time when he had started working in Putten. Because of all the goings on around the birth, they had barely paid attention to it yet. But when on a Sunday afternoon Nant was lying down for a while, Ben decided to have a closer look at the site where their new house was going to be. He walked to the edge of the village – unaware of what was waiting for him there. The relevant lots lay around a nicely landscaped park. He looked again at the number that was mentioned in the letter and arrived at a piece of land where five duplex residences were going to be built. He immediately liked the fact that the gardens behind the houses would border straight onto the park. As he walked forward a bit, he did not notice that someone was following him.

'Doesn't look too bad, does it?' he heard suddenly.

Ben turned around and looked into the friendly eyes of a man who stood looking around in a relaxed manner – his hands deep in his pockets. He indicated with his head the lot that Ben was standing on and asked: 'Did you get that one assigned?'

'Yes…' said Ben, 'at least, if I understood properly.' He took out the letter once again and showed it to the man. He glanced at it and gave it back.

'That's right,' he observed and nodded again – now straight ahead – and continued: 'And that's mine! So it seems that we are going to be neighbors.'

He took his hand from his pocket and extended it towards Ben.

'Pleased,' he said, 'Lub Vonhof.'

Ben introduced himself also and looked closely again at his future neighbor. He seemed a bit tired. His chin pressed into a bright red scarf that had been tied high underneath a dark, loose jacket. Ben estimated that he was roughly ten years older than he. And, as he always did almost automatically, he calculated that the man must have been born just before or during the war. Usually he avoided talking about the war as much as possible. But this time he had a strong presentiment that it would happen. It had to do with a certain bond that he felt from the beginning. Intuitively, he knew that the man carried a story that touched on his own. It had happened before. He could never explain it, but it was always right. Apparently he had a kind of antenna, with which he received those signals from a person, as soon as there were corresponding emotions.

'Do you live in Putten already?' he asked.

'Yes,' answered Lub, 'but I have to retire for health reasons. Catering, you know. I sold the business on January 1st, but I can stay there until we have found something else. And I have to say that this pleases me. Nice small street... no traffic passing your house and a park instead of neighbors at the back.'

As he rubbed his moustache and beard with his thumb and index finger he slowly turned his gaze on Ben and asked: 'Would you be interested to combine forces for the drawing of the plan and looking for a builder?'

Ben smiled in surprise: 'Yes... that seems a good idea.'

'Great...' Lub reacted enthusiastically, 'that's great. Do you feel like going over to *De Waag*, then we can drink to that. Or is that a problem? I mean, because it is Sunday?'

'Well,' said Ben, 'it would be a problem for my boss and for most of our clients in Putten. That's why I would not do it as a matter of course. Just out of respect. Also, my wife is a Christian. She is also not used to it, but I myself have no problem with it. My "Sunday" is over. That was yesterday.'

Lub looked at him with surprise and asked: 'What do you mean...?'

'Because I am Jewish,' answered Ben.

'Oh...?' said Lub, 'I hadn't noticed yet.' A moment later he added: 'That means that your parents survived the war?'

Ben confirmed that and explained: 'Yes, my mother was in hiding on a farm in Nunspeet. My father and also his twin brother survived *Auschwitz* – as the only ones of the Elburg *kehilla*. In fact, that is why I exist.

And for a few days now we also have twins.'

Meanwhile they had left the largest part of the park behind them already. On a grassy wall at the edge of the park was a bench on which they sat down. In the distance the tinkling of a few fountains could be heard and apart from that, the silence was carried by the sounds of songbirds and ducks. Lub sat deep in thought – with his elbows leaning on his knees – staring ahead.

After a while he sat up straight and looked at Ben: 'This is really special, isn't it, such a meeting, because my father too has survived the camps – together with his brother – as one of the few.' At that moment, Ben received the confirmation that his presentiment had been right, and he also realised that his flight from Elburg – to break with the consequences of all the suffering that the Germans had inflicted – had been in vain.

From talks with his colleague Anton van der Hoeven, it had become clear to him that in Putten there had also been a tragedy during the war - even greater in size than the one in Elburg. More than 600 men had been taken away here, of which less than 10% had survived. Of the more than a thousand children, who lost their father at the same time, Anton had been one.

From what Anton had told him about it, he had tried to imagine what the village must have looked like after that raid. Over 90 houses had been burnt down – and therefore as many families were left homeless. Hundreds of families were bereft of their breadwinner, just before the infamous hunger winter. How do you get through that – with only children, old people and all those defeated and broken widows left?

It took more than six months before the first lists with names of the men who perished arrived at the municipality. As long as her husband's name was not on those, Anton's mother had kept her hopes up. And in spite of the fact that none of those who came back could tell her anything about him, she kept waiting for him. Until one morning she found an envelope in her letterbox from the Red Cross, with in it the wedding ring of her husband and a note that mentioned the place where he had died…

'But do you know what the problem here was…?' asked Lub and continued after a short silence: 'See, in your case whole families were taken away. Here only the men. Then, when those who survived came back again, they were overwhelmed by questions from all those women who were still hoping for the return of their husbands and sons.

Most of the time they could not give them certainty and sometimes they had to disappoint them. The question why those men had stayed alive and theirs not, roused, besides feelings of mourning, also a certain resentment. That was not easy for those who had returned. Sometimes they were publicly pronounced as liars, when they said that someone had passed away. Because someone who had returned earlier, whom they had asked also, had said that he had still seen that person in another camp. In the course of time they clammed up and withdrew. There was no professional help or counselling and in the village all the attention was directed at those who died and their families. It was understandable but all the same, those who had returned were left alone with their own trauma. The only thing, for which they were still approached, was to attend memorial services. Once the queen was expected to come to the *Oude Kerk* for such a memorial service. The mayor approached my father personally to invite him for that. "Vonhof... good man", he said, "if you come, I'll make sure that you can sit next to the queen". But my father shook his head. "You know what you should do?" he said, "you sit next to her and give her my best regards, because I am not coming". He poured two drinks, lifted his glass and added: "Let the dead rest and give the living all the best... cheers".

Those men did not feel like sitting in the first row in their Sunday best, like a kind of hero, in order to add lustre to such an event. It served no purpose. It only increased the sadness and loneliness of all those widows.'

It had become dusk already and they decided to walk on. Silently, each preoccupied with their own thoughts, they walked together to the center of the village. Ben thought about what Lub had told him. It all sounded dismally familiar and he asked himself why, of all places, he had ended up in Putten. Should he be happy with that or not? As the son of someone who had also survived the concentration camp, Lub was his fellow-sufferer in a way. But would it be good for him to be confronted with that all the time, when they became neighbors? He tried to imagine it, but could not really assess the effect that this could have on him.

As they passed the *Oude Kerkhof*, Lub told him: 'Last week they buried a man here who was also in the camp with my father. For a few days he was really upset by that. And do you know what I find so strange? I mean… he goes all to pieces about someone dying here, while in the camp he saw stacks of corpses, including people he knew, and that hardly bothered him…!'

Ben nodded. He recalled the explanation that the Jewish psychoanalyst Viktor E. Frankl – who had also survived the camps – gave for that in his book *Man's Search for Meaning*. If you are confronted with – or are part of such extreme, unthinkable atrocities, the mechanism with which you normally take in and deal with something like that, seems to become blocked. What you see and experience does not seem to really penetrate. He had particularly appreciated that according to Frankl, the meaning of existence is mainly determined by the desire to make a difference. Freud may have contended that, for a human, lust is the greatest incentive to live, and Adler that it is the need for power, but those were debatable, intellectual theories. Frankl's theory, on the other hand, was entirely based on what he himself had experienced as a prisoner in the hard reality of the concentration camp. There he saw that prisoners who knew that they still had to perform a task, had better chances of survival. The desire to still be significant for the world and for their loved ones, that was what gave them the strength to endure the most bizarre circumstances. It had been characteristic for the attitude of uncle Bram, and obviously also for the man that he was going to meet now: Lub's father.

When they reached the end of the Achterstraat, they crossed the Kerkstraat and after a few more steps they stood in front of *De Waag*. The crossed, dark beams in the white stone of the façade of the old building reminded Ben of a classic pub, somewhere in the English countryside, rather than an average restaurant on the Veluwe. It emanated something of tradition and history and he liked that. He had the same feeling about *De Heerdt*, the restaurant across from his place of work. Centuries ago Perrol – infamous leader of *The Black Gang* and enemy of Jan van Schaffelaar in the war of Utrecht – used to be a regular visitor there. Just like *De Bonte Os* in Elburg, they were buildings that showed in every detail that they had already survived many generations. Inside the sagging and cracked walls both sad and exuberant scenes had taken place at the long rough tables, and emotions had been shared that touched the soul of life. When you entered, you smelled the aroma of the years that had stuck to the furnishings and the walls.

'Where did the name *De Waag* come from?' asked Ben.

'It was like this…' Lub explained, 'my father was a butcher, first somewhere else, a little bit outside the center of the village, but later over there, in that building.' He pointed at the butchery next to *De Waag*. 'And this used to be a barn that belonged to it. Inside, were some large scales on which the animals that he bought were weighed before he butchered them. But the farmers too, who went to the market with their cattle, had their animals weighed here first. They were given a note that mentioned the correct weight. Any "product" that was sold by weight, could be weighed here. Hence *De Waag*. Later my father sold the butchery and he altered the front of the barn to an auto-buffet and bar. Afterwards, when I entered the business, we also included the back part and made it into a restaurant annex pub – as it is now.'

It was the first time that Ben came inside and he immediately liked the atmosphere. In the middle there was a large U-shaped bar, to the left behind him a massive habitués' table, and to the right a fireplace had been installed. The first guests were already sitting around the fireplace with a pre-dinner drink, looking at the menu. At the end of the bar there was a half-open kitchen with a narrow passage that led to the restaurant in the back.

'You see,' Lub posed, 'most visitors like to be able to glance into the kitchen as they walk to their table. The advantage of such a separate space in the back is that the people there are not bothered by the guests at the bar. Anyway, after dinner they often return to the bar for another drink.'

'Yes,' Ben admitted, 'it looks cosy. I can imagine that it appeals to people and that they like to meet each other here. It looks like home – quite genial.'

As he looked at a man putting some logs on the fire, the true reason for his visit disappeared from his thoughts for a moment.

'That is Henk, the new owner,' said Lub.

As Ben greeted him, he heard a door open behind him.

'Good afternoon, everyone…!' a voice said enthusiastically.

Ben turned around and saw a man who radiated joy of living. Two sparkling eyes, full of fun, lit up his full round face. The shape of the wrinkles near his mouth and eyes made Ben believe that he must almost have been born with a smile on his face. Therefore he was quite surprised to hear that this man was Lub's father. Such a relaxed and friendly fun-face on someone who had had such traumatic experiences rather surprised him.

Lub introduced his father to Ben. Then he told him about their meeting; that Ben's father was also a camp survivor and that they were likely to become neighbors. At this Vonhof called out: 'Hendrik, give these boys a nice beer and me a coffee.'

They sat down at the bar and when Henk put their order in front of them, Vonhof said, pointing at his cup of coffee: 'I can't have alcohol anymore, that's why. Whether I'll ever get used to it, I don't know, but I guess it is better this way. I like gin better than the cat likes milk and in the long run that comes home to roost. The doctor warned me: "At the most two drinks a day, Vonhof, otherwise that's it for you". I said: Dear man, in that case I stop completely, for two drinks a day are not worth wetting your mouth for!'

'I understood from your son that you have also experienced a few things,' Ben started the conversation.

Vonhof stared at his cup and stirred his coffee with his spoon, deep in thought. His round head nodded slowly. 'Yes,' he said after a while, 'and it was so unreasonable. I mean, the punishment was not at all in proportion to the crime. They sent more than six hundred men to a terrible death as a revenge for an ambush, in which only one person died. Of course, they were frustrated, because they were losing the war. Note when it happened, the south of our country had already been liberated! The krauts did appeal several times to the perpetrators to step forward, but they remained silent. They were brave enough to shoot that German from the relative safety of an ambush, but when it came to being a real hero and saving six hundred human lives, they bolted. And when some time later you, who are innocent, are walking around in a camp like that in such a stupid monkey suit, and you feel the blood seeping into your pants, because they shaved you down below, well, then you feel really cheated.'

'In which camp were you?' asked Ben.

'In *Neuengamme* more than any other,' answered Vonhof, 'that was both a labor camp and an execution camp. Because I am a butcher by profession, I got a job in the kitchen. And I think back with much gratitude to all those whose hunger I was able to relieve with the bits of meat and bread that I smuggled back to our hut. You had to be extremely careful with that, for if they caught you, that was it. My brother worked in a hut where men made parachutes. They worked in groups of twenty. At a certain moment it was noticed that one particular group had sabotaged the job. Those men used to make small tears in the material, so that a German parachutist would crash without fail. We were told about this at the following roll-call and we all had to watch how that whole group of twenty men was hanged. I was terrified that my brother would be among them. The first was brought to the scaffold. Then the second, who had to hang the first. Then the third had to hang the second, and on it went until the last one climbed the scaffold. Only when he had been hanged by a German, did I know for sure that my brother was not among them. Even though that was a relief, this event is always the first to come back to me whenever I think about that time. One of the last in that row was a handsome young guy. As soon as he realised what was happening, he went completely berserk. I have never seen anyone resist death like that. Two *kapos* could barely restrain him, however much they beat him and tied him up. He shrieked and fought till the very last, it was horrible. It went to the marrow. The crowning disaster was, that the man next to me could not deal with it and fainted. An SS-man walked over to him, kicked him a few times and roared: "You there, get up!" But he remained motionless with his head against my foot. I looked at it, heard a bang and just saw a trickle of blood running down his neck.'

He fell silent, shook his head despondently and drank the last sip of coffee. Ben looked at him and noticed that – in spite of the charisma that he still radiated – there was for the first time a broken sound in his voice.

'Is it difficult for you to talk about this?' he asked.

'No... not really,' said Vonhof, 'but you don't want to bother everyone with it, do you? Lub just told me that your father has been through a similar experience and therefore I assume that you are really interested. They say it is good to talk about it a lot; that would help to deal with it. And I do believe that it is true, but it will never explain to me how it is possible that evil can take possession of such a large group of people in such a short time. Hell lets loose and it does not bear thinking that it could happen again. You can talk about it however much you want, but that is something that you can never explain to someone who has not been through it himself. One long, terrible nightmare it is. Usually it is only one event that you always see in great detail. The rest eventually becomes one large mess of images about death and destruction, which does not really seem to penetrate to you.'

Ben recalled Frankl's theory. 'Is that so?' he asked, very interested. 'Does that apply to everybody?'

'I think so,' Vonhof assumed, 'at least it applied to me and those whom I knew. Last week we buried a good friend of mine. He was in *Kamp Ladelund* with his father and two brothers. They had a very bad time there. First they had to walk quite a distance early in the morning, and then they had to dig tank pits in that muddy mess in the north. Digging the whole day, up to your knees in cold water, with hardly anything to eat. One day the father advised his sons to save a piece of bread till they went to bed. Hunger prevents you from sleeping, you know, no matter how tired you are.

One night that friend of mine lay in bed crying with hunger and finally he crept to his father. Very carefully he took his piece of bread from under the straw mattress, ate it and fell asleep a bit later. The next morning it turned out that his father had died that night. His brothers also did not survive, but my friend has never had another day in his life without guilty thoughts that he had contributed to the death of his father. During the time he was ill I visited him regularly and whenever we talked about the war, it was always that which he remembered first.'

When Ben walked home through the Kerkstraat later on, he felt more strongly than ever before that his father had still kept the most upsetting event of his life from him. And before he went to bed that evening, he closely examined again an old picture of Jacob and Abraham van Zuiden, taken after they had both become Bar Mitzvah. At that time they were still a unit, the one a copy, a mirror image of the other. The same character, the same humor. But after the war his father's face and life had been covered with a veil of melancholy and devastation. In the case of uncle Bram this was much less obvious. For a long time he had been unable to explain this. But now, after the meeting and the talk with the old Vonhof, two names kept running through his head more strongly than ever before… Ischie… and "De Schim…"

Very soon this intuition turned out to be right…

8

It was already half a year ago that Ben's youngest sister Leah had left for Israel. After a month of vacation and four weeks of working in a *kibbutz*, combined with language studies, she had started the real practicum with a national daily newspaper.

From Tel Aviv, where she stayed with uncle Bram and aunt Roza, Ben and Nant received a card congratulating them on the birth of the twins.

In the letter that was included, she wrote: *Having twins appears to be hereditary and because papa is also one of twins, I think it is very beautiful that this line now continues via you. Especially because of that special bond that you have. Anyway, now that I am here, it has become really obvious to me how much more cheerful uncle Bram's view of life is than papa's. On the outside they look as alike as peas in a pod. It startles me each time, especially when I meet uncle Bram unexpectedly. Even his voice and mannerisms are exactly those of papa, but emotionally there is a great difference. Papa has obviously been damaged much more. On the one hand it is clear that that has to do with the war. On the other hand, I cannot understand it, because they both had the same experiences there.*

In any case, uncle Bram and aunt Roza are a wonderful couple. They are well-matched. The other day, when aunt Roza had one of her bad days due to her rheumatism, uncle Bram said something like "her circumstances could never become as bad as they were during the camp period". She looked at him with disdain and reacted; "Pff... listen to that ... he has only survived Auschwitz and already he thinks he is Job". Uncle Bram put his hand on my shoulder and sighed: "Well... my dear child... and that is your aunt – even worse – my wife... God protect you from such mazel!"

After the rather intensive and primitive time at the kibbutz, it is wonderful to be their guest again in this last period. Ruben lives in Natanya and Els is temporarily at home again – now that she has finished her psychology studies. As of September 1st, she has a permanent appointment as therapist with the "Simon Wiesenthal House" here in Tel Aviv. That is a treatment centre for traumatised survivors of the Shoah. Yesterday I went with her to that place. I made an appointment with two of the people whom I met there, for an interview that I am going to use for a report about that house.

Els is really a great girl. The energy that she has… and the sense of humor… She gives her opinion straight – whoever she is talking to – exactly how she thinks about it. She takes her work very seriously and has great sympathy with the people around her, but when you go out with her, you are in for a surprise! The first thing she is going to save up for is a trip to Holland. You'd better get ready for that!

By the way, I did not know that Els really is called Esther, named after the eldest sister of papa, just like our Esther. And I also did not know that this sister was not taken away together with the other family members at that time, but was in hiding for a few years with a farmer in Oldebroek. There they changed her name to Els for safety's sake. After the war, Uncle Bram heard from that farmer how she was caught in the end and put on transport after all. When he told this to his daughter later, she started to call herself Els also – out of a certain respect for the aunt that she was named after. Quite wonderful really – and it fits her very well, because it sounds a bit pluckier than Esther. I wonder why papa never told us that.

Well – I'll finish now. How things are going for me here, you'll be able to read in the letters that I sent papa and mamma. I do want to say, though, that it has been a very special experience till now. Much of it is strange to me and new and yet it is familiar. It probably sounds very illogical to someone who is not Jewish. But you know, yesterday in the "Simon Wiesenthal House" I met an old man who was born and raised in Russia. He said that, of all the countries in the world, Israel is the only one where immigrants are not bothered by nostalgia.

That is what it has to do with. As a future journalist I should not really finish with a cliché but at this moment I don't see how I can say it more clearly than this: I was born in Holland… I am at home in Israel! Or, as that old man said yesterday: "Russia is in my head… Israel is in my soul!"

Two big kisses for Sjaak and Sarah and two for you!
Lots of love
Leah

'Well,' Ben declared as he put the letter on the table, 'she has become a lot more mature in this half year.'

'Maybe she was already, but you had not noticed it yet,' Nant said, 'I have always thought that you treated Leah too much as the little sister and only took Esther seriously.'

'Really…?' Ben asked surprised.

'Yes,' Nant assured, 'and you yourself probably don't notice that at all. You may get along easily with all sorts of people, but when push comes to shove, there are only a few that you take seriously. And now that we are talking about it… your father called. He wants to see you. I saw on the calendar that you have to do a job of window dressing in Zwolle on Tuesday next week, so I said that you would pass by him on the way back in the evening. And please go to my parents then too for a minute. My mother still has a box with my old baby clothes and toys for us.' And as her face slowly wrinkled into an impish smile, she concluded: 'She has already asked several times when those two little darlings of ours are finally going to be baptised. Then you can explain that at the same time!'

In their conversations about the spiritual aspect of their children's education, they had agreed that neither of them would try to convince their children of the right of one of the parents. As balanced as possible they would confront them with both religions – emphasizing in everything as much as possible the similarities. Their common deep conviction was that God was the Creator of their children. Both came to terms with the symbolism of the "dedication". In this ceremony, you confess in the middle of the congregation that your children first of all belong to their Creator, and as parents you promise to tell them about that and to raise them according to His rules, as He has given them in His Word – the Bible. Ben had accepted that the New Testament would play an important role in that. He had understood by now that it is made specifically clear in there that the Eternal One also had wanted to have a covenant with non-Jews, to which his wife and children belonged. Just as – according to the Torah – circumcision is the sign of the covenant of God with his chosen people Israel, adult baptism by immersion has that function for those who do not belong to that people, according to the New Testament.

On the other hand he had a great problem with the baptism of children by sprinkling. He could not find any legitimate indication for that, either in the Old or in the New Testament.

Still, he decided to attend such a baptism the following Sunday in the *Dutch Reformed Church*. A former colleague had invited him to the baptism of her daughter. He had agreed to come out of respect. However, he realised that now his experience could be useful in the unavoidable discussion about it with his mother-in-law.

When – during the service – the moment for the baptism had come, he listened with mounting amazement to the minister, who – lofty above a humble crowd – read the baptism form severely and without emotion: *Because baptism has now taken the place of circumcision...* He was taken aback by the certainty with which they went dead against the truth of the Torah. There it was mentioned clearly that circumcision is not a temporary, but an eternal covenant of God with His people. He could not imagine that Jesus – who had been circumcised himself for that reason – would have done away with it, in contravention to God's will. In his mind's eye he saw fragments of the first circumcision service in their family... the understandable emotion of his father when he as *gevatter* had held his first grandson Ruben

– the oldest of David and Thera – on his lap during that age-old ritual. But the images of the accompanying festive mood and of the blessings that were pronounced, were rudely interrupted by the voice that spoke about what else was written about baptism in the *Dutch Confession of Faith*: *He has abolished circumcision that used to involve blood and instituted instead the Sacrament of Baptism.* And further on: *We, on the other hand, believe that they should be baptised and sealed with the sign of the covenant, just like small children in Israel used to be circumcised, based on the same promises that were given to our children.*

He was aghast at how with this text the Biblical truth had been twisted, adapted and completely taken out of context. Again it was the old story of the spoiled latecomer that kept squirming and wriggling in order to take the place of the eldest, the firstborn son. The spirit of Christian superiority – as had been exhibited so subtly, but none the less clearly by Andries on that particular final evening at the *Free Evangelical Youth Society* – now again appeared to him as an anti-Semitic threat. And again he was overwhelmed by that vague fear of the schoolyard of his youth. Now it was not a matter of children that accused him directly of having "killed" Jesus, but adults who with their silent docility obviously all thought that child baptism had taken the place of circumcision, and therefore confessed indirectly that the Church had taken the place of Israel. He looked around him and wondered how many were really conscious of it and how many had followed this generations-long tradition blindly, without thinking.

In spite of the fact that many people greeted him with a short nod as he left the church, he felt a stranger in their midst. The clearly present Christian dominance with which they surrounded him, stood like an invisible enemy opposite the Yiddish *neshome* - his anchoring point from which he was slowly becoming detached. And roaming on a treacherous sea – full of threatening anti-semitic dangers – he started to feel the paradox of a secret longing for Elburg – his home port that he had just escaped with such conviction. Recently it happened more and more often, that when he had to work on Friday during the shopping night, he was thinking about his family members who were celebrating the Sabbath evening at that moment. When he saw how his brother and sisters conducted their life, every now and then he was swamped by a mild melancholy, and he was not so sure any more whether he had taken the correct decisions in his life. And as he walked home from the church – his head full of conflicting thoughts – he had to admit grudgingly that he even started to miss his mother's commentary. 'What were you looking for anyway with those "baptised"?' he heard her complain. A faint smile of wistfulness showed on his face and suddenly he understood what, in her view, was the difference between a "Christian" and a "baptised person". She was very consistent in that. "Christians" to her were non-Jewish believers that had been "correct" during the war, that cared about Israel and that were considered *besedder* – alright – by her, purely on the basis of her female-yiddish intuition. All the others were "baptised people" to her and you had to be wary of those. Basically "Christians" were supporters and "baptised people" adversaries.

On his return, Nant wanted to know how he had experienced the service.

Ben stared ahead silently, shook his head and said, upset: 'Terrible…! That child baptism… that is all wrong…! That is supposed to have taken the place of circumcision, they say. Well… tell me where it says that in that Bible of yours. They just invented it themselves in order to take the place of Israel. And the worst thing is, that most of the people who were sitting there do not even realise it, I think. To my surpise they give their children Jewish names.

Do you know what that child of my former colleague is called?' he asked, raising his voice and moving his arms passionately.

Nant saw his fierce eyes and experienced misgivings. She had never before known him like this. Until now, he had always withdrawn into silence if something bothered him. The eruption that she witnessed now moved her especially because of the impotence it showed. But the wild gaze and the aggressive tone of voice frightened her. She shook her head in denial and asked cautiously: 'What…?'

'Naomi…!' Ben shouted, exaggerating the sound. 'Naomi van de Broek…! What are they thinking of…!'

Nant shrugged. 'But isn't that a nice Biblical name for a girl…?' she said.

'You mean a Jewish name!' reacted Ben fiercely and curtly, 'and that does not belong to a baptised person. I don't call my children Hasan or Yusuf either; those names do not belong to our culture, to our people and to our religion, do they? Excuse me, but you have to realise that my parents did not call me Benjamin because they thought it sounded nice, but because that name, just like those of my brother and sisters, has been inherited and used throughout the ages right through all the misery. They do not only underline the identity, marked by much persecution, of our family, but of our entire people. You as outsiders can look at that and learn about it with respect, and as far as I am concerned with a certain involvement, but other than that you have to leave well enough alone. You should leave things where they belong and a Jewish name does not fit a Christian.'

He got up and walked to the door. 'Naomi van de Broek…' he muttered, shaking his head. 'Really, don't you hear that that does not fit?' he insisted and continued without waiting for her reaction: 'That sounds just as illogical as Lubbert Cohen or as… as…'

First he slammed the door of the room and then also the front door behind him and walked into the quiet Sunday evening of the Kerkstraat. At the end he went left, hesitated a moment but then entered *De Waag*.

His hesitation was due to the fact that it was Sunday. He did not mind to be seen at *De Waag* any other day. The pub had a good reputation and a respectable clientele. *Het Rode Hert*, a little further down the street, was a different case. Everything was a bit more chaotic there. In the daytime, a lost sales rep would have a fried egg sandwich there and elderly men would play their game of pool. However, towards the end of the afternoon, the first notorious drinkers would appear on the dot and during the evening the habitués' table was usually occupied by a set group of hardened card players. The stakes were always high and many a newcomer had left the pub totally ruined. Through the years it had developed into a refuge for those who – for whatever reason – had problems toeing the line as "proper" citizens.

Louis de Bourbon, a short, untidily dressed bourgondian – descendant of an old and distinguished French noble family – attended regularly. After an eventful life as a writer, poet, journalist, resistance fighter and later even mayor, he had retired to the peace of the *Putter Bos*. There he lived in a wing of the stately property *Groot Spriel*.

Dressed in a worn hunter's jacket and with a large French cap on his head, he usually bicycled towards the end of the afternoon to the village for his shopping. Then he first had three or four "old gins" at *Het Rode Hert,* followed by some chopped steak with onions. Among the people he met there regularly were his friend and colleague-author Jan de Vries, whose book *Young people leave home* was being transmitted as a radio play and sometimes also Wijnand Wildeman, a painter- window dresser. The latter had recently lost one of his best clients. It concerned a chic ladies' fashion business in Het Gooi. Wijnand, who usually could tolerate a few drinks, apparently had consumed a bit too much during lunch on that particular day. Overcome by the heat of the midday sun that had considerably warmed up the shop window, he had fallen asleep behind the window – stretched out between the mannequins and the clothing – to the great amusement of the passers-by.

Louis enjoyed stories like that. Sometimes he made notes of such events or remarks for his books or poems.

He was also well acquainted with the writer Antoon Coolen. With him he shared the love of the common workers who were guided in their needs and joys mainly by a natural urge and the voice of the heart.

With "uncle Kees" – another regular client of *Het Rode Hert* – he had once visited the latter's clandestine gin distillery, deep in the woods near the *Solse Gat*. It was an experience that Louis later used in one of his novels. On another occasion, when it became clear that the wife of the publican was pregnant, he spontaneously wrote the poem that was later printed on the birth announcement of the little Petra…

> *What is these days*
> *our most saddening loss?*
> *That love and companionship*
> *from the heart have been tossed.*
>
> *And yet, each child born,*
> *in love and care conceived*
> *proves that now – as before –*
> *life is love received.*

When Ben entered *De Waag* Louis was sitting near the fireplace in the company of a gentleman and two ladies, enjoying a coffee and liqueur. He only came here when he had guests of standing, with whom he dined copiously. Ben took a seat on one of the bar stools and at his question, whether Lub was there, Henk phoned upstairs, and soon he appeared.

'It is good that you have come,' he greeted Ben, 'I intended to call you tomorrow. You see, in the past week I have met someone who is willing to make a building plan for a duplex for a reasonable price.'

Ben agreed to make an appointment, after which Lub drew his attention to Louis and told him what a special person he was.

'Because of his French name and descent, I once asked him where he was born. "In Holland", he assured me, "but… I saw the light of day on French soil!" If I could guess how that was possible, he would give me one of his books, but if not, it would cost me a bottle of French cognac. He earned the bottle, but I got the book anyway.'

When Ben indicated that he would like to read it, Lub went to get it for him. He read the title: *The red colour of the sky* and looked at the personal note of the author in the front of the book:

> *A substantial story for Lub with liquid consequences for me.*
> *Best regards*
> *Louis de Bourbon.*

'But uh… what exactly happened at that birth…?' asked Ben.

'Well,' Lub explained, 'it was really quite simple. According to him, the four legs of his childbed were standing in pots with French soil during his birth. It could be true, because those French people are as chauvinistic as they come.'

'Whether you should call it chauvinism, I don't know,' said Ben, 'you can also consider it as something symbolic to express the bond with the country. For instance, we have the custom to put a small bag with soil from Israel underneath the head of someone who has died. That person is then buried in Holland, but in a sense also on Israeli soil. That too is a symbol to emphasize the unique relation we have with that country.'

In the meantime Ben had noticed several times that Louis was observing him and eavesdropped the conversation. When their eyes met again, Louis got up and invited them for a drink.

An hour or so later Ben walked home and noticed how, due to this special meeting his vexation about the church service earlier that evening, had almost disappeared.

Nant was also relieved and secretly surprised about the quick about-face. She was not really happy that he had been to a bar by himself on Sunday evening, but because of its good effect on Ben she did not talk about it at that moment.

Ben told her about his meeting with Louis de Bourbon.

'He claimed that I reminded him of someone. When I mentioned that I came from Elburg, he smiled in surprise and said: "That's it… now I know… you look like David Hamburger". He said that that boy also came from Elburg. He was born during the war and was out of town at the time of the deportation. His father, however, was there and was taken away. After the war his mother moved with him to Oss, where her family lived and where Mr. de Bourbon was the mayor at the time. He knew the family well and mentioned that David was a very intelligent boy, who recently became a lawyer in Nijmegen. So…' he concluded with a broad grin, 'I look like a lawyer… what do you say to that…?'

Then the smile slowly disappeared from his face again. Absentmindedly he stared ahead and considered: 'Hmm… I'll ask my father about that next Tuesday…'

That particular Tuesday evening, as he was travelling from Zwolle on the way to his parents-in-law in Oldebroek, Ben was preparing himself in the car for the expected question about the baptism of the twins. Too bad that at the *Free Evangelical Congregation of the Netherlands* they practised child baptism, contrary to all the other Evangelical denominations, where the adult baptism is customary. Determined to discuss the subject with his parents-in-law only together with Nant, he walked into the kitchen of the farm a while later.

In a certain sense he was lucky, because at that moment, besides his parents-in-law, uncle Evert was also sitting at the kitchen table. The latter was complaining about his son, whose wife – it turned out – had left him for someone else.

'I told him from the beginning,' Evert said to Ben, 'don't start so young, I said, that woman doesn't seem right, but of course he didn't listen. Tcha, and when another stallion enters the meadow… you can wait for it!' He shook his head despondently.

In the silence that ensued, Ben looked questioningly at this mother-in-law.

'Would you like a cup of coffee, kid?' she asked.

'No, no,' said Ben, I'm in a bit of a hurry because I still have to see my parents too.'

'That's fine,' she said. Visibly upset by her brother's bad news, she handed him the box with stuff for Nant and continued: 'Here you are. Please come again soon, all of you.'

Ben nodded, said good-bye to his parents-in-law and tapped uncle Evert on the shoulder. 'All the best with you!' he wished him.

Evert sighed: 'Thanks kid… and you, take very good care of that pedigree horse of yours, for they are becoming for ever rarer.'

Fifteen minutes later Ben rang the bell at his parents' home on the Westerwalstraat in Elburg.

'Mamma isn't there?' he asked, after his father had let him in.

'No, she is babysitting for David and Thera,' Jacob answered, as he walked towards the kitchen. Till then he had been sitting in the living room. Ben noticed that because of the folded newspaper and the cup on the table next to the club seat. He knew that his father liked to sit there because it was restful for him. Through the large glass doors he had a nice view of his garden and the city wall with its high oaks behind it.

'We could sit in the room,' Ben proposed.

'Well,' Jacob reacted, 'it's almost dark outside and anyway, let's stay with what we are used to, don't you think?'

He smiled, poured a cup of coffee for Ben and then they sat – as always – in their familiar places opposite each other at the kitchen table.

After talking a bit about Nant and the twins and also about working and living in Putten, Ben said: 'Sunday evening I met a man who knows a certain David Hamburger, a boy who was born during the war in Elburg and who later moved with his mother to Brabant.'

Jacob gave a start, it was clear that it took him by surprise. 'David Hamburger…' he repeated slowly. He was silent for a while and then said: 'David is the only child of my dear childhood friend Sal Hamburger.'

For a moment he considered leaving it at this short bit of information. It would be difficult enough already for him to speak about what he had planned to tell Ben. And now this came as an extra. On the other hand, he had realised more and more – especially since Ben had left home – how good and special it was to be able to partly entrust the surplus of emotions to his son. To be allowed to store it there, specifically, in that "part of him", had brought him – in retrospect – relief, and had given him the feeling that it was safe there. He had always made a mental vow to never burden his children with his traumas. But now that all four were leading an adult life, he had to admit that Benjamin was the one who was predestined from childhood to help him carry that – still heavy – load. Therefore he decided after all, to share the great sadness about the loss of his childhood friend Sal Hamburger with him…

'It often happened that people thought that Sal and I were brothers. In a sense it felt like that to me too, for we were not average friends, but soul mates. I loved that guy. That may sound weird, but he was such a unique human being. Very spontaneous and smart. And he had such a great sense of humor… we laughed a lot. But what made him so extra-ordinary was that he was such a good person. A peacemaker. He despised quarrels and injustice and would do anything to solve and dispel situations like that.

Although Brammie and I are obviously alike in many aspects, in some things it was even more so with Sal and me. During a *Habonim camp* he started to go out with a girl from Brabant, whom he later married. They came to live in Elburg and during the deportation she was visiting her parents with her son – David. Sal died in the camp from dysentery and she went back to her family in Brabant after the war.'

'Did you see each other sometimes in the camp?' Ben asked.

Jacob shook his head: 'But one day, when we had to take the dead from the huts to the crematorium, I found him. Mordecai wanted to pick him up, but then I told him who that boy was and how much he had meant to me. We then said *kaddish*, after which I lifted him up and…'

His voice faltered, and after he had tried a few times to swallow the lump in his throat, he finished his sentence in a broken voice… 'I carried him by myself to the crematorium.' He took his handkerchief from his pocket, blew his nose and wiped his cheeks dry. Then he shook his head and stammered disconsolately: 'He weighed nothing… terrible…'

Ben sat staring ahead, upset. He tried to imagine what you would feel when you have to say good-bye to your best friend in such a terrible manner.

Meanwhile Jacob had stood up and walked to the room. Deep in thought he stood in front of the window for a while and peered into the darkness. Then he walked back again to the kitchen. He poured another cup of coffee for Ben and, after he had sat down again, he said: 'But what I really wanted to tell you… "De Schim" is dead.'

Surprised Ben looked at his father and asked: 'Oh…? But uh… who was that anyway…?'

'It is quite a story,' said Jacob, 'but I'll try to keep it short. First I want to say that I have always appreciated that you never asked me about "De Schim" and Ischie. I know it is on your mind, but in a little while you will understand why I have waited to tell you.'

'Ischie was the youngest in our family. He was born with the Down syndrome. A mongoloid, a very sweet kid. Luckily he was very healthy otherwise and so – in his own way – he enjoyed life immensely. He had a very cheerful character and none of us considered him to be a burden or a worry. On the contrary, he added something to the atmosphere in our home. He considered me to be his oldest brother and was quite attached to me. Because

Brammie used to tease and challenge him, that bond between us became only stronger. He always called me "Sapie". When we arrived in *Auschwitz* and had just stepped out of the train, one of those Germans picked him out immediately. Roughly he pulled him by his arm away from my mother and chased him onto the path to the gas chambers. We lost sight of him and walked with the throng to the end of the platform. At a certain moment I was walking as the last of our family on the outside and suddenly I saw Ischie further down, crying and in a complete panic. He tried to walk back to the platform, against the flow. But one of the SS-men also saw it and shot him down from behind, just like that. Because he still moved when he lay on the ground, that man walked over to him and gave him the coup de grace. Then he pushed him off the path with his foot, like a piece of rubbish.'

Ben recalled that evening on the graveyard in Oldebroek, where his father had told him about children who were shot like rabbits, but immediately he concentrated again on the continuation of the story…

'For just a moment I clearly saw the face of the murderer of our Ischie. Later I also saw him from time to time in the camp. But until recently I used to meet him time and again here in Elburg…'

He described the man who was the spitting image of the SS-man, but that person did not seem familiar to Ben.

'It was an NSB-man of the lowest kind. One of those who were in league with the enemy only to better their own cause. The first thing he did, when we had been deported, was to rob our houses together with some of his comrades. Joop Cohen, the only one who managed to escape and to find refuge with Hendrik Westerink, here in the Westerwalstraat, saw it with his own eyes. From the attic window he saw how they entered his butchery on the Beekstraat and took everything that had any value. It did not bring the man much happiness. After the war most Elburgers ignored him. He never married and a few weeks ago he died in complete loneliness. Gérard told me that there were only four people at his funeral.'

Jacob peered at the empty cup that he slowly turned around in his hand. Meanwhile, Ben looked at the face of his father and he had the impression that he could keep his emotions under better control now, than when he had spoken about Sal Hamburger. Probably that was – Ben supposed – because of the unexpected confrontation with the memory of Sal. The story about Ischie and "De Schim" was not less upsetting, but he had prepared himself for that and consciously decided to tell it.

'So,' Ben said, 'every time when you met that man you were reminded of the murderer of your little brother.'

'Yes...' Jacob answered and while he lifted his head he continued: 'but that did not happen every day, mind you. Sometimes weeks passed in which I did not see him. He was quite aware that most Elburgers didn't want to have anything to do with him, so he only came to town when it was really necessary. If he would see me or Joop Cohen, he would look around fearfully and disappear immediately. It was in fact a very pathetic and miserable person. For me it was very painful that he always reminded me of that horrible event, but he really was not guilty of that – but he was guilty of the death of our Esther. He dragged her away personally from her hideout and handed her to the Germans. He received seven guilders and fifty cents for her. That was the amount the *Krauts* paid if you brought them a Jew. That was how much our life was worth then...'

Now Ben told about the letter from Leah and about what uncle Bram had told her about Esther. Jacob nodded in confirmation: 'Yes, that's right. But there is one thing that Brammie does not know. I'll tell you so that you may understand better why I am so loath to go back to *Auschwitz*.

Esther was the oldest in our family and I got along very well with her. Brammie and I were next, then Ruben, Leah and our Ischie was the youngest. On the day that our family was deported, Esther was the only one who was not at home. She went in hiding afterwards with a farmer in Oldebroek called Helmig. A very special person. After the war I visited him regularly. As far as I can judge: a *tzaddik*! A Christian who roused deep respect in me. Big and strong like Goliath, but his real strength was within. A man who lived with God and the Torah. He did not know what *kosher* meant, but he kept to the food laws more carefully than many a Jew.

One evening, when everyone was already in bed, they were warned by neighbors that there was a raid in the village. As quickly as possible every one was brought to safety. There were two cupboard-beds in the large living room. Helmig and his wife slept in one and in the other was Esther, at that moment very ill with high fever. Helmig carried her from the bed and took her to the cow barn. There he put her down behind the cows in fresh straw. It wasn't a very clean spot, but it was safe. Soon after, two Germans entered, accompanied by "De Schim" who asked if they had any Jews in the house. Helmig just looked calmly at him without saying a word. "It is forbidden to lie, but staying mum is not a sin", he thought. Quickly they searched the farm but found no one. When they were about to leave again via the living room, "De Schim" turned around and walked over to the cupboard-beds. He looked and felt, then asked Helmig – pointing at the other bed: "Is that where you sleep with your wife?" Helmig assented – because it was the truth – whereupon the man growled: "So how is it possible that this one is also warm?" Salvation from this awkward situation had everything to do with Helmig's knowledge of the Torah. In spite of the seriousness of the situation he looked at "De Schim" with compassion and answered with a deep sigh and shaking his head: "Man, man… I can tell that you do not know the laws of God, because there it is written that you have to sleep separate from your wife when she has her unclean days".

For the moment Esther seemed saved by that, but "De Schim" was obviously suspicious, for a few hours later he came unexpectedly running into the room again and found her in the cupboard-bed. Sick as she was he took her along anyway and handed her to the Germans.

Later, when Mordecai and I regularly had to pick up the dead in the camp, I found her one day in the sick hut and I carried her myself to the crematorium – just as I did with Sal. And that…' he swallowed a few times, looked ahead sadly and confessed: 'that I have never told Brammie.'

༄

When Ben drove into Putten late that evening, the village was covered with a quiet, misty haze. Cautiously he opened the front door and climbed the staircase. Only in the kitchen was the light still on. There was a note on the table. He picked it up and read:

> *Hey… Van Zuiden, you are out of luck. The woman of your youth and woman of your life is already asleep. I'll hear tomorrow how you got on.*
> *Sleep well. Johanna-Aleida.*

He smiled, walked to the fridge and opened a bottle of beer. Then he entered the dark living room and looked out towards the lit-up tower of the *Oude Kerk*. Thin wisps of fog floated through the shafts of light from the floodlights and light of the streetlanterns.

He saw that someone had put flowers in front of the large memorial stone on which the text: FROM HERE THEY WERE DEPORTED was written.

And although just a few days ago he had had such a bad experience within the walls of the old building, that same building now suddenly conjured up something of respect and even a certain degree of solidarity. "From here they were deported" it buzzed through his head, as he looked at the old walls and the high windows. And gradually these turned into those of the *shul* in Elburg.

For a moment his attention was drawn to a long trail of white smoke that rose from behind the building. But almost immediately he realised that this must come from the furnace that stood in the space built purposely adjacent to the church to house it – just outside his field of vision. When he saw the smoke dissolve in the wisps of fog and the drizzling rain, he turned around and went to bed.

That night the emotions of the past few days took their toll. At the mercy of a seemingly arbitrary string of incoherent and threatening images, a frightening nightmare swept him into the dark night…

… In the church the minister appeals to all Jews to be baptised right away on the pain of death. In a panic, he tries to beat a path through the crowd that wants to keep him back. Someone trips him up, another pushes him over, it seems endless. When he finally stands outside he sees dark smoke rise from the chimney of the furnace shed next to the church. Two men carry his sister Esther inside, one holding her feet and the other her hands. He attacks them and Esther falls to the ground with a thud. The men look at her and start to laugh loudly. Quickly he picks her up in his arms and runs into the Dorpsstraat. At *De Heerdt* he sees through the window that Gérard is sitting at a long table with "Red Kobus" and "The Bellows", but he cannot find the door. And when he thumps on the window, they all continue to laugh and talk. They don't hear him. The two men continue to pursue him. Their laughter sounds hollow in the deserted street. He runs for his life, but his legs become more and more heavy and he sees Esther's head wildly shaking back and forth. Exhausted and paralysed with fear, he stumbles on. Then his pursuers grab him on both sides. The eerie sound of their laughter and of their unintelligible strange words reverberates through his head. Completely exhausted he allows himself to be led away. They stop at the memorial stone on the wall of the church. They force him to read the text but he turns around and sees how they are emptying his apartment above the shop in the Kerkstraat. "Look", one of the men whispers in his ear in a provoking, sadistic tone of voice, "there is "De Schim" with your wife and children…"

"NOOO!" he shouts and with his last strength he tries to release himself from the grip of the men…

Nant woke up with a start from that horrible shout and the wild movements next to her. Frightened, she turned on the lamp on her bedside table and looked at Ben who lay staring at the ceiling with wide-open, dazed eyes.

'Hey… what's the matter?' she asked cautiously and stroked his dark hair that contrasted strongly with the white pillow and his pale, sweaty face. Slowly he turned his head towards her and looked at her with that same absent gaze. After a deep sigh he blinked and slowly sat up.

Sitting on the edge of the bed, he wiped the sweat from his brow with his shirt. Then he got up and walked without a word out of the bedroom to the kitchen.

After a while, Nant followed him in her peignoir. She sat down opposite him and looked at the strong young body… The wide shoulders and the dark skin underneath the white shirt. That strong head with the thick long black hair. Strength and charm all over, but at that moment also just vulnerability and loneliness.

Cautiously she put her hands on his arms that rested on the table top.

'Hey… are you OK again…?' she asked.

He lifted his head up slowly, looked at her and answered, still upset: 'I am OK… it was only a dream, but now I finally understand what it would be like if you have to go through something like this almost every night…'

9

The following years were characterised by the building of the new house and the move, but also by two pregnancies of Nant with far-reaching consequences. When she became pregnant again – only a little over a year after the birth of the twins – complications occurred due to her high blood pressure. Her body retained fluid and on examination it was found that the protein level in her urine was much too high. These were the early signs of what turned into a serious pregnancy intoxication six months later. Nant and Ben lived through two anxious months in which the lives of mother and child were constantly in danger.

After eight months the baby was delivered by Caesarean section. It was a girl and they called her Lilian, named after Leida, Nant's mother.

Because the blood pressure problem was uncontrollable, the doctor advised strongly against a possible next pregnancy. The possibility of having another pregnancy intoxication and to die of it was a reality. But sterilisation or the use of contraceptives still roused a natural resistance in Nant – even though she realised the necessity for it. She needed time to take a decision about it. But in the meantime she got pregnant again and when she became fully aware of it, it caused her inevitable fear. She finally realised that she had to face the fact that it was irresponsible to ever become pregnant again. Too much was at stake.

Things went reasonably well for half a year, but then complications occurred again. Blood loss and early contractions landed her in hospital. An ultrasound showed that the bleeding was caused by a placenta that was too low. As the baby grew in the uterus, Nant experienced daily blood loss. Only with complete bed rest she would have a chance to carry out the pregnancy.

She was put on a drip with contraction inhibiting medication. And thus she had to spend the remaining two to three months of her last pregnancy chained to her hospital bed.

Towards the end of January there was a period in which Ben hardly had any window dressing to do due to the seasonal sales. His employer also cooperated to let him take care as much as possible of the daily running of the household and to visit Nant every evening. In that time his worry about the consequences of being the neighbor of a "fellow sufferer" disappeared like snow in the sun. Lub and his wife Gea sympathised and helped as much as they could. In addition, their children, who were already a bit more grown up, enjoyed babysitting and playing with Sjaak and Sarah and the little Lilian. The bed rest was clearly good both for Nant and the baby. Everything indicated that the damage to the placenta had been limited. However, she kept losing blood and as soon as more than eight months had passed, the doctors decided to initiate the birth. One April morning Ben got a call from Nant that he should come to the hospital right away because the delivery would be induced.

He left straight from work without taking the time to tell anyone about the impending event. During the drive an anxious feeling gradually took hold of him. It was not fear or worry – as it had been the last time at the Lilian's birth. It had more to do with a premonition of Nant… "You'll see, this is going to be a special child", she had told him several times already. Of course she could not explain it and therefore Ben had very sensibly taken that remark at face value. He had ascribed it to the fact that she had been lying in the hospital for many long, lonely days with time to worry. In normal circumstances – at home with three small children – she would have had much less time for that. Also – in his opinion – an additional factor was that Nant realised that this would definitely be her last pregnancy. However, now that the baby was about to be born, he had to admit that this thought had started to dominate him too. Fragments of events and conversations went through his head disjointedly…

… The crash during that champions' game in which he had ended up unconscious… The great sadness of his father that, in a sense, had taken root in him… The "flight" to Putten that turned out to be partly in vain…

But when, a bit later, he walked beneath the high trees from the parking lot to the hospital, he became calm and only heard his father tell quietly and with conviction about the promise that the name of his descendants would not be blotted out from Israel.

When he arrived in the corridor he saw Nant being wheeled out of the room. On the way to the delivery room he walked next to her, held her hand and looked at her pain-contorted face. He felt the strength with which her hand, during a mounting contraction, squeezed his, which gave him a very special sense of solidarity with her.

Because of the action of a stimulating medication the contractions followed one another in quick succession and within a few hours the birth of Robertus was a fact. Named after Bertus – Nant's father – he would be Robert van Zuiden from now on.

After the normal lusty crying bout, he lay – just six pounds, due to his early birth – contentedly on Nant's chest.

Because of the complications a number of routine examinations had to be done and Ben was advised quite early to say good-bye and come back in the evening during visiting hours. Somewhat bewildered he left the delivery room. With mixed feelings he walked through the long quiet corridor to the elevator. Gratitude filled him that their last child too had come through the rather unusual pregnancy well – as it seemed now. But in that cold, sterile environment he could not really deal with his emotions. He looked around and saw only doors, windows and here and there a trolley with medication or linens. Suddenly he stopped in surprise… There he saw his father – calm but purposefully – walk towards him. Obviously he had stood waiting near the elevator. With a serious face he looked at Ben and asked: 'Well…?'

Flustered but at the same time incredibly happy that right at that moment there was the person with whom he felt such an intense bond, he stammered: 'Papa… I have… we have another son…!'

They embraced and Jacob asked: 'Is everything alright with Nant?'

'Yes… eh… yes, yes…' Ben reacted and he continued in utter surprise: 'but how did you know it was going to be born today…?'

Jacob grabbed his son's shoulder: 'I did not know, but I hoped it with all my heart because today is such a memorable day for us.'

With a voice trembling with emotion, Jacob answered Ben's questioning look… 'Your son, my boy, is my first grandchild to be born on *the day after Passover…*'

At that moment Ben recalled Nant's premonition that it would be a very special child. It filled him with awe, and secretly he was ashamed for the laconic manner in which he had taken that.

'Come,' he said, 'come along,' and shortly afterwards he knocked on the door of the delivery room.

Ben politely asked the nurse who opened the door whether he could show his son to his father. She nodded with understanding and together they walked to the bed where the nurse continued what she had been doing: to put an elastic string with letter beads that spelled the name *Robert van Zuiden*, around the small wrist of the baby. Jacob looked at it and read the name, murmuring softly. Then he put his hands around Nant's face: 'My dear, congratulations with this special child.' Carefully Jacob took Robert in his arms, lifted him and said: '*Shalom zakhar…* Robert van Zuiden, son of the covenant, may the Lord bless you and keep you, may He make His countenance shine upon you and give you peace.'

Gently he kissed his grandson on the forehead and put him back again into the arms of his mother.

Nant looked into the moist eyes of her father-in-law and felt a tear drop on her arm.

More than a week after the delivery Nant and Robert were discharged from the hospital.

When, back at home, they entered the baby room and Nant saw two small soccer shoes hanging over the baby bed, she asked: 'What for Pete's sake does that mean?'

'Oh,' said Ben, 'your brother Jan hung those there. You are not to remove them for any reason, "because", he said, "if that is the first thing that boy sees in his life, then I guarantee you that he'll be a good soccer player later!" '

Nant shook her head, put Robert in his cradle and walked smiling to the living room.

Amongst the many wish cards there was one from Leah, who was living in Israel again. She had finished her studies in Utrecht, and the practicum time with the newspaper in Tel Aviv had resulted in a part time job there. The rest of the time she worked and lived in a *kibbutz* near Zichron, between Tel Aviv and Haifa. Besides sending them her warm congratulation on the birth of their son, she also wrote that it was very likely that she – together with their cousin Els - would come to Holland in the fall for three weeks vacation.

On a beautiful Sunday morning in August Ben and Nant walked with their children to the building of the *Evangelical Congregation*. Sjaak and Sarah walked next to them and each in turn helped to push the pram in which Robert lay, who would be dedicated that morning.

Lilian – still too little to walk the whole way by herself – sat on a small chair that was attached to the front of the pram. Like a little princess on the driving box of a coach she called to the animals in the park and the church-goers on the street in her own, mostly unintelligible toddler language.

Many women and girls who were on their way to the *Hervormde Kerk* carried a plastic bag in which they kept their hat. For some reason they did not want to wear them as they walked in the street and they only put them on just before entering the church building. Lilian obviously had no idea that in those circles it was not customary for women to attend a church service with uncovered head. She associated the bags with those that she always took with her to the kindergarten, with her sandwich, some fruit and a drink of juice. When a woman passed them, Lilian pointed at the plastic bag and called with a high voice: 'Mommie, the lady also take blead…? And appels… and juilce…!'

Ben smiled. He thought it was interesting to see how the differences in character of his children became apparent at such a young age already. Even with Sjaak and Sarah you saw now already - although they were twins – how different they were from each other. When they were still in the playpen, Sarah would sit playing or dreaming quietly for hours. Sjaak on the other hand tried everything to get out of there as soon as possible. He pushed his sister against the bars, then climbed on top of her and dropped over the railing.

His inborn resistance against being shut in was probably the reason that around that time he liberated a number of birds. A neighbor, three houses away, had an aviary with tropical birds, some of which were unique. Little Sjaak thought that they should be able to fly freely just like all the other birds in the park, and at an unguarded moment he opened the door of the aviary. It took the owner days of work with a catching net. He did catch most of them again, but a couple had – literally and figuratively – flown the coop.

When they arrived in the meeting hall Ben was seized by a vague sense of discomfort. He knew that it had to do with the fact that he still felt himself to be an outsider in this Christian world. Raising his children in a religion that was diametrically opposite his own kept – in spite of his respect for Nant's religious background – calling up a kind of resistance in him. And again he had to face the fact that the effect of "fleeing from Elburg and marrying a non-Jewish woman" had turned out completely different from what he had expected at the time. His Jewish identity had been strengthened by it rather than weakened. It reminded him of how Einstein had once expressed this duality. On a tile that used to hang on their kitchen wall at home, it said: *Schau ich mir die Juden an, hab' ich wenig Freude d'ran. Fallen mir die Anderen ein, bin ich froh ein Jud zu sein.* (*When I look at the Jews, it does not make me very happy. But when I consider the others, I am happy to be a Jew.*)

In the meantime the service had started and as he looked around he saw several raised hands, with which the believers intended to emphasize their songs of praise. After three songs had been sung, the pastor announced that now the son of Ben and Nant van Zuiden would be dedicated, so that all the children could witness it before they went off to their own meeting. He invited Ben and Nant to come to the front with their children and all the other children of the congregation were allowed to stand around them. Then the pastor took Robert in his arms and prayed. All of this passed Ben by, but the end touched him deeply, mainly because it came so unexpectedly.

'During the preparation,' the pastor said, 'my attention was drawn to a prophecy from the Old Testament, with which I would like to end this ceremony.' He put his hand on Robert's head and said: Robertus van Zuiden, I bless you in the name of the Father, the Son and the Holy Spirit. Thus says the Lord, Creator of Heaven and Earth and of your life: *He shall lead the heart of the fathers back to the children and the heart of the children to their fathers.*'

Ben was startled and for a moment his head felt dizzy. Very clearly he experienced the parallel with that other "family promise" that said that the name of his children would not be blotted out from Israel. He could only observe that these words were linked to that promise and were even a confirmation of it. It just surprised him that they came from this Christian corner. It occupied his mind all day. Even though he had looked into Christianity quite a lot lately, that had in fact only been a theoretical activity till now. The hypothesis that had been formed through this now turned out to have developed into an absolute truth; namely that the Eternal One was revealed – not only by His people – but actually also through Christians. He recalled what his father had told him about Helmig, the just farmer from Oldebroek. How he – as a Christian – lived according to the Torah more meticulously than many Jews. When Ben asked Jacob how he could explain that the inquisition and the crusades could have taken place and that people such as Hitler and Luther had prided themselves on belonging to Christianity, his father had answered him that they had absolutely not understood the teachings of the Jewish rabbi – after whom they named themselves – and had in any case interpreted these wrongly. Their words and acts were definitely not in accordance with the message of Jesus: *to love God above all else and your neighbor as yourself.* And again an expression of Einstein, which his father had quoted at that time, came to mind: "When you see the faith of the prophets and the message of Jesus Christ without any interpretations and additions, you are left with a message that can heal all the wrongs of humanity". The fact that this was the conviction of a Jewish scientist had impressed him even more than the content per se.

Late that evening Ben decided to have a stroll around the park before going to bed, to put some order into the diversity of his thoughts. Apart from someone walking his dog, the park was deserted. Now and then a duck quacked and, besides that, there was only the splashing sound of the fountain. Sitting on the armrest of a bench, he peered across the dark surface of the water of the pond that was lit by the full moon. He thought of little Robert: the child that according to the doctors should not have been born, but that had been called "son of the covenant" by his grandfather, immediately after his birth. Only now he realised that never for a moment he had feared the outcome of the pregnancy. Also in Nant he had never noticed anything like that, although both of them were very much aware of the risks.

A gentle breeze rustled through the trees and shrubs and for the first time that day he became quiet inside. From an endless distance unspoken words drifted peacefully into him…

"Their name shall not be blotted out of Israel", and…"He shall lead the hearts of the children back to their fathers". Words that accompanied him home and that gave him, although he could not explain it, the certainty that they were linked with the life of the little Robert. He looked up, to the moon – just like the earth only a dot in the endless universe. Somewhere in that immeasurable space was the Origin of laws and structures that determined and guarded the correct balance and rhythm in the universe. He could not understand it, that mystery of order and connection of all things, but it had given him the strong conviction that there had to be an intelligence of an immensely high level behind everything. Its "Name" pervaded him at that moment more than ever before - due in particular by the pattern of the developments in his own life. *Hashem*, the Eternal One, Creator of Heaven and Earth and at the same time Director of his life and that of his children. And suddenly he saw very clearly – for the first time – the perspective, the connection of all those promises and events in his life. They did not stand on their own and did not take place arbitrarily or by accident. On the contrary. With a mixture of surprise and wonder he realised that they were linked with what was put in his heart – both at the very start of his life and also later as an adult – by the Lord: *This is my covenant that you will keep between Me and you and…your descendants.*

For Ben the month of September of that year was dominated by the meeting with Els, who – as planned – came to Holland together with Leah for a three weeks' vacation. The first days they spent in Berlin where Els attended a congress and Leah visited some people and museums – partly for her job. Then they went with David and Thera to Antwerp to celebrate the Feast of Tabernacles there. Afterwards they spent a longer period in Elburg and the last four days they stayed with Ben and Nant in Putten.

'You'd better brace yourself, boy,' said Jacob with a sigh of relief to Ben, after Saar and he had delivered the ladies in Putten, 'that Els… she is a darling, but a real adventurer, a cross between an adolescent and a prophet.'

That characterisation turned out to completely true. She faced everyone openly, honestly, but above all plainly. She gave her opinion immediately in unmistakable wordings. During the conversations and discussions that they had, it struck Ben how the restlessness in her behaviour could suddenly turn into attentive listening and even into a somewhat emotional attitude whenever it concerned the underdog. Driven by a natural sense of justice, she convinced you – short and snappy – in unpolished terms of the absolute guilt of the perpetrators. But with just as much emotion she pulled you along in her involvement with the victims. It was the unconditional faithfulness with which she served the latter group in her daily work – in the midst of the hard society of her birth country – that gave her the right to speak.

For the children of Ben and Nant it was a complete revelation. That unhindered, spontaneous behaviour appealed to them especially.

The regular visitors of *Het Rode Hert*, where she had ended up already on the second day of her stay in Putten, revived completely during her exuberant presence. She didn't come home before midnight. Leah had left much earlier and had gone to bed, like Nant. Only Ben was still up and just when he was getting a little worried he heard the garage door slam.

A bit later Els dropped into a chair opposite him and told him with satisfaction: 'Wow, that was really a good evening. Tomorrow I am going to Friesland with Louis de Bourbon!'

Baffled, Ben looked at her and asked: 'What… why Friesland?'

'Well…' she answered laconically, 'Louis is an interesting man. He wanted to know if I had any hobbies and I said: "Drawing". And now he wants to take me to the museum of… well, I have forgotten the name. But that man – self-taught – appears to have made very original drawings and paintings.'

'Jopie Huisman,' said Ben.

'Yes, that's right. Louis thinks I have to see that because it suits me to a T. "I am sure it will appeal to you and inspire you", he claimed. Well… I am curious.'

When Ben asked what she liked to draw best, she was silent for a long time. It seemed to him that she was considering whether or not to answer the question.

'People,' she admitted in the end, rather curtly. 'And objects that have to do with people or their story. But it really is therapy rather than hobby. As a child I used to suffer a lot of headaches. At least, that is what I called it. In fact they were the result of especially bad, frightening dreams that I could never reproduce. Most of the time I would wake up by myself, but sometimes it was accompanied by sleepwalking or with loud calling and shouting. My parents would wake me up and then I always just said that it was due to the headaches. I did not want to bother them with those dreams. And anyway, I could not have reproduced them. I only remembered extreme fear and hollow voices, but the concrete situations, with which they were all linked, seemed to have been immersed in a large black hole. I remember very well how scared and sweaty I used to be and how utterly tired. After such a nightmare I often did not dare to go back to sleep. I used to listen to classical music a bit and sometimes I started drawing. The result was that I would be completely knackered the next day. Once my parents had an extensive brain examination done, but nothing special was brought to light. After puberty it became a bit less but it has never gone completely. I call it "the ghost" that entered my life once in some way. Fortunately it is no longer as dominant as it used to be, but there is still a vague fear inside me… slumbering and elusive. I have talked about it once with a certain Bronia. A very sweet, wise woman with an unlikely life story. She lives with us in the Simon Wiesenthal House, is of Polish descent and can paint very well. According to her, my problem is that I am too intensively occupied with my job, I get too involved with my patients and do not maintain enough distance. "Therefore it is important to have something for yourself, apart from this work", she said. Now I have to show her every time a drawing that I have made. She gives me tips and advice, for instance how you can give more depth to something with a shadow and that sort of thing. And sometimes she gives me an assignment. It is really a matter of the tables being turned. I mean… something like a doctor who is helped by his patient. I doubt that Bronia's diagnose is right, anyway. In my case, that fear has a completely different origin, I think. But that does not take away the fact that drawing has a very salutary influence on me. By nature I don't have much patience but when I am drawing I can lose myself completely in it.'

Ben nodded with understanding. 'Hmm…' he said, 'I also have such an amateur-psychologist. A friend of my father. He has insisted already several times that I should write down everything that, in my opinion, has to do with my depressions. I never made it beyond a few short poems, but I must admit that it really does give a kind of tranquillity, when you concentrate on something like that.'

Els got up and while she absentmindedly ran her fingers through her hair, she walked towards the window. She looked outside for a moment, then turned around and asked: 'Is anything left of the wine that I brought?'

Taken aback by her candour, Ben looked into the eyes that appeared to reflect such an essential and intimate part of himself.

Her ever present, slumbering fear had to have the same origin as his… so often already he had asked himself why he did suffer from that and his brother and sisters didn't. But now that it turned out to be also present in one of the children of his father's twin brother, he experienced a very strange feeling of recognition.

'Hey… hello!' The words sounded in the quiet room, 'I asked you something. What about it, anything happening?'

She smiled and made a clarifying movement with her wrist.

Ben went to the kitchen and came back with a bottle of wine and two glasses. He poured, lifted his glass and said, pensively and well-considered: 'Well… Esther van Zuiden, *lechaim*, on the emergence of the hidden dimension of our relationship.'

'Yes… *lechaim*…' she repeated slowly and continued: 'in fact I was a bit aware already of that special dimension through conversations with Leah. Otherwise I would probably not have broached the subject with you. It does not surprise me, for at work I am confronted daily with the phenomenon "second generation syndrome". Although, in our case you should really talk of "third generation syndrome". For our fathers had to deal with the murder of their parents also. Still, at times I doubt whether my fear has to do with that. You see, in your father it is obvious that he has a war trauma. But in mine that seems not to be the case, or not as much. At least… I never noticed.'

'Still,' said Ben, 'I am convinced that the name of your "ghost" is anti-semitism. And it is not just because of what you observe in your direct environment. That which has taken root in you by tradition is also at the base of it. I mean: your father may seem an optimist at first sight, but that does not mean that inside him the images of the terrors that he experienced and sounds are not stored also. And that has, consciously or unconsciously, also had an influence on the person he has become, the person who has fathered you.'

Els looked attentively at her cousin. She had to admit that what he posed interfaced with certain hypotheses that she recalled from her studies. And now that she got confirmation of these theses from the lips of a direct kinsman – who spoke with the authority of someone who was personally involved – they suddenly became much more credible.

'So,' she asked, 'you hold that you can "inherit" your fear, so to say?'

'Yes...' Ben assented, 'I think so, yes. I am not a scientist, of course, but I am convinced by now that you inherit more from your forefathers than just a few physical, concrete characteristics. Take for instance the déjà vu phenomenon. You can only explain that by means of genetics, really. Because... how else can you explain that in one city or environment you feel like a stranger and threatened, and in another city safe and protected, when there is no demonstrable cause or reasonable explanation for it.'

With that Els moved to the edge of her chair, put her glass down resolutely and said with a raised index finger: 'Now that you say that! I experienced that very strongly in Elburg. The typical square shape of the city, the building style and the dark colours, all of it is totally different from Tel Aviv, our "White City". Still, some of those alleys and certain sites near the harbour seemed familiar to me. Just like the synagogue and the canal with those old trees. It was as if I had been there before but could not quite remember when. Oh yes... and do you know what was also special? For the first time in my life I had a herring at one of the fish stalls. You know exactly how they clean them and then eat them raw, just like that. Well, all those men were laughing because I was looking at it with such a disgusted face. That fishmonger says to me: "You want a herring too, miss?" Really, I shuddered all over. But that man claimed that it was so good and so healthy and that no one had ever died of it. So I tasted a piece and what do you think? Delicious! And then I had that same experience again. It was hardly in my mouth and it seemed that the smell and the taste were familiar to me in some way.'

'Yes, that's what I mean,' said Ben, 'you can be sure that your father loves them too and has eaten them regularly when he still lived here, for mine is crazy about them too, and so am I.'

Suddenly going to bed was no longer important. The openheartedness that had developed between those two people, who until recently were barely aware of each other's existence, had meanwhile created the need to dig further, to search further and to share more. A spark had passed that had lit their curiosity about each other. Common areas, that were in principle there already in the time when Ben was still called Benjamin and Els was still called Esther, became apparent spontaneously – after years and miles of separation. Just like Ben defused his emotions at times in poems, Els turned out to do that in drawings. They shared their preferences in types of music – from Vivaldi to Pink Floyd – and…both turned out to be lovers of a good glass of wine.

Towards four a.m. the wine was finished and fatigue hit. Els lay shattered in her chair and informed Ben sleepily that she was going to bed.

'One more question,' said Ben. 'You have been here for almost three weeks and have clearly noticed that your roots are here in Holland, even though you were born in Israel. Do you feel more Dutch or Isreali?'

She thought about it for a while and confided: 'You know… especially during my stay in Elburg – the city and the atmosphere at your parents' home – I really felt very strongly that my roots are here. It has done me a world of good to confirm for myself that in principle I am Dutch – an Elburger. Sill, during this vacation I have also focussed on what, in essence, is my one true identity. And in fact that has nothing to do with the fact that my parents were born in Holland and I in Israel, but with the deeply routed consciousness that I am Jewish – that is even more authentic and essential. It rises above all other things. And do you know where I experienced that most during this vacation?'

Ben shook his head: 'No… where…?'

'In Antwerp,' she said. 'For me in that city too, everything was different from Tel Aviv. Until we sat down at the table at Thera's parents' place for the *shabbes* meal and Mrs. Hoffman lit the candles and pronounced the blessing. Then all the differences in distance, culture and language just fell away. The next morning we all went to *shul* and there I had the same experience. There too, I was very deeply aware of the strong, age-old bond that we as a people have. In whatever corner of the world you are and how lonely you may feel there, as soon as you enter a synagogue, you are at home.'

Ben stood up and walked towards her. He reached his hand out to her, pulled her up from the chair and embraced her.

'Esther van Zuiden,' he said, 'Sunday morning you are going home again and I'll take Leah and you to Schiphol and wave good-bye, but this… here, this night, that was our good-bye and I'll never forget it… *shalom aleychem*,' he whispered softly and kissed her on her forehead. She wrinkled her eyebrows and stared at him with open mouth.

'What is it?' Ben reacted, 'did I say something wrong?'

'No. no… not at all,' she answered, 'but it's so weird, my father does exactly the same thing at such moments… an embrace, a *shalom aleychem* and a kiss on the forehead…'

After a short night's rest Els had a long, intensive day with Louis. Tired but satisfied, she returned home in the beginning of the evening. Leah had been to Oldebroek with Ben, Nant and the children and then to Elburg to say good-bye to her parents. Some time later the four of them walked to *De Waag* for a farewell dinner. Els told them how impressed she had been with the work of Jopie Huisman. Both the almost photographic paintings and the more casual atmosphere paintings, but also the original subjects, had appealed to her and inspired her beyond expectation. Other than that she did not say much and was unusually quiet and a bit withdrawn.

Back home she promised – in reference to their conversation of the night before – to send Ben an article by a doctor William Rivers, based on his experiences during and after the first world war.

'The title is: *A therapy of remembering instead of trying to forget,*' she said, 'and the essence of it is that recalling and reliving events that led to a trauma in the long run have a more salutary effect on the victims than suppressing them. It seems contradictory, but in the practice of our work I have seen that it is true. In those who try to suppress and forget it, it comes back all the more violently at night in the subconscious.'

Nant did not join the conversation. The subject was too far removed from her. Still she sensed intuitively that there was a link between what was being said and Ben's depressive moods.

The next morning Leah and Els said good-bye to Nant and the children and then were taken to Schiphol by Ben. After checking in, Els took an envelope from her bag and gave it to Ben.

'There's a poem in there that Louis made for me. I copied it for you. I'm curious what you think of it,' she added with a mischievous look.

He put it in his coat pocket and waved until they had left his sight, and walked out of the departure hall to the parking garage. As he drove on the A1, direction Amersfoort, it became gradually quieter on the road. It was obvious that the greater part of Holland was still deeply immersed in the Sunday rest. At a gas station he stopped, bought a cup of coffee and walked to a bench on the parking lot. The sun barely penetrated the clouds that floated in long grey veils above the meadows. He thought of Leah… for many years his little, lank sister and now such a beautiful, adult woman. So strong and well-balanced and… so at home in Israel. Without her mentioning it, he had noticed from everything that her choice was definite and that she had found her new home in that old world.

The cold humidity sent a shiver down his spine. Quickly he drank his last sip of coffee and when he wanted to walk back to the car, he suddenly remembered the envelope that Els had given him. He took it from his pocket, took out the poem and as he read it, his face wrinkled into a smile of recognition…

SOMETHING ELS

It's that introvert mildness
that exuberant wildness
far above mediocrity
that maketh this woman.
But righteous or rebel
anxious or rash
makes no difference to me
for the woman I see
is the sum of these parts
a real 'something Els'.

PART 3

10

In the following years Ben and Nant's life was mainly defined by the raising and supervising of their children. Ben kept working as a window-dresser on his day off, but he had dismissed two clients so that he could be at home more often in the evenings. Nant enjoyed heart and soul her fulltime job as a mother; she was totally involved in it.

Sjaak and Sarah turned out to be intelligent and good students. After grade school they both went to the athenaeum and gained nice report cards. Lilian had a more practical nature and resembled Nant most. She had a cheerful and easy character and was always ready to help out. Studying to her was a necessary evil. However, the prospect of working as a care-taker of handicapped people motivated her sufficiently to acquire the necessary theoretical knowledge for this. Robert, too, had a distinct loathing for studying, but it was impossible to motivate him. He could walk around for weeks on end with an attitude as if nothing interested him. Taciturn and listless, he lived from one day to the next and said no more than what was absolutely necessary. If it was really unavoidable, he answered briefly and uninterested with only "yes" or "no". Even the request of the *KNVB* to join the regional selection team of C-juniors did not change a thing.

Nant did feel sorry for him, but she could not deal with it. Her spontaneous, no-nonsense attitude often affected Robert the wrong way and caused him to withdraw even more. This caused Nant to be confronted for the first time with a sense of complete helplessness; the result of a development that – to her – was quite unnatural and unacceptable, namely losing contact with her child, her own flesh and blood. The inability to comfort him and break through the dejection caused a feeling of estrangement and quiet sadness in her.

Clearly she saw in him the same attitude that his father had, but she also noticed that this suddenly touched her more, now that it concerned her own child. She was aware of Ben's depressive moods, had tried her best to understand them, but when that turned out to be impossible, she had kept quiet about them and more or less accepted them. Towards Robert, however, it was very obvious that she lacked that ability to see things in perspective. Because of the indelible link between mother and child, it occupied her intensely. However much she tried to understand his behaviour and attitude, she did not get a grip on it.

Even though she saw little or nothing of her own strength and tradition mirrored in him and though he closely resembled his father in just about everything, it did not diminish the fact that he – just as much as her other children – was part of herself. Hadn't she felt him grow and move below her heart? It had been this unusual pregnancy – also due to the anxiety with which that had been surrounded – that had created in her something extra, something exclusive in relation to this child. Still, she saw in him – as the years passed – more and more clearly the traces of the race whose silent history he carried within himself. And intuitively she sensed that the particularity of this "son of the covenant" – born on *the day after Passover* – above all had to do with that.

Towards the end of the last year that Robert was in grade school, Ben and Nant had a talk with his teacher, master Zandbergen. Of course, this man had also noticed the big difference between Robert and his brother and sisters, whom he had also had in his class.

But in spite of Robert's moderate school results, he thought that Robert had a few talents that were worth while. He should train himself in that direction.

'You see,' he said encouragingly, leaning backward in a relaxed manner, 'the advantage of children who do not like studying is that in them you can see very clearly what their natural talents are. For they do enjoy those things and they apply themselves more or less automatically. In Robert's case those are: drawing, language and sports. As far as sports go, I am not telling you anything new, I assume. The fact that our school has won first prize in the annual sports day for grade schools two years in a row, we owe for a major part to him. I understand that after water polo and tennis he has now decided for soccer and that he has even already been scouted by the *KNVB*. As I am saying… because he excels in so many sports, training as a sports teacher is certainly an option.

Tcha… as far as drawing goes, there he distinguishes himself specifically by two essential characteristics, namely an inborn creativity and a strongly developed sense of perspective. Of his own accord he turns each assignment into something original and the depth and proportions are always correct. He is also the only one who, without a word from me, always puts a title above his drawings. So in view of that I see possibilities for him in the graphic sector of the advertising world. He would have to apply himself to finish secondary school first, but I would not worry about that too much just yet. For very often you see that, once children are convinced of their choice of profession, the motivation to study for it follows by itself.'

This positive approach of Robert pleased Ben and Nant, as did the prospects that were outlined for him and with which they were confronted totally unexpectedly.

'Boy,' Nant reacted visibly relieved, 'how nice that you look at it that way. To be honest, I have never thought of that. That is because at home he is so different from the other children. Usually very quiet and withdrawn…'

Zandbergen looked at her with surprise. 'Oh…?' he said, 'I never noticed that in class. Quite the contrary even. Here he is very witty. He has plenty of friends and…' he continued with a smile, 'he also can't complain about the interest of the girls. Even though studying is not his hobby, I can't say that he sits there apathetic and uninterested. That's why I thought it was so strange that he adamantly refused to come along to the *Memorial space*.'

'Did he not tell about that at home?' he asked when he saw the surprised looks on their faces. Ben and Nant both shook their head, after which Zandbergen explained that in the last year of the grade school someone from the *October 44 Foundation* always came to tell about the cause and consequences of the raid in Putten. And that afterwards all the children went along for a visit to the *Monument* and the *Memorial space*.

'Well, when the time came and everyone walked to the corridor, Robert was the only one who stayed in his seat. I tried to explain to him that it was part of the lesson and that therefore he also had to come along. He just stared ahead, shook his head firmly and was silent. Intuitively I sensed that I should not force him, but I did not understand it. Specifically because I know that you are not from Putten originally. When we came back I saw through the window of the classroom that he was still in his seat and was writing with great concentration. The minute I opened the door he quickly folded the paper and put it in his pocket. At the end of the afternoon I gave all the children a booklet in which the whole story of the raid is described, with their name and a personal note in the front. When I reached Robert during the handing out, he again stared ahead defensively, shook his head and said nothing.'

Zandbergen took the booklet from the drawer of his desk and handed it to Ben. He opened it and read:

> *For Robert van Zuiden*
> *on the occasion of*
> *leaving grade school.*
> *Don't ever let soccer be more than*
> *a side-issue in your life.*

*You can draw and write all your life
and I hope that those talents will give you
satisfaction for a long time.*

*Lots of success
Best regards,
Master Zandbergen*

'That's nice,' said Ben and gave it to Nant. 'I'll keep it safe, for there will certainly be a day in his life when he would like to get it after all.'

He stood up and wanted to say goodbye, but Zandbergen did not seem to notice. He sat staring ahead absent-mindedly. Then he slowly lifted his head and asked in an almost apologetic tone of voice: 'Could I ask you a personal question…?'

Ben sat down again and said somewhat surprised: 'Uh… yes, of course.'

'You are Jewish, aren't you…?'

For a moment Ben considered the unexpected question. He nodded in agreement: 'Yes, I am, but my wife isn't. But… why?'

'Well… you see…' Zandbergen answered with a slight hesitation, 'that particular afternoon I asked Robert at the end of the class for an explanation for his behaviour. "I have enough sores of my own", he grumbled. And when I made it clear to him that I did not understand what he meant by that, he said: "Only six hundred of your people were murdered and you never stop talking about it. But of our people six million were killed and I never hear anyone mentioning that. The only thing I hear is that it is our own fault. A punishment of God because we killed Jesus!" Then he turned around and walked away. We have not mentioned it again since then, but I wanted to let you know.'

'I never noticed that this occupied him so,' said Ben when they walked home through the park later.

'I did,' said Nant.

'Really…?' Ben reacted upset. He walked to the wooden fence of the pond and peered thoughtfully across the surface of the water. Nant went to stand beside him, stroked his arm and comforted him: 'Hey, that is not so strange. I see him a lot more often than you… and then, a mother senses that sort of thing better anyway.'

'What do you mean…?' Ben asked abruptly.

Nant searched carefully for a good example. 'Take Sjaak and Sarah. As you know, they think it is interesting that they have both a Christian and a Jewish background. And Lilian…she could not care less what and who she is and where she comes from, as long as she has fun and is happy. But of all our children Robert is by nature the most Jewish and I think he finds it confusing that he has a Christian mother. I believe that he thinks about that a lot. He never disliked going to the Jewish lesson on Sunday afternoon. I mean, isn't that significant in a child who hates studying? And you know, on the one hand I may love him most of all, maybe due to that unusual pregnancy. But on the other hand he is furthest removed from me. In fact I knew already before he was born that he would be a special child. A dreamer… a thinker. Take that writing in class that Zandbergen mentioned. By accident I saw that paper lying in his room and I glanced at it. It mentioned "circles" and "wounds", but I couldn't make head or tail of it. He had crossed out a lot… and his handwriting is so sloppy… I think that you should try to talk with him sometime, for a lot is going on inside that boy that we are not aware of and that I, for one, know nothing about.'

'And you think I do know about it?' Ben asked.

'Yes, I'm sure of it,' she assured, 'for it has to do with you and with uh… well, let's say your family's problem. You should not underestimate those dreams of his either. Sometimes at breakfast he sits there and it seems as if he already had a difficult day behind him. Dead tired and quite out of it.'

Ben was alarmed and that was not only because what Nant said was new to him. She had mentioned those dreams of Robert before. How she could barely wake him from such a nightmare – that was often accompanied by talking and sometimes with screaming. And how confused and afraid he then was, unable or unwilling to speak about it. But because he himself was such a deep sleeper he had never noticed it. However, now he heard – in a flash – the echo of Els's story. He had not, or rarely, told his children about his father's suffering. Specifically because of the impact it had had on him, he wanted to avoid as much as possible to burden them with it. And if it was ever mentioned, he had always very consciously tried to emphasize the present and the future. With some satisfaction and a certain gratitude he had seen the effect of this expressed in the development of Sjaak and Sarah and certainly in that of Lilian. But had the after-pains of evil now found entry in the soul of that son who was such a "Van Zuiden" in every respect…? Had the past caught up with him once again…?

His face radiating dejection, he shook his head. And after a deep sigh he shouted desperately: 'God, does it never stop…?'

It was then that Ben decided very consciously to spend more time and attention on Robert.

The first concrete step that he undertook with that aim was to take Robert to Amsterdam. In the *NIW* he read that there was an exposition of the works of the painter Marc Chagall, a Russian Jew by origin, in the *Jewish Historical Museum*.

After they left Putten it remained quiet in the car for a long time. That did not bother Ben at all, because it was quite familiar to him. It seemed as if he saw himself at that same age sitting beside his father. First thinking about something for a long time and finally posing a question – short and snappy.

'Is *Ajax* a Jewish club…?' Robert asked suddenly, while still looking ahead.

'Not really,' Ben answered, 'that is a myth. My father once told me how that soccer club came into being. Before the war most Dutch Jews lived in Amsterdam. And by far the most of those lived in the eastern part of the city, for that is where the diamond-cutting establishments were located where many Jews were working. And you know, *De Meer* was adjacent to Amsterdam-East. You could walk there, so to say. For that reason alone most Jewish boys that wanted to play soccer went to *Ajax*. In addition it was a Sunday club so you didn't have the problem of playing soccer on the Sabbath. But as far as I know only Sjaak Swart and Bennie Muller really made it to the top. *HEDW*... now that really was a Jewish club. You could only become a member if you were Jewish. But, if I may ask, what brought that up?'

'Well, most boys at *Rood-Wit* are *Feyenoord* fans and a while ago in the cafeteria they were talking about it once again. I said that I thought *PSV* was the best club and then the trainer said with a weird little laugh: "Oh, I thought you would be an *Ajax* fan". A few others also laughed and because I did not understand that, I wanted to know what exactly he meant. And then he said: "Because *Ajax* is a Jewish club, of course".'

Ben explained how each club had its own culture and atmosphere. That the bond with a club is often even more important than the quality of the soccer playing.

'*Feyenoord* for instance,' he continued, 'is associated very strongly with the working class and that's why it has so many supporters with *Rood-Wit*.'

'Was that why you preferred me to go to *Rood-Wit* instead of to *SDC*?' Robert asked.

'Yes... amongst other things,' said Ben. 'For me the feeling of solidarity is more important than the principle: "performance above all". In underprivileged groups people are always more dependent on one another than among the well-to-do. You don't only see that in soccer, but in all of society. In my youth I always felt very strongly that our family – and therefore I myself also – belonged to a minority. That is why I have so much respect for my father. And with that I mean specifically what he has achieved with *Van Zuiden Fashions*, in spite of his trauma. David took that over and expanded it perfectly, but my father was the one who laid the foundation. He raised us above the wanderers and the down-and-outs to which we belonged originally, and he has gained much respect for that. So take care that you never make yourself out to be better than you are, and above all don't forget from where you came. As long as your behaviour is entirely based on that, you'll be at peace with yourself and feel at home in a club like *Rood-Wit*. That club is also a bit smaller and therefore more clearly structured. And the most important thing is, that it is a real amateur society that does not pay its players nor does it get them from outside in order to proceed up the ladder. For that always happens at the expense of its own young people.'

Ben hoped for a reaction, specifically about the aspect: "being at peace with yourself", but nothing came. He could almost hear Robert think but he knew that it was absolutely no use asking him something now. He glanced sideways at Robert and again it seemed as if time had stood still and he saw himself sitting there. There was a very clear parallel with the family to which he used to belong. Everything about his sisters and specifically his brother was identical to the situation now, in his own family. He knew why Robert – just like he himself used to do – often withdrew in silence. And because he also knew quite well how difficult it was to find words for all those feelings, he understood that his son only needed one thing at this moment: silence… respectful silence while they were together was characteristic for them, and thus they entered the *Jewish Historical Museum* a bit later.

Robert looked rather fleetingly at the paintings and Ben had the impression that it did not really touch him. *Rabbi with synagogue scroll* was the first painting that he looked at more attentively.

'Well… what do you think of it?' Ben asked.

Robert shrugged. 'I don't know,' he said. 'The colors are rather nice but other than that it seems a bit childish. That man may be world famous but I find it rather simple. No, I can't say that it appeals to me.'

As Robert walked on ahead, Ben stayed behind, moved by one of the poems of Jacob Israel de Haan that could be found here and there between the paintings.

> RESTLESS
>
> *Will I find in Jerusalem*
> *the peace and quiet*
> *that never came to*
> *restless me in Amsterdam?*
>
> *O foolish doubt*
> *not here or there*
> *you'll find your rest or unrest*
> *but only in your mind.*

Jerusalem and Amsterdam automatically translated into Elburg and Putten. Carefully he read it again and he had to agree secretly that he too had made the same error in reasoning. For his departure from Elburg had not made a different person of him.

In the meantime a woman had accosted Robert because of his attention for the painting *The White Crucifixion*. She told him what Chagall wanted to say with this – in Jewish circles rather controversial – subject. Because of her knowledge and the authority with which she spoke, Robert took it for granted that she was an employee of the museum. He looked at the black clouds above the cross and at the man who was hanging from that cross, clothed in a Jewish prayer shawl as a loincloth, while the woman explained why the ray of light was not shining at the cross but behind it.

'Whatever you think about Christianity,' she said, 'the murder of Jesus remains one of the most remarkable events in both Christian and Jewish history. If ever there was a place where Judaism and Christianity approached each other very closely, it is Golgotha. There Jesus laid the foundation for Christianity and at the same time showed His solidarity with the suffering of His own people. For first and foremost He was a Jew and He was – just like millions of others of His people – also innocent and also murdered in a terrible manner. Just think of the similarity between, on the one hand, all those Jews that were herded to the transport vans – jeered at by the people amongst whom they had always lived – and finally arriving completely broken in the camps, and on the other hand how Jesus had to go His way to Golgotha in similar circumstances.

They were all humiliated and just as the last possessions were taken from the Jews in the camps, so at the foot of the cross the murderers of Jesus threw dice for the only thing He possessed: His cloak. But the most moving similarity must be that He, like so many Jews in the concentration camps, wondered where God was at that crucial moment. Chagall wanted to portray in this painting that in the dark periods of life, when God seems to be absent, He in fact is really there.'

Robert looked at the ray of light in the painting that depicted the presence of God and – without Jesus being aware of it – shone behind Him. And at that time he, too, could only ask that question that millions of others had spoken in despair.

'But if He was there… why did He not do something…?'

'You should not ask questions the answer to which you are not, or not yet, able to understand,' the woman spoke calmly but determinedly.

'And why would I not be able to understand?' asked Robert.

She put her hand on his shoulder: 'Because you are a child of this modern time. Someone, on the other hand, who has been influenced by Jewish thinking leaves more space for the mystery – knows that there is a Higher, a perfect Intelligence and accepts the difference with his own limited knowledge and abilities.'

'But I am Jewish!' said Robert. He surprised himself; more so with the half lie than with the half truth that he had spoken so spontaneously. Still, he was happy with it, because he had allowed himself to be led, not by who he was according to the "letter of the law", but by how he felt inside. And that was more Jewish than Christian.

The woman gave a friendly smile and said with emphasis: 'From now on pay close attention to the number four.'

At this cryptic remark Robert looked at her in utter surprise. He wanted to ask for an explanation but she continued calmly: 'And remember Chagall's message that, however dark it may be in your life, the Eternal One is always there. Even if you do not notice it at all, the light of His presence is always behind you.'

He pondered that for a while and then said: 'But as long as I do not notice that He is there, I still have to live alone with my fears.'

For the first time in his young life he had put a name to that which tired him so and literally jammed him. And he knew that it was the calmness that this unknown woman radiated, her involvement and the authority with which she spoke that had led him to be so open.

'Fear always has a cause,' she said, 'Don't push it away and do not close yourself to it, but seek it out, for what has passed, is not finished, but determines present and future… In remembering is the deliverance.'

Robert turned his eyes to the figure on the cross and thought of the nights in which he woke from his nightmares, when around him it was so dark and frighteningly quiet. And when he concentrated on the ray of light behind the cross, he heard again within him that last, dominating remark… "in remembering is the deliverance". He felt a merciful peace come over him. And strangely, he knew that, even though the circle of fear that surrounded his existence had not yet disappeared, from that moment on it was breached. He also realised how much that woman had contributed to it and he felt an honest need to thank her for that. He turned his head towards her, but to his surprise he looked… into the eyes of his father.

In confusion he searched where she could be, but she was nowhere to be found.

'Are you looking for someone?' Ben asked, when Robert had returned to him.

'Yes… that lady whom I was just talking to,' he answered absentmindedly, and his voice held both confusion and despair. 'I wanted to thank her and ask her more about uh… about the number four…'

A vague sensation of discomfort now took hold of Ben also. Something was going on here for which he had absolutely no explanation. With a question in his eyes he looked at his son: 'Sorry, I have been standing here for quite a while next to you looking at that painting, but I did not see any lady…! Do you want to continue looking or shall we leave?'

Robert nodded resignedly and in silence they walked out of the museum to the car. Both of them were preoccupied with the mysterious woman. In Robert the meeting with her had caused a sense of relief. All sorts of images of injustice and innocent suffering, but also thoughts about the invisible presence of God in his life, mingled – still somewhat disconnectedly – through one another. But something in his subconscious assured him that sooner or later it would liberate him from that oppressive circle of fear. And that had everything to do – he sensed it clearly – with that last remark, with which the woman had ended their strange meeting… "in remembering is the deliverance". A new perspective had been handed to him just like that, as a gift from Heaven. It made him aware of the fact that, just as his future was partly determined by his past, the deliverance lay in the remembering…

His father's voice startled him from his reveries.

'Let's get a sandwich from Sal Meijer,' he proposed.

That was fine with Robert and so they parked the car a bit later in the Scheldestraat. As they walked past *Restaurant TEL AVIV* Ben remarked casually that this was a "*kosher* style" restaurant and that Sal Meijer – diagonally opposite – was a sandwich shop, pre-eminently a meeting place for Jews.

'It'll be busy there for sure, now, at the end of the afternoon,' he expected.

'What do you mean by "*kosher* style"?' Robert wanted to know.

'That the food there is allowed, as far as the food laws are concerned,' explained Ben, 'but that not everything was butchered and prepared U.R.S. – under rabbinic supervision. According to orthodox Jews it is not really *kosher* then. They then call it "*quosher*" – *quasi kosher*.

Take for instance my mother. She always used to have chickens brought especially from Enschede because they were butchered U.R.S. there, but my father thought that was nonsense. "A chicken is *kosher*, period!" he used to say, "and "Unburdened by Rabbinic Supervision" is also U.R.S.".'

Although the furnishing of the shop reminded Robert more of the cafeteria of a soccer club, he had to admit that it had a special atmosphere.

The simple tables – with white Formica tops – were almost all occupied by men, clearly sons of Israel judging by their looks and gestures. Ben told Robert in a low voice that the man who sat near the long wall was a big businessman, who had his reserved place there – near a telephone that was hanging on the wall next to him.

They walked to the counter and ordered a salted meat sandwich. As they waited Robert said softly: 'Those two men over there near the window… I know them… they attended our last selection match in Ede.'

Ben recognised them too now: 'Those are those old *Ajax* players that I mentioned in the car; Sjaak Swart and Bennie Muller.'

As if they sensed that someone was talking about them, the two interrupted their conversation and looked first at Ben and then at Robert. Then one of them got up and came towards them.

'Robert van Zuiden, isn't it…?' he asked, as he shook their hands. 'Nice to meet you, I am Bennie Muller. Really, that is quite a coincidence because we were just talking about you. Won't you join us?'

With their sandwiches in their hands they walked to a table near the window. There Bennie Muller showed them a piece of paper on which Robert's name was mentioned also, and that explained their presence at that match in Ede.

'The scouting that Sjaak and I do, now and then, is mainly for our good friend Mircea Petescu. We help him to organize a soccer tournament for C-juniors in Romania once a year. Over there, talented players do not get nearly as many chances to be discovered and make it to the top as here in Holland. To be honest we had just decided not to approach you. Not because you are not good enough. It is rather a surplus problem. In your position we have plenty of players at the moment. But we will certainly pass on your name to *FC Zwolle*, so that they can keep an eye on you. We did that for Robbie Nieuwenhuis, that blond guy from Harderwijk, too. He now plays in the first team there. He also came along to Romania once, together with my son Danny.'

He turned towards Ben and said, pointing at Robert with an approving smile: 'He's a bit a "Piet Keizer type". I mean… that slow pace and then he seems to stop for a moment, while he is actually surveying the game situation. And as soon as an opportunity presents itself, all of a sudden he accelerates tremendously and runs free. He has a good pass and a good understanding of the game. In fact, the only thing he should work at is his finer technique. But that boy will make it, I am convinced of it.'

Robert laughed shyly. The praising words of those *Ajax*-bigwigs and their promise to pass on his name to *FC Zwolle* rather overwhelmed him. Terms like "turning point" and "breakthrough" went through his head. And the thought that maybe now already the foundation was being laid for a career as a professional soccer player caused a strange tension in him. While Ben suddenly recalled the opinion of Master Zandbergen: "don't let soccer be more than the most important side issue in your life", he felt a hand on his shoulder.

'Hey... Bennie van Zuiden!' a voice rang out behind him, 'what brings you to Mokum, man? Is it boring in the *medina*?'

Ben got up and shook the hand of John, a representative of *De Levita – Men's fashions*, and also of the man who accompanied him.

'This is one of my colleagues,' said John. 'Mr. Barend of the sales department.'

Ben looked at the man whom he only knew from the telephone: 'How nice to see the face that belongs to that well-known voice. Oh... by the way, this is my son Robert.'

'Yes, we had gathered that,' reacted John. 'Really, he is your spitting image.'

He pushed a few chairs to the table and continued: 'So you are spending a day in Amsterdam together. Tcha... every Yid has to return to Jerusalem now and then.'

While the men analysed the situation at *Ajax* and the fashion trade in great detail, Robert saw how that was accompanied by fits and starts with a passionate raising of voices and exuberant gestures. He saw his father, too, follow suit. And although he hardly ever saw him like that, he sensed that it had to do with "feeling at home", here among his own people. And as he observed him, the characteristic differences between his parents suddenly became very clear to him. Where his mother was a straightforward person who frankly admitted all that she felt and thought, at a certain moment for her it was over and done with, and she put a full stop to it. His father on the other hand definitely also had his own opinion, but he always kept open the possibility to adjust or supplement it. He always kept asking, kept searching. To him things were never quite finished, but everything remained open to discussion.

Silently Robert looked from one person to the other. He was amused to notice how they kept quizzing each other and were not always satisfied with each other's answers. More and more clearly he saw the big difference between the two cultures that were united in himself... Christians who tell each other: "this is it" and Jews who quiz each other: "why is it so…" Christians who want to convince each other and Jews who want to learn from each other. Christians who want to "preach" and Jews who want to "learn".

'I think that John resembles uncle David a bit,' Robert said later, when they drove out of the city on the way home.

'Yes,' said Ben, 'I think so too. By the way David still does business with *De Levita* and John already used to come to us in Elburg when the business was still my father's. At that time he still lived in Enschede. It was he who always brought my mother the *kosher* chickens.'

Ben also told him that only a fraction of the Jewish community in Amsterdam was left after the war… That *De IJsbreker* – a large billiards pub on the Weesperzijde – also used to be such a popular meeting place for Jewish merchants at that time. And he recalled the fact that his opa used to go to Amsterdam by boat several times a month, together with "De Voas" – a colleague-pedlar from Oldebroek. Both had a large cart full of farmer's butter and eggs that they peddled in the more well-to-do quarters of town and afterwards they would return with materials, threads, ribbons and other wares that they had bought.

Robert paid scant attention to the stories. He looked at the long lines of cars between which they moved at a snail's pace, and he left his father's words where they belonged: in the far, unknown past. His head was too full of words and images from the present. He saw and heard the man who predicted an attractive future for him as a soccer player, and he thought about the mysterious woman who, in the quiet of the museum, pointed the way to a life without fear. Again he saw her unbelievably clear eyes and heard her calmly spoken words – full of knowledge and authority – as truths from which there was no escape. And between the slowly moving lines of cars he saw the scene of *The White Crucifixion* again.

'Why do Jews have such loathing for Jesus?' he suddenly asked.

'Because the Church has always claimed that He is the Messiah,' answered Ben, 'and I think that history has taught us that that cannot be true. What I mean is that it is clearly written that the arrival of the Messiah will be accompanied by peace and justice. And that is far removed from the hate and jealousy of the Christians, for which millions of Jews have been and still threaten to be sacrificed. For us, Jesus is, just like many of his contemporaries like Hillel and Gamaliel, no more and no less than one of the many Jewish rabbis. His teaching could not be faulted. The only thing is, most Jews never got around to studying it because they were discouraged by the manner in which his followers dealt with it. And I am sure I would not have studied it if I had not married your mother.'

Robert just nodded. Intellectually, he accepted his father's explanation. Emotionally, however, something inside him said that Jesus really was more than just an average Jewish rabbi.

In the meantime they had left the freeway and were driving through meadows and past farms from Nulde to Putten. Robert looked at the impressive clouds that floated above the wide landscape. He recalled the face of Jesus on the cross and for some reason that image too was connected with the truth that he had been handed that afternoon… "What has passed is not finished but determines present and future".

11

During his last season at the C-juniors Robert was invited to play a test game at *FC Zwolle*. Gert-Jan, trainer-coach of the A-juniors at *Rood-Wit*, accompanied him. At the entrance of the complex they were welcomed and told that they could present themselves in the players' area below the stands.

Although Robert was usually quite matter-of-fact about his soccer talent, now he felt a certain anxiety take hold of him. Until now, the fact that he was a good soccer player had only brought relaxation and had given him a lot of enjoyment of the game. In fact, his technique with the ball, playing around an opponent, setting up a good attack or giving a perfect pass, that's what gave him more pleasure than winning a game. Now however, another aspect was added, because it could possibly play an important role in determining his future. He had never really thought about it and he asked himself if he would really like that and also if he had enough talent for it.

Timidly he looked around at the overwhelming accommodation of the soccer business where he found himself at the moment. The luxurious changing rooms and showers, the bar and the players' home, the high stands that enclosed the field; it was all very impressive compared to what he was used to.

It turned out that twenty six players had been called up. Four would function as substitutes. Gert-Jan received – just like the other coaches – a list with the names and numbers of all the players and a schedule of their placement. After that the coaches sat down in the stands. Apart from a few personal duels, that were not very successful, Robert played a good game. His passes were – as usual – exact and from a high first move he even scored a great goal. After he freed himself cleverly, he sprinted with impressive speed into the penalty area and headed the ball, with a well-timed high jump, unstoppably into the goal. Halfway during the second half he was exchanged.

After the game they were offered a drink in the players' home and they were told that they would all be personally notified about a possible sequel. In a relaxed atmosphere they still talked for a long time. Gert-Jan met someone with whom he had played soccer many years ago, and Robert rehashed the whole game with a boy from Barneveld who played with him in the *KNVB* regional team.

'Well...?' asked Gert-Jan when they left the stadium, 'what did you think of it?'

'I felt that I have never played as well as tonight,' was Robert's opinion. 'Everything went fine.'

'Well, really... everything?' Gert-Jan reacted down-to-earth. 'I think you proved that you are a good soccer player. But they already knew that, otherwise they would not have invited you. The few that they'll continue with are those who have mastered everything, and in the personal duels you twice made mistakes in tonight's game. So... we'll wait and see.'

And indeed, two weeks later there was a letter with the announcement that they had decided to refrain from cooperation for the time being. But if Robert would improve both his fine technique and his speed, they would certainly be interested in him in the future. They wished him a lot of success and promised to keep watching him.

As a result of this, a talk followed with *Rood-Wit* in which it was agreed that after the summer vacation – at the start of the new season – Robert would be included in the A-selection of the juniors. In addition, it was agreed that he would sign up immediately at the local sports school for power training, so that physically too he would reach the level of an average A-player. Gert-Jan realised that in spite of the equivalent level that could be reached by this– both technically and physically – there would still be a difference between Robert and the rest of the group. At 18 years old you experience life differently and are occupied with entirely different things than at 14 years. He would also have to prevent that jealousy would insert itself into the group. He decided that as soon as the new A-selection had been definitely put together, he would demand that Robert – in spite of the age difference of the boys – would be accepted as an equal. They should be well aware that only then they would profit from it as a team and would –collectively – become stronger.

Meanwhile, Robert's progress in sports was in shrill contrast with that in school. Where in the first year of the *MAVO* he had just barely made the grade, in the second year his school record was so poor that he had to repeat the year. When he came home late on the evening of the last training of the C-juniors – with afterwards in the cafeteria a pleasant closing of the season – he found only his father still up.

Sjaak and Sarah were attending a school camp and Nant and Lilian had just gone to bed. Ben was doing his administration. He preferred to do this at the kitchen table; he could concentrate better there. Usually it was quieter there than in the living room and the lighting was better, too. Robert walked over to the fridge and poured himself a glass of milk.

'Would you also like to have something to drink?' he asked.

'Uh… yes,' Ben answered, bent over a table full of invoices and bank statements, 'better give me a beer.'

When Robert put it in front of him, Ben had a flash back to identical scenes from his own youth.

'Sit down for a moment,' he said, pointing at the chair opposite him, taken off guard at the thought of sitting as a father opposite his son at the kitchen table.

For a moment that strange parallel took control of him and he was amazed at the scene that was played out, as if planned, before his eyes. In spite of the emotions, he tried to concentrate on that which he wanted to discuss with Robert as a result of a visit earlier that evening by his brother David.

In a way he would like to motivate him also to do better at school, but he realised that he hardly had the right to speak. He knew the cause too well. It was not so much laziness, but an inborn dislike to study material that did not interest him in the least. When he was at the *School for Retail Trade* he himself had only considered languages, advertising and window dressing worth the effort. He had profited particularly from the window dressing techniques he had learned at that time – specifically of materials – and it had given him satisfaction. He regretted that Robert had to re-sit a year, but it would have been rather hypocritical to reproach him for it.

In addition he had in a certain sense also "failed to passed" with regards to soccer – in spite of his talent. Romania was cancelled... *FC Zwolle* was out of the picture... On the one hand, he did not mind that very much. Of the thousands of boys who dream of a career as a top soccer player, only a few ever achieve that in the end. On the other hand, he had to admit that he was sorry after all that he himself – even though he was a talented soccer player – had stopped just like that from one day to the next, and had never really discovered how much he could have achieved. Still occupied with all these thoughts, he put down his pen, poured his beer and looked at Robert.

'Listen... son,' he started, 'you probably think that I am very disappointed that you did not pass. Of course, that is partly the case, but I am really not very surprised. You are just different from your brother and sisters. I know exactly what you are feeling, for I was just like that. I did not dislike school, just studying. Still, you have another four years to go, so you'll have to try to make something of it.

What I wanted to discuss with you is that David was here this evening. He had been to Amsterdam for purchasing and came by on the way home to talk. When we talked about the children and I told him about you, he said that maybe he knew a nice summer job for you. One of his friends, a certain Martin Westerink, started his own advertising studio recently. Design logos, signage of cars, billboards, that sort of thing. As a starting entrepreneur he does not have any salaried personnel as yet, but he is looking for a young, cheap temp. It would be a nice opportunity for you to enter that world and get some experience. For the advertising world is typically a specialty in which more value is attached to creativity and experience than to education and certificates.'

Robert looked doubtfully at his father and asked: 'But do you think that I am suited for that?'

'Yes, I think so…' Ben confirmed, 'and I am really not the only one! Wait a minute.'

He went upstairs and came back with the little book that master Zandbergen had wanted to give Robert at one time.

'Look in the front!' he said, 'master Zandbergen was someone who was able to judge. He was convinced even at that time that you'd be suited for that. You have a feeling for language and a talent for design, and take it from me: there is nothing that gives a person more satisfaction than to be creatively occupied.'

Amazed at the praising words of master Zandbergen, Robert took his time to ingest them. Then he closed the book and pushed it aside. For a few moments he looked ahead thoughtfully and considered: 'Yes… maybe he is right. I have never yet thought very consciously about what I want to be later.'

He fell silent again and Ben sensed that his son was about to share with him what went through his mind at that moment.

'Uh…' Robert started hesitantly, 'you just said that I have to go to school for another four years.'

'Yes,' Ben explained, 'because school education is compulsory until you are eighteen. That is to say, you are allowed to start working when you are sixteen, but only in combination with some kind of training.'

'Well… you see,' Robert said, 'this is not so much about school as about the number four. When you mentioned that I suddenly had to think again of that lady in the museum in Amsterdam. She told me then that if I doubted the existence of God in my life, I should pay close attention to the number four. But what does it really mean? Do you understand that...?'

The question took Ben by surprise. He saw the tense look in Robert's eyes and understood that he had been thinking about something completely different than he. The lady in the museum he had not seen at all... the number four... It was a while before he had switched from the rational to the spiritual.

'Four...' he repeated slowly, 'first, of course, there is the name of God that we are not allowed to mention and that consists of four letters: JHWH. Tcha... and the only other thing I know is that the number four is connected with our life here on earth. I mean the four elements that make life possible: fire, water, air and earth. And then there are the four seasons and four wind directions. And to be able to function as people on this earth, we have been given four limbs.'

After a slight hesitation he continued: 'But... whether that woman meant all of that?' he shrugged, spread out his hands and concluded: 'Tcha, that I really don't know, son.'

He looked at his watch and remarked: 'What I do know is... that I am going to put these papers away and that we are going to bed.'

They stood up at the same time. Robert put the empty glasses and the beer bottle on the sink unit and as he walked to the door, Ben said: 'One more thing... You know that in the Jewish tradition numbers mean more than just something numerical or mathematical and that there is a relationship between letters, numbers and conceptions. That is to say... letters have a numerological value and do you know what the "God's name number" is?'

Robert shrugged his shoulders: 'No, no idea.'

'Seventeen,' said Ben, 'for that is the numerical value of JHWH. The letter J is one, the H is five, and the W is six. And do you know what you should think about when you are in bed...?' He looked at Robert seriously for a moment, before he finished his sentence: 'that in our family there are only two persons whose name consists of seventeen letters: Benjamin van Zuiden and Robertus van Zuiden… exactly these two… both no interest in studying but both with talents and a name to be grateful for. He patted Robert's thick long hair a few times and said with a contented smile: 'Sleep well, boy!'

The next Sunday afternoon Ben and Robert were driving to Elburg. David had called his friend of the advertising studio immediately after the visit to Ben and set up a meeting for Robert. On Saturday Ben had received a phone call from his father to tell him that David Hamburger had called. David had to be in Elburg on Sunday afternoon and had asked if it was convenient that he came for a brief visit. David's mother had recently died and among her possessions he had found a few old photographs of his father together with his friend Jacob van Zuiden.

Ben had noticed a certain resignation in his father's voice when he told him about it. He guessed the cause for that and also that this was the reason why he wanted Ben to be there when David came.

'Do you know that man who is visiting opa?' Robert wanted to know.

'Yes and no,' reacted Ben. 'David is the son of Sal Hamburger. Sal was my father's best friend long ago and he died in the camp. The reason why he asked me to be there too is that he dreading the confrontation.'

'Did he not meet him ever before?' asked Robert.

Ben could hear and understand the amazement in Robert's voice.

'The problem is,' he answered, 'that on the one hand my father would want that very much, but at the same time he realises that it will bring back many memories of a time that he wants so badly to forget. He knows now already what the price will be of a meeting with David Hamburger.'

Ben felt how Robert turned his head towards him and saw that he looked at him questioningly: 'Long, terrible nightmares;

that is the price. Therefore he avoids as much as possible anything that can bring associations with the camp.'

'Everything...?' Robert repeated. 'What other things bother him then?'

'Ah, my son, believe me, so many things... remarks... barking dogs... barbed wire... sounds and faces... photographs and reports in the paper or on TV, people who carelessly throw away food... really, the list is endless.'

In the meantime they had entered Elburg. As they approached *De Bonte Os*, Ben said: 'I'll give you another example.' He slowed down to a snail's pace and pointed out to Robert the iron braces that were attached to the side wall of the building. 'I used to go here sometimes with my father, and once when we walked towards the place I asked why those braces were there. My father looked at them, but shook his head and said nothing. I sensed that he knew, but did not want to talk about it. But I did not understand why not. Later I asked the same question of his friend Gérard. He explained to me that the tradesmen who used to fetch their trading goods with horse and wagon here, attached their horses there during their visit to *De Bonte Os*. And according to Gérard the reason that my father did not want to talk about my question was that most huts in *Auschwitz-Birkenau* used to be horse stables that also had such braces attached to the walls.'

Ben dropped Robert at David's, at *Van Zuiden Mode,* and arranged with him that he would come on foot to the Westerwalstraat after the talk with Martin.

Martin lived only a few streets away. David returned home after he had introduced his friend to his nephew from Putten. Martin then invited Robert to come with him to Wezep where the advertising studio was located. On the way down there Martin told him that, after his parents-in-law had closed down their farm, it had been agreed that he could use the empty stone barn for five years under very attractive conditions. After that, if the enterprise would be successful, he would be able to buy both the barn and the farm.

A bit east of the centre of Wezep they took a left turn to the farm that was situated about fifty meters up-country.

'You see,' said Martin when they entered the large barn, 'an additional advantage is the great space and the wide, high doors. That allows me to park trucks and semi-trailers up to eighteen meters long inside.'

On the left hand side were first a showroom with reception, then an office, a design- and sketch room and finally a storeroom with a large cutting table and shelving with wide rolls of adhesive foil in all the most current colours. The large windows provided sufficient daylight and a nice and restful view across the extensive meadows.

He showed Robert a design for trucks that transported flowers. 'This is a nice assignment,' he said, 'that I got last week. It concerns four trucks.'

For a moment the number four niggled with Robert but right away he concentrated again on what Martin was telling him: 'This is the name of the company and the logo. They go above the windshield, on both doors and as large as possible on the sides of the cargo-space, together with a strip of flowers underneath – as if to underline it. A truck like that has to be finished in one day. Monday next week they will bring the first. They collect it again in the evening and bring the second one for the next day right away. So one job keeps you busy for a week and that is impossible on your own. There are parts for which you just have to be with two people. So, as far as I am concerned, you can start a week from tomorrow.'

On the way back Robert told him that he could stay with his grandparents so that he could have a ride with Martin from Elburg to Wezep. If things went to their mutual satisfaction – they agreed – they would discuss a possible extension at the end of that first week.

'Shall I drop you off in the Westerwalstraat?' Martin asked when they entered Elburg again.

'No,' said Robert, 'that is not necessary. Just let me out over there, then I'll walk along the canal.'

He thanked Martin and, after the car had moved on, he swept his eyes from the old Vischpoort along the buildings in front of him. He decided to walk to his grandparents through the center of town rather than via the Westerwal, and crossed the street diagonally towards the town hall. Directly across was the small gate that gave access to the synagogue behind. He peered at the Hebrew letters that were written high above the stone gate. Even though he had no idea what they meant, they seemed familiar, even inviting. Without thinking he crossed the street and, as he walked through the gate, a strange emotion overwhelmed him. Slowly – with an increasing feeling of piety – he walked down the small, stone path to the old synagogue. And with each step that brought him closer, he sensed as it were how these surroundings had been filled through the years with the heavy silence of the long-vanished hymns and prayers of his forefathers.

Looking up at the high windows he was startled by the grating sound of a door that opened and closed. He looked sideways and saw the bent figure of a man, who, after closing the door, turned around and walked towards him with a large black file in his hand. He looked at Robert intently and slowly his face wrinkled into a wide smile.

'If I am correct, you are one of the kids of Benjamin van Zuiden,' he said.

Robert nodded and the man continued as he shook his head: 'Boy, oh boy, you really look like your father!'

The man told him that he was a member of a choir that was allowed – as was the musical society – to use the building as rehearsal space.

'Would you like to have a look inside?' he asked.

'If that is allowed… yes, please,' Robert reacted surprised and he took the key that the men handed to him.

'Here,' he said, 'lock the door properly when you leave and give the key to your opa. Just tell him that I'll pick it up tonight.'

He patted Robert's shoulder. 'See you around… and say hello to your father.'

'Yes, that is fine, sir,' Robert stuttered, 'but… from whom…?'

The man answered with a smile: 'Tell him from "De Balg", then he'll understand right away.'

Once inside, Robert walked past the stairs through the porch and via the communicating door he entered a large, square space. Slowly he walked to the middle. The emptiness overwhelmed and oppressed him because he remembered all those murdered people that used to fill this synagogue.

When he had controlled his emotions again he looked around. The only thing in that hollow, deserted space that still reminded of the interior of a *shul* was the trellis work of the women's balustrade, to which the staircase in the porch seemed to lead. All along the walls were music stands and cases with musical instruments. On the site of the *bima* was a square raised wooden platform for the conductor and on the lectern in front of it there was – instead of a Torah scroll – a musical score. Against the high wall opposite him the closet, meant for the holy Torah scrolls, had been replaced by a huge cabinet full of shiny cups, cheap pennons and medals, surrounded by kitschy embroidered, meaningless banners. With a deep sigh he had to conclude that the sanctuary of his people had deteriorated into a common clubhouse for the local band and the rehearsal space for some choir.

Just as he wanted to leave the building again his attention was caught by four framed drawings that at first sight were almost identical. They were somewhat dwarfed by the exuberant display of prizes above, but in the meantime the sun had moved so far west that its soft orange rays placed – via one of the three high windows – the drawings in a heavenly light. Again he was reminded of the remark of the woman in the museum… "pay attention to the number four". He walked over to the wall and sat on the edge of the wooden platform. One by one he scrutinized the drawings carefully and he saw that on each of them the same bush was depicted, but every time in a different season. The first bush had leaf buds, the second was covered in blossoms, the third had fall colors and the fourth bush was completely bare. The background in all four was the same: an open field with a narrow column that rose high above two rather dilapidated barns. It reminded him of the bushes along the sandy road near the farm of his opa in Oldebroek. Even though he did not really understand what the link was between the drawings and the place where they were hanging, they made an extraordinary impression on him. They were original and the style even seemed – just like the subject itself – to be vaguely recognizable. There was something familiar about it, but he could not explain why. In vain he searched the enormous quantity of images that were stored in his memory.

Suddenly he was startled by a soft creaking of the floor. A little behind and to the side of him stood a girl, who looked at him with a disarming smile. Apparently he had been so deep in thought that he had not even heard her enter.

'Hi…' she said, 'am I disturbing you?'

Bewildered, Robert looked at her. She had a distinctly beautiful, but above all friendly face. He did not know her and therefore he was amazed at the sudden warm sensation that washed completely over him.

Somewhat confused he stammered: 'Uh… not really. I was just looking at those drawings and I don't really understand why they are hanging here. I mean… this used to be the synagogue, right?'

'Certainly,' she answered with assurance and a serious face.

'Then what…?' Robert asked, 'has a shrub like that to do with it…?'

She sat down next to him. First she put down a file on the ground at her feet and then she gazed with concentration at the four drawings.

'Hmm… you know,' she suggested after a while, 'I think that the person who made them comes from Elburg, or in any case from this area. Look at it… those barns, they are typically those old barns that you often see here behind the farms. But those columns…?'

After some hesitation she shrugged her shoulders: 'I don't know, it could be that they are of one of those two dairy factories, in that village down the road. I came by there this afternoon and they look a bit like that. In any case, it is obviously the shrubs that matter more. And why the pictures are hanging here, I also don't know. Maybe as a symbol for the four periods in a person's life: being born, growing up, getting old and dying. By the way, I am Deborah Hamburger, but you can call me Debbie.'

Robert shook her hand, introduced himself also and asked if she lived in Elburg.

'No, I live in Nijmegen,' she said, 'but I am busy doing a history project about the Jewish community of Elburg. I have already been to see someone of the Archaeological Society and I have also taken some pictures of a few old buildings where Jewish people used to live, of the Jewish cemetery and here just now of the gate with the *shul* behind it.'

'But how did you get here?' Robert asked.

'Oh, my father took me,' she answered. 'He was going to visit someone and we have arranged a time when he is coming to pick me up here at the gate.'

'Wait a minute,' Robert said, 'You did say Hamburger, didn't you…? But then your father is now at my opa's house. He was going to get a visit from the son of his old friend: Sal Hamburger.'

'Yes, that's right!' Deborah said surprised, 'Sal Hamburger was my opa.'

She fell silent for a moment and then spontaneously put her hand on Robert's knee. 'Jeez…' she reacted astonished, 'so our opas were friends… that's really a coincidence.'

Both were thinking of the great injustice that had put an end to that close friendship. It gave them a special feeling of kinship that neither knew how to deal with. Silently they looked at the four drawings and felt how – here in this deserted space, from which their people and tradition had disappeared – those linked them in a mysterious way to one another.

'So you are also Jewish?' Deborah finally broke the silence.

Robert shook his head. 'Half,' he answered, 'on my father's side.'

'Oh, but that does not matter at all,' she said with an infectious smile as she bent towards him confidentially, 'for if you later marry a Jewish girl…' She waited for a moment, spread her hands and continued gaily: 'then everything will be alright again!'

They talked for a while together about their families, but when they heard the penetrating sound of a car-horn, Deborah got up hastily: 'That is my father, I really have to go.'

Robert got up too and they regarded each other shyly for a minute, searching for the proper words. Deborah stood on her toes, put a hand on Robert's shoulder and softly kissed his cheek. A moment longer she looked intently at him with her sweet eyes and whispered: 'Bye Robert van Zuiden… see you later!'

At the door she turned around once again: 'Don't forget… you can call me Debbie!' She waved and went outside.

Robert stayed behind in a daze and asked himself what had just happened. He knew plenty of nice girls, but he sensed that something entirely different was going on here. 'Deborah Hamburger…' he said slowly, and carefully he rubbed the cheek that she had kissed. Till this afternoon he had not know she existed, completely unexpectedly she had entered his life and before he had realised it, she had also disappeared from it again. And yet… it seemed as if they had known each other for ever.

Absorbed in thought, he walked to the communicating door and before he closed it, his gaze swept the empty *shul* once more. He determined that, now that the sun no longer shone through the windows, the glow of the drawings had also disappeared. They were only vague silhouettes, modestly withdrawn in the shade of the large, ostentatious prize cabinet.

Once outside, he locked the door, looked once more at the high windows and then walked down the path and took a right turn into town. Here and there he looked at the old steps and gables of the monument-buildings he passed and he wondered which of those Deborah would have photographed. Almost tangibly he saw her again in his mind's eye, and the words that she had said to him reverberated within him. He felt an overwhelming desire for her, but whether that had to do with being in love or with something else… he did not know.

Only when he walked into his grandparents' home did he realise how long he had been away. Ben asked him where he had been all that time and let him know that he had already called home to say that they would be back a bit later. Robert sat down at the table and reported succinctly about his visit with Martin to the advertising studio in Wezep, mentioning that he could start there in a weeks' time. He handed over the key of the synagogue and told them about the meeting with "De Balg", but he did not mention that which had made the deepest impression on him that afternoon.

Meanwhile Saar had put a cup of tea and a piece of shortcake in front of him. 'Nah,' she said, 'then I'll put the guestroom in order for you this week, but before you are going to work with Martin you have to have a haircut. Much too long! You obviously hate the barber as much as your father!'

Jacob saw how Robert, as he drank his tea, was looking at the picture that was lying on the table.

'Well… what do you think?' he asked, 'which of those two handsome guys would be your opa?'

Robert picked up the photo and as he looked at it he felt again, as it were, how Deborah put her hand on his knee. "Jeez…" he heard her say again, "so our opas were friends… what a coincidence". Gradually he saw the lines and the shape of her face change into that of one of the two boys in the picture and he was even a bit startled by the same characteristic smile. Because of that he knew immediately which of the two was his opa.

'That one!' he pointed decisively.

'Are you sure…?' Jacob asked.

Robert nodded utterly convinced: 'Yes… I am one hundred percent sure!'

For a moment Jacob looked at his grandson thoughtfully and he had to admit: 'Well…that is clever, son, for both your oma and your father pointed out the wrong one.'

'What did opa think of Mr. Hamburger's visit?' Robert wanted to know when they drove back to Putten.

'Well,' Ben considered, 'what shall I say. I think that it meant more to David Hamburger than to my father. He heard things that were new to him and now has a better image of his father. For opa it was in fact only recalling old memories and I doubt whether that was really good for him.'

'Was it that bad, then?' Robert asked.

Ben considered the question for a moment before he said: 'I think… what makes it bad for him is the great contrast. How their friendship was and how it ended. From what I understood, those two really were soul mates and that in itself is already quite rare. I have read somewhere that in astrology models were developed from which you can deduce whether two people get along well together and complement each other or not. Your sign and even the day and time of your birth are supposed to be decisive in that. I never really made a study of it but I do believe that when – in whatever relationship – there are two characters that fit together in a unique way, you could speak about soul mates. Two people like that seem to know it right away at the moment when they meet for the first time.'

'Then that is something different from falling in love,' Robert concluded. The remark escaped him because it was that which occupied his mind so completely.

'No,' said Ben, 'not really something else, but rather more.'

Robert looked ahead thoughtfully and mused about that strange concurrence of circumstances through which he had had such a remarkable meeting with Deborah. He thought she was pretty and nice, just as he thought other girls were just pretty and nice, but with her there was also something more, that he could not express. He recalled the old photograph and the striking likeness between Deborah and her grandfather, the bosom pal of his own grandfather, and he wondered whether that which had made that friendship so remarkable could have an effect in the descendants of both.

As if Ben had guessed his son's thoughts, he remarked: 'By the way, how come you were so certain which one was opa on that picture?'

Robert shrugged. 'Well…' he answered matter-of-factly, 'just a matter of looking closely!'

'What now, looking closely,' Ben spluttered, 'I have known my father much longer than you and I have also met David Hamburger now, of whom it has been said that he resembles me, and still I did not see any likeness on that photo at all.'

'Well,' said Robert with a secretive smile, 'I did!'

On the evening of that eventful Sunday, when Robert was in bed, his tired mind could hardly put his thoughts and emotions in order. Right up to the moment at which he finally fell asleep he was searching for an explanation of the feelings that Deborah had stirred in him and that he had never before experienced like that. He recalled that she told him that she – just like he – was the last to be born in a family with four children. That reminded him of the four drawings in the synagogue and eventually again of the woman who had urged him: "pay attention to the number four". That woman in the museum, who was she… and where had she disappeared to so suddenly at that time…? He saw her clearly and heard her say again: "What has passed, is not finished, but determines present and future…"

The laughing faces of two boys looked at him and in one of them he saw very clearly the lines and shape of Deborah's face.

Then one walked away, while he took the other in his arms... This image combined, as it were, with again those same words... "What has passed, is not finished but determines present and future". Inside him the awareness was growing stronger that there were invisible lines that seemed to lead from the far past to an unknown but assured destination.

Since the meeting with the woman in the museum he had not had another nightmare. But that night it hit him again with force...

... Carrying a dead, skinny Deborah in his arms he ran along the sandy path near the farm in Oldebroek. Chased by men with high black boots, who time and again jumped up out of the bushes and tried to take her away from him. Near the barn that he ran passed a band was playing party music below a large price cabinet. Behind the barn an enormous fire was burning. He could not go back and did not dare to go forward. As they laughed and made scornful remarks, the men that were chasing him made a half circle behind him. From the fire in front of him an old, tall skinny man walked towards him with big slow steps. With a cruel smile he reached for Deborah, stretching out his arms...

Nant woke up from a loud scream that ripped through her. She looked to her side and once again was amazed that Ben just kept sleeping. In the bathroom she quickly got a glass of water and walked to Robert's room. Cautiously she sat down on the edge of his bed, as he lay looking up with big scared eyes. Nant recognised that scene by now; she had already experienced it so often. That frightened look and the typical smell of cold sweat. But still... as a mother it cut into her soul time and time again. Carefully she wiped the sweat from his face, put her hand against the back of his head and pulled him towards her.

'Hey...what happened, son?' she asked, as she handed him the glass.

Robert took a few sips of water. He took a deep breath and murmured softly: 'They... they wanted to throw Deborah in the large fire...!'

As he pronounced her name he seemed to return slowly to reality. He gulped air, lay back again and then stared fixedly at the ceiling.

Nant got up and observed: 'Well, fortunately it is over and your head is empty again. You'll see that you will sleep quietly now, and you can sleep in as long as you want, for you are on vacation.'

At the door she turned around once again and asked, to divert his attention from that bad dream, with a mischievous smile: 'By the way, who is Deborah…?'

To her satisfaction she noticed that that question changed his staring scared look into a vague smile.

'Mom,' he said, 'go to bed, you don't know her.'

'No, now I want to know,' Nant reacted teasingly as she walked back into the bedroom.

With some irritation Robert sat up again and repeated imperatively: 'Mom, to bed!!' But Nant kept gazing at him stoically, with a daring look.

'Okay…' he said, raising his hand in resignation, 'she is pretty and nice and uh… I can call her Debbie. Sleep well!'

'Well,' Nant concluded with satisfaction, 'you just think of that pretty Debbie of yours, then it'll be a very good night yet… sleep well!'

After visiting relatives in Oldebroek and Elburg Robert stayed behind at his grandparents' the next Sunday afternoon.

'Oy,' Saar said, feigning alarm, 'still not been to the barber! Nah,' she continued, shaking her head, 'come along, then I'll show you the way to your room.'

'Oma…!' Robert sighed, 'I know the way!'

As if she had not heard him, she toddled ahead of him and when Robert put his weekend bag on the bed, she cried: 'Off the bed with that bag … there!' Imperatively she pointed at the corner of the room and then at top speed she poured out such a wealth of information on the running of the home that only half of it went in.

When Robert entered the living room again, Jacob remarked with a smile: 'Not so easy, is it? But just think, after a few weeks of staying with your grandmother military service will be a breeze later.'

After dinner Jacob said: 'When the weather is reasonable I usually go for a stroll after dinner. Do you feel like coming along?'

Before Robert could answer, Saar, busy with cleaning up, warned: 'As long as you do not take the boy to the pub, for that – God save us – won't do him any good. The people there are not the most distinguished!'

Via the Westerwal they walked to the north side of the town, where they sat down on the bench near the two old canons.

'This is one of my favourite spots on the walls,' Jacob confided to him. 'Later I'll show you another one.'

Their gaze swept the harbor where pleasure yachts had gradually taken the place of the fishing boats. Jacob told Robert how the construction of the Afsluitdijk had been the death blow for most of the Zuiderzee fishermen. How Eibert den Herder – an old fisherman from Harderwijk – had waged a real crusade all by himself to convince the "great lords" in The Hague that no good could come from such a rigorous measure. 'Of course he was concerned above all about the interest of the fishermen, for whom the closing would have enormous consequences. But he also pointed out the dangers of this – to him – arbitrary meddling with creation. He was aware of the laws of the water and knew that the powers that were freed in a severe storm could discharge themselves in that large gulf of the Zuiderzee; for that was how it been for centuries. "As soon as you close off that possibility", he warned, "those powers will head for the most vulnerable part of our coast". When in 1953 a spring tide coincided with a northwestern storm, it happened exactly as Eibert had predicted and the biggest flooding disaster of our history took place.'

Robert gazed ahead and recalled how his father had told him recently that his opa used to go by boat from Elburg to Amsterdam. And while he realised that since the closing and reclamation not much was left of that tumultuous Zuiderzee but a recreational lake for watersports, Jacob got up: 'Come along… I'll show you that other spot also.'

At the harbor they met an older couple that was also taking an evening stroll.

'That must be one of Benjamin's,' the woman said, 'that is easy to tell.'

'Is he also going into the "kleerosie"?' the man asked.

'No,' said Jacob, 'Robert belongs to the creative branch of the family.' Proudly he raised his index finger and added: 'And… to the soccer branch!'

'Well, my boy,' said the man, 'if you play like your father and grandfather, it'll be alright. The name is well-known; I'll be watching you.'

'What for Petes's sake is "*kleerosie*"?' Robert wanted to know as they walked on again. 'Is that Yiddish?'

Smiling, Jacob shook his head and explained that it was old-dialect for clothing. 'If you had a clothes business in the past, like I did, then you "worked in the *kleerosie*".' He told how the woman of the couple had been married before with a certain Deet. 'Deet was a fisherman, but when he was at home he did not behave exactly like the ideal husband – to the woman's great sadness. Drink, other women, you name it. He died quite young of a heart attack, and when I extended my condolences to her, her reaction was: "You know what he was like and I am sorry but I can only say what David wrote in one of his psalms… My evil "deed", you took it away graciously!".'

Meanwhile they had walked quite a ways along the Oosterwal, when Jacob sat down again on a bench. 'This is that other spot I wanted to show you,' he said when Robert sat down next to him. 'Here I have sat many times with your father when he was about your age.'

Robert sensed that he was going to hear something that had nothing to do with history of the town or its inhabitants, but with his own. He looked across the meadows and although the barns and the high chimney of the dairy factory in the distance reminded him of the four drawings and of his meeting with Deborah, he listened attentively to what his grandfather told him.

'For here you are exactly between the last two remnants of the Jewish *kehilla* of Elburg. There is the *shul* and there the cemetery.' He fell silent for a moment, then pointed straight ahead and continued: 'And there, way beyond the horizon, is Poland.'

'Do you think of it often?' Robert asked.

'Yes… you could say so,' Jacob acknowledged, 'and as I grow older, even more often. That is because our forefathers came from there, and as you know, the most intensive period of my life occurred there. By the way… you should stop addressing me the formal way. I know that one should and in company – certainly in that of your oma, it is OK, but when we are together with just the two of us it bothers me, because it supposes a distance between us that is not there.'

Robert looked at his opa without understanding. In a familiar gesture Jacob put his hand on his shoulder. 'After all we are linked together in a very special way,' he continued, 'and not only because you are such a good soccer player.' He mentioned his unique relationship with Benjamin and that he saw that line continue in Robert. He mentioned the link with the prophecy of Mordecai. That, although he – Robert – was born from a non-Jewish mother, his name would not be blotted out from Israel and that he was his only grandchild who was born on *the day after Passover…*

At that moment Robert realised for the first time that there was a likeness and kinship not just on the outside, but also deep within him, in that abstract area of his spirit. That his features resembled his father's and also his grandfather's, he could see for himself. That he had inherited from them his soccer talent, his creativity and "Jewish feeling" had also become clear. However, now he understood that in that tradition certain characteristics had been transmitted that were not so concrete and visible. The certainty that his opa had already known about that for a long time took away his diffidence to pour out his heart to him.

'I often have such awful dreams,' he confessed, 'and I can suddenly become fearful without knowing what of. Could that have to do with it?'

Jacob nodded. 'I knew about those dreams and that fear,' he said. 'Not that your parents told me, but I saw it somehow and I sensed it. And yes, that has to do with our family bond. The suffering that we – as a family – saw and experienced in the camp was too much to be processed in one human life. And that "surplus" is then taken over by one or sometimes more of the following generations. A kind of inborn sensitivity for the suffering of your forefathers and the fear for a repeat. I cannot really explain it properly, but I see it happening in Benjamin's life and in yours. Experts call it the "second and third generation syndrome". Whatever it may be, there is one consolation! Namely that it will end during your life, and that then it will really be over.'

'Oh…?' Robert asked. 'Why…?'

'Not because I just happen to think that,' Jacob answered, 'but because it is written in the Torah that the consequences of sin will have their effect till the third and fourth generation. It even says that not before the fourth generation the measure of injustice will be full. So you should not suppress that fear that you mentioned, because the sooner you know from where it comes, the faster it will disappear. And in your case it will then definitely be gone, because – counting from my parents – you are the fourth generation.'

Now Robert started to see the "number four" really in a very remarkable perspective. His brain reeled at the realisation that it was most likely this "number four" that the woman in the museum had meant. Again, he wondered who she had been…

'Come,' said Jacob, after they had sat quietly for a while, 'it is time to go home and convince your grandmother that we really have not been to the pub.'

In silence they walked past the cemetery along the Oosterwal, crossed the road, and as they walked down the Westerwal Robert asked: 'Opa, do you believe in chance?'

'Well, you know,' Jacob said, 'this morning I read a letter in the Elburger newspaper from someone who complained that our mayor hardly ever sees the people any more. I walk out the door to run an errand and the first person I meet who talks with me is the mayor. You can call it chance, but in essence it does not change anything in my life or in the course of things in the world. *Mazel* and bad luck also have to do with that kind of coincidence. But quite apart from that, I know that there is a Creator who directs the world – and therefore also my life. I know that because I have experienced that He is involved in my life and does not let go of me – His creation. During the deepest point of my misery, when I had lost all courage, my friend Mordecai showed me that and he was right. "Everything is *bashert*", that was the last thing he said to me.'

'*Bashert*…?' Robert repeated.

'Yes,' Jacob explained, 'that means that everything is directed towards a pre-ordained destination. And now that we are talking about that,' he continued with a smile, 'I also have a question… about that picture last Sunday, you know, that David Hamburger gave me. The reason that you knew absolutely certainly who I was… that was not because you recognised me, but Sal. Am I right or not?'

Robert felt a weird mix of alarm and amazement. 'Uh… yes, but how do you know…?' he stammered, rather upset.

Jacob put his hand on Robert's shoulder. 'I know that David had another reason to come to Elburg that Sunday afternoon. But you don't have to explain anything to me. There is time for that later… There is a time for everything!'

That evening Robert noticed with satisfaction that the thoughts his grandfather had given him had instilled a strange but pleasant calm in him. His fear seemed to have acquired a "name" and might have come close to being exposed. Finally a ray of light broke into that dark space within him. With the comforting certainty that he had been given the correct indications to escape finally from the negative spiral of that gloomy labyrinth, he fell asleep.

The only one who appeared in his dream that night was the friendly woman from the museum who emphasized once again what his grandfather had said that afternoon… "Don't suppress your fear, but search for the cause, for in remembering lies the deliverance…"

The experience of his first practicum week in the advertising studio had such a positive effect on Robert that he felt even less like going back to school after the vacation. Because the satisfaction was clearly mutual, it was agreed that – if there were sufficient assignments – he would continue working as long as possible.

That Friday evening he went straight from work by train from Wezep to Putten. Opposite him sat a pretty young woman of Surinam descent. She seemed to hardly notice that he sat down opposite her. Relaxed, supporting her left elbow with her bag, she looked out of the window, deep in thought. Robert sized her up attentively and estimated that she was some ten years older than he. She had a nice figure, clad in faded jeans, a tight pink sweater and a short, brown jacket of thin, supple leather. What intrigued him most, however, was the remarkable calm and self-assurance that she radiated. He wondered what she was thinking of at that moment, with that contented expression on her face. In spite of the fact that he did not know anyone in his own environment that was of Surinam origin, she seemed familiar to him. As he wondered, looking at her dark eyes, whether he might have seen her somewhere before – or whether she resembled someone he knew – she took a deep breath and obviously dismissed the subject of her musings. Slowly she turned her gaze away from the window and looked at Robert with a friendly, vaguely sensual smile. It startled him and he felt himself blushing. She pretended not to notice and took a plastic bottle from the bag. At her leisure she untwisted the cap, poured a bit of white fluid in the palm of her hand and rubbed it onto her hands and fingers in a gracious, almost ritual manner. In one fluid motion she replaced the cap on the bottle and replaced it into her bag. Then she relaxed her back against the seat and looked at Robert.

'Tired…?' she asked.

Robert smiled shyly and admitted: 'Yes, because for the first time in my life I have really worked and after that you are tired in quite a different way than after a soccer game.'

'But you did like the work?' she asked.

'Oh yes, certainly,' Robert answered, 'it is with an advertising studio. I helped to put the signs on four trucks and did all sorts of other jobs. This weekend I have to think about a name and a logo for a sports school.'

'And… do you have any ideas yet?' she wanted to know.

'No, not yet,' Robert said. 'the problem is that it is not just going to be a hall full of toning machines; they also want to do yoga and that sort of activities.'

'Hm… interesting,' she reacted and with her attractive light Surinam accent she continued – in response to the questioning look in Robert's eyes: 'Those people obviously understand that a good condition does not only have to do with your body but also with your spirit. Nothing is separate, you know. Everything hangs together… And that is how balance, harmony and depth are created in your life… the past and the present… intelligence and feeling… body and soul. You know the expression "a sound mind in a sound body?" Well, it has to do with that. It does not only concern your body, you know, but your body and your soul. That is the direction in which you should think, according to me, when you make a design.' Smiling, she added in a familiar tone of voice: 'Both for the sports school and for your own life.'

The train reduced speed when they approached the station Harderwijk. She got up, zipped her bag shut and shook Robert's hand. She looked at him intently for a moment and said: 'See you again some time, right!' Then she turned around and as she left the coach those last words reverberated in Robert's head... "See you again some time!" That sounded as if they had met each other before, but he was absolutely sure that this was not the case. At the same time a vague, strange doubt came over him, that was strengthened when from the platform – as the train started moving again – she looked at him for another moment with that intriguing, self-assured smile and waved at him.

As the train left Harderwijk he gazed absentmindedly at the landscape, while what he had just heard gradually shaped itself into a name and logo for the sports school... *BODY and SOUL* – for the right balance... *BODY and SOUL* – for a complete condition. He pictured various possibilities to have the lower curve of the B and the upper curve of the S flow into one another. That same evening he withdrew to his room and made three design sketches based on the name *BODY and SOUL*.

Only when he had finished did he realize the important roll that the Surinam woman had played. He recalled her in all her beauty and attractiveness and he was taken aback by the sudden desire for her that he felt within himself. In fact – he told himself – there was no similarity between them whatsoever. The age difference, her skin colour and accent, her culture and background, she was his opposite in everything he could think of and yet...

He put a new piece of paper in front of him, picked up his pencil again and waited patiently until the storm of his thoughts had died down and only quietly rolling sentences were left...

BODY and SOUL

*A thousand people
past me flow
in a long
and endless row.
Then suddenly
there's you
with peaceful eyes
that so bemuse me
and confuse me
a polar wave that stole
my heart, my very being
my body and my soul.*

12

With mixed feelings Bart Rozendaal left the small sports complex of the soccer society *Rood-Wit* immediately after the end of the game. As an exception he did not go with the set group of supporters to the cafeteria for the "third half" but walked straight to the parking lot.

In the past week Jannie van der Hoeven had died and this Saturday afternoon there was an opportunity for condolences at her home until 6 pm. Jannie had been married to Bart's friend Anton, but as a result of the raid she had become a widow at a young age. She was left behind with two little girls and pregnant with a son, when Anton was deported from Putten with all those other men, never to return. She had not remarried and Bart had kept regularly in touch with her as well as with the children. And now that she had died, he definitely wanted to extend his condolences to the children in order to share this loss with them personally.

He always dreaded going to the village. Without fail he was reminded, more or less, of that particular Sunday – October 1st 1944 – the day of the attack on a car with German officers. When the perpetrators did not give themselves up, in spite of repeated summonses, 660 boys and men were herded together – as a retaliatory measure – and deported the next day to *Kamp Amersfoort*. A large number of women and children were also arrested, but they were allowed to return home later in the day. Of those who were deported a few dozen were released during their stay in Amersfoort, but over 600 were transported to concentration camp *Neuengamme* near Hamburg. From there the majority were spread across twenty or so concentration camps elsewhere in Germany. Only 49 men – himself included – survived the terrors of those camps and returned home after the war. Every time when he went to the village he was reminded of it... How they tried to flee when the Germans entered their neighborhood... The panic... The trip to the Kerkplein, packed together in an army truck... The machine-guns at all the important crossings...

The secret hope that the memories would fade as he grew older turned out to be futile, as was the expectation that the sharp clarity of the images would wear off as time went by. During the past few years he even noticed that it became ever more difficult to find the strength to suppress the emotions and memories. And this time it would certainly not succeed, for Anton junior – who had been born half a year after his father was deported – had meanwhile grown up in his likeness. And that, that unavoidable recognition, was one of those surreptitious but incredibly vicious parts of the indelible process of Bart's war trauma. Days could pass during which nothing or no one reminded him of that dark period of his life. Then his vegetable garden, his family life and the many activities at the soccer club *Rood-Wit* occupied him to the extent that it seemed that the past had faded, had even almost disappeared. But then such a relatively short period of beneficial peace and happiness was rudely disturbed again – often completely unexpectedly – by the recognition of a face. Suddenly he would see somewhere the son of one of the victims. On the street or at a birthday, during a reception or in the cafeteria... they popped up anywhere, unexpectedly... the sons whose fathers he had watched dying in the camps. Men from after the war, living in peace... but to him they appeared at such a moment to be revived ghosts from the hell of *Ladelund* or *Neuengamme*. Sometimes, if such a person looked at him inquiringly, he would apologize and ask hesitantly: "Excuse me, but are you maybe the son of...?" And if that then turned out to be the case, he only nodded and withdrew quietly. The shock of such recognition always signalled the end of his peace of mind and the beginning of the umpteenth nightmare.

Absorbed in thought, he drove slowly out of the car park in the Veenhuizerveld neighborhood and turned in the direction of the village. Fifteen minutes later he parked his car beneath the high linden trees next to the church, opposite *Van Ganswijk Ladies' and Gents' Fashion.*

As he walked to the Kerkstraat he recalled the temporary shop – on the square in front of the property – that had been put there at the time of a radical restoration of the fashion shop. Together with his colleagues of a local contracting business he had helped erect it. After the re-opening of the totally renewed and expanded shop Mr. van Ganswijk Sr. had asked him if he knew a good destination for the temporary shop that was no longer needed. That was why since then the wooden building had been the cafeteria and boardroom of *Rood-Wit*.

Without reproaching him in any way and in a very friendly manner Mr. van Ganswijk had asked Bart once why he never went to church any more. He had been raised with it, after all. But at a very young age he had started to experience doubt and unease because of the way of life of some well-to-do village "church-people", which went straight against the teachings of the Bible. And later, after his return from the concentration camp, his enthusiasm had disappeared completely and he had gradually taken his leave from it. The degrading circumstances in which he had seen his family members and friends die, did not fit the image that he had had as a boy of the "Good Shepherd", who would go through fire and water to save his sheep from the claws of the enemy. He had also not understood why some of his believing fellow-villagers had submitted so uncomplainingly to their undeserved punishment. Their faith seemed to take away the need to voice even the smallest protest against the hard work, the lack of food and the bad quality of it and the brutal treatment. Often the farmer's sons, who were used eating well at home because they had to do heavy physical labour, died first due to the lack of it.

Because he thought of himself in the first place and because he did anything and everything in order to survive, he had survived. It had not made him an atheist, but for him the experiences in the camps had undermined the biblical truths considerably. It had caused the window through which he used to look at the peaceful, safe image of Sunday school and church to become soiled and full of cracks.

Before he entered the empty Kerkstraat he turned around for a moment and looked across the deserted square to the wall of the *Oude Kerk*. FROM HERE THEY WERE DEPORTED, he read on the large stone memorial plaque. Angry about all that injustice he frowned grimly. Apart from a few pigeons that were searching the street for something edible, the village seemed deserted. But in the few seconds that he stood there, the space around him filled with the images and sounds of that particular Sunday in October 1944... Again he heard the cursing and ranting of the German soldiers that pushed the arrested men with the barrels of their guns to the Church Square and to the school next to the *Oude Kerk*... He saw himself again – with some thirty other men – standing against the wall of the pub next to the church... The anxious hours for this group of men, who had been herded together and set aside to be shot... Standing by helplessly as the women and children were herded into the church... The shouted commands of the German soldiers and the stamping of their hobnailed boots... The machine guns that were set up everywhere...

As he turned around to enter the Kerkstraat he suddenly noticed that on the elevated stone platform on the square stood a plinth with a small sculpture on it. He wondered when that had been put there, for it was the first time that he had noticed it. Curiously he took a few steps towards it to see what it depicted and was startled... Two male figures of which one – bending deeply – lifted another from the ground. Below it was a metal plaque engraved with the text: *The Good Samaritan*. He shook his head, wanting to know who had had the crazy idea to put a sculpture of *The Good Samaritan* at this very spot from which 660 men and boys had been deported – the majority to be tortured to death in the end. The person from the parable of Jesus that told about the love and pity of God for miserable and oppressed people; the Saviour who lifts them up, takes care of them and delivers them from their seemingly hopeless situation. How painful… for it was that Saviour, that good Samaritan who had been so obviously absent during those terrible days in which they were arrested and then deported.

'And of that they have to remind the few who returned by means of such a sculpture… what are they thinking of,' he muttered.

As happened so often, now also the images from *Ladelund* appeared in his mind again. He saw himself return with the group after a long day of work in the wet peat-swamps. Cold to the bone, exhausted and hungry. The strongest carried the corpses on their shoulders of those who had succumbed and put them down in the roll-call area. Comrades who had died that day but who had to be taken back to the camp. The number of men that had left early in the morning had to be exactly the same on their return in the evening. Dead or alive, that made no difference.

"The Good Samaritan", he muttered, shaking his head. He had not encountered him. Not then and never… But then he suddenly saw in his mind's eye the figure of pastor Meyer from Ladelund. The man who, using his position and endangering his own life, helped dozens of men to survive by taking care of their wounds and appeasing their worst hunger. Bart himself owed his life to him too. Suddenly he realised that – as in the parable – that "Good Samaritan" had also come from the land of the enemy. A German no less, who had been so moved with pity, that he risked his life. And at that thought the little sculpture acquired a glow of beauty after all… Yes, he thought, it is beautiful after all, but it is just in the wrong place…it really belongs on the square of the church in Ladelund, for that is where I met him, not here in Putten.

He walked past the building of *Van Ganswijk Fashion* into the Kerkstraat and rang at the house of Van der Hoeven.

'Rozendaal... man, that is great. Come in!' Anton said warmly. He had always appreciated it very much that Bart used to visit his mother from time to time, in spite of his own war trauma. After he had hung up his coat they walked, talking, into the living room. The spacious L-shaped room emanated an atmosphere of sobriety. The classical furniture of dark oak was still in exactly the same place where it had been put long ago – timeless and solid. On the chairs that stood in a half circle in front of the fireplace mainly neighbors and family members were seated. Inconspicuously Bart looked around the circle and saw Ben van Zuiden, Anton's colleague. Both had worked for years at *Van Ganswijk Fashion* and Ben's son Robert was still one of the most promising players in the A-selection of *The Reds*, as the club *Rood-Wit* was often called. But there were rumours that *The Blues* – as *SDC*, the other soccer society in Putten was popularly called – were interested in him and that had been bothering Bart for some time already. He had seen boys leave so often. With regret and a feeling of helplessness he had had to watch how *The Blues* then harvested richly with the talented players from his club and that he felt sore about.

Bart saw there was an empty seat next to Ben and gratefully he used the opportunity to seek some distraction and to suppress the earlier bad images that still went through his mind.

'We won three-zero!' he whispered to Ben, who in his turn asked softly: 'And... did Robert play well?'

Bart frowned, and as he slowly turned his head towards Ben he said in a worried tone of voice: 'Yes, very well... but uh... Van Zuiden, I would like to talk to you later about that son of yours!'

He drank a cup of coffee, participated in a hushed voice in the conversation and listened to Anton. With carefully chosen words Anton spoke about his mother's sick bed, about her struggle and how she had suddenly received the miraculous certainty that she was allowed to enter the "glory of the Lord…" How they had been amazed by that sudden calm, after a long period of uncertainty and fear. That unearned grace, that is what they had asked of the Lord and He had granted it. Visibly impressed, he concluded: 'Yes, miraculous… and then you see that where we – people – are powerless, the Lord wants to help…'

Slowly and soundlessly, Bart sighed and he looked down without speaking, his head bent. Beyond the patterns in the old Persian carpet he saw the little sculpture of *The Good Samaritan* and in his head the echo of Anton's words kept buzzing: "Where people are powerless, there the Lord wants to help".

After a while he walked together with Ben and some family members to the room where Jannie lay. They looked with sadness at the delicate, sunken face and someone whispered something unintelligible.

Once outside again Ben looked at Bart's seasoned face. In a friendly tone he asked: 'And Rozendaal, what's eating you?'

'I would like to hear straight from you whether it is true that Robert has been asked to play for *The Blues*,' Bart answered.

When Ben assented, the old man shook his head with disillusion.

'It's such a darn shame, Van Zuiden,' he said, 'that the test game that Robert played with *FC Zwolle*, did not bring anything. Then at least the club would have had something to be proud of, but of this… of this I am not proud… of this I only become dejected. Look at all that extra time and attention that a trainer like Gert-Jan has spent on that boy. Thanks to that he was only half a year with the A-juniors and now he plays already for almost a year in the first team, when he is only barely seventeen. And you'll see that he will really make it with *The Blues* and then they will take the credit for it again.'

Ben smiled. He could imagine Bart's disappointment very well. That's why he decided to reassure him, even though he had promised Robert to keep mum about it for the time being. For he had a soft spot for this man, which had to do above all with the man's war past that was comparable to that of his father in a way. This exception – he knew for sure – would be OK with Robert.

'Rozendaal,' he said. 'then I have good news for you after all, but it has to stay between us, deal?' Bart nodded, and then Ben confided: 'One of these days Robert will really cancel his membership with *Rood-Wit*, but not because he is going to play for *The Blues*. He is going to *FC Zwolle*. He just received a confirmation in writing yesterday. He'll play for one year with the A-juniors and then it'll be decided whether or not he gets a contract.'

'Right...' Bart reacted visibly relieved, 'that really is good news, even though I'll be sorry to see him go and not only because he is such a good soccer player.'

Ben looked at him in surprise and asked: 'Oh... what other qualities does he have then?'

'I don't know if you should call them qualities,' Bart continued, 'there is something in that boy that attracts me for some reason, but it's difficult to describe.' He hesitated for a moment. Then he said slowly: 'It's like this, Van Zuiden, if Robert is in good shape, it is a real pleasure to see him play. Then he is so concentrated on the game that he does not see or hear anyone outside the field. After the game also, with the other boys in the cafeteria – he is a sociable guy. Never the talker, never a loudmouth, but very witty. Still, at other times he walks around...then I can just tell that something is bothering him. It just seems then as if... yes, how should I say that...?'

He swept the empty street with his gaze and then said: 'Take that game when he got "red", a month ago. Boy oh boy... what a bad show. From the start he paid no attention. He kept looking at the public instead of at the ball. His passes did not arrive; he got stuck all the time, lost every duel and to add insult to injury he attacked an opponent with a stretched leg for no reason. Frustration pure and simple! The trainer asked him for an explanation, of course, but in vain. "A bad day… can happen to anyone", more than that he would not say. But during the next week, after the training, I talked with him for a while and then something came to light, I have to say, but whether that was all…?'

Ben looked at him questioningly and Bart continued: 'Well, you also know his frustrations of course. You are present at all contacts with sponsors, parties and receptions, but on Saturday afternoon you are hardly ever watching. Because of your work, of course, but still… and what bothered Robert most was that – on that particular Saturday afternoon – your father was not there either.'

'Tcha…' Ben said with a sigh, 'it is understandable from his point of view. My father is still crazy about soccer. He used to play the game himself, heart and soul. He still follows everything on TV. And then of all people it is the grandson – who has such a special place in his life – who is the only good player in the family, but he never goes to watch him. I always save the game reports from the newspaper, the club magazine and the presentation guide for him. And I know that whenever there is a positive report or a nice picture of Robert, he shows that full of pride to his friends in the pub. That Saturday afternoon that you mentioned, my parents were visiting us. Robert knows as well as I do that the women always go into the village to shop and have a coffee in *De Heerdt*, and he had doubtlessly counted on it that my father would come to watch him. But you know, Rozendaal, in the past he never came to see me either and I did not understand that at all when I was about Robert's age. In the meantime I know the reason for it and I think the time has come to explain it all to Robert too.

In any case… there'll be a lull in the business now and I think that I'll come to watch again in two weeks time – at the home game.'

Bart smiled: 'I'll remind you of that, Van Zuiden. Then we can have a drink together afterwards!'

'Or two!' Ben reacted happily and they said good-bye with "see you in two weeks…"

Still pondering their conversation, Bart left the Kerkstraat and after he had passed the square with the sculpture, he was startled by a car that slowed down beside him, just as he wanted to cross the street. He turned to the right and stopped at the bottom of the church tower. To his surprise he saw that the car had a German number plate. It did not happen often that Germans came to Putten. A kind of collective shame obviously kept them from doing that. Bart wondered, therefore, what caused the man to drive around here, at this time of the day.

He walked towards his own car and just as he wanted to start it, he saw in his mirror that the man walked past the church, in the direction of the Kerkplein. There he halted, put his hands on his back and looked around the deserted square. Only his head moved slowly from side to side. Bart felt a shock pass through him. Completely taken by surprise he watched the man with wide eyes. Taking deep breaths he looked away, and to the wall – straight ahead – where he had stood the particular Sunday. He felt again the same fear of long ago, when he was threatened with being shot on this spot.

He rested his head on the steering wheel that he grasped with clenched hands. A dull pain crept up slowly from his neck and kept thumping in his head, and his stomach turned with a feeling of nausea.

'It can't be true, it can't be one of those sadists…' he whispered.

He had often wondered what he would feel or do if he ever met one of them. Now he knew and it was very different from what he had imagined. Strangely enough it was not a question of revenge or aggression. On the contrary, a unusual feeling of helplessness had taken possession of him. The thumping in his head changed into dizziness, and the nausea caused a tendency to retch. As in a nightmare the images mingled without connection. And in the quiet of the evening the sounds of fear and panic from a far past echoed through his head.

He did not hear the knock on the window of his car and he also did not notice that the door was carefully opened. Only when a hand was hesitantly put on his shoulder, he reacted. With tears in his eyes he looked at the man who asked him full of concern: 'Are you feeling alright, sir… can I do something for you…?'

Bart looked at him in confusion. In a reflex he turned his head to the right and saw that the German had disappeared. He looked at the empty car near the church tower and managed to stammer: 'But… are you… uh… the person who was just standing there… was that you…?'

The man confirmed that, scrutinizing Bart's face, and then asked cautiously: 'May I ask you… are you maybe one of those who were deported from here in the war…?'

Bart nodded silently, at which the man extended his hand: 'Me too…! My name is Willem de Vries.'

Hesitantly Bart shook the extended hand and stuttered: 'But… I thought that you… I mean… because of that German car…'

'Yes, I understand,' De Vries interrupted, 'and I am very sorry that I caused you a few awful moments that way.'

With a look at the sign on the wall next to him he concluded: 'It looks like this is a pub. I propose that we drink a cup of coffee here together, then I can explain.'

And thus Bart heard the story of Willem de Vries that evening…

… After the failed attempt of the allies to cross the Rhine in September 1944, he was evacuated – at 19 years of age – together with his parents and two sisters from Arnhem to Putten. The initially safe and quiet accommodation was to be of short duration and it would have a terrible consequence… For on October 1st 1944 not only residents but also evacuees and others who were accidentally in Putten were arrested and deported.

The sadistic pleasure with which Kotälla and his cronies humiliated and mistreated them during their stay in *Kamp Amersfoort*, made Willem fear the worst with regards to what was still waiting for them. And from those first days there in *Kamp Amersfoort* only one thought dominated him: try to escape! It turned out to be impossible from *Kamp Amersfoort* but when after ten days they were transported to Germany, he was continuously on the look-out for a chance. Quite soon he saw some people jump in a panic from the train. Some survived that, others didn't. They landed badly or they were hit by the gunfire of the German soldiers from the train. It only resulted in stricter guarding and soon a warning followed: "If one person jumps from the train, another one on the train will be shot".

A few kilometres outside of Almelo the train stopped and stayed there a whole day. Because of a bombardment the railway was damaged in such a way that it was impossible to continue. At that place escape was not feasible. Around five o'clock a few fellow-prisoners were allowed to fetch water from a farm and pull some tubers from the ground, but the machine guns in the field were aimed continuously on the train…

De Vries fell silent and stared outside with eyes that saw nothing, to the church wall and a part of the Kerkplein. In front of him his coffee stood untouched and a heavy silence filled the pub. Slowly he turned his head to Bart again and spoke with a halting voice: 'I don't know what you felt at that time of course, but I can tell you that I have never felt so afraid and so lonely as then. The gnawing hunger, the cold and the stink of all those people, pressed together in one space… And there, in that carriage, I felt the spirit of evil and Kotälla's satanic deeds as a heavy threat around me. The fear for the multiple terrors that were most likely waiting for us gradually surpassed the fear of being shot during an escape attempt. It may sound absurd, but that fear turned out to be – in hindsight – a good counsellor. A kind of "friend" who encouraged me and in the end gave me the strength to do what I did… Near the town Rheine I jumped from the train in the night, and as you can see I survived. A stiff leg… that is the only thing I still have. A bullet hit me in the back of my knee, went straight through the patella and came out at the front. The pain was terrible and I lost a lot of blood, but finally I reached a farm. Fortunately "good" Germans were living there. They wanted to have nothing to do with Hitler and the Nazi-regime. During my extended stay in that family I fell in love with the eldest daughter whom I married a few years after the war. Via the farmer's life I later ended up in the trade of agricultural machines and I have just come from a large trade fair in Amsterdam. On the highway I suddenly saw PUTTEN on a sign and…'

He waited for a moment and looked outside again before he continued: 'I know what happened to most of us who were deported and believe me, I am well aware that – in comparison with them – I have just had a great deal of luck…

And… what happened to you?' he asked.

Bart shrugged and answered: 'Well, on the one hand you could say that I too was lucky because I survived, but on the other hand…'

It was quiet for a long time as he stared fixedly ahead. Finally he said: 'But… - I can say that to you – the older I get, the more often I ask myself who had the better deal, those who died or those who survived… How can you function as a husband, a father and grandfather or as chairman of a soccer club when you have come from hell… the hell of *Neuengamme* and of *Ladelund*. Apart from the few who returned, there is not a single living person in the village who really understands that!' He blinked, took a handkerchief from his pocket and blew his nose. Then he wiped his eyes dry and spoke with difficulty: 'It was so terrible, kid… so… so…'

Moved, Willem watched the impressive, authentic and living proof of the damage wreaked by the people to which he had delivered himself up so completely. He had experienced it as a real mercy that there were also "good" Germans during the war. That he had even married one of them caused him at that moment a kind of guilt that bordered – as he noticed – on treason. Powerless he sat there – the trader with the gift of the gab – searching for the correct words but he did not find them. After a long silence he asked hesitantly: 'Have you ever considered uh… going back to the camp…?'

Bart shook his head. 'No, I really don't want to see that again,' he assured, 'I just want to forget.'

Later, when they were outside again and said good-bye, Willem gave his card to Bart. 'Here is my phone number,' he said. 'If ever you change your mind, then please call and we'll go there together. I travel through Holland regularly, so I can pick you up and take you home again. You can stay with me.'

Pointing at the little sculpture of *The good Samaritan* Bart proposed: 'Then we can take that along too and put it where it belongs.' He told him how pastor Meyer in *Ladelund* had managed to alleviate his misery somewhat just in time. Glancing at the German number plate on Willem's car, he concluded: 'Tcha, there we are, as two of the few dozen who survived, and both of us owe it to a German…'

Half an hour before the start of the game Ben reported to the boardroom of *Rood-Wit*. As the representative of a main sponsor he was welcomed warmly. At his question why Bart was not present he was told that he had been off colour for two weeks already. "A touch of the flu", they said, but because he felt that something worse could be the matter, Ben resolved to look him up after the game.

At the field he concentrated on the game and specifically on Robert's share in it. It had been a while since he had seen him play and he clearly noticed progress. Robert's dedication had become more serious and he radiated more alertness and passion. In just over a year his posture and attitude had developed from that of a playful adolescent to that of an adult athlete. Ben reacted modestly to the positive remarks that he heard from supporters here and there. However, as soon as Robert was involved in an attack, and – head and shoulders forward – he immediately went after his prey with the power and grace of a predator, Ben felt his blood boil and inwardly he was bursting with pride. The similarity to himself caused him to have a déjà vu-like experience at some moments, but it also convinced him that this likeness of him would "make" it in the future. For a long time there had been that vague worry about the quiet, withdrawn life of Robert. That introvert world of his own, that gradually took a special place in the homogeneity of their family, had sometimes caused Ben a fear of estrangement from exactly that person who was essentially closest to him. But since he had graduated – just barely – from the *MAVO* and started to work permanently for Martin Westerink, he seemed to be freed from a heavy pressure. One day a week he followed a course "Advertising and Design" at an educational institute in Utrecht and now that the transfer to *FC Zwolle* was finally a fact, it seemed that his life had gradually acquired direction and purpose. All together, it had made him an adult in a relatively short time.

After the game Ben drove directly to Bart's small, farm-like working-class house. Due to the idyllic location at the edge of extensive forests, the majority of similar dwellings had been bought through the years by well-to-do villagers and people from the cities. They then had built luxury bungalows there, so that the area with the old working-class houses had gradually changed into a posh country housing estate. Bart was one of the few who had consistently declined the more than generous offers. His parental home was not for sale at any price. "Here I was born", he always said, "and from here I shall leave again. What my children do with it later is their business, but I am never going to leave!"

When Ben drove into the yard Bart's wife emerged from the chicken coop with a bowl of eggs.

'I've come to see how Bart is doing,' Ben said, 'at least, if it is convenient.'

'But of course, Van Zuiden,' she cried, 'just go inside and cheer up that old grumbler.'

Through the low doors he walked via the small kitchen to the living room where Bart was sitting at the table in front of the window. Ben shook his hand and sat down across from him.

'Well... how is it going?' he asked. 'I have just been at *Rood-Wit* and there I heard that you are not feeling very well.'

Silently Bart peered through the window at the horses that walked in the meadow in front of the neighbors' house. Ben more or less recognised the mental state in which Bart seemed to be. The fact that he had not even asked whether his club had won, meant in any case that he was emotionally in worse state than physically. Ben realised that he could do one of two things now. Either wish him improvement with a single word and a friendly pat on the shoulder, or show understanding for that from which he really suffered. Even though it was difficult, in view of the sensitive subject, he decided for the latter.

'It's the war, isn't it!' he determined simply. He felt how his words remained suspended heavily in the silence of the room.

Bart slowly turned his head and looked at him with wide, dull eyes.

'And the camp...!' Ben added.

Bart nodded dejectedly and started to speak about the meeting with Willem de Vries. About the moment at which he saw that Willem was watching the empty Kerkplein and what that had roused in him.

'And then... one thing follows the other. I had a bad flu for a few days and the fever causes such terrible dreams. In the daytime too that misery keeps going through your head. My wife said yesterday: "You should not bottle it all up. Talk about it and tell me something about it. You'll see that it brings you relief".'

He shook his head and sighed: 'She just does not understand that that is impossible. It was too bad... so terrible... so brutal, so...'

'Yes,' Ben agreed softly, 'I know...'

Frowning, Bart looked at him. 'What do you mean?'

'My father survived *Auschwitz*,' said Ben, 'and you have to take it from me that I have come to understand what that meant to him. In the course of the years I became a kind of sounding board for him within our family and because of that his fears and dreams have, in a certain sense, influenced my life also, and even that of Robert. Of course that cannot be compared at all with experiencing it personally, but it brought us somehow closer to that of which you say cannot be explained.'

In the silence that followed both let their thoughts wander… Bart recalled Robert during his quiet, absent-minded moments that he had never been able to explain, while – strangely – they seemed familiar to him. And Ben wondered if Bart had a sounding board at all, a container into which he could pour the surplus of his emotions.

'Have you ever considered going back to the camp?' he suggested.

'You are the second person in a short time who asks me that,' Bart answered. 'The man I told you about just now, Willem de Vries, also wanted to know that. If I call him, he'll pick me up just like that. I can stay with him and he'll also take me home again.'

'Well, that's a nice offer,' Ben said. 'If I were you I'd consider it. It seems conflicting but you'll see that you'll be able to deal with it better afterwards. To forget it or to suppress it is impossible; it was much too intense for that. And as you grow older and your mental resistance decreases, the images and memories are only going to increase. If you go back to the place where it all happened, it may be possible to leave the greater part behind there. I know that some men have done it and that was their experience. They were relieved in a certain way and afterwards they felt that they had really left something behind and had closure. As far as I can judge you have nothing to lose – only something to gain.'

Bart considered it for a while. Then he looked at Ben and admitted: 'Maybe you are right. I have talked about it a few times with Henk Vonhof. He went back and he said something similar to what you are saying now. But then… Henk is a completely different person than I. He has a different make-up, but maybe that does not really matter. I don't know, but I shall think about it.'

'You do that,' Ben advised him and got up. He shook Bart's hand, put the other hand on his shoulder and concluded: 'And something you have to start thinking about now also is that club of yours. This afternoon they beat the second top of the league: 4-1 and therefore they could, if everything goes well, be champions this time next week!'

On the way home Ben wondered if Bart would manage to go back. At the same time he realised that he himself also had never yet followed the advice that Gérard had given him years ago. Whenever "the ghost" – as Els had called it – reared up in him and made him downcast, he resolved to start writing. But as soon as that thin veil of vague fear had been driven from his head again, he did not get around to it and it remained just a resolve. Now and then a poem, that was all.

Unexpectedly the importance of the self-analysis that is started by writing was pointed out to him once more – and now from a completely different side.

An unknown lady entered the shop where Ben worked. Immediately he felt a kind of kinship with her. A very subtle, but nonetheless real signal, just as he had received that time when he met his neighbor Lub for the first time.

She had seen a shirt for her friend in the window but was doubtful about the correct size. After Ben's remark that she could always exchange it, she smiled: 'That is going to be rather complicated for I live in France.'

'Well,' Ben reacted, 'that is quite a journey just for a shirt.'

When asked if she originated from this area, she told him

that she was born in Rotterdam during the war and that, because of the bombardments of Rotterdam by the allies of late 1941, she had moved soon afterwards with her family to Putten.

The magic word had been spoken and hung – as a confirmation of his vague feeling of solidarity – between them.

'And that is why you come back now and then…? Because of the war…?'

Somewhat reserved and surprised by that direct approach, she looked at him inquisitively and confirmed: 'Yes, amongst other things. But I also still have family and acquaintances living here. After all, an important part of my life happened here and now and then I have to go back for a while.'

'If I may ask,' said Ben, 'and I hope you don't mind – it is not curiosity but real interest – was your departure to France a flight?'

For a moment it remained quiet. Then she answered: 'No, I went to live in France to write my third book… but if I may ask something too… why the interest?'

At that moment Anton came back from his coffee break. Ben beckoned to him and said: 'This is a cousin of mine from France. We haven't seen each other for years and are now going to have a cup of coffee in *De Heerdt*.'

'Cousin from France,' she repeated, smiling, when they walked outside, 'and you have no idea who I am and what my name is.'

He extended his hand: 'Ben van Zuiden, pleased to meet you.'

'My name is Marijke,' she said, 'Marijke Spoor.'

They sat down at the table near the window with the view of the *Oude Kerk* and a part of the Kerkplein behind.

'OK,' Ben continued, taking up the thread of their conversation, 'my question whether your departure for France was a flight stems from the fact that my departure from Elburg – where I spent my youth – was just that. That had to do with the consequences of the war.'

He briefly told her how the suffering of his father had influenced him, with all the inherent consequences. And that – to be honest – he had to conclude and admit now that that flight had solved nothing.

'It's the path of least resistance. You cannot leave your fear and the incurred traumata behind. You bring them along, wherever you go. Within yourself - that is where you have to solve it… but how does one do that?'

In the silence that followed Marijke gazed pensively outside. Her right hand rested on the spoon with which she had just been stirring her tea. Ben wondered what images and thoughts went through her head at that moment. It struck him that nothing in her attitude and aura gave him the impression that he was sitting opposite a "damaged" fellow human being. On the contrary, her calm and well-considered manner rather gave the impression of a balanced woman, who had organised her life well. He concluded that if she was born at the beginning of the war she had to be about eight years older than he and that she looked well for that age. Whatever had been lost or broken in her life, she had managed to control it in such a way that one could not tell from looking at her.

She looked at Ben again and repeated his last remark thoughtfully…

'I went into therapy when I was still young, because of depressions. It did not occur to me that the war experiences, and specifically the raid, were the cause. The Jews were the war victims in my opinion. The war was not mentioned in my first therapies. Years later, when the depressions became more and more serious and I had treatment in the *Sinai center*, I discovered that I too was a war victim. The fact that I could gradually acknowledge this was a big step on the road to recovery. Part of the therapy was writing down my war story, something I dreaded. But I persevered and I am happy about it now. It has helped me to deal with my trauma. Only then the time was right to start the autobiographical novel that I had in my head for a long time already.'

As Ben sat listening attentively, he realised that he should now take Gérard's advice seriously. Marijke had – speaking from experience – confirmed and underlined the importance of it once again.

He nodded in resignation: 'Years ago I was advised to write things down, also as a kind of therapy. I still have not gotten around to that, but when I hear this…'

He looked at his watch and continued: 'I fear that my fifteen minutes' coffee break is long over. Sadly I have to go back to work.'

They said good-bye and agreed to meet again somewhere – if possible – during a next visit of Marijke to Putten.

That evening when Ben wanted to finally start writing down his story, he noticed that he was distracted by that unexpected meeting with Marijke. And when he saw the parallel of the search within herself and her last name "Spoor", the sentences formed – like so often – into a poem rather than into a story.

SPOOR

Among the words unspoken
a veil that cloaked the past,
which opened and revealed to me
your struggle long and vast.

Among the words unspoken
was shown the perfect child
who gazed outside at the old stone church
with eyes so calm and mild.

Among the words unspoken
as your eyes the square explored
it was with awe I realised
the amazing metaphor.

Among the words unspoken
"Spoor" its meaning I sense
and compares this portion of your life
in perfect coincidence.

Among the words unspoken
this thought impressed me more
I realised I was witnessing
a part of Marijke's spoor.

13

From the moment that Robert became part of the selection of A-juniors at *FC Zwolle* his life consisted almost completely of work and soccer. He did both with pleasure, with great dedication and also with a lot of success. From Monday to Friday he worked with Martin Westerink, and after work he reported to the sports complex around 6 pm for training. The Saturday was mainly spent by playing a match. Only Wednesday evening and Sunday were free.

For the time being he lived with his grandparents and drove down to work in the morning with Martin. In the evening he would then go by bus to Zwolle and after the training back to Elburg. Due to the combination of his feeling for languages and his creativity, he became gradually better at designing original logos and in-house styles, and through the experience he was also gaining the dexterity in the execution, which improved as time went on.

As far as soccer was concerned he was rather surprised that from the start he played better and easier than at *Rood-Wit*. He discovered that, if your fellow-players and opponents play at a higher level, you yourself start playing better too. The only thing that he had to get used to in the beginning was the speed in which the ball was played around. That was much higher than he was used to and it asked for a lot of practice and concentration. The opportunity to use his talent optimally and effectively resulted in the fact that quite soon he became one of the better players. After the winter stop he participated fully in the training of the first team, and one month before his nineteenth birthday – at the start of the new season –he was offered a contract. The evening after the signing he called home from Elburg. Ben was not at home and Nant picked up the phone.

'Hey... mom,' his voice was cheerful, 'I just wanted to let you know that from today I am officially a professional soccer player!'

'Go away!' Nant cried spontaneously. 'Do you really have a contract?'

'Yes,' Robert said, 'I signed this afternoon. Now all of a sudden I have two salaries, but the problem is that I barely have time to spend it. Not that it applied to today. First I had to treat the boys of my team, then I bought a bunch of flowers for oma and just now I have come back from the pub with opa. And there it was not just two beers, for most of his friends were there too! And now that I am at it... I would like to treat all of you on Saturday evening. We are playing at home in the afternoon and then I'll come to Putten immediately after the game. Would you please reserve a table for six at *De Waag*?'

'Yes, that is fine... but uh...' Nant stammered, completely overwhelmed by the exuberance of her usually quiet and withdrawn son, 'but that is really not necessary, boy, that is too much!'

'Mamma... don't nag!' Robert reacted with determination, 'you have no idea how proud and happy I am with this contract and how I enjoy my work. But now that I am not at home permanently any more and have a totally different life from before, now... well, let's say... only now do I appreciate that I was rather lucky with the stock that I come from. And I think this a good opportunity to show my appreciation.'

With this he stirred a very tender chord with Nant. The emotion shut her up like a clam.

'Hey, hello. Are you still there?' Robert asked after that unusual silence.

'Yes... but... you know...' Nant said.

'Sjaak has recently acquired a girl friend in Amsterdam and she is coming this weekend for the first time to Putten.'

'Oh…?' Robert asked surprised, 'what girl is that then?'

'I don't know yet,' said Nant, 'I only know that she is called Tamarah and studies the same subject as Sjaak.'

'Tamarah…?' Robert repeated thoughtfully, 'is she Jewish, maybe?'

When Nant confirmed this, Robert said laconically: 'Well, then she can come along for half the price!' Then he concluded the conversation with: 'OK. We'll see each other Saturday evening. Now I am going to tell oma that Sjaak is going with a Jewish girl. She will be even happier with that than I am with my contract.'

Even though Robert was spot on with that last remark, it escaped him that it made an even stronger impression on Jacob than on Saar. And that had everything to do with the fact that the fulfilment of the promise "that the name of Israel would not be blotted out of all his posterity" had come closer again because of it.

Many people from Putten were proud that a real soccer prof had come from their village. In the shortest possible time it was known among the true soccer fans. And when the Van Zuiden family entered De Waag that evening, Robert was congratulated on his contract immediately by various guests that sat at the bar and around the fireplace.

During the meal the usual bits and pieces were exchanged first and Tamarah had to submit to a veritable cross-examination.

'So now we have a rich brother,' Sjaak stated teasingly.

'Well,' Robert said, 'as far as money goes you should not expect too much of such a first contract, it's a nice little extra, no more. Although, oma thought it was far too much. "Golly what a *mezomme*", she said, "just for running after a ball a bit!" But opa was so proud; he follows everything I do.'

For a moment he looked pensively ahead and then asked Ben: 'That he never ever comes to watch a game, does that have to do with the war too, you think…?'

Ben nodded: 'Yes, but also with a very intense event during the last game that he himself once played.'

Briefly he told them how, during that specific game, his friend Arie Westerink had been struck down by a heart-attack and died in his presence. 'After that he came to watch one of my games one more time. It was the most important one I ever played. We won, became champion and for the first time in history SC Elburg was promoted to the highest class. Still both of us have a bad memory of that particular game: I, because I became unconscious during a tackle, and opa, because immediately after he entered the sports park he was confronted with memories of the concentration camp. Then too it was the old story of those associations that we have talked about before. The iron arch above the entrance of the sports park where the letters *SC Elburg* suddenly changed into *Arbeit Macht Frei...* Changing rooms became huts... Announcements over the loudspeakers sounded like commands... Ushers changed into soldiers... An outsider would find it hard to imagine, but it just happens and you have absolutely no control over it.'

Ben's story rather subdued them all and for some time it remained quiet at the table, until Nant – very subtly – steered the conversation to a lighter subject. 'I still have a present for you,' she turned to Robert, 'everyone just thinks that your soccer talent comes from the "Van Zuidens", but you should not underestimate the part my family played in it.'

Robert opened the little box that had been handed to him, took out a pair of miniscule soccer shoes and looked at his mother questioningly.

Nant told them with a laugh: 'My brother Jan had hung those in your cradle even before we both came back from the hospital. He insisted that I left them there "because", he said, "if that is the first thing that boy sees, then I guarantee you that he will be a good soccer player later!" She leaned backwards in a relaxing manner, spread her hands and stated matter-of-factly: 'I did leave them there and... this is the result!'

'Does such a contract mean that you now have a basic place in the first team?' Ben asked.

'No,' Robert explained, 'you have a basic place for a year in the senior selection. You start in the second team and go along with the first team from time to time as a substitute, and in this way you yourself have to bring about both the extension of your contract as a permanent place with the first team. But the weekend after the end of the competition we first have a tournament in Germany. There I play with the A-juniors once more. Then I have two weeks vacation and at the end of July the training starts again already.'

When, after leaving *De Waag*, they walked through the village and via the park to their home, Nant took Ben's arm and looked full of pride at their four wonderful adult children who – busy talking to one another – walked ahead of them. She pressed herself closer to him: 'Hey… Van Zuiden, it is really something, when you look at it… a Jew from Elburg and a farmer from Oldebroek, and look at what came from that. That deserves a thanksgiving, doesn't it?'

Ben smiled at the original way in which she put into words exactly what he himself felt at that moment. 'My dear,' he answered, 'you are totally right and therefore we should do that now your way.' With a wide gesture he threw his hands high into the air and shouted at the top of his voice: 'Hallelujah…!'

Surprised, the children stopped their conversation and looked around. Sarah, the most level-headed of them all said: 'Hey papa, we do know that you love mamma, but you don't need to exaggerate!'

At home they opened another few bottles and the talks and discussions continued into the small hours.

Although Robert had pleasant relationships with various girls, none of them had led to a serious friendship. At the thought of a steady relationship he always recalled Deborah. For a long time he had wondered whether the memory of her had to do with love or with the special circumstance in which they had met one another that time. They were then at an age at which you did not yet think of going steady. However, the idea that by now she could have a steady boy-friend could sometimes oppress him, just like that, and immerse him in a feeling of melancholy and sentimentality. He realised more and more that, beside mutual physical attraction, it also had to do with the secret of the links from both their pasts. All in all, it increased his longing for her in such a way that one day he decided to contact her. He called the lawyers' office in Nijmegen and was connected with her mother. The reaction to his question whether he could speak with Deborah, was brief and rather business-like. Deborah was studying in America and it was not yet certain whether she would come home for vacation this summer. He should try again at the end of July… Then the connection was broken ruthlessly.

As the message sunk in that she was – for the time being anyway – unreachable for him, the desire to meet her again grew even stronger, and he noticed only now that she had never really been away from his subconscious. The fact that he could do nothing but wait, with in addition the fear that maybe she had long since forgotten him or had a boy-friend in the meantime, roused a vague uneasiness in him. Too bad he could not call again until the end of July. Because his work and especially his soccer career would occupy him more than ever in that period, he resolved now already to start calling a little earlier. And thus he started the closing of the competition and the preparation of the tournament in Germany with mixed feelings.

In the group of more than twenty boys with whom he trained every week, there were two who, from the start, had taken him under their wing in a natural way. They became an important sounding board for him, both on and off the field: Rob Nieuwenhuis from Harderwijk and Bert Konterman from Rouveen. They, too, had ended up with *FC Zwolle* in an identical manner at the time, and now they had been playing in the first team for a few years already. Both were endowed with – besides their soccer talent – a sober perspective of life that had a balancing effect on Robert. He built on their experience and took their advice seriously. For the imminent A-juniors' tournament in Germany – in which they themselves had participated several times in the past – they only had one important bit of advice: "Just take care that you make the final! For that is where the scouts from the really big clubs are and if you can make an impression anywhere, then it is there".

On a Thursday they left from Zwolle by tour bus to Berlin. The next day the qualifying rounds would be played; on Saturday the quarter- and semi-final and on Sunday the final.

After passing the German border, a vague feeling took possession of Robert. Strangely he realised only now that he was going to a country with which he really did not want to have anything to do with; a country that his family never mentioned. He was the first of his family to visit the land of the erstwhile enemy, on his way to honor and success. The fact that he would have to take on very disciplined opponents like *Werder Bremen* and *Bayern München* caused him a dejection that for now was hard to explain. During dinner and the evening with the group it remained in the background, but once he was lying in bed it came to the surface. The sound of the trains that thundered past the hotel, wailing sirens and other sounds that belong to a large city penetrated into his hotel room and kept him from sleeping. Peering at the ceiling he remembered Rob Nieuwenhuis and Bert Konterman and heard them say again how important it was to reach the final, because of the large public and – even more important – the scouts of the big clubs who would be present then. But imagine that there would be a "breakthrough" or "discovery…" would he be proud that it had occurred in Germany of all places? He heard his father tell them again during the dinner at *De Waag*, how the Germans had damaged and destroyed his opa's optimal enjoyment of the soccer sport. And he wondered what it would do to him when later on the field he would face one of the descendants of those who were responsible for that, and who, in addition, had murdered so many millions of his own people. Would it paralyse him or would it motivate him even more? He did not know but he hoped that neither the one nor the other would happen and that he would be able to concentrate completely on the game. His head full of disconnected images and thoughts he finally fell asleep.

An hour later Piet Abbringh, the team-leader with whom he shared the room, shook him awake from a bad dream. Silently they sat opposite each other – at the edge of the bed – staring ahead. Then Piet got up, fetched a glass of water and gave it to Robert.

'Well…?' he said after a while, 'are you alright again?'

Robert nodded without saying anything.

'Do you want to talk about it?' Piet wanted to know.

Slowly Robert lifted his head and looked into his team-leader's clear, steel-blue eyes that showed only compassion. As fragments of the nightmare still went through his head, he realised at the same time that he had especially good luck to share his room with this particular man. Piet knew both Elburg and Robert's family very well. He had come to live there just after the war and for many years he was a teacher at the local secondary school. Both his pedagogic and social qualities made him especially suitable for the function of team leader.

In his dream Robert had obviously said and shouted some things, but he realised that he did not have to explain the cause of those to Piet. Now that he asked, he felt indeed the urge to talk with him about it.

'Yes,' he said deliberately, 'I would like that some time. But I think that maybe now we should sleep, for I want to be fit for tomorrow.'

The next morning after breakfast they left with the bus to the stadium that was about ten minutes' drive away from the hotel.

The sixteen participating clubs were divided into four pools of which number one and two would proceed to the quarter final.

The ballot for *FC Zwolle* was not really favourable but even so they became second in their pool. They had better luck with the ballot for the quarter final. They won and then had to play the semi-final against *Steaua Boekarest*.

Gradually Robert felt an enormous tension build up inside. The final was now really close and he imagined what it would be like to reach it. In all the years that *FC Zwolle* had participated in the tournament, it had happened only twice before that they had reached the semi-final. The thought that he could contribute to his team becoming the first in history to reach the final, made him quite upset. However, as the time approached at which the game was going to start, he felt another, stronger feeling inside. A strange emotion that even forced the sportive importance to the background a bit. It was overshadowed, as it were, with an inexplicable sense of an imminent climax that would influence his whole life. He recalled images of his dream of that first night in the hotel and they made it clear to him that his attempts to gain insight into his fears and uncertainties would lead to results before long. Because of the relaxation this gave him, he started the game with extra concentration a while later.

Lately he had developed a strong tactical judgement. From his favourite position as attacking midfielder he caused surprising attacks time and again. His frustration was often that his fellow-players then did not always pick that up. Instead of participating in such an attack, they played the ball back, which caused the chances that he created to be lost.

The only one who did have the same attack attitude was his mate René who usually played in the position in front of him. Apart from their soccer qualities, there was the extra link between them – hidden from the outside world – of their similar Jewish background. Automatically that was partly responsible for the fact that they adapted themselves to one another more and more. They found each other blindly, just like the royal couple Luc Nilis and Marc Degreyse at *Anderlecht* during that time.

That duo was their great example. It always gave them a kick to see the spectacular actions and the "one-twos" of that famous couple. And as soon as a similar action of their own was successful, it did not matter at all which of the two scored ultimately, because they felt as if they had scored together. Through this two-in-one a trick had developed of its own accord, that they themselves called "scoring the Zwolle way".

Just half an hour into the first half of the semi-final suddenly an excellent opportunity for this presented itself. The pressure on *FC Zwolle* was great and it was a miracle that *Steaua Boekarest* had not yet used one of the many chances that they had created. Because of the big difference in power, the defenders of *Steaua* gradually played more to the front in order to decide the match as soon as possible. In the space that was thus created, the ball was played to Robert on the left and he saw René take off through the middle. 'Yesss... René... "the Zwolle way!" ' he shouted, as he passed the ball to him in the sprint and ran towards him. René's whole body language indicated that he was going to shoot the ball into the right corner, but with the sole of his foot he stopped it, so that Robert could easily shoot into the left corner. And thus *FC Zwolle* reached the intermission – in no proportion of mutual strengths – with a 1-0 lead.

The players of *Steaua Boekarest* clearly felt that they had been shown up by the underdog. They started the second half provoked and extra motivated and they won the match – quite appropriately – 3-1. Even though it was a pity that they had not reached the final, everyone at *FC Zwolle* was reasonably satisfied with the result achieved. That evening they went into town together, ending with the traditional visit to discotheque *Le Village*. Late at night they returned to the hotel, which caused most of them to barely make breakfast. Piet announced that the intention was that everyone should get their belongings and that they should leave their rooms tidy. They would leave around noon to attend the final that would start at 1 pm. After the match and the official closing of the tournament they could drive home straight away. Then he approached Robert and asked: 'What do you think of walking to the stadium together?' He looked at his watch and continued: 'that'll take about an hour, so if we leave in half an hour we'll have plenty of time.' Robert agreed and after having informed the trainer, they put their bags ready in the hall and left the hotel as planned.

The city was still slumbering in the pleasant repose of the Sunday morning. Piet seemed to know the way quite well. On a city map that he had taken from the hotel desk he pointed out to Robert how they could walk through the park behind the station to the stadium. Via narrow paths that wound alongside a brook they reached a wide avenue that ended at an enormous memorial column, called the *Victory column*. Around the foot of this column there were a dozen or so wide steps, on which here and there people sat to rest, enjoying the nice view. They also sat down on one of the steps and looked at the view for a while without speaking. Until then, they really had only talked about soccer… about the necessity to never be satisfied and always remain critical of yourself… about the attacking attitude of Robert and that he –because there was such a need for that – would certainly get a base place with the first team… that he had become more mature, had a more positive presence during games and knew how to leave his mark… however, now they both seemed to search – in the peace and quiet of the park – for the proper words to share for which they had really sat down there.

'Is it the first time that you are in Germany?' Piet started the conversation.

Robert nodded and kept looking ahead silently.

'And,' Piet tried to elicit a reaction, 'how did that work out?'

Feigning indifference Robert shrugged, thought for a moment and had to admit: 'Not too bad, really. They are no longer our enemies, are they? But on the other hand… they did destroy my opa's life. And by that they also damaged – partly – the life of my father and me.'

'And do you often dream about that?' Piet asked.

'Yes… quite often,' Robert confessed, 'and the crazy thing is that you are dealing with something that you did not even experience yourself. It is caused by a fear over which you have no control, because you don't know exactly where it comes from and how it came into existence.'

Piet thought about that. Then he looked at Robert and said resolutely: 'Listen, dear boy… deep in your heart you know very well where it comes from… and where it came into existence. And you have never – literally and figuratively – been so close to that place as you are now. Your vacation has started, so what is keeping you from getting on a train here and travelling to Poland. *Auschwitz* is the only place where your fear will get a name. For there it will become visible and tangible for you, so that you will possibly start to understand and – more importantly – will be able to find closure, at least partly.'

As he listened to Piet, Robert had gradually experienced a pleasant feeling of deliverance within himself. The words of his team leader had almost sounded prophetic. His strong advice engrossed him completely. He realised that it also joined up seamlessly with the words of his opa… "the sooner you know where it comes from, the sooner it will go away", as well as with those of the mysterious woman in the museum… "what has happened is not past, but determines the present and the future" and with those of the Surinam woman on the train… "nothing stands on its own, everything is connected: body and soul, intellect and feeling… past and present".

'Hmm… yes,' he said, inwardly convinced, realising that so many sayings of totally different people all pointed in the same direction. 'I think that is really not such a bad idea.'

And thus Robert van Zuiden – on that beautiful Sunday morning, in the centre of Berlin – made the decision to go back, as the first of his family since the war had ended, to the origin of the trauma of his grandfather and of the symptoms he himself experienced.

However, at that moment he could not guess that this trip would bring about a definite change of direction in his existence and would determine the rest of his life.

After the final and the festivities around the prize presentation the bus took them first past the station. Piet walked inside with Robert and lent him enough money for the next few days. When the ticket for a single fare from Berlin to Kraków had been bought, they said good-bye. Robert thanked Piet at length once more and promised – as soon as he was home again – to let him know how he had experienced the visit to *Auschwitz*.

After he had waved good-bye to his team, he searched for the nearest hotel and called home. At first Ben thought, when he picked up the phone, that enthusiasm about reaching the semi-final and scoring against *Steaua Boekarest* were the reason for his son calling home. But soon he understood that this was not the case.

'What I am actually calling about,' Robert said, 'is to tell you that I am not coming home today. For tomorrow morning I am taking the train to Kraków and then…to uh… to *Auschwitz*.'

For a while silence reigned. Ben didn't quite know what to do with the sudden emotions that this short and matter-of-fact announcement evoked in him. With some difficulty he tried to put the thoughts that flashed through his head in order. 'Yes…sorry,' he excused himself after a while, 'you are taking me by surprise and I really don't know what to say.'

'Papa,' said Robert, 'you don't have to say anything about it now. We'll talk when I get back. I'll call as soon as I know when I arrive in Amersfoort.'

'Make sure that you are back before Sunday in any case,' Ben insisted, 'for that is when my father celebrates his birthday. He put it off a week especially for you and for Leah, who comes back from Israel on Sunday.' Then he wished his son all the best for the emotional and exciting days that he was undoubtedly going to have.

That evening Robert went to bed early, after having had something to eat in the city. The next morning he bought a map of Poland in the station's bookshop, as well as a soccer magazine and a regional newspaper which had a comprehensive report of the tournament. Then he changed some money and ambled to "platform 2", where other people were waiting already. Next to him stood a handsome woman in her middle sixties with a girl of about fifteen, who – as he soon gathered – was her granddaughter. They spoke English with a pronounced American accent and judging by their appearance he wondered if they were Jewish and might have the same destination as he.

Only after the train had left the station – on the dot – at 9.04 did he notice how vast Berlin really was. From the center they rode for half an hour through residential quarters, between high office buildings and busy, large industrial areas. Only after the stop at station Berlin Ostbahnhof did the view became gradually more open and rural. As all this passed in front of his eyes, his thoughts were with the unexpected situation in which he found himself and for which he was totally unprepared. What would he find there and what kind of an effect would it have on him…?

'Good morning, tickets please!' he heard suddenly. He started from his thoughts and handed the conductor his travel documents. While the man examined them attentively, Robert looked at him carefully and felt a strange, sick feeling inside. There stood a German in uniform, checking whether he – a boy of Jewish extraction – had the right to be taken to *Auschwitz* by train.

'Thank you very much and have a good trip,' the man said kindly as he returned the papers to Robert.

After this incident Robert tried to distract himself and immersed himself in the German paper, specifically in the extensive report of the tournament. The play of *FC Zwolle* was described rather positively. In the part about the semi-final against *Steaua Boekarest* his name was even mentioned and the action of René and him that had led to the 1-0 lead was described as "surprising and original".

When around noon two customs officers entered his compartment to check the passports, he realised that they had already passed the German-Polish border. The train reduced speed and stopped at the station of Zary. On the map of Poland he looked where that place was and he tried to find *Auschwitz* at the same time. According to Piet it should be in the neighborhood of Kraków but Robert could not discover it anywhere.

In the compartment in front of him sat a man and a woman of about sixty. She was seated left of the corridor, he on the right. Meanwhile it had become clear to him that they had Polish nationality, but he could not assess the kind of relationship they had. On the one hand, the almost intimate manner in which they sometimes talked together gave the impression that they were a couple. On the other hand, that impression was denied by a cold distance between them. Their frequent long silences even bordered on indifference.

He considered which of the two he would approach with his question where exactly *Auschwitz* was and in the end he chose the woman. In his best German he accosted her, and she motioned him to sit beside her. She spread the map out on the table and underlined the place name Oświęcim, a bit west of Kraków. Robert looked at her without comprehension so she explained to him in broken German that the name of the concentration camp is different from the name of the city, and that therefore it was not mentioned on the map.

Back in his own place, he thought about that for quite a while. All concentration camps, also those outside of Germany, had – as far as he knew – the same name as the community in which they were located, except *Auschwitz*. Slowly, one letter at a time, he took in that name once more and was surprised by the figments of his own imagination. At first he thought that Oświęcim had maybe not sounded sufficiently "German" and that therefore it had simply been changed to *Auschwitz*. Still the suspicion remained that possibly there was more to it. His sense of language, combined with the knowledge how deeply the Germans used to despise his people – had essentially wanted to exterminate it completely – caused him to suppose that in a cryptic and cynical manner it was indicated that it would be a "*witz*" to think that one could get "*aus*". A word pun that could have emanated from the same sort of sick mind as the macabre slogan *Arbeit Macht Frei*. For those who asked what it meant were mockingly and with sadistic pleasure informed that there was only one way to get out of the camp: by way of the chimney!

As he gazed at the timeless landscape of small patches of forest alternating with endless, marshy plains with in the distance a dark ribbon of woods, a feeling of melancholy gradually took hold of him. He thought back to his great-grandparents. How they – because of increasing *pogroms* – fled their native country Poland. And how a pitiless enemy had taken them back many years later after all. Only those turned out to be safe who, having arrived in western Europe, had then also crossed the ocean to America.

Around two o'clock the train passed through the suburbs of Legnica. The city was defaced by neglected, grey residential blocks with a dish antenna on each weathered, wooden balcony. In shrill contrast a part had been given a bright, flashy color here and there. In between all the houses, farms, station- and industrial buildings there were hardly any new buildings to be seen. Practically everything was old and decrepit. Here and there a bare factory chimney rose up – far above everything -, as a silent witness of a disappointing economy and absent prosperity. From broken windows of deserted houses fluttered fragments of curtains and on a siding, just outside the station, completely rusted train carriages stood – as if they had grown into the grass and weeds – waiting to be turned into scrap some time.

When during a few kilometers – shortly after leaving the station of Legnica – the rhythm of the wheels on the rails sounded even louder than before through the compartment, he was reminded of his opa. He had been – when he was about as old as

Robert was now – on his way to the same destination. In a train coming from France and with only one intermediate stop: *Westerbork*. There they were overloaded, in spite of the instruction that was attached on signs to the outside of the carriages: "8 cows or 5 horses at the most". He couldn't stop himself thinking about the purpose of his trip and seeing the bleak, deserted landscape gradually gave him an oppressed feeling. At a certain moment he noticed that it came close to that same indefinable fear that so often accompanied his dreams. But now he experienced it for the first time in full consciousness. A wave of loneliness broke over him and he felt the cold sweat on his forehead.

The need for some distraction made him decide to look for the restaurant car. All tables were occupied, but when, holding his coffee and two sandwiches, he looked around again carefully he saw that a place became available in the back on the right. The woman he had seen with her granddaughter on the platform in Berlin got up. He walked over to them and asked if their places were free.

'Yeah, sure!' the woman pointed invitingly at the stool behind the high table that she had just left. 'Sit down.'

Robert saw that the girl was looking at him shyly and said: 'If you don't mind, I'd rather sit in your granddaughter's seat, because I prefer to travel forward instead of backwards.'

The woman smiled fleetingly and answered: 'That's a good attitude son, I recognize that. But believe me, dear, once you have my age, the only important thing left is to reach your goal and it doesn't matter one bit anymore whether you reach it backwards or forward.'

As she walked away from the table she turned casually to her granddaughter: 'Come on Debbie, get up for this handsome young man!'

Robert was startled when he heard the name. He looked at the girl who had stood up in the meantime and briefly put his hand on her shoulder: 'Thank you, Debbie. You have a beautiful name. I guess: officially it's Deborah, am I right?'

She nodded, blushing, greeted him timidly and quickly followed her grandmother.

Faster and in a completely different way than expected, Robert had been provided with a distraction. Contentedly he looked out. And although thick, dark rain clouds made the view even more sombre, he noticed a pleasant relief inside. And that, he knew only too well, had everything to do with that one name. It had reminded him of his "own" Debbie. Although – geographically – he became more distant from her all the time, inwardly he felt how he came – right now – closer to her than ever. Her image chased away the dark shadows in his head and he looked forward to contact her after his return from Poland. And he made up his mind that he would not let himself be brushed off so easily again but would want to have – if she were not in Holland – at least her telephone number.

After the pleasant turnabout in his mood he returned to his compartment an hour or so later. He took the soccer magazine from his bag, but after having read a few sentences his eyes grew heavy. For another moment he looked out and thought of the lines from the past that, besides his personal feelings, linked him to Deborah Hamburger from Nijmegen. And as he tried to imagine what she would look like – more than four years later – he fell asleep.

The crunching and squealing noise of the brakes and the mild jolt with which the train came to a stop, woke him up. Somewhat confused he looked outside and saw that they were in Gliwice. Vainly he tried to remember what he had dreamt about. On the platform the clock showed 16.45 and from the loudspeakers came an unintelligible, croaking voice.

He watched the arriving and departing passengers and – as had happened earlier that day – he was struck by the fact that most people – especially the women – were well dressed. It was in shrill contrast to the impoverished conditions of the country in which they lived. The same applied to the young people, who with their West-European clothes, make-up and hairdos seemed to want to indicate that they wanted to free themselves from that desperate state. But that this was accompanied with some despair could be read clearly in the tired eyes in their often grey faces. Slowly the train started to move again and just when he leaned back comfortably he heard behind him how the sliding door that gave access to his compartment slammed shut. In a reflex he turned his head around and saw a woman in the corridor who looked at him with friendly but penetrating eyes. She pointed at the seat opposite him and asked in English whether she could sit down there. Robert nodded. The obvious modesty with which she spoke felt familiar and she even seemed vaguely known to him. She looked like…like…He almost had it but not quite. Those eyes and that expression, her shape and the manner in which she rubbed her hands when she had sat down, he had seen that somewhere before. Thinking deeply, with wrinkled eyebrows, he looked at her pale face and was startled when she looked up from the book that she had meanwhile taken from her bag. With a reassuring smile she asked him whether he was on the way to Kraków.

'Uh… yes,' he said, still half in thought. But when he had told her what the final destination of this trip was, he saw that her face acquired a serious expression.

'But then you are better off getting out in Katowice,' she advised. 'That is the next station and from there you can reach it much faster than via Kraków.'

He pulled out the map and soon saw that she was right. In view of having to buy a train ticket there and having to find out at what time and from which platform the train to Oświęcim would leave, he asked her whether the railroad personnel spoke English or German. She seemed to think about that for a moment. Then she took a notebook out of her bag and wrote calmly in an uninterrupted rhythm: INFORMACJA-POCIĄG DO OŚWIĘCIMIA O KTÓREJ JEST GODZINIE, PERON-TOR.

She handed the note to Robert and while he looked at the text, he wondered whether she was someone who originated from an English-language country and spoke the Polish language perfectly, or whether she was Polish and spoke fluent and accent-free English. Just when he wanted to ask her that, she said, pointing at the note: 'Take that to the ticket counter for a ticket and for information about the time and platform of departure. The ticket will cost about five zloty.' To his surprise she gave him a ten zloty bill and said: 'Use that for paying your ticket and save the change carefully until you are in *Auschwitz* and throw it as a substitute entry fee in the glass bowl that is standing in the large hall at the entrance.'

Robert wanted to protest but sensed that it would be to no avail. Rather shyly he accepted the bill and put it together with the note in his breast pocket.

Meanwhile the train had reached the suburbs of Katowice. The woman bent forward confidentially and put her hand on Robert's arm.

'Listen,' she said, 'I know that you are not going to visit the camp as an average tourist, but that you have a special reason for it. When you are there you should concentrate very well on the things you hear and see. Don't allow any thoughts from your normal daily life, but look around carefully and…'

She fell silent for a moment, bringing Robert's attention to a peak, '… and listen especially well to "the old man" and to "the fourth woman", for they will play an important role in the final of your personal struggle. Don't be afraid. You won't be sorry, on the contrary. After you return to the heart of the fathers, the sadness about the past will soon die. *See! The winter is past; the rains are over and gone. Flowers appear on the earth.*'

Slowly the train entered the station. As Robert looked at her, moved by all that she had said, she added: 'One more thing. Make sure you know from which platform the train to Oświęcim leaves, OK?'

Somewhat taken aback he nodded. Then he got up, turned around and took his bag and jacket from the luggage rack above.

As the train came to a stop he thought about the correct words to say good-bye to his extra-ordinary fellow-traveller. He wanted to do so very sincerely but when he turned around, her place was empty and the seat looked as if no one had sat there at any time during the trip. Confused, he looked around where she could have gone to so quickly. He glanced into the next compartment, searched the platform and, still looking around carefully, entered the hall of the station building. But he could see her nowhere.

He took the note from his breast pocket, took it to the only one of the five windows that was open and went to stand at the end of the line. A sweet, mouldy smell hung heavily between the old damaged walls. Cleaning and maintenance seemed not to have been done for a long time. Everywhere there were pieces of paper, chewing gum, used train tickets and cigarette butts on the floor. Everything around him breathed an atmosphere of decline and neglect, in contrast to the ultra-modern, clearly structured layout and strict organisation of the station in Berlin.

The man behind the window looked at him with a dull gaze and without any kind of greeting, as Robert shoved the note and the ten zloty bill towards him. Without interest the clerk put the train ticket, a five zloty bill and some change in front of him and raised three fingers to indicate that the train was leaving from "platform 3". Via the tunnel Robert walked there and on the announcement board above the platform it said, indeed, that the train to Oświęcim would leave in a little less than half an hour – at 18.20.

After fifteen minutes an announcement in Polish was made via the loudspeakers, of which he did not understand anything, but which had as a result that everyone left the platform and walked via the tunnel to another platform. Five minutes later the announcement was repeated. Now he listened more closely and heard that the word Oświęcim occurred in it. The announcement board, however, remained unchanged. Having become a bit uncertain he looked around nervously. When a train entered the station and it became clear that it would stop at the platform opposite, he recalled the remark of the woman… "pay attention from which platform the train to Oświęcim leaves".

As fast as he could he ran through the tunnel to the train that was about to leave. 'Oświęcim?' he asked, panting, the last passenger that got in. The man nodded and quickly Robert jumped on the train too. Almost immediately the doors closed behind him.

In the compartment where he sat down there were diagonally opposite him – at the other side of the corridor – two girls of about eighteen. One of them looked with interest at the logo and text on his sports bag, whereupon she whispered something unintelligible to her friend. When she looked at him, he repeated, just to be sure: 'Oświęcim…?'

Reassured by her confirmation he looked outside where a drizzly rain came down on the dusky and dreary landscape. Noticeably less comfortable than what he had been used to until Katowice, the old, worn out carriage rattled and shook on the subsided and therefore irregularly spaced rails. The sound of the steel wheels on the spaces between the lengths of rails thundered continuously – without rhythm – through the empty space of the compartment. The faded red synthetic upholstery of the narrow hard seats was either blotched or destroyed or – just through wear and tear – ripped.

He stared at the empty seat in front of him and in his mind's eye again he saw the woman who had so suddenly disappeared. He wondered how she could already have known at that time that the train to Oświęcim would leave from another platform. Both at the window and on the announcement board something else had been announced. How could she have disappeared so suddenly anyway…? Had she sat there at all…? Had it not been a dream…? For now too he saw her there almost tangibly, when she was really not sitting there… What was it with these mysterious women in his life? This was already the third time that something like this happened to him. But the note that she had written for him was clear proof.

"Pay close attention to the fourth woman", he heard her say again. Four… the number four… Suddenly he saw it and he knew whom she resembled. The calm tone of her voice and the clear blue, almost transparent eyes were those of the woman in the Jewish Historical Museum in Amsterdam, but her figure and her graceful movements were those of the Surinam woman, that time in the train from Wezep to Harderwijk. Both women seemed to have been transformed, as it were, into the third. Pondering about the origin of this strange phenomenon and also about the question what all this would lead to, he was startled by the conductor who entered the compartment. With a loud slap the thin wooden door closed behind him. Bracing himself with his legs spread to keep his balance the conductor stoically punched the ticket that Robert handed him and gave it back without greeting or even looking at him. After that Robert was unable to pick up the thread of his musing again or to discover any pattern in all those words, sentences and images that went through his tired mind.

The train stopped for the third time. At the previous station no one had gotten off or on the train. However, now he saw a man – with a package under his arm – walk hurriedly to the side of a ghostly, dark station building. There he placed the package – probably nothing more than an empty bread tin – on the rear carrier of his bicycle and disappeared into the dark of the night. Up till now Poland held little attraction for Robert. But that it had at the same time something familiar must have to do – he thought – with the fact that for many generations his forefathers, who were shaped by the culture of this country, had lived there. Fragments of it would undoubtedly still be in his genes and could be the reason for that vague, elusive feeling of solidarity. But he would never feel at home here. The contrast with Holland was too great for that.

He felt the gaze of one of the girls fixed on him and looked at her. Rather shyly she tried to indicate to him that Oświęcim was the next station and also the final stop of the train. "Final station

Auschwitz", flashed through his mind and he was swamped by an unfathomably profound loneliness. Gradually an oppressing feeling of uncertainty took possession of him and he wondered desperately whether he had underestimated the effect that this place would have on him. "Don't be afraid", he heard again, "the old man and the fourth woman will play an important role in the final of your personal struggle". And suddenly he remembered that special moment when they were starting to play for a place in the final of the tournament. Strangely, there had suddenly been no question of the usual tension before such an important game. At that time and also after the lost semi-final, he had felt instinctively that it was not over yet and that – in some way – the true final for him was still ahead.

The sound of creaking steel sounded loud through the old compartment when the train passed some switches. The first lights of the city came into view and soon he noticed that Oświęcim was much larger than he had imagined. As he alighted he greeted the girls, who joined a group of young people on the platform. Walking from the station to a taxi stop, he suddenly discovered the nearby *Hotel Globe*. With the pleasant expectation of a shower, a warm meal and a good bed he reported – tired and dripping with rain – to the hotel lobby. However, it appeared that there was no room available at all and he was advised to try at the *Hotel Olimpijski*. That turned out to be at the edge of town, so that he took a taxi after all, which dropped him – fifteen minutes later – at the entrance.

Ahead of him was a large group of Jewish people, including many men with black coats and hats. They had just arrived by touring bus from Antwerp. It raised an anxious suspicion that here too – thanks to them – all would be full.

He joined the group and as unobtrusively as possible he shuffled past a few people now and then while they were busily talking to one another. Inside, there was a loud buzz of Flemish, Yiddish and German and soon he saw the reason why there was so little progress. At the desk there was only one woman who had to deal with the usual, time-consuming formalities of every guest, before a room key was handed out. When it was finally Robert's turn, he was pushed aside roughly by a large, black-clad man who caused some extra delay. With violent gestures he complained about the fact that there was no elevator, whereupon he was informed that this was rather usual for a hotel with only one story. Because his wife – due to a hip ailment – could not climb stairs, the man demanded a room at ground level, but that turned out to be unavailable. Still gesticulating, he then went looking for someone who would change rooms with him.

'Reservation?' the woman asked Robert.

He shook his head and looked at her imploringly. After he was informed curtly that all the rooms were taken, he walked away from the desk dejectedly.

In despair he pushed through the people to the corner of the lobby and sat down on one of the chairs that stood around a rectangular glass coffee table. Gradually the crowd diminished and the hum subsided. One after the other disappeared through the corridor or via the stairs to his or her room. The door opened and some twenty boys – busily talking – passed him. In view of their training suits with the word POLSKA on the back, he surmised they probably belonged to some national sports team. They sat down at a long table in the dining room behind him and almost immediately were served a hot meal in large bowls.

Robert felt tired and lonely. He could not remember having ever longed so much for a shower, a hot meal and a bed. Leaning forward, with his elbows on his knees he stared at the ground – racking his brain about what he could do now. He could ask the coach of the sports team whether maybe one of them had a room in which there was still a free bed. But if not, then… he was so preoccupied with this that he barely noticed that the door opened again and shortly afterwards a bag thudded to the ground in front of the desk.

'Reservation?' he heard in the background the woman with her monotonous voice ask for the umpteenth time.

'Yes,' it sounded resolutely through the meanwhile empty and quiet space, 'Hamburger, New York!'

It startled him from his thoughts and with half-open mouth and disbelieving eyes he looked at the woman who stood at the desk, filling out a form. Black curly hair hung, glistening with rain, to her shoulders and the collar of her jacket. For a moment he did not understand what was happening. As if in a trance he got up, feeling light-headed. With bated breath he walked towards the desk and waited till she was handed the key. She bent over, picked up her weekend-bag and put its strap on her shoulder with a languid movement. Slowly she took a few steps in his direction, meanwhile carefully tucking away her passport in a small bag that she wore around her neck. Then she lifted her head and looked straight into the eyes of… Robert van Zuiden! Taken by surprise by that unexpected confrontation she also was open-mouthed with pure amazement. Her arms fell as if paralysed to her sides, causing her heavy bag to slide off her shoulder and land with a dull thud on the ground. In that moment all sounds around them seemed to disappear completely into the background.

Robert saw how the girl that he had met for the first time four years earlier in Elburg had grown into a beautiful young woman. Her hair hung wet with rain around her tired face. Even though her body had become taller and had filled out, her long face was still exactly as he remembered it… That typical Jewish nose and her large, wonderfully brown eyes that stared at him in a daze.

'Debbie…?' he said with a voice that trembled with emotion.

She nodded slowly at which her mouth formed the well-known, somewhat impish smile. 'But…' she stammered, as they embraced, 'how did you get here… just at this very moment…?'

Robert felt her wet hair against his cheek and deeply inhaled its smell. He looked at her. 'That is a long story. I have been looking for a long time for something that I hope to find here. And this afternoon in the train I suddenly knew very certainly that

– besides looking for answers to important questions – I have also been looking for a long time for uh…' He smiled shyly and then continued: 'for you!'

'You don't say!' she said with surprise and embraced him again. 'And I have been looking for you,' she whispered, 'really!'

When Robert told her that he could not get a hotel room here because the hotel was completely booked, she said with determination. 'Wait… I'll organise that for you right away.'

For she recalled that at the time when she made the reservation only a double room had been available. She walked to the desk and explained the situation, at which the woman asked for Robert's passport with indifference and pushed a form towards him.

After having taken a shower, they took a taxi to a restaurant in the center of Oświęcim. In the back seat Debbie snuggled against Robert.

'I can still hardly believe this,' she murmured. 'The place where we met each other for the first time – that old synagogue in Elburg – that was already so special, those four drawings, the friendship of our grandfathers and… well, you and me. But this… I mean that both of us would make such a journey to such a crucial place at the same time without knowing that of one another! That can't be a coincidence, can it…?'

Robert put his arm around her and, deep in thought, caressed her arm. 'No,' he agreed finally, 'it certainly is no coincidence, but what it is then…?'

He mentioned that he had called once but that her mother had reacted rather coldly at that time.

'Oh…?' she said astonished, 'she never mentioned it.' She shook her head and continued with a cute smile: 'When I came home that evening from Elburg, she asked what it had been like. I told her that I had met a very nice boy, but when it became clear that your mother was not Jewish she said very severely: "Deborah, forget that boy; a paternal Jew can never be your *besherte*!" She is very conscientious and principled when it comes to that.

That was also the reason that she encouraged me to go and study in New York. Not so much because of the studies, for you can do those in Holland too, but because there I would have the best chance to meet a rich Jewish partner.'

'So now you have a problem,' Robert concluded.

'I have a problem?' she chuckled, 'come on, she has a problem!'

The taxi stopped in front of a bistro-like restaurant and the driver pointed out a nearby taxi-stop from where they could be taken back to the hotel later on.

The evening passed quickly. They told each other what had happened in their lives the past few years. And in between the sentences, emotions of amazement and delight about their miraculous reunion gushed continuously. Besides the fact that her grandfather had died here, Debbie's visit to *Auschwitz* was also part of a study tour. She was following a two-year course for history teacher at the *Columbia University*. The events and developments that had led to the eruption of the Second World War formed a substantial part of her final thesis.

From New York she had travelled via Amsterdam to Warsaw. There she had visited the remains of the infamous ghetto, as well as the *Jewish Historical Institute*, that holds extensive documentation about the eventful history of the Jewish population and about the uprising in the ghetto of 1943. From there she was going to take the train, first to *Auschwitz*, then to Kraków and finally to Berlin.

'In Berlin I am staying for a few days with a fellow-student,' she told him. 'We are going to visit a few important sites there and she wants to introduce me via her grandfather to someone who used to cooperate closely with Oskar Schindler. Depending on the information, such an interview could, of course, become a very authentic part of my thesis. On Sunday I'll go to my parents for a vacation in Portugal with them immediately afterwards.'

'Coming Sunday...?' Robert repeated pensively.

'Yes,' she answered, 'why...?'

'Well, you know,' he explained, 'Sunday afternoon my grandfather in Elburg is celebrating his birthday. And I am sure that if I would introduce you – the granddaughter of his best friend – to him as the woman of my life, that that would be the very best present I could give him. If need be, I can take you to Nijmegen that same evening.'

'It's a deal,' she said, 'I'll call you as soon as I know when I am leaving Berlin.'

Long past midnight they were the last to leave the restaurant. Walking to the taxi stand, they talked about their plans for the next few days, but both felt that the day that would dawn in a few short hours would make by far the greatest impression on them.

Silently they sat – huddled closely together – in the taxi on their way to the hotel. The rain had stopped and a full moon illuminated the quiet streets of Oświęcim. After a sombre, clouded period the sky above *Auschwitz* seemed to have cleared that evening. Not until they lay down in bed did they feel how tired they really were. Tenderly the soft moonlight shone into their room. Overwhelmed by what had happened to them that day, the grandchildren of Jacob van Zuiden and Sal Hamburger lay quietly thinking, only a few kilometres away from the empty huts of *Birkenau*. Robert leaned over slowly towards Debbie and kissed her. She stroked his hair. 'Hey, how about – before we go to that special place tomorrow – we promise each other now, that we… that we will stay together for ever?'

At that unique moment Robert felt something float away from him that had always oppressed and inhibited him. The unknown power that had held him captive in an unbreakable circle of fear and threat seemed finally to falter thanks to the strongest of powers… love! An indescribable feeling of relief and happiness went through him and made him look speechlessly into those beautiful questioning eyes of "his" Deborah.

With a smile he nodded at her: 'Oh yes, as far as I am concerned we'll stay together for ever. Only… I do think that in that case you have to be just as happy with me as I am with you.'

She thought about that for a moment, then looked past him through the window and said: 'Look behind you, please.'

Robert looked at the moon that from miles away – from somewhere in the endless universe – illuminated the darkness around him. With a questioning look he turned his head back to her, at which she declared: 'Robert van Zuiden, I love you… all the way to the moon and back!'

In spite of the long tiring day, Robert woke the next morning as usual at seven thirty. In a reflex he looked to his side and then turned around carefully. Leaning on his elbows he closely examined Debbie's face – again fully engrossed in the happiness that had befallen him. She lay still deep in sleep – breathing peacefully – on her right side, with her face towards him. Her mouth was closed and seemed to underline the words that it had spoken. He looked at her sensual lips that had given him a taste of her love. And again he saw how those lips – beautifully and honestly – had shaped the words that still sang like music in his head: "Robert van Zuiden, I love you… all the way to the moon and back".

Very carefully he stroked the clear, lightly tanned skin of her soft cheek. Languidly she opened her eyes, smiled and groaned softly: 'Hey, good morning.'

He kissed her: 'Now if you can do your utmost to wake up properly, I'll go and get us a nice breakfast in the meantime.'

'First a cuddle,' she said, 'otherwise I don't really wake up.'

When Robert entered the still rather quiet dining room, he was just in time, for by the time he had loaded his tray, a rather large number of guests had arrived, including the majority of the group from Antwerp.

'Well,' he announced when he re-entered their room, 'fortunately I was ahead of those hungry "people of Israel" from Belgium.'

They sat down at the table near the window from where they looked out on a large bus station on the other side of the road. Scheduled buses drove off and on in all directions.

'We could go by bus,' Debbie proposed. 'There has to be one that stops at the camp.'

Robert did not react. Absent-mindedly he stared outside. Clutching a spoon between thumb and index finger, he slowly stirred his coffee and his other hand – with the remains of a cheese roll – lay motionless on the table. Reflectively Debbie observed him for a while and then stroked his arm. 'Hey, what's eat'n you?' she asked.

With a sigh he looked at her. 'Don't you find it a weird feeling, now that the meaning of our life has doubled as it were, to go to a place where one and a half million innocent people had their life taken away. Didn't all those people also have loved ones and expectations for the future, just like we now?'

Debbie nodded agreement: 'Yes, of course, it is more than terrible when that is taken away from you just like that – and in such a brutal way. But the result of that for me personally is, that I – just because of it – experience my freedom very consciously and intensely. I realize very well that I belong to a generation that still experiences the psychological consequences of what our grandparents went through in the Second World War. At the same time, I want to prevent it causing a shadow to lie across the most precious possession that our generation has, that is to be able to live in freedom based on a Jewish identity.'

'But,' Robert wanted to know, 'aren't you afraid that it'll happen again? That from one day to the other you'll be declared outlawed and can be murdered just like that, just because you are Jewish? The Germans now have become decent people, compared to what they were. And Hitler – who came into power in a democratic way at the time – may be dead, thank God, but what is still very much alive in this world that is anti-semitism.'

He took a sip of coffee and ate the rest of his roll. Now it was Debbie – in her turn – who sat staring outside, deep in thought.

'I won't say that you are wrong,' she said deliberately a while later, 'but still I think that you let yourself be influenced too much by the events of one period in history. The political and economic circumstances that led to the Second World War and the Shoah are now absolutely out of the question. Through my studies I have been occupied with this for some time and I must say, the better I get to know the past, the better I understand what happened and the more realistic my hope for the future becomes. Only when you know what the circumstances and causes for a war have been, you are able to recognize wrong developments and to prevent a repeat. That is the interesting thing about history. You start to understand better why things happen as they do.'

'So,' he said, 'what you are really saying is: "What happened has not passed, but determines the present and the future".'

'Uh… yes,' she stammered surprised. 'Say that again.'

Slowly and clearly Robert repeated the remark that the woman in the museum had given him and in the same breath he quoted also the Surinam woman who had pointed out to him that nothing is separate and everything – including past and present – are linked.

He looked at Debbie's face that radiated a mix of surprise and amazement, and suddenly he recalled what the "third" mysterious woman in the train to Katowice had said: "The old man and the fourth woman will play an important role in the final of your personal struggle". With an inexplicable but nonetheless overwhelming certainty he was deeply convinced at that moment that "the fourth woman" could be no one but "she" who had definitely entered his life yesterday and who still sat watching him with amazement.

'Jeez, that's wonderful,' she said, 'where did you get that? I mean, who said that?'

'Oh,' Robert answered, 'that too is a long story. I'll tell you sometime soon, but now we really have to leave.'

She got up and took a map from her bag. 'I'm writing it down first. I still need a motto and a good title for my thesis. This quote is really too long for a title, but it is usable, because it says exactly what I want to demonstrate.'

'Oh,' Robert proposed laconically, 'I also know a shorter one, with the same meaning. Write down: "In remembering is the deliverance".'

It was quite difficult to explain to the ticket-clerk that they wanted to go to *Auschwitz* by bus. But eventually they walked with a ticket to the platform and boarded a bus to Kraków. The driver appeared quicker on the uptake and promised to warn them when they should get off.

'What is this?' Debbie asked. 'That man at the ticket office talked about a museum, but *Auschwitz* isn't a museum, is it?'

'Still, that is what they call it here, obviously,' Robert said, 'for I just saw a large sign at the side of the road saying MUSEUM AUSCHWITZ with an arrow at the bottom. Look, there is another one!'

'Really... where did they get that idea,' she reacted indignantly. 'For heaven's sake, what kind of cultural or aesthetic value can be found in the macabre remains of a concentration camp? A place that was Hell for one and a half million people you don't call a museum, do you!? As soon as I am home again I am going to send a letter about it to the Polish embassy.'

After ten minutes' drive through the center of Oświęcim the driver gave them a sign. They were the only passengers to get off and looked – after the bus drove in front of them further into town – to a part of the dark wall with barbed wire that surrounded the camp. They crossed the street and walked down the parking lot that was already rather full with touring cars, buses, cars and taxis. Here and there the drivers – smoking – stood talking together. As two groups of school children walked past with the usual noisiness, a sense of disillusionment assailed Robert. Where he had ended up now had nothing to do with the image of this place that he had created for himself. There was absolutely no question of a devout silence and forlornness that he had imagined at the site where people had been abused and killed in such a terrible manner. He was taken aback by the spontaneous association with the entrance of *Bobbejaanland,* the family recreation park where they used to go on a day trip for many years – as a tradition – with the family during the annual summer vacation in Belgium.

As they walked to the entrance they passed a "souvenir" stand and with a feeling of distaste he looked at the display of books, posters, slides, videos and postcards. But the notice: "For sale only here: The only official *Auschwitz*-information guide" forced him inside anyway. The conversations between clients and salesmen in this "shop" did not differ at all from those in the stands and stalls of the summer fairs in Putten. The guide contained maps of *Auschwitz* and *Birkenau.* With a recommended route and descriptions with photos of the "places of interest". With the thought that the information guide could possibly serve a purpose that day or maybe also later, he bought a copy of the Dutch-language version and walked out again, pondering about the question whether or not his grandfather would like to look at it.

With a downcast face and a touch of incomprehension, Debbie looked at the booklet that Robert had in his hand and without saying anything she walked to the entrance. She seemed tense and this had to do – he assumed – with the same mixed feelings that possessed him too. They entered the building that – as an entrance area – had been built in front of the camp proper. To the right was a cafeteria where the school children were enjoying chips and cola. In the melee some boys were tossing empty plastic bottles back and forth between each other and Robert was amazed that none of the leaders urged them to be a little quiet. Suddenly he discovered – in the middle of the hall – the rectangular glass container that the woman in the train to Katowice had mentioned. The bottom was covered with a thick layer of paper money and coins. He put his hand in the pocket of his jeans where he had kept the five zloty bill and the handful of change. Just as he wanted to take it from his pocket, he was startled by Debbie's loud voice. He looked back and saw her stand at the door that gave access to the area of the camp. She was engaged in a rather heated discussion with a man in uniform. Quickly he walked over.

'He says that we have to pay first before we are allowed in,' she said crossly.

The man turned to Robert and – pointing at the ticket windows behind him – explained again patiently that they had to buy an entry ticket first for just three zloty, before they could visit the camp with a group led by a Polish-, German-, or English-speaking guide. With the same ticket they could then go by bus to *Birkenau* and back later. Robert, contrary to Debbie, thought this was reasonable.

'Come on!' she cried, gesticulating excitedly, 'I don't want any guided tour from you. Let all those tourists and school kids pay just like they do at any museum or recreation park. I am coming just to remember my opa, who was murdered here. And you want me to pay for that…? What *a khutzpe…*!'

She walked away angry, whereupon Robert apologized to the man and asked him to come along with him for a moment. In the meantime he took the five zloty bill and the change from his pocket and having reached the glass container, he said: 'This is more than six zloty. If I put this in here now, could we then go in on our own, without a guide?' The man nodded in resignation. He watched as Robert threw the money into the container and then returned to the door again. Robert walked outside where Debbie – hands deep in the pockets of her jacket – stood staring ahead with a sad look. He stood beside her and cautiously put an arm around her shoulder.

Slowly she turned her head towards him. With moist eyes she looked at him and with a voice that had completely lost its fierceness she proposed: 'Shall we take a taxi to *Birkenau*? After all our grandfathers were there, and there is nothing for us here.'

'Come on,' Robert insisted, 'it is OK. I have talked with that man and we can go in. Not with a group, but just us, together, you and I.'

'You did not pay for it, did you?' she asked with something of a threat.

Robert shook his head and answered, scout's honor: 'No… really… I did not!'

Walking back he recalled the miraculous guidance of the woman in the train, who had anticipated this whole situation already and had solved this problem in advance. In spite of the riddle of the true identity of the three mysterious women, it was they – like extra help from "outside" – who had led him to the place where he was now. At the same time there was something that convinced him that they would bring him also closer to "the secret" of his opa. Here – in the hell of *Auschwitz* – he had managed to survive and in spite of that terrible experience, he still had – with help of his friend Mordecai – retained the certainty the Eternal One was concerned with his life. As in his mind's eye he saw the ray of light on the painting of *The White Crucifixion*, he heard his grandfather, during that particular evening walk on the walls of Elburg, say again: "All is *bashert*".

'Hey… what are you thinking of?' Debbie wanted to know.

Robert smiled reassuringly. 'Oh,' he reacted, 'of a lot of things at the same time.' He kissed her and concluded: 'But in the end of you… my *basherte*!'

In the meantime they had reached the end of the hall again. With a look of understanding at Robert the man opened the door and so Robertus van Zuiden en Deborah Hamburger walked down the path that led them to the *Auschwitz* camp that was wrapped in a sacred and deep silence.

Everything around them was clean and well-cared for. Nothing was left of the stench and the dirt, the noise and the tortures that had characterized this place for so many years. And yet they sensed – also because of that strange cold silence – the shadow of death and the spirit of cruelty hanging around them heavily.

Debbie sighed: 'This is really what you could call a "dead silence".'

They approached the infamous entrance arch with the text ARBEIT MACHT FREI. Although intellectually they knew that they could pass underneath without any danger, still an indefinable sense of evil and threat came over them. Robert stopped and stared at it mesmerized. Debbie, who had walked ahead a few steps, turned her head and walked back again.

'What is the matter?' she asked.

'Something is not right,' Robert determined.

She glanced at the arch and shrugged.

'Don't you see it?' he insisted and continued: 'The letter B is upside down…!'

'Hmm… yes,' she said, 'you are right. But apart from that one letter the rest is also nonsense. As if there were a glimmer of a chance that labor would give those poor people their freedom back. Only death made them free!'

In the information guide Robert read that the camp had been a Polish barracks complex. On both sides of the main paths there were long rows of identical high stone buildings that were called "blocks". In blocks 4, 5 and 6 exhibitions had been set up.

The interior was tidy and fittingly modest. On the walls of the various spaces hung enlarged photographs of shaven-headed men and women with empty eyes in sad faces, who were herded into the gas chambers; of children who were separated from their mothers, and of piles of burning corpses. There were also pictures of little boys that showed the bizarre results of the experiments of doctor Mengele.

Debbie and Robert said little. Deeply impressed by the horrible images, they walked past various display cases in which lay the remains of confiscated objects that the Russians had found at the time of the liberation of the camp. One was full of old suitcases on which names and addresses were hastily scrawled. In others there were prayer shawls, shaving brushes, protheses and shoes. Every object lay there as a silent witness of the life that had been taken from the erstwhile owner. And more than ever before Robert realised there – seeing all these personal possessions – that, as he had heard an old rabbi say once – not six million Jews had been murdered, but six million times a Jew was murdered.

In the next room that they entered a glass wall had been constructed along the full length, from half a meter above the floor to the ceiling. The enormous space behind it was completely filled with human hair, all sorts of colours mixed, here and there still plaited. During the war that was taken by train to factories in Germany to be made into yarn. A few examples of clothing that had been made of it were hanging on display in a show case.

Meanwhile Robert stood looking a bit further on at a large, oblong glass container that held part of the administration, reports and photographs of Mengele's practices which had been found. Mengele preferably worked with handicapped people and twins, whom he injected with poison and sterilised and whose skin or other body parts and sometimes even sexual organs he transplanted. Hundreds of people died at his hands and the few who survived would be severely disfigured for the rest of their lives. When Robert wanted to walk on again, he looked around and saw that Debbie was still standing in front of the display case with clothing. As if petrified she stared with a drawn face at a dark beige long pair of underpants. Such pants used to be made mainly for German soldiers. He walked over to her and gently stroked her back. She sighed deeply and slowly turned her face towards him.

With wide eyes in which only despair could be seen she stammered: 'It is so…so bizarre…!' Then she turned completely towards Robert and put her head on his shoulder. Failing words he continued to gently stroke her back. She looked at him and said with a voice that almost cracked both with anger and pure impotence: 'Where did they get the idea… warm underpants made of human hair…! Is it possible to despise and humiliate your fellow men more…?'

Robert put his arm around her. 'Come, let's go outside.'

'Yes, please,' she agreed. 'I really need some fresh air.'

Along the main path that ran past the blocks, groups of visitors were walking everywhere. Now they met someone who was crying softly, then again someone who put an arm comfortingly around someone's shoulder. The silence was strange and oppressive, in spite of the large number of people. Not even a bird was to be seen or heard. Obviously they knew instinctively that the atmosphere here was not suitable to fly, leave alone sing.

The square between block 10 and 11 was closed off by a high stone wall. As they walked towards it Robert read in the guide, that the camp prison used to be in block 11. Anyone who had received the death penalty because of an offence – however small – was put against the wall naked and executed. That was the reason why the windows of both buildings that looked onto the execution area were blacked out.

At the foot of the wall dozens of tealights were burning and the ground was covered with flowers. In spite of the fact that both here and in *Birkenau* most people had been killed in the gas chambers, this "death wall" seemed to have become a special memorial place, where survivors and relatives wanted to show their sadness about their dead loved ones.

A group with a female, German-speaking guide entered block 11 just before Robert and Debbie. They joined the group and heard that everything in this block was still in its original state. They walked past the offices, the arrest cells, the "courtroom" and the washrooms where the condemned people had to undress for their execution at the "death wall". The guide mentioned that the punishment system that was applied by the SS was clearly meant to destroy as many prisoners as possible. And that stealing of food, defecating during work time or working too slowly were reason enough to land a person in block 11.

They descended the stairs to the cellar, where it became apparent very soon what kind of horrors the comdemned people had to submit to, if they were not condemned to death. There was a vaulting horse on which prisoners were whipped, a pole on which they were hung by their hands that were tied behind their backs and also a portable gallows. Besides the normal cells there were special punishment cells. If they judged that for a certain infringement a shot in the neck was too mild a punishment, then such a person was locked in cell 18 until he died of hunger. Cell 20 was airtight and pitch dark so that most people slowly suffocated from lack of oxygen.

Clearly upset, the visitors followed the guide to a large space, at the back of the cellar and indicated with: cell 22. In the middle four stone containers had been constructed, 90 cm square and about one and a half meter high. The small space between the four walls was just large enough for four prisoners, who had to stand there, naked – jammed together – for three times 24 hours. They were not given any food or water, so that during that period in each container one or more people died. Only after the three times 24 hours the dead were taken out – together with those that were still alive.

Filled with horror and lost for words, Robert and Debbie looked at the stone containers. In their mind's eye they saw the emaciated, naked bodies with a corpse hanging in between. They heard the groaning in the hollow, chilly space and smelled the stench of urine, faeces and decomposition. Everything clashed with the respect that Jews have for the sanctity of life and also with the reverence with which they deal with their dead. This had nothing to do with punishment and not even with hatred any more. This was pure sadism in its most extreme, satanic form. The fact, that many German soldiers had participated so massively in it, frightened them. What they were seeing was what a person was capable of when the evil inside is no longer kept in check and can do what it wants unrestrained. Detached from the respect of life, people obviously can degenerate into something less than beasts.

Debbie held her hand in front of her mouth, closed her eyes and swallowed a few times. Then she looked at Robert and said disturbed: 'I've got to get out of here… I can't stand it any more…'

Once outside she took a deep breath and they walked back in silence. A bit further down Robert saw a girl sitting on the ground, with her back against the wall of block 10 and with her face in the direction of the execution place. He stopped, looked again carefully and then knew almost certainly that he had met her – with her grandmother – in the train.

'Debbie…?' he asked hesitatingly.

Surprised she looked up and smiled. The other Debbie turned back, when she heard her name, whereupon Robert introduced her to the girl.

'Grandma is over there,' she said, pointing at the "death wall".

Robert looked at the people that were standing near the wall. Slowly "grandma" came walking back to them. In her hand she held a handkerchief with which she carefully dried her cheeks. She kept looking at the ground and only when she was just a few steps away from them, she looked around, searching for her granddaughter. When she recognised Robert she looked at him silently, with an intensely sad expression. For a moment he did not know at all what to say or to do. Looking at the woman in whom down-to-earth self-assurance had completely changed into utter defeat, he spread his arms in pure impotence. As tears rolled down her cheeks, she walked towards him and put her head on his shoulder.

'I shouldn't have come,' she sobbed. 'They've killed them all… I'm the only one left…'

This intimate expression of solidarity with a woman, whose name he did not even know, made a deep impression on Robert. He sensed that it all had to do with the place where they stood and with the people to which they both belonged.

Debbie was also moved by the scene. Comfortingly, she held her namesake close and she resolved firmly once again to write a letter to the Polish embassy. The indescribable emotions that this place dislodged in people made it everything but a museum. They walked away together and Ruth – as the woman had introduced herself in the meantime – told them that they were staying in Kraków. Because Robert and Debbie were going there the next day also, they arranged to meet each other at noon near the statue on the large marketplace, in order to have lunch together. After saying goodbye Robert and Debbie turned into a side path towards the Dutch pavilion in block 21.

On large photo- and information panels a clearly-structured overview was given of the Jewish community in Holland up to and including the second World War. Debbie made a few notes for her thesis and Robert was struck by two things in particular. The first was the original sign that used to hang on the platform from which his grandfather had left with the text: "WESTERBORK-AUSCHWITZ – do not detach any carriages. The train must go back to Westerbork closed".

The second was a poem by Leo Vroman. Before they left the building he borrowed Debbie's pen and note block and copied it…

> *Let tonight the tales be told*
> *of how war ended long ago*
> *and if repeated hundredfold*
> *every time my tears will flow.*

The last area they visited was the gas chamber and the crematorium that were located together in one building outside the enclosure of the camp. It looked like a bunker and inside it was remarkably quiet. It was obvious that everyone was deeply aware that here the greatest respect possible was imperative. Only soft weeping and the whispering of comforting words filled the cavernous grey concrete space.

A sign mentioned that "only" 70.000 people had been killed here. Most of the total of one and a half million victims had been killed in the four gas chambers of the camp *Auschwitz II- Birkenau* that was located three kilometers away.

Robert and Debbie both felt how they were also overwhelmed by a very specific emotion. It was oppressive to stand there where countless times the Nazis had herded together and confined hundreds of naked, shaven people. In their minds they saw and experienced how those defenceless, innocent people slowly suffocated within 15 to 20 minutes due to the Zyklon B gas that flowed from the showerheads in the ceiling.

In a daze they walked to the incineration ovens into which the dead bodies were then pushed by other prisoners. And here too they could not deal with their emotions. They knew from stories and books that this had really happened, but to see with their own eyes the original ovens that were especially designed to incinerate tens of thousands of people, caused them to shiver to the depth of their souls. Only now did they realize that it would be impossible from a survivor of this Hell to ever be able to lead a normal life, when for weeks or even months at a time you had nothing else to do than to incinerate gassed fellow sufferers.

Robert stared at the flowers and the tealights around the ovens and felt light-headed. Inside, something seemed to have burst open and he was confronted with so many thoughts and images that he became dizzy. Everything ran together… He saw his opa – as a boy of his own age – take corpses to the crematorium day after day and he felt the unbearable emotion that Jacob must have felt when he carried his sister Esther and also his friend Sal… The face of the innocently dying Jesus on the painting of Chagall intruded upon him and voices of mysterious women sounded through the ray of light behind the cross… he was still preoccupied with all this when– without paying attention to Debbie – he walked outside, deep in thought… "However dark your life may be, the Eternal One is there"… "Fear always has a cause. Don't push it away and don't close yourself for it, but seek it out, for in remembering lies the deliverance"…"The sooner you know where it comes from, the sooner it will be gone"…

In the meantime he had sat down – a bit away from the building – on a tree trunk. He gazed at the clouds floating past, high above the now superfluous wall with barbed wire and the unmanned watch towers that stood there without purpose. After some time had passed he gradually felt calm and balance return. Just when he realised that he had left Debbie alone in that macabre space, he felt a hand caress his hair. She sat down next to him, put her arm around his waist and her head on his shoulder. He inhaled her scent deeply and cherished the softness and warmth of her body. "Listen carefully to the old man and to the fourth woman", mild words sounded inside him, "after you return to the heart of the fathers the sadness of the past shall soon die. See! *The winter is past; the rains are over and gone. Flowers appear on the earth*".

With the images from that destructive ghostly place still on her retina, Debbie stared quietly at the rose that lay on her lap.

"That is for opa Hamburger", she had said to Robert when she bought it in the stall outside the camp. He then told her how and where his opa had found his friend Sal and had carried him from there to the crematorium.

Robert was quiet too and broodingly he looked out of the window of the bus with which they left the city on their way to *Birkenau*.

When a little later they walked towards the infamous "gateway of death", both of them were more and more aware of the realization that they were now walking on the soil where their family members had experienced such a terrible time and unmentionable misery. Debbie looked at the rusty rails on which the trains used to enter – through the gate – the vast camp.

When they arrived in the main watch tower above the gate, they looked out across the desolate plain that was surrounded by concrete posts with barbed wire and wooden watch towers. Most of the hundreds of huts had disappeared. Of some only the red brick chimney was still standing. As dilapidated gravestones – full of unwritten names – they seemed to honour with difficulty the memory of all those innocent people. Straight below them they saw the train rails that went into the camp for a kilometer or more.

Halfway down was the long concrete platform. On arrival at that place old people, sick people, pregnant women and children were sent straightaway to the gas chambers by the Nazis. Those who were still capable of working ended up in the concentration camp. They had to work under atrocious circumstances or had to come along with Mengele for "research".

'Look,' said Robert, after he had studied the information and the map in the guide, 'there, at the back to the right was the sick bay. Shall we go there first?'

Debbie nodded, and they descended the stairs of the main watch tower again.

Silently they walked along the railway to the ruins of the four gas chambers and crematoria at the very back of the camp; two on the left and two on the right side. Immediately before the liberation by the Russians the Germans had blown them up in order to destroy the proof of their atrocities.

As they walked from one corner to the other, they stopped at the large international monument. Then Debbie turned towards the right and asked, pointing ahead: 'So opa died somewhere there?'

'Yes,' Robert assented, and he put his arm around her shoulders. Slowly he turned her towards him again, looked at her full of sympathy and continued: 'And there they scattered his ashes.' He pointed at the pond in the distance. With a mix of both aversion and respect, they walked there together. Filled with dismay, they stared at the grey, murky water. With reverence and a lump in his throat Robert listened to the Hebrew words that Debbie murmured softly… *"Al ele we'al ele anie bochiya"* – "for him and the others I weep". They were the words from the bible book Lamentations that are read on *Tisha Be'aw*, the mourning day of the Jewish year. She took a few steps forward and remained standing motionless for a while at the edge of the pond. There she knelt, took the rose by the end of the stem and put it – as far as she could reach – carefully on the surface of the water. She bent her head and Robert saw from the softly shaking movements that she cried.

In the meantime the cloud cover had increased and some long gusts of wind chased across the vast plain. The already gruesome surroundings became even drearier.

Debbie wiped away her tears with the back of her hand and clung tightly to Robert's waist.

'It's not only to do with my opa,' she explained, as they walked back again along the railroad. 'I never knew the man. It is above all the madness through which this crime – maybe the largest and worst in history – could have taken place. It is unimaginable that someone develops such an idea and that there are then so many that execute it. All those innocent people… and all those thousands upon thousands of defenceless children. And why…?' She shook her head dejectedly and after a deep sigh she asked with an intensely tired voice: 'Hey, shall we go? I really have seen enough!'

Robert would really have liked to enter one of the huts, but because of Debbie's state of mind he agreed with her wish. Although he also had to admit that he was more than full of all the impressions, he had a vague feeling that something was still missing. Something was floating through his mind… a vague, elusive expectation of something that had to do with the words of the three women.

He was startled when Debbie suddenly stopped and – listening very carefully – tilted her head a bit.

'What is it?' he asked surprised.

'Don't you hear it…?' she said.

Robert looked back at a row of huts. Dark shadows flitted across the long buildings. Now he also heard very far away – carried by the wind – the thin, sad and rather out of tune sound of a violin. Resolutely he walked back and after a few steps he turned right onto the sandy path that ran past the huts. Astonished at that sudden resoluteness – which she noted for the first time in

Robert that day – Debbie followed him. It struck her that as the sound grew closer he quickened his step.

'Hey, what's the matter?' she asked.

'I don't know,' Robert snapped. 'I only know that I have to go there!'

The large wooden door of the last hut was ajar and a few people just came out. Inside it was rather dark. Here and there a few visitors shuffled past the wide wooden plank beds that stood three-tiered along both walls. In the middle – along the full length of the hut – there was a square stone wall of about fifty by fifty centimeters. The long row of round holes at the top clearly inferred that this had served as toilet for hundreds of prisoners. The only heating in the hut was by means of a stove with a stone chimney and a flue that went from there throughout the entire space.

Although a minute earlier he had wanted to look at the inside of such a hut – a picture of which he had seen in the information guide – now Robert seemed to be barely interested. Almost in a trance he walked to the other side where the creaking, sometimes false sounds of the violin came from. Debbie followed him at some distance and she suddenly recognized the melody. It was the *Song of Deliverance* that told about the expectation of the Messiah. She knew that it was exactly at this place that it was sung by all the prisoners or hummed as a *nigun*, just before they were herded into the gas chambers.

In the meantime Robert had reached the violin player. Wide-eyed and strangely moved he stood looking at him. And at that moment he knew with absolute certainty that he had reached the destination and purpose of his journey. After the meeting with the "fourth woman", this had to be "the old man" he was facing now.

Slowly the man – who sat in a wheelchair – lifted his head and looked at Robert with a tired but piercing look. Then the weathered face with heavy eyebrows and wrinkled eyelids folded itself into something like a smile. He put his violin and bow by his side on the wall and extended a trembling hand: 'I knew that someone would come today... and so it is you... son of my brother Jacob.'

'Mordecai...?' Robert asked hesitantly, as he carefully took the extended hand. The old man nodded whereupon Robert sat down next to him on the wall. A very extra-ordinary, astonishing feeling flowed through him. He mentioned that he was not the son but the grandson of Jacob van Zuiden. It barely seemed to register with Mordecai. He only saw the young man that was the spitting image of the friend whom he had last seen more than fifty years ago. Even when Robert introduced Debbie to him, he kept staring closely at the face of the "son of my brother Jacob".

Finally a deep sigh seemed to lift him out of the memories. Slowly he turned his gaze away from Robert and looked at Debbie.

'This is my friend,' Robert repeated and added this time: 'And my future wife; Deborah Hamburger... granddaughter of Sal.'

Debbie came closer, shook his hand and sat down next to Robert. Mordecai turned his wheelchair towards them and looked at her attentively.

'Sal...? Jacob's friend...?' he asked with disbelief in his cracked voice. Both nodded and they saw how tears of emotion rolled down the weathered, wrinkled cheeks of "the old man". A few times he looked from one to the other and then spoke with holy amazement: 'Praised be to the Eternal One who sees justice done to those who love Him.'

In the silence that followed they let the meaning of those words penetrate deeply. Debbie was the first who broke the silence.

'Do you come here often?' she asked.

'Yes,' Mordecai confirmed, 'regularly. Only lately no longer for I am sick and I feel my end approaching.'

She looked into the tired, sunken eyes in the sallow face. Cautiously she asked: 'Does it help you to deal with what the Nazis did to you and all those others?'

For a few moments he looked at her silently. The question seemed to affect him. Then he gazed around the semi-dark, grey space and moved his head up and down a few times. 'Yes,' he confided. 'but essentially it was not the Nazis who did this to us. They only carried out what the devil himself told them to do. It was his destructive voice that sounded from their mouths and his sadistic look that radiated from their eyes.' He looked around once more and concluded: 'Oh yes, it was his continuous fearful presence that made this place a hell.'

Robert noticed that the meeting with this remarkable man engrossed his attention completely. Hesitantly he asked: 'You said that you knew that I would come today, but… how did you know that…?'

Again it seemed as if this question did not really penetrate to Mordecai. Absentmindedly he stared ahead. In the end he slowly turned to Robert and told him: 'Yesterday evening I was lying in bed thinking about my disease that prevents me from playing the violin properly any more. I feel and know how it should be, but my muscles no longer have the strength to carry it out. I thought about the time here in the camp when we, together with Jacob and Brammie, performed for the Germans. And when I fell asleep I dreamt of a party at which Jacob was the focal point. It was a peaceful scene. A lawn with behind it a row old, high trees and Jacob was standing there – very quietly – intensely enjoying his children and grandchildren. I wanted so badly to play the *Song of Deliverance* for him, but I couldn't. They all stood looking at me very strangely because of the creaking, false tones. And then suddenly my son, for whom I have been looking all my life, appeared. He walked towards me. I gave him the violin and he played so wonderfully… so purely, that everyone fell silent. At that moment I woke up with the strong urge to go back just once more to the camp. It was the first time that I had dreamt about Joshua and secretly I hoped it would be him that I would meet here.'

He took the old case that stood against the wheel of his wheelchair, put the violin and bow inside and closed it. His trembling hand lay resignedly on the case as he looked at Robert and asked him: 'Is there maybe anyone of Jacob's children that plays the violin?'

Robert nodded in surprise: 'Yes,' he said, 'aunt Leah.'

Mordecai caressed the lid of the case. 'I had hoped to be able to give it to my son,' he confessed, 'but this way is also fine.' He handed the case to Robert, looked at him with piercing eyes and asked him: 'So would you give this to the daughter of my good friend Jacob?'

Deeply impressed and unable to utter a word Robert accepted the case.

Debbie, who also was quite moved by everything that was happening, bent towards Mordecai, put her hand on his and asked: 'Was uh… or is Joshua your only child?'

He nodded and told them how he had managed to prevent Joshua being landed in the camp as a baby, but that all attempts to find him after the war had come to nothing. 'If he is still alive… then he is the only family member that I still have,' he said. 'The others have all been murdered here… all.'

A few steps away from them stood a middle-aged woman, patiently waiting for quite some time already. When Mordecai had finished speaking, she walked slowly towards them. A bit shyly she greeted Robert and Debbie and put her hands on Mordecai's shoulders with care.

'We really have to go now,' she said softly, 'for it is getting much too late for you.'

Mordecai nodded and caressed her hand. 'This is Zanna,' he explained. 'Zanna means "God's gift of grace" and that is what she is to me. She is a daughter of the baker in Bochnia where I have always worked and she takes care of me like an angel.'

With a modest smile Zanna wanted to pull the wheelchair backwards, but Mordecai motioned her to wait a moment. With his one hand he took Robert's hand and with the other Debbie's.

'Greet my dear friend Jacob,' he said, 'and be blessed, children. Be guided on your path through life by the Torah and wait for each other if one of you lags behind. Pass on what has happened here to the generations before you, so that it will not happen again. Be happy that you belong to the fourth generation after the Shoah. Four is the middle; the turning point in the perfect row of seven. From that point on the sadness of the past shall change into hope for the future, as it is written: *See! The winter is past; the rains are over and gone. Flowers appear on the earth!*

A cold shiver ran through Robert when he heard from the mouth of Mordecai the echo of the words that the "woman on the train" had also quoted. In addition he also finally understood why the "woman in the museum" had enjoined him to pay attention to "the number four". The explanation of Mordecai seemed like a liberating revelation of a mysterious secret. It was as if in his mind the last fog had lifted, so that finally the entire landscape became clear and recognisable to him. It made him listen with even more respect and awe to this remarkable man…

'The arrival of the Messiah is near,' Mordecai continued. 'I'm getting more and more convinced that it won't be long any more. Pray that he will come soon, for then, children… then there will finally be peace on earth, as it is written. *Many peoples will come and say: Come, let us go up to the mountain of the LORD, to the house of the God of Jacob. He will teach us his ways, so that we may walk in his paths. The law will go out from Zion, the word of the LORD from Jerusalem. He will judge between the nations and will settle disputes for many peoples. They will beat their swords into plowshares and their spears into pruning hooks. Nation will not take up sword against nation, nor will they train for war anymore.*'

He fell silent for a moment. Then he released their hands and spread his own with difficulty – trembling with effort – above their heads. The Hebrew words that Mordecai spoke at this memorable place would become, for Robert van Zuiden and Deborah Hamburger, the ultimate confirmation of the unique bond for the rest of their lives. In holy awe they let the age-old blessing penetrate into the depth of their souls… *The LORD bless thee, and keep thee: The LORD make his face shine upon thee, and be gracious unto thee: The LORD lift up his countenance upon thee, and give thee peace.*

Silently they watched how Zanna pushed the wheelchair through the hut and how they disappeared from sight through the half-open door.

Robert stared at the old violin case that lay on his lap. As he wondered what this gift would mean to his opa, he felt how Debbie put her arm around his waist and laid her head on his shoulder.

'My, my, what a day, isn't it!' she sighed.

Together they walked in silence to the exit of the hut. Robert's head was full of images of the strange ways by which he had finally ended up in this place. It all occupied him so much, that he did not even notice that Debbie had walked away from him. Only when she called his name, did he start from his thoughts and looked around. She beckoned to him and said in a tone of voice in which both tension and enthusiasm could be heard: 'Hey, come have a look!'

She stood near one of the plank beds that were fastened to the wall of the hut. He walked over and looked at her questioningly. She took him by the shoulder, pushed him carefully forward a bit and pointed at the narrow gap in the wooden wall. Still in a daze about all that had happened that day, he peered through it. Suddenly he understood Debbie's excitement. What he saw was a high brick chimney in front of which a hut and a bush, exactly as depicted on the four drawings in the synagogue of Elburg!

Early the next morning they left with the bus from Oświęcim to Kraków. Tired out from all the impressions made by the visit and with a niggling headache, Debbie had gone to bed the night before almost immediately after dinner. Robert had gone down to have a drink, and before going to bed he had first tried to write down his feelings. After an hour or so he was happy with the result and he had copied it – on a new sheet of paper in nice, even handwriting – for Debbie.

Lost in thought Debbie looked out the window of the bus and let the streets and buildings of Oświęcim pass before her eyes. The ample night's rest had revived her. The tiredness had gone and she did not have a headache any more. In addition she felt how the tension, which the images and emotions of the previous day had roused in her, had diminished. For the first time she could look back on it with more equanimity and she even managed to place it partly in the perspective of her theoretical knowledge.

Robert's gaze went from the violin case that lay on his sports bag next to him in the aisle to Debbie. He recalled Mordecai's instruction to wait for one another, should one of them lag behind. The plait in which Debbie's thick hair had been tied together and the long peak of her baseball cap accentuated the characteristic shape of her face. Her length, her figure and aura, her character and background, it all could not be better and more beautiful, he thought. And just like the previous evening when he was writing the poem for her, an intense feeling of gratitude flowed through him. There was also an inner peace and a deep conviction that his fears and nightmares would decrease – as a result of the "law of the number four", as Mordecai had explained – and would disappear completely for the rest of his life in the end.

'Hey, Hamburger,' he said, 'what are you thinking of?'

'What…? Oh…I was thinking of that bush that we saw yesterday through that crack in the wall,' she answered. 'And that we were probably standing there on the same spot as the person who made those four drawings. I was thinking that the person must have found courage in that. I mean… he must have looked at it in the fall and the winter and seen it come into flower again in the spring and the summer; that must have been an encouragement to not give up.'

'Anyway, I am very curious about Kraków,' she said, changing the subject. 'It is supposed to be a really beautiful city. I recently read that the old centre is on the World Heritage List of Unesco as one of the twelve most valuable cultural monuments in the world. It is a miracle that all those beautiful old buildings did not get damaged in the war.

After about an hour they entered the city. When they had alighted, they walked to the station hall, where they stored their bags and the violin case in a locker. Then they walked along the Wisla river and via the beautifully landscaped *Planty* – the green belt – to the centre of the town. On the *Rynek Glówny*, the immense central square, it was lively and busy. Because of the fact that Kraków is the oldest and largest university city of Poland, they saw many people of their own age. They sat down at one of the many pavement cafés. Debbie looked around: 'I am going to buy a city map at that bookstall. Can you order a cappuccino for me?'

Robert's look that followed her was full of love as he gazed across the sunny square. For the first time he felt really at ease in Poland. This atmosphere, amidst all those beautiful old buildings that obviously attracted so many different people, rose far beyond the poverty of the neglected countryside.

Between the cathedral-like church, the gothic-style mansions and the famous, hundred meter long cloth hall the pavement cafés were full of mainly students and tourists. In the middle of the square there was a large statue around which children were feeding the pigeons. All kinds of people sauntered at leisure between the colorful stalls with flowers, fruits and souvenirs. Everything he saw and felt was in harmony with the rest, and when in this beautiful peaceful décor Debbie came walking towards him again, he was overwhelmed by an intense feeling of contentment and happiness.

Again he had to think of that particular moment, just before the game for a place in the final of the tournament. How – very strangely – the tension had suddenly flowed out of him, because something indefinable had made clear to him, that there was going to be another, much more important final. Now he knew for sure that not the tournament in Berlin, but the meeting with both "the old man" and "the fourth woman" had been the true destination of his voyage. He - as the child of the fourth generation - had been allowed to leave the past behind with Mordecai at the place where it all happened, and in Debbie he had been given at the same time the ultimate purpose for a new beginning. A scene that he would never have dared to imagine beforehand. "Everything is *bashert*" he heard again. It reminded him of his poem that was inspired by it and for which he still had to find a title. "*Bashert*" was possible, but it was too yiddish for a Dutch text. "Pre-ordained" then, he thought, or uh… "Destination"… Yes, that was right.

He started from his thoughts because Debbie put her hand on his knee.

'Hey, are you alright?' she asked.

With a broad grin he looked at her and said: 'Deborah Hamburger, woman of my youth and woman of my life, I could not be any better!' he kissed her and continued: 'Those are not my own words. That is what my father always says to my mother and he in turn got it from his father.'

Silently Debbie looked across the peaceful square, drinking her cappuccino.

'It is impossible to imagine, isn't it,' she argued, 'that from here seventy thousand people were taken to the camps. That was at that time maybe more than the total population of Nijmegen and Putten together. Se-ven-ty-thousand people, whose right to live was taken away just like that, simply and solely because they were Jewish. What could that be? I mean…what, do you think, is essentially the cause of anti-semitism?'

'My father is convinced that it is jealousy,' Robert declared, 'but according to my mother it is the devil.' He smiled and told her about the spontaneous simplicity with which Nant often approached complicated issues. 'The reason that it is the devil - according to her - is that from the beginning that bastard has wanted to destroy everything that belongs to God.'

'In fact it is the same as what Mordecai said,' Debbie observed.

'Exactly!' Robert said, 'and therefore it can happen again just like that. You may say that the circumstances of those times have changed but the real enemy has not changed. Racism and hatred of foreigners still exist in this world.'

'OK,' Debbie admitted, 'but look at how long we have been living in peace already in our modern western world. We and our parents have never experienced a war ourselves and that is partly due to the fact that people were frightened by *Auschwitz* and became more alert after the Shoah. Nations have united more and more since then and the longer you work together, the smaller the chance of war becomes.'

Robert let it sink in for a moment. He ordered another two cappuccinos and observed: 'You are really an optimist, aren't you?'

'Yes!' she said very convinced, 'and you'd better take into account that this will only get worse now that I am in love! In any case,' she continued, 'you still owe me an explanation about your trip here and also about those two quotes of yesterday morning.'

Robert told her of the meetings with the three mysterious women, how after their first meeting in the synagogue of Elburg his soccer- and social career had taken off and why he was advised by Piet in Berlin to go to *Auschwitz*. 'And,' he said finally, 'do you understand how – after all – I can only conclude that all this must have been "guidance from above?" '

For a moment Debbie looked ahead quietly. Then she nodded slowly and said, clearly impressed: 'Wow, how special… what a story! I already thought it was miraculous how our relationship came about, but this is really very remarkable.'

'You know,' Robert confided, 'for me it is an enormous relief that I have put an end to something right here in Poland – the country of my forefathers – and that at the same time I found a new purpose in you.'

'So,' Debbie asked with a slight hesitation, 'when you said yesterday to Mordecai that I was your future wife, you really meant it…?'

'Yes, of course!' Robert insisted, 'it is abundantly clear that we are meant for one another!'

'Now, come on then,' she called, as she jumped up, laughing happily, 'let's go and buy rings right away!'

After having settled the bill they crossed the square and walked in the direction of the cloth hall. In front of the colossal main building a large arched gallery – in gothic style – was built along its full length. There a multitude of stalls with flowers, art objects, jewellery and souvenirs. A large sign pointed towards the entrance of the National Museum in the main building, where an exposition of 18th and 19th century painting had been put up. A bit further along there was a similar sign in front of a travel agency on which – under the heading SIGHTSEEING – the following offers were mentioned: a boat trip along the Dunajec river, a coach tour to the salt mine in Wieliczka and another one to the *Museum Auschwitz-Birkenau*.

Debbie walked to the desk and asked the man whether he was the owner. 'Yes madam,' the men answered enthusiastically, in the supposition to be able to sell a trip for two.

'What can I do for you?'

Curtly she indicated that he should follow her and when they stood together in front of the advertising sign, she pointed fiercely at the last offer and snarled at him: 'This-is-not-a-museum, you idiot!'

The man became angry and Robert had to do his best to calm them down, which he managed with a lot of effort.

Silently they walked on and Robert saw how Debbie's tight-set facial expression gradually relaxed when she stopped in front of a jewellery stall. It made his head swim; literally every square centimeter was full of rings, chains, earrings, pendants, etc.

'Don't you like this one?' she said enthusiastically, and continued without waiting for his reaction: 'I think this is amber.' She held up the chain with the oval orange stone. 'Is this amber?' she asked the woman who stood squeezed tightly in the midst of her livelihood. The woman nodded. 'Yes, you see!' Debbie reacted.

'That's what I thought. Nice isn't it? Or do you like a round stone better? This one, for instance.' She held up a chain with a similar stone, but round in shape this time. She looked at him inquisitively.

'I think the first one is much nicer,' Robert remarked.

'Really?' she asked, 'but round is nice too, isn't it?' she stood in front of the mirror, compared them carefully once more but then put both of them back. Then she walked on.

'Hey, hello!' Robert called, utterly surprised, 'you liked them, didn't you? Why don't you buy one?'

'Let's look over there first,' she proposed, as she walked to the stall on the opposite side. 'Ooh… come quickly,' she called over her shoulder to Robert, 'here they are also in green. That is nice too… green.' Again she held one up and asked: 'Or do you like orange better…?'

'Sweetheart,' Robert sighed, 'we were going to buy rings, weren't we?' He looked demonstratively at his watch: 'If that is going to take as long as that chain, we'll never make the meeting with Ruth at noon and then we should be happy if we manage to catch the train tonight.'

Because this did not seem to impress Debbie very much, he insisted: 'Listen! Tell me now which one you like best, then you get that from me as a souvenir of this trip and then we can go look for rings.'

'I think uh… this one,' she said. 'Yes, I like the green better, the colour is deeper than that orange, don't you think so?'

'Yes,' Robert assured, 'much deeper!' and he paid quickly.

As they walked away from the stall she kissed him spontaneously on the cheek: 'Hey, many thanks. That was sweet of you… And I am really very happy with it!'

'Well, so much the better,' said Robert, 'only, now we are still facing the second half; I hope that does not go into extra time!'

To his amazement that was not so bad. Quite soon they found rings that they both liked. Each of them paid for one and they decided to wait until they found a fitting location in the course of the day to exchange them officially.

In the meantime it was 11.45 and when they walked to the end of the gallery, they suddenly discovered Ruth and her granddaughter near a souvenir stall. Ruth was gesticulating effusively and having what seemed to be a rather irritated dispute with the owner.

'A good morning to you too!' Robert interrupted her argument.

She turned around in surprise, briefly greeted Robert and Debbie and said: 'Look at that there!'

They glanced around the stall full of woodcarving artefacts. Shelves full of little men in *lederhosen* with overflowing beer jugs in their hands; father Christmases with enormous beards and… Jews with sad, drooping faces, wearing long, black coats, large hats and with long beards and exaggerated large hooked noses.

'Is that not terrible?' Ruth observed indignantly, and without waiting for an answer: 'To humiliate Jews to funfair caricatures! When all the time it was they – with their intelligence and craftsmanship – who helped to make this city so beautiful and great. That lady should be ashamed to want to sell something like that.'

Robert took Ruth by her shoulders and calmly walked away with her from the stall to the end of the gallery. In the meantime he wondered whether this violent reaction – such as he had also experienced a few times with Debbie – was typical female or typical Jewish. Or, he thought, did the confrontation have to do with expressions of humiliation of Judaism – and maybe subconsciously – with fear of discrimination and its possible consequences. In this sense he could understand their criticism but he himself would never make such a scene about it.

Outside, in the sun on the large square Ruth calmed down quite quickly. She told them how they had enjoyed the surroundings and the many shops, as well as the beautiful art galleries and museums in the city. They sat down at a pleasant pavement café and as they talked, it turned out that Ruth lived in a New York suburb that was called *Great Neck*.

Debbie in her turn mentioned that she studied in New York and knew that suburb, because a fellow student with whom she sometimes spent the weekend lived there.

'It is just like Israel there,' Ruth said to Robert, 'we have eight or nine synagogues and even more restaurants!'

In the meantime the waiter stood waiting for the second time already to take their order. Before Ruth – as the last one – had made her choice, the man had been subjected to a veritable cross-examination about the kind of meat and the composition of the filling of one of the many sandwiches that were on the menu.

'Grandma, please!' her granddaughter sighed. 'It-is-just-a-sandwich!'

But grandma took no chances, food had a high priority for her, it appeared, when she finally made her decision.

Did Debbie ever had a sandwich at DELI on Second Avenue, she asked. When this turned out not to be the case, she bent forward, put her hand with familiarity on Debbie's arm and spoke seriously and with dedication, as if it concerned a witness statement under oath: 'Dear child, as soon as you are back in New York, I'll pick you up and then we are going to have a "pastrami on rye" there. That is chopped liver with mustard and sour pickles. The meat is smoked in the cellar and it takes seven to ten days to season it properly, but then you have never tasted anything like it…!'

Robert smiled. The endless and passionate discourse about food reminded him of his "lodgings" in Elburg. Opa had said recently: "Your oma still loves her pots and pans the most… we come second place".

In spite of the fact that a pinch of curry could have been added and that the pickles were a bit soft and bland, the sandwich on the whole got a passing mark from Ruth.

While she was eating, she told them that she often took one of her grandchildren along on a trip after they had become Bar or Bat Mitzvah. 'They themselves can choose a destination,' she explained.

'Debbie wanted to go with me to "the camp", that's why… My children and grandchildren are the only family members that I have and…'

'Grandma,' said Debbie, when there was a pause, 'there's curry all over your mouth.'

With a paper napkin Ruth wiped her mouth and she ate her sandwich in silence. Everyone sensed how the word "camp" remained like a dark cloud over their table and had all of a sudden chased away the pleasantly relaxed atmosphere.

After a long silence Debbie stroked Ruth's arm and asked: 'Yesterday you said that you should not have come. Are you sorry that you went?'

She looked around the square, heaved a sigh and confessed: 'I had considered it often, but what always kept me from doing it was that I could not assess properly whether it would be good or bad for me. The fact that Debbie wanted to go finally tipped the scales.' She stroked her granddaughter's back gently and declared: 'She is very interested in my history…'

For a while she seemed to consider whether or not she would open that book with its many black pages. But then she started, calmly and deliberately.

… 'For me the war years themselves were not the worst. We were four children at home. My twin brother Ruben and I were the youngest. An ideal position. My older brothers always caught the first smacks and they had the strictest upbringing. When we were eight years old Ruben and I were taken to a hiding place in Friesland. My mother insisted that we should go together because we were so close. "Ruth and Ruben" sounded like a unit and that is how it was. The large farm was very remote and we barely noticed that there was a war going on. We were never really afraid, until the moment – a few months before the liberation – when the words sounded, that have haunted me the rest of my life… "Open up, open up"! Two German soldiers first pursued Ruben who wanted to run away. When I saw a chance I also started to run, as fast as I could. First through the meadows, where I jumped over ditches, and then I hid in a wide patch of reeds. I heard a German approaching. With his rifle he beat wildly at the reeds. I took a very deep breath and went under water – as long as I could. Afterwards I stood in the water for hours until I could not manage any longer because of the cold. Very carefully I then walked back to the farm and that same evening the farmer took me to a safer hiding place. After the liberation I went to a foster family and that is when my war really began. Every day I waited for the return of my parents and my brothers. Time and again I heard of others that they had received notification from the Red Cross that their family had perished. Every day my fear mounted, only in 1948 the bad news arrived that my parents, brothers and everyone else in our direct family had been killed in the gas chambers also. A Jewish couple that could not have any children, adopted me and shortly afterwards we emigrated to America. There I met my husband with whom I had a rich and good life. Four years ago he died. I recognize his features very clearly in our children and also those of his parents, but in what I and my children resemble my parents and my family… that I don't know and I shall never know. There is not one person left with whom I can compare or whom I can ask…'

With a sad look she stared ahead for a while, engrossed in herself. 'To talk about it helps, the wise men say, as does visiting the camps, but whether it will help me…? Materially I – and this applies now also to my children and grandchildren – have had a rich life, but it has no foundation. The great enemy has shattered that permanently and since that time the war is a sleeping tumor in my life and there is no doctor or therapy that can get rid of it. Someone once said: You can take a person out of the war but you can never take the war out of a person. And that is right.'

With reference to Ruth's life story they kept talking for quite a while and the afternoon was half over when they finally said goodbye. Ruth insisted strongly that Debbie should contact her as soon as she was in New York again and Robert was very welcome too of course.

'Who knows we might come together on our honeymoon,' Robert proposed. 'A trip through the United States would be fantastic.'

With the aid of the city map they walked to the old Jewish quarter *Kazimierz*. That was supposed to be the location of the factory of Schindler that Debbie wanted to look at in connection with her thesis, and also in view of the interview, in Berlin soon.

When after quite a walk they entered the district, it struck Robert that the old buildings here were almost all still intact. Sometimes he stopped in front of one of the synagogues that they passed and considered whether that would not be a fitting place to exchange rings. After all they were here in what could be called the erstwhile Jewish heart of Poland.

When they arrived in the Szerokastreet – the central square-like main street of *Kazimierz* – he saw a synagogue with its doors wide open.

'Shall we look inside?' he proposed.

Debbie hesitated and said, pointing at the *Jordan Jewish Bookshop*: 'You go, then I go in there for a minute to see if there is anything interesting for my thesis.'

Robert entered the age-old synagogue and admiring the beautiful gothic vaulted roof – high above him – he climbed the stairs to the space behind the women's balustrade that had been made into a museum. It showed old utensils, but also photographs and documents about the way in which the Germans had finished off the Jewish community of Kraków. And there he suddenly fully realised that, although the district looked very Jewish, its soul was no longer there. The *klezmer* music that sounded from the cafés, the Hebrew letters on shops and buildings, the *kosher* restaurants, the old synagogues, theatres and bathing houses, that all had remained, but the Jews themselves were gone. The authentic life was gone. Only the envelope was still there and the once lively quarter had been reduced to a hollowed-out, silenced museum-like curiosity.

He went out again and when he saw Debbie still walking around in the untidy book- and souvenir shop, he sauntered around the square for a while. He stopped in front of the restaurant *Noah's Ark*. Next to the entrance there was a wooden case with inside a yellowed paper with menu suggestions. After the entry "Krupnik" it said that this was a soup with beef, barley and Jewish-Lithuanian carrots.

'Were you able to make a choice?' a cheerful voice behind him said. Debbie put her arm around his waist and she looked at the menu too over his shoulder.

Robert pointed at the relevant entry and remarked: 'Well, I was just wondering what the difference is between ordinary carrots and Jewish carrots.'

'Tcha, I don't know that either,' she said, 'but I do know that we have them!'

'What…?' Robert asked surprised, 'what do you mean?' What do we have?'

Chuckling about the fact that he had not understood the pun right away she answered: 'Jewish roots of course!' she glanced at the menu and proposed: 'By the way, shall we go and eat here later? Look at that, carp in *kosher* vodka or Israeli wine,… great! That will give us a good sleep and then we are in Berlin in no time.' She looked at her watch, took the map and said, without waiting for an answer: 'But then we do have to hurry, for the train leaves at 21.10.'

After a short search they entered the Lipowastreet and stopped in front of an old –two storey high – factory building with a round façade.

'This should be it,' Debbie noted, 'number 4.' She took a few pictures, then they walked together across the parking lot and tried one of the doors. When it turned out to be open they carefully entered and arrived in a stairwell. As if it was the most normal thing in the world Debbie climbed up.

'Hey…!' Robert whispered, 'you can't just go inside like that all by yourself.'

'We'll know soon enough,' Debbie said resolutely. 'I have to see this!'

Arriving at the first floor they heard the monotonous sound of some machine behind a door. Debbie knocked and a middle-aged man opened the door. His few remaining hairs hung straggly around his pale face. Silently and without interest he looked at them.

Robert saw that Debbie accompanied her request to see the factory with a certain charm in her movements and even in the tone of her voice. She mentioned her thesis and how important she thought it was to describe the history as neutrally and objectively as possible. That therefore it was necessary to mention that during the time of the awful evil that the Germans had done, there had also been people who – endangering their own lives – resisted this and chose to do good.

The man actually came out of his shell. He touched Debbie's shoulder and gestured with his head for them to enter. They now stood – it appeared – in the former office of Oskar Schindler. While Debbie took pictures the man explained that since Schindler's death no enamel wares were produced any more and that there was a publishing company in the building now. Then he walked ahead of them to the large hall where hundreds of prisoners were ostensibly put to work, but were in fact saved from certain death that way. Here in this space Schindler and his men had taken care of hundreds of wounded and sick people and brought their condition back up to par with proper, dosed nutrition.

Here too Debbie took several photographs and Robert took some of her with the big hall as a background.

'You were flirting with that guy,' he said when they walked back across the parking place to the Lipowastreet later.

'Yes… that's right,' Debbie agreed, 'and you saw what it brought me. You would never have succeeded with that *mishponem*.'

When they had passed the gate, she turned around and looked up. 'Look,' she said, 'this is where they should have put that arch with *Arbeit Macht Frei*.' Carefully she looked at the factory building once more, passed her gaze across the façade and the parking lot and proposed: 'Shall we put our rings on here, after all this is a unique place.'

Robert looked hesitantly around. 'Those rings mean that we promise each other eternal faithfulness, don't they?'

'Certainly,' Debbie declared, nodding enthusiastically.

'Well,' was Robert's opinion, 'then I think the old *shul* where I was this afternoon is a much nicer place. It is in the heart of one of the oldest Jewish quarters in the world and in addition our very first meeting was also in a synagogue.'

At that moment each of them separately had the same idea and they looked at each other in the same instant.

'Are you thinking what I am thinking?' Debbie asked.

'Yes,' Robert confirmed, 'Sunday afternoon in the old *shul* of Elburg.'

She nodded contentedly. 'Yes,' she noted, 'that is the place... our place.'

After they had ordered a carp at Noah's Ark, Debbie asked: 'And, what did you think of it?'

'Of that factory?' Robert wanted to know. 'Tcha, it is an old heap, isn't it. It could use a dollop of paint here and there, because essentially it was built in rather a remarkable style.'

'Hey, come on,' she protested, 'I mean inside of course.'

'Well,' Robert noted matter-of-factly, 'the same thing applies.'

With a pitying look she shook her head and said: 'What did you think of being in such a memorable place? In the office of Oskar Schindler and in the space where he saved one thousand two hundred people from a certain death?'

'That he did that is fantastic, of course,' Robert had to admit. 'But in proportion to the millions of dead it was only a drop in the ocean.'

'Hey,' Debbie said with a voice full of indignation, 'you can't say that. Think of the offspring of those one thousand two hundred people who would otherwise never have existed. You know that it says in the Talmud that whoever saves one life, saves the world?'

Robert nodded.

'So,' she said emotionally, 'that's what it is about. Schindler was a hero because he dared to do battle with the powers of evil. In the circumstances in which he was at the time, it was extra courageous of him – as a German – and therefore it is extremely important to be mentioned. What was also quite remarkable was: although with him there was no question of any religious involvement, he acted completely according to the exhortation of the Torah: *You shall not follow the majority in evil.*'

Because of the passion with which Debbie spoke, Robert had started to listen to her more attentively. 'For you, history is clearly more than dates and events, isn't it?' he asked.

'Oh yes,' she reacted, 'much more. Take that saying "that history teaches us that we learned nothing from history". That is only partly true according to me and I regard it as a real challenge to confront people with facts from history from which – according to me – we did learn and can still learn.'

With a smile Robert supposed: 'So it is possible that there will be discussions later in the class of "Miss Hamburger".'

'I hope so, yes,' she said.

Around eight o'clock a few men on a small platform started to make preparations for a musical performance, but they had barely any time left to enjoy it. With cheerful *klezmer* tones in the background they left the restaurant and walked quickly to the station. There they retrieved their bags and the violin case from the locker and at 21.10 left Kraków, clothed in peaceful dusk, behind.

After more than an hour the train entered the station of Katowice, where Robert had gotten off on his way down. Seeing the platform and the old, dark station building evoked in him again the state of mind he had been in at the time. He saw himself searching full of amazement for the mysterious woman. On leaving the station they passed "platform 3" where he had been waiting in vain for the train to Oświęcim. What he saw was known and unchanged in fact, but everything he felt was a new reality that had energed in two days. Again he was amazed at how both a closure of his old existence and a true rebirth of life had taken place twice in 24 hours.

Outside the city the train made a long, faint curve to the northwest and entered – after the sun had set behind the forests at the horizon of a wide plain – into the dark Polish night.

Berlin had just made it through the morning rush hour when the train eased into the station at 08.10 a.m. Debbie first phoned her fellow student to say that she would arrive around noon. Because Robert's train would only leave at 11.34 a.m. they sauntered through the modern building to the restaurant on the first floor where they enjoyed a leisurely, large breakfast.

In silence they looked at the busy street scene. They saw a continuous stream of arriving and departing buses and taxis with people of all ages and nationalities. It reminded them both of the fact that their ways would part soon and that they would have to say goodbye to each other for a long time. At a certain moment their gazes crossed and Robert looked into the moist, sad eyes of Debbie. He caressed her arm as he tried to find the right words.

'Hey,' he said encouragingly, 'we stay together "forever", don't we…?'

She looked at him with wide eyes and nodded imperceptibly.

'So,' he continued, 'what is half a year compared to "forever"?'

'It is eight months,' Debbie said aggrieved, 'at least… if I pass.'

'You'll pass for sure,' Robert predicted, 'and the fact that we won't see each other for a long time increases that chance. The same applies to me. In the coming year I'll have to concentrate fully on soccer. If I don't create a foundation now, I can forget the rest. So in fact it is better for both of us to not be close together for a long time. And if both of us reach our goal because of that, then the reward will be so much greater.'

They drank another cup of coffee and towards eleven o'clock they walked to the taxi stop.

'I really won't stay in Berlin any longer than is necessary,' Debbie assured when she had put her bag into the taxi.

Robert gave her the envelope with the poem that he had made for her and he wrote his telephone number on it. 'Call me as soon as you know when you are arriving in Amersfoort, then I'll pick you up.'

They said goodbye and embraced closely.

When the taxi drove off, Robert walked back again to the main entrance of the station. After a few steps he was startled by a shout behind him: 'Rooobert!!'

He turned around and saw that the taxi was standing at the traffic lights and was just driving on. Debbie was leaning as far as possible from the window, and cried at the top of her voice: 'To the moon and back!' She kept waving till Robert was out of view. Then she fell back, relaxing, opened the envelope and read…

DESTINATION

Walking in circles
through the streets of my life
hoping for happiness
with wounds that just might
be second-hand injuries
and therefore not real
who ordered this dream,
this life so surreal?

*But then there was you
like a distant light came
on herediraty wings
and helped me proclaim
a generation long sleep
washed away by your sight
that rose on my morning
and conquered my night.*

*For in you I found that
which was lost long ago
I'm immersed in your presence
and re-birthed in your glow
for after years of regret
and nights so alone
my destiny is found…
I finally came home.*

14

It was one of those rare, muggy summer days, when it doesn't cool down in the evening or even at night. Lost in thought Ben van Zuiden was standing in his garden and gazed across the lawn that was brightly lit by the moon, while countless stars glittered in the sky. The leaves of the trees and shrubs barely moved. The whole evening Nant, Lilian and he had been sitting here on the covered terrace listening to the remarkable and impressive events that Robert had experienced in the past week.

Now that the others had gone to bed, Ben took the time to let everything settle in place. Fragments of all those strange events flitted like elusive wisps of mist through his head… The sympathy and valuable advice of Piet Abbringh with whom Robert – yes, with him of all people – had shared a room during the tournament… The reunion with Deborah Hamburger who – independently from Robert – had also chosen that special destination at exactly the same time… And then the remarkable meeting with Mordecai whose wise words finally led to the solution of a search of many years… He heard Robert say again: "In that silent hut I experienced the final of my personal struggle".

Till this point he had been able to follow everything. Even though the concurrence of circumstances had been extra-ordinary, there was a rational explanation for it. For Ben the elusive aspect, however, was the struggle that his son had gone through all those years. He had never been able to get a grip on that. The latent fear that became apparent at times during the night, but remained unmentioned otherwise… The long withdrawals into silence… He had recognised them all as traces of those typical "Van Zuiden-inheritance", but still he had never been really able to exert any positive influence, that brought about any change. And now he had to admit that Robert had found the correct direction and – as it seemed – even his destination from an entirely different source.

It all had started at their visit – years ago – to the Chagall-exposition at the *Jewish Historical Museum*. There – in some mysterious manner – his eyes were opened. From that moment on he learned to deal with his problem in a more balanced way and seemed to have gradually found a different track in his life. The enjoyment of his job and soccer had certainly given him an extra stimulus. But what, essentially, had been the secret that had made his son mature into a stable, adult guy…?

He recalled fragments of what Robert himself had told them about it that evening… *The White Crucifixion*… The number four… The unique relationship with Debbie, who was the granddaughter of his father's best friend, no less… The woman in the train… The influence of Mordecai… And again he wondered what or who was really the linking factor. What logical explanation was there for the entire process that had now come to a conclusion?

From the park a soft wind rustled through the bushes. As he heard the swishing of the leaves he felt that the need for an answer to all his questions slowly evaporated. A strange metaphor explained it to him suddenly. He heard the wind and he saw the leaves move, but could not discern the cause of the displacement of that air – let alone understand where it came from. He recalled that late evening walk through the park, years ago. It was on the evening of the Sunday on which little Robert had been dedicated. There too – under a clear starry sky – the sound of the wind had brought peace to his worried mind. At that time the invisible, but tangible presence of the Eternal One had reminded him of the promise for his life: *This is my covenant between Me and you and your offspring*. Now again, that was foremost in his mind. Hadn't Robert, just like his brother Sjaak, linked himself with heart and soul to a Jewish partner? Suddenly he realised

– straight through all his questions – that this in particular was the fulfilment of what had also been promised to him from on high, namely, that the heart of his children would be led back to the fathers and that their name would not be blotted out from Israel.

After breakfast Robert was sitting with his mother on the terrace enjoying a cup of coffee when the telephone rang. Enthusiastically Debbie informed him that she would arrive in Amersfoort that same afternoon at ten past five already.

'Yesterday afternoon,' she told him quickly, 'my friend and I visited that former co-worker of Schindler and that was very interesting. A very special man who gave me a lot of unique information and even photos and documents for my thesis. Yesterday evening we went out and now I am calling from a museum. My train leaves at eleven thirty and I have to go now. Love you. See you tonight!'

With a smile Robert shook his head. 'That girl is in a hurry!' he said. 'She'll be here tonight already.'

'Well, that is nice,' Nant said, 'I am really very curious. Tomorrow we'll have a big dinner, for Sjaak, Tamarah and Sarah are also coming home for the birthday of opa Van Zuiden.'

In the course of the afternoon Robert called opa to tell him that he wanted to come by the next afternoon to introduce someone to him. Also he asked him if he could pick up the key of the synagogue from his friend once more.

'Yes, that is fine, my boy, but tell me first how you have been.'

'Opa,' Robert answered, 'I am so happy that I went. It has done me the world of good and that has to do, above all, with what we have talked about together before. I have met your friend Mordecai and he has confirmed it all. He sends you his warm greetings. But the most exciting thing that happened to me there… that I will tell you about tomorrow!'

After the telephone conversation Robert drove to Amersfoort and picked up Debbie from the station.

That evening too was, just like the previous one, dedicated mainly to their remarkable meeting and unforgettable journey.

The next morning they left early for Zwolle where Robert showed Debbie around the stadium. At the office he picked up his training and match-schedule for the next few weeks and when they were drinking a cup of coffee at the players' home, Piet came in. Robert paid him back the money he had borrowed and thanked him extensively for his golden advice.

'Look,' he said pointing at Debbie, 'what a terrific bonus this trip gave me!'

Via Wezep, where Robert showed his place of work and introduced Debbie to Martin, they drove to Nant's parents in Oldebroek. There they joined them for lunch, and at the beginning of the afternoon they arrived in Elburg. Because of the vacation crowds, they parked the car on the large parking lot just outside the old town.

In the shadow of the high oaks on the Westerwal Jacob van Zuiden sat in the garden waiting for his grandson. The fact that it was Robert of all people who – as the first and for the time being the only one of his offspring – had gone to visit *Auschwitz* had occupied him intensely for a few days already. However, strangely enough, it had not caused him depressing or restless nights. For the first time he felt that there seemed to be some distance between his present circumstances and the past. A kind of numbness that had dulled the sharpness of the paint seemed to have created some space in his mind. Now he could even look forward with interest to Robert's experiences and discoveries. In the tone of his voice relief had sounded, which gave him the impression that after all, it had been a correct decision to go there. That Robert came to visit him now, especially – a day before the birthday celebration – only confirmed that suspicion. That he had met Mordecai was something that he had secretly hoped for, but had not really dared to expect. The only question that remained was what the "most exciting" thing had been, that he had experienced there.

In the meantime Robert and Debbie had walked via the Westerwal to the entrance of Jacob's garden and saw the old man staring ahead, immersed in thought. A forced little cough by Robert startled him from his reveries. He got up and walked with a big smile towards them. Robert put his arm around Debbie's shoulders. He said, elated: 'Opa, four years ago, when you had a visit from David Hamburger one Sunday afternoon, I met his daughter Deborah here in the synagogue. You were the only one – I think – who sensed that at the time.'

Jacob nodded, smiling.

'And after all these years,' Robert continued, 'we found each other again – in *Auschwitz* of all places, and now I'll never let her go again.'

Jacob gave his grandson a searching look and then asked: 'Do you mean that, boy?'

'For sure, opa,' Robert assured him. 'I have taken Deborah Hamburger into my heart forever, and the reason that I asked you for the key of the synagogue is that we want to confirm that there today.'

Jacob looked at Debbie carefully and thought he recognised in her face vaguely the features of his dear friend. In a totally unexpected way he felt linked again with him and for a moment it seemed as if time had disappeared. As he embraced Deborah Hamburger, tears of holy amazement and intense gratitude rolled down his face following the furrows of his cheeks. After this moving event he took the key of the synagogue from his pocket and just as he handed it to Robert, Saar came out.

'I thought I heard something,' she called. As she cast a curious glance at Deborah, she walked towards Robert. She took his head between her hands, gave him a firm kiss on each cheek and asked: 'And, how was your trip?'

'Very good oma, and look,' he said gesturing to Debbie, 'may I introduce the woman of my life to you: Deborah Hamburger.'

'Hamburger…? Saar repeated slowly as she took Debbie's hand in both of hers. 'The daughter of uh…'

Debbie laughed radiantly. 'Yes,' she confirmed, 'the granddaughter of Sal.'

Saar put her hands to her cheeks and cried, shaking her head: 'Oh my, oh my, oh my, it can't be. That such a thing can happen to me in my old age, oi oi oi. First Sjaak and Tamarah and now you... come here, dear child, may you be blessed and may the Eternal One give you health and strength enough to be present at the wedding of your grandchildren.' She kissed Debbie exuberantly and kept stroking her arm.

Jacob pulled Saar towards him: 'Now you see that in the end all is well with our Benjamin?' Because Debbie looked at him rather surprised at that remark, he explained to her that Saar had been rather upset at the time when Robert's father married a non-Jewish woman. She nodded with understanding and said: 'I am going to have a similar problem with my mother and therefore it is just as well that I'll already be engaged when I come home tomorrow.'

'What...?' Saar cried, 'are you engaged already...?'

'Not yet,' Robert reacted, 'but we are going to do that now!'

Via the Westerwalstraat they walked along the canal to the center of town. The shops and catering facilities did good business with the hordes of sauntering tourists, but once Robert and Debbie had passed through the small gate and walked on the path towards the synagogue, all the noise of the summer crowds suddenly seemed very far away. The sight of the old building that was so special to them gave them a pleasant feeling of tranquillity.

Debbie took Robert's arm: 'In your poem you wrote something about coming home, didn't you? Well, to me this also feels a bit like coming home after a long journey.'

Robert nodded and he thought of previous generations that had also shared and celebrated the deeper values of life with one another in this building. And when he realised how both Debbie and he were part of that past, again he heard the words:

"What has passed, is not finished, but determines present and future…"

Inside everything was just about the same as they had found it four years ago. Now too, the sun sent her generous rays through the high windows. Silently they walked to the spot where they had said goodbye after their first meeting. There, between the wooden platform and the prize display case – below which the four drawings were still hanging – they slid the rings on each other's finger. And in a long embrace they cherished the thought about the strange way in which they both had "come home". For another moment they looked – but with very different eyes now – at the four drawings, that had acquired such an authentic dimension for them.

Then they disengaged from the silence of the old prayer house, that on this nice summer's day had been used once again for its original purpose: to keep up the relationship between the Eternal One and His people.

Back in the garden at the Westerwalstraat they received congratulations. Saar admired the rings, wished them *mazel* and *brogue* - happiness and blessings – and then walked busily back and forth with tea and doughnuts.

Robert explained how Piet Abbringh had – after intense conversations – advised him during the tournament in Germany to go to Poland and reported extensively about all that had happened to him during those days. The experience with the woman on the train, the reunion with Debbie and the meeting with Mordecai.

'Everything was impressive,' he said, 'and also what Mordecai said agreed with all those things that you had pointed out to me earlier. The fourth generation in which the remnants of inherited traumas disappear and which is followed by a new period. But what still impresses me most is how in those few days everything fitted together and seemed to be directed from on high. I mean, it seems that you are right, that indeed everything is "*bashert*".'

After Robert's frank testimony it remained quiet for a few moments. In the distance the sound of sirens sounded shrilly above the buzz of the city. And in the high trees on the Westerwal the pure song of a blackbird interrupted the monotonous coo-ing of the wood pigeons and the loud cawing of a few fighting crows.

Jacob had to process all of it first and he stared ahead absent-mindedly. The story of everything that Robert had experienced, but above all the conclusion he had drawn from it, had made a deep impression on him. He also appreciated that his grandson, out of reverence for his opa, had not at all mentioned the terrors of that time with which undoubtedly he had been amply confronted. Still he felt a certain need to share something about that with him. His intuition told him that he had to, because Robert had – for the same reason as Benjamin – a right to it.

He lifted his head slowly and looked at Robert. Although it took some effort, he asked in a controlled tone of voice: 'And the camps, boy… How did you find those…?'

'Well, you know,' Robert proposed, 'if it does not bother you too much, I would like to talk about that with you in peace and quiet once. At home I have an information guide with maps of *Auschwitz* and *Birkenau*. I could take those along next week. I mean, there is no hurry, is there?'

He got up, put his hand on Jacob's shoulder and said cheerfully: 'First we are going to have a party tomorrow. Your birthday and our engagement; and anyway, it is nice to be all together again for once. By the way… at our home the party has already started, for everyone is coming to Putten this afternoon already in view of your birthday party. Therefore we should really go now too.' He addressed Debbie who had been listening quietly. 'Hey beautiful, are you coming?'

She got up, hesitated for a moment and then said to Jacob: 'Tomorrow evening I am going home again and then for eight months to America, so I won't be seeing you for a long time. But there is one thing that I would still very much like to know of you…'

Jacob looked at her kindly and said: 'Tell me, my dear. What do you want to know?'

'Those four drawings that are hanging in the synagogue,' she asked, 'can you tell us who made those?'

Jacob nodded in confirmation and then answered slowly: 'Yes… yes, I can.' He looked at Saar and remarked: 'I think that I'll walk along a bit with them.'

With a look of understanding Saar agreed.

They left via the garden gate and climbed the rather steep stairs up the Westerwal. At the top they waved at Saar once more. Then they walked leisurely between the trees and sat down on a bench. The wide branches of a colossal weeping willow hung down to just above the surface of the water and between the water lilies and the green algae a group of ducks slowly swam past.

Jacob had sat down between Robert and Debbie and then it became clear why he had been thinking that long.

'Listen,' he started, 'before I answer Debbie's question, I have to tell you something… As a child I had just one great passion: drawing. One of my most beautiful memories from my youth is that my mother once took me after school to that large bookstore of Hengeveld on the Vischmarkt. There I was allowed to select a drawing-case, pencils and crayons and also a large sketchpad with fifty pages of drawing paper. When you know that my father in those days could barely take care of his family with his trade, then you'll understand that I thought this was very special. The good woman had saved for it from what little household money she had, just to stimulate me. In the fifth grade I had a teacher who could draw and paint fantastically. He gave me free lessons after school. For instance, I had to put my left hand on the table in front of me and draw that, but also a vase with flowers; a bowl of fruit; an old canon on the walls; the Vischpoort and the harbor; you name it. I liked it so much that I planned to continue, whatever happened. But the war broke out and when Brammie and I returned to Elburg after the liberation as the only ones of our family, we found our little house completely plundered. My drawing case and sketch pad had also disappeared. However sad that was, Brammie and I had survived the camp and we did not want to succumb now, come what may be. With the help of my father-in-law we fixed up the house. First the shop at the front, and later the remainder was furnished as a living space. By nature I have always preferred to be creatively active rather than be in trade, but there was nothing for it. Saar and I wanted to get married and I had to pay Brammie's share, so we had to make money. *Van Zuiden Manufacturen* it said on the window, very posh. Your oma served in the shop in the daytime and for a number of years I still went with a pushcart to clients that lived outside. When the children grew up it was soon apparent that David would be the most suitable successor. I gave him a lot of responsibility at a young age. Still, at that time I had never dared to dream that he would create something this large and beautiful. He did not inherit that from me, but from his mother's side. His name may be Van Zuiden, but in all the rest he is the spitting image of my father-in-law. Tough and businesslike, sometimes boarding on indifference. To him, life rests on three pillars: money, money and more money. In the past I have often talked to him about the fact that there are higher values in life, and that happiness has to do with entirely different factors than money and material riches. He accepts that from me and even listens to it, but it does not really penetrate. In the sensitivity and creativity of Benjamin, however, I have – already since his early years - recognised much of myself.'

He turned to Robert, tapped him on his knee and added: 'And of all my grandchildren you are the one who resembles me most. In our talks I feel that you and your father have become extensions of me, as it were, and I recognise that especially in your soccer talent and creative aptitude.

Anyway, about those four drawings… you have visited *Auschwitz* and – I assume – have seen and heard enough to be able to imagine that, when you go through that in full consciousness this causes such damage in your life, that it can never be repaired.

Apart from Benjamin and you, your grandmother and my friend Gérard are those that have managed to ease the pain for me. Saartje de Lange was my first and great love and she still is. She has kept me in balance with her glorious simplicity and honest solicitude and thus warmed my life with a pleasant *neshome*. As years went by, Gérard became a vessel for me in which I could let my misery overflow. Many times he has insisted that – as a therapy – I should write down my "story". "For then a few positive memories will also come back and you need those desperately for balance", he would say. Because I never managed to do that, he once advised me: "Didn't you use to be able to draw well…? Well, if you can't write it down to get rid of it, draw it! In all that misery there has to have been something which gave you support and courage". And when I thought about that, I suddenly remembered the bush in the camp. It was winter when I arrived in *Birkenau*. My plank bed stood more or less in the middle of the hut and there was a rather wide gap in the wall that we tried to close with old rags against the cold. Through this gap you looked at a bare bush that seemed to be dead. But when spring arrived, it grew buds and in the summer you could not recognise it any more, it flowered so beautifully. When in the fall it gradually became bare again and seemed to be dead, I knew that it would survive, however severe the winter might be. Just like me, it had to go through the cold and the pain, but sooner or later it would flower again. And thus that bush became a quiet friend, who gave me hope and courage to not give up.

As I had seen it in each season – as far as I could remember – I then sketched it and afterwards I gave all four to Gérard for his good advice. But he thought they should not be with him but in the *shul* and that is how they ended up there.'

Softly Jacob put his hand on Debbie's knee: 'I admit, it was rather a long introduction, but now you know that not only did I make those drawings, but also why.'

'Boy, that is beautiful,' Debbie thought, 'now I also understand from whom Robert inherited his drawing talent.'

For a peaceful moment of silence they sat together thinking.

'Anyway, I can assure you,' Debbie added after a while, 'that your memory did not abandon you. I mean, what you drew resembles the reality. That bush, the hut with the chimney behind it, they are still there, almost exactly the same. We have both seen it through the same gap in the wall. It was in that hut that we met Mordecai. When we were already on the way out of the camp, we heard the sad and rather false tones of a violin in the distance. We walked to the hut where the sound came from and found an old, sick man in a wheelchair there. He immediately recognised Robert as "the son of my brother Jacob". But somehow or other there was also a certain disappointment in him for he had dreamt that night about a reunion with his son Joshua, who played on his violin. Therefore he went back one more time to "his" hut with a vague feeling that he would meet his son there and then he would give him his violin. Due to his illness he could no longer play in tune. But when he found Robert there instead of Joshua, he asked whether one of your children played the violin, maybe. When Robert told him that aunt Leah played the violin, he put the instrument in the case and asked us to take it and give it to her.'

With a worried face Jacob looked ahead.

'So my old friend is very ill,' he remarked with sadness.

'Yes,' Robert confirmed, 'he even indicated that he felt that the end was near.' He looked at Jacob: 'Would you not like to meet him once more?'

'I have never had the courage,' Jacob answered, 'but lately it seems as if something is changing. Tomorrow afternoon I'll discuss it with your father, for if I go, then with him.'

Together they walked to the end of the wall. There Jacob turned left to go into town. Robert and Debbie turned right to the parking lot. When they had left the old rampart and wide city canal behind, Debbie suddenly stopped, perplexed. 'Hey Robert,' she called, looking back at the city wall.

Robert walked towards her and looked at her questioningly. She remained staring ahead in a daze for a few moments and explained: 'That garden of your grandparents...' She shook her head and continued in a louder voice: 'and the dream of Mordecai about the meeting with his son...'

'Yes... what of it?' Robert asked matter-of-factly.

'What of it?' Debbie repeated, lifting her hands. 'Mordecai clearly indicated that it happened during a party of which your grandfather was the focal point, in the midst of all his children and grandchildren... And that it happened on a lawn, bordered by a long row of old, high trees...'

*

Because Jacob's birthday was in the summer, it was always celebrated in grander style than that of Saar in the fall. In the small house on the Westerwalstraat there just wasn't enough room for a large number of people.

On the morning of the party Esther turned up early to help her mother to prepare everything.

'Shalom, papa and congratulations,' she greeted Jacob warmly and immediately went to work. Jacob considered himself fortunate with his children and he was really happy about the fact that – now that Leah would also be coming – his family would be complete again for the first time for ages.

The previous evening David had set up the market stall - on which he displayed special offers during the summer evening fairs - in a corner of the garden. In the course of the morning he put the coffeemaker from the shop there and gave his father a box with five bottles of Jacob's favourite wine.

'Here's hoping that you can keep drinking them in good health, at least as long as I can deduct them as expenses,' he said, chuckling. 'For,' he added with a serious face, 'when that is no longer possible, then the deal is over and you'll have to revert to water.'

They had a cup of coffee together and David mentioned that at his workshop in Poland a new manager had been appointed whose name was Jeda. 'I explained to him that my grandmother also had that name and came from Poland,' he continued, 'but I should have thought twice before doing that. He wanted to know everything and kept asking questions. Finally I told him: "Now you have to quit. I did not even know the good lady. I only know she was called Liese and if you want to know more about her, you'll have to call my father". So I gave him your phone number.'

'Well,' Jacob reacted casually, 'who knows, I may look him up soon.'

Utterly surprised, David looked at his father, who did not get a chance to explain because Thera and the children wanted to congratulate him. Shortly afterwards Ben and Nant arrived with their children including Tamarah and Debbie.

David had walked to the stall and stood pouring coffee, handing out large pieces of Saar's homemade apple- and chocolate cake. Thera praised her mother-in-law for the delicious chocolate cake and wanted to know exactly how she had made it.

'Thanks,' Jacob said when he was also handed a piece of the cake, 'take some yourself too.'

'Well,' David said laughing, 'I think I'll stick to the applecake for if I understand properly we'll be having lots of chocolate cake in the near future.'

Jacob, listening to the expansive explanation of his wife about the proper method of preparation, said with resignation: 'Yes, son, Meyer Sluyser knew it already: "The cookbook of the Yiddish kitchen keeps more Jews together than the holy Torah".'

Robert, who was discussing the developments in soccer with his cousin Ruben, suddenly heard his name mentioned. He looked around and saw that David was talking to Debbie and beckoned him. He walked over to them, whereupon David asked inoffensively: 'Hey, Robbie van Zuiden, have you lost your marbles?'

Robert, who by now knew his uncle, answered calmly: 'Sure… why?'

'Why…?' David repeated shaking his head and pointing at Debbie: 'Who allows such a pretty gal to go by herself to the other side of the world for eight months, for Pete's sake? Do you want to get rid of her? Don't you know that those Americans are crazy about those beautiful tall girls of ours?'

Robert smiled and proudly showed his engagement ring. Then he took hold of Debbie: 'This is the woman of my youth and the woman of my life, and she'll never leave me!'

An hour or so after the coffee Esther put a large pan of soup on the stall. Then she brought trays with sandwiches: salmon, tuna, beef sausage and salted beef. In her most beautiful dress Saar walked around enjoying her children and grandchildren and encouraging them continuously to eat well.

'I don't know, mam,' David said with a worried face, rubbing his stomach theatrically, 'but according to me that salmon is spoiled.'

'Ah, shut up, boy,' Saar said, dismissing the teasingly meant but nevertheless hurtful remark, 'may my innards explode if that salmon is spoilt. Look at those children eating... as if they are recuperating from a severe disease!'

David put his arm around her shoulder lovingly and pacified her: 'Just a joke, mam. Your sandwiches are delicious but I am waiting for the fried chicken legs. You do have them this year again, I hope?'

In the course of the afternoon the next-door neighbors as well as "De Balg" and Simon Steinmetz and their wives joined the company, and to everyone's surprise Gérard turned up a little later with a miserable little dog on a leash.

'What is this, my friend?' Jacob asked, pointing at the nervous yapper of an indeterminate race.

'Ah,' Gérard sighed, 'after that heart attack my doctor keeps telling me that I should take a hobby. In order to stop his nagging I have bought a dog and called it "Hobby".'

'I was just telling them,' Jacob explained, gesturing to "De Balg" and Simon, 'that I am seriously considering going to Poland with our Benjamin soon. He and I have discussed it this afternoon already.'

Gérard nodded in agreement. He lit a cigar and clearly indicated – with a meaningful look at Jacob as well as Ben – his satisfaction and contentment with it.

Simon's wife stood catching up on the news with Saar. 'Boy oh boy, it is really busy in Elburg!' she said.

Saar put her hand familiarly on her arm and said in a very worried tone of voice: 'It is just ter-ri-ble. It is like Sodom and Gomorrah with all those holiday visitors. They make noise till the early hours and walk around the streets with barely enough clothes on to cover their shame. A respectable person wouldn't want to leave home any more out of sheer annoyance.' When she saw that Debbie approached them, she quickly mentioned at low voice: 'That is the girl-friend of our Benjamin's Robert. She is Jewish, her father is a lawyer and she studies in America. And yes… they are already engaged.'

'I think I'd better join you here,' Debbie proposed with a semi-serious face, 'for I feel that you are gossiping madly about me.'

'My dear girl, where do you get that idea?' Saar denied. 'I only told her that you got engaged yesterday.'

'And…?' Mrs. Steinmetz asked, 'when are you getting married?'

'Getting married…? Debbie repeated, 'not for the time being. If all goes well I can only start earning my first money in a year or so.'

'Dear girl,' Mrs. Steinmetz advised seriously, 'don't wait too long. My mother used to say: "Getting up early and marrying early does no harm and procrastination only improves cheese, but not a marriage". And that is true!'

'Ladies,' said Jacob, who in the meantime had joined them, together with Robert, 'may I interrupt you for a moment and ask Deborah to come with Robert and me to receive their engagement present?'

'Yes, go ahead,' said Saar and she nattered on with her friend about the far too loose morals of today's youth. Debbie however was rather surprised. She gave a questioning look at Robert when they walked into the living room via the garden doors.

'When we said goodbye yesterday,' Jacob said, 'I walked into town to return the key of the *shul*. But first I went inside for a moment to pick up your present.' He opened the wardrobe, took the four drawings out and placed them next to one another on the table. Speechlessly Robert and Debbie looked at them.

'The reason why I want to give the drawings to you,' he explained, 'is that they have played such a remarkable role in your meetings, here and over there, and because…'

His voice faltered, whereupon he turned slowly to Robert and added: 'and… because I see so much of myself in you. Specifically my vanished passion for drawing I have seen return to life in you, as it were.'

Deeply moved Robert and Debbie searched in vain for words. Finally they turned to Jacob, embraced him and let the silence say that for which they could not find words.

When they had mingled with the guests again, it took a while before they could change over again to the festive bustle. They were still too full of everything that had taken place around the four drawings. Jacob's gesture, together with his emotional words, still preoccupied them. Their rather absent-minded attitude almost made the impression that they had landed in the wrong party.

Saar was still exchanging confidences with Mrs. Steinmetz as if nothing special had happened in the meantime.

At the table where a group of men sat, and where Jacob had sat down too in the meantime, David stood complaining to Gérard with busy gestures.

'You should trim the hair from in front of the eyes of that *meshugene* Hobby of yours,' he said a bit peevishly.

Gérard casually blew a cloud of cigar smoke into the air as he muttered: 'That doesn't bother him at all.'

'No…??' David cried excitedly. 'Then why is that *shlimil* pissing on my shoes?'

Simon burst out laughing and remarked: 'It was really a good idea of the doctor to advise you to take on a hobby. Even I am getting a lot of pleasure out of it!'

The whole event seemed to pass by Jacob. He had already looked at his watch several times and his gaze regularly turned to the open garden doors. Continuously he looked around searchingly until he finally saw what he had been waiting for. Tanned by the Israeli sun and attired with her inseparable hair band, Leah entered the garden from the house. Surprised, Saar whooped with joy and quickly walked with arms spread towards her daughter; 'Oi, oi, my little Leah,' she said, caressing her daughter's arms with concern, 'do they give you enough to eat over there, my love? You haven't gained an ounce in all that time!'

'Mam, please,' Leah sighed, 'let's talk about something else first, alright? I would like to introduce a friend of mine, but first I have to greet papa and congratulate him.'

In the meantime Jacob had already approached her. He looked at the tall figure and her calm, self-assured attitude. The intriguing thing about her was, he had always thought, that – in contrast to her brothers and sister – she could not be fitted in a definite "Van Zuiden- or De Lange- frame". Even though she had the characteristic oblong face with the long nose and wide mouth of the "De Langes", inside she had manifested, to his great joy – in spite of a bit of miserliness and business acumen – more and more clearly the Zionistic and anti-material character of the "Van Zuidens". In addition, she was also the only one of his children who kept up the musical tradition of "his" side. In her last letter she had written that she had been taking violin lessons again recently. Altogether, this reunion after such a long time caused a deep, intense gratitude in him and spontaneously he spread his arms.

Suddenly, however, he stood stock still. His arms fell, - as if hit by acute paralysis – straight alongside his body. He felt how a slight dizziness came upon him and how his heart beat louder and faster. The people around him faded into ghosts, surrounded only by resonances of monotonous, distant sounds. Completely disconnected from reality and overwhelmed by an awesome amazement, he stared at the man who, together with Lea, came towards him casually and with a somewhat irregular gait. He examined the man with an intense look and was taken aback by the striking resemblance with his friend Mordecai, the way he remembered him from his youth. Then he took a deep breath and whispered – almost unintelligibly – in utmost amazement: 'Joshua!?'

Time seemed to stand still. Everyone stood looking breathlessly at what happened there in the middle of the lawn. Joshua – sensing that he was the focal point of all that sudden interest, but unaware of the reason – looked helplessly from Jacob to Leah and then to the spectators, that stared at him silently.

Upset, Leah walked towards her father. She embraced him first and then looked into his moist eyes. 'Papa… what is happening here…? What is this…?' she asked.

Bewildered, Jacob shook his head and stammered, looking from one to the other: 'How come that you… I mean, how… how is it you know each other…?'

'Come on,' Leah decided resolutely, 'let's sit down, then I shall explain…'

'Joshua is a very talented violinist,' she started, 'and because we both are part of a group of close friends in Tel Aviv, I am having private lessons from him as one of a few. The reason, why we have travelled together to Holland, is that next week he is going to an international congress in Amsterdam for Jewish war children of the second and third generation. With the information he hopes to get there, he is then travelling to Poland.' She translated quickly into English what she had just said, whereupon Joshua himself – with Leah as interpreter – told his story.

… 'In 1947 I arrived via the Red Cross and the Alijah Youth in Israel with a group of orphans. There I grew up in a *kibbutz*. I was told that I originated from Poland, that my name is Joshua and that my parents died in *Auschwitz*. Still I sensed

– strangely enough - more and more often that this last fact is not true and that they are possibly still alive. Probably the desire is the father of the thought, but because time is running out, I have finally decided to look into it now. At the congress both experts and fellow-sufferers will attend to exchange experiences and data. Hopefully I can get some clarity there about the fate of my parents and about the question whether I still have brothers or sisters…'

Apart from a few playing children, everyone stood or sat in a circle listening spellbound to Joshua's story.

Jacob was completely convinced by Joshua's voice and his whole comportment – even more than by what he had heard – that he was eye to eye with Mordecai's "lost son". Intently he watched him and asked with some hesitation: 'Aside from playing the violin, can you sing well too?' Joshua nodded, whereupon Jacob asked: 'Are you by any chance the precantor of a large synagogue in Tel Aviv?' This too Joshua confirmed, and because of the flabbergasted look on his face, Jacob considered telling him that this had been revealed to him once in a dream. On second thought, he decided to wait with that after all.

'I still have two questions,' he said, 'and you'll have to forgive me if they are rather intimate by nature. But you'll understand soon why it is so important for me to know. Is it correct that you had a club foot since birth… and that you have not been circumcised?'

Joshua slid to the edge of his chair. He spread his arms in plain bewilderment and cried: 'Yes, that's right! I have a club foot and indeed, as a child I was not circumcised. That happened later.' He looked at Jacob in confusion and then asked with a cracking voice: 'But… but how do you know all this and… and how do you know me…?'

Briefly Jacob told him about his friendship with Mordecai and how the latter had managed to prevent that his newborn son Joshua ended up in the camp. 'That happened a few days before the boy was going to be circumcised and before they were going to see a specialist in Kraków for treatment of his club foot. Because of these similarities, your talent for playing the violin and the physical likeness, I am practically certain that you are Mordecai's son. And if that is indeed the case, then I can tell you that you do not have any brother or sisters, for your parents had not been married long before they were deported to *Auschwitz*. Your mother died there, but your father – and this we know for sure since last week – is still alive. My grandson Robert and his friend Debbie met him and what that was like they'd better tell you themselves.'

Robert looked at Debbie and proposed: 'You tell him; you speak better English than I.'

Debbie – impressed with all she had heard, just like the others – stared ahead with eyes that saw nothing.

'What? Uh… yes, that is alright,' she returned to reality, 'then you go and get the violin, please.'

Pensively she slowly stepped forward a few paces. She looked at Joshua and had to take a deep breath before she spoke with a clearly emotional voice: 'It has taken me so much by surprise, what I am experiencing here, that I don't really know where to start. But in any case the most important thing I have to tell is that there is still another reason to accept that you indeed have to be Mordecai's son. Robert and I met him in a hut in *Birkenau* where he played his violin with great difficulty, sitting in a wheelchair. He explained to us that he had come to that place because of a dream the night before. In that dream he was at a party at which his old friend Jacob was in the midst of all his children and grandchildren. It was happening on a lawn with behind it a row of high, old trees. Mordecai tried to play the *Song of Deliverance* at that party, but because of his disease – that has taken the strength from his muscles – he did not succeed. Then completely unexpectedly – in fact exactly like it happened here just now – his son, for whom he had been looking in vain for many years, appeared. He took the violin from him and played that same song, very beautifully and in tune. Then he woke up and decided to go back to the camp once more, with the help of the woman who takes care of him. He recognised Robert immediately as "the son of my brother Jacob", as he said. What he told us was – together with the thoughts that he gave to us – extremely impressive and valuable for us. Still, he was clearly disappointed too, because he did not meet his own son, something he had secretly hoped for. And that had undoubtedly to do with the fact that he is seriously ill and – as he said himself – feels the end approaching. He asked whether one of the children of his friend Jacob played the violin. When that turned out to be the case, he put the instrument in its case and said: "I had hoped to be able to give it to my son, but this is alright too". Then he gave the violin to Robert to...'

At this point her voice broke and tears filled her eyes. She looked away from Joshua and wiped the tears from her cheeks with the back of her hand. While Thera, who stood behind her put an arm around her shoulder and gently pulled her close, Robert walked over to Joshua and gave him the old case.

Carefully Joshua put it on his lap and – exactly as his father had done before he gave it to Robert – caressed the rough, damaged surface a few times. Then he opened the case and carefully took out the old violin and the bow. It took a while before he had tuned it to his satisfaction. When that was done, he rested the bow on his knee and a silence fell in which even the wind and the birds seemed to hold their breath. Then he gently laid it on the strings and filled the air above the Westerwal with the crystal-clear, pure tones of the *Song of Deliverance*.

Breathless and deeply moved, Debbie watched with teary eyes the children and grandchildren of Jacob van Zuiden, the lawn and the high, old trees behind it… Her eyes searched for Robert and she sensed that he too was very much aware that they were witnessing the miraculous fulfilment of Mordecai's dream.

When the last sounds of the impressive song about the coming of the Messiah had floated away, Joshua rested the bow on his knee while it remained completely quiet. Everyone sensed that applause was not appropriate here. David was the first to break the silence. He walked towards Joshua, put a hand on his arm and complimented him. Then he introduced himself and gradually an animated conversation developed between the two of them. After some time others also approached Joshua and something of the relaxed atmosphere returned.

From his chair in the corner of the garden Jacob saw all this happening and he recalled the prophecy of Mordecai. Words that had worked like an ointment on his deep wounds of being lost and lonely and that had been engrained into his memory ever since… "As I have delivered you from the yoke of the pharaoh of yesteryear, so I shall deliver you from the yoke of this oppressor. I shall return you to the city of your birth. In the midst of her inhabitants you and your children will live as a sign that I have not forgotten my people. Just as Passover is the day of my covenant with my people, so *the day after Passover* will be the day of my covenant with you and your descendants. I shall be with them so that their name shall not be blotted out of Israel…" In his mind's eye he saw Mordecai leave the hut after that, playing the song that he had just heard– as purely as then – played by Joshua and that had washed over him as a heavenly "encore" to the fulfilment of that old prophecy.

Here he was sitting – so many years later – in the city where he was born, in the midst of his children and grandchildren "whose names were not blotted out of Israel". One after the other he scrutinized them and was impressed with each person's specific contribution with which they had illuminated the darkness in his life, and by which a blanket of comfort and gratitude had gradually covered his great sadness. Benjamin - the son who grew from rebel to friend and who had helped bear the pain of this trauma by opening his heart for him in a natural, self-evident way – stood talking to Joshua. Although he could barely understand them, he knew what they were talking about. In a few days, maybe, he would travel with them to Poland. And there – on the most beautiful birthday of his life – a great longing for the country of his mother and the country of Mordecai and Joshua suddenly welled up in him. A desire also for the perception and recognition of the colors and smells, of the accents and customs in the country of his forefathers. It lifted him out of that long, slumbering fear of the confrontation with *Auschwitz*. Already he felt it as a victory that was attained only thanks to the miraculous guidance of the always Present and eternally Faithful One in his life… *Hashem*.

Unwittingly he moved his head up and down and enunciated that name once again softly and full of respect. Then he looked sideways to the high, old trees on the Westerwal. Cautiously but full of purpose he got up. He opened the little gate and walked to the top. There, a softly rustling wind invisibly carried the words that rose from the depths of his soul. High above the old oaks of the city wall they floated on still, pure tones full of gratitude and holy awe straight to the Center of his being… *Boruch Atoh Adonoi E-lo Heinu Melech Ha'olam… Praised art Thou, oh Lord our God, King of the world…*

GLOSSARY

Yiddish

Bar Mitzvah	Literally: "Son of the covenant". The celebration of religious adulthood at the age of thirteen. From that age on a Jewish boy is counted as a full-fledged member of the community
Bashert	Preordained
Besedder	Alright, OK
Bima	Elevated area in the middle of the synagogue from which the Torah is read.
Brogue	Blessings
Chochem	Sage, often used mockingly
Chupah	Traditional Jewish marriage canopy
Chutzpah	Impudence, cheek
Devarim	Deuteronomy
Falderappes	Common people
Fatherjew	A child with only a Jewish father
Goy	Non-Jew, gentile
Goyim	Non-Jews, gentiles
Habonim	National Jewish Youth Society
Holocaust	Greek word for sacrifice. Because sometimes Jewish people protest the use of this word – a sacrifice was brought voluntarily - the Hebrew word Shoah is used.
Hashem	God – literally "The Name"

Yom Kippur	Day of Reconciliation
Kaddish	Special prayer to remember the dead
Kevater	The person who brings the child into thesynagogue for the circumcision
Khutzpe	Effrontery
Klezmer	A type of music
Kehilla	Jewish congregation or community
Kol Nidre	Prayer at the beginning of the evening service on the Day of Reconciliation in which God is asked for an annulment of all the promises made to Him in the past year.
Kosher	Permitted according to biblical prescription
Lamed-Vav	Collective name of 36 subsequent just people who according to the Talmud have taken upon themselves the suffering and sins of the people from the beginning of time, in order that humanity would find grace in the eyes of God and through which the world could remain in existence.
Lechaim	To life. Toast pronounced when drinking wine or other alcoholic beverages.
Mazel Tov	Congratulations
Medina	Hebrew word meaning country
Menukha	Rest, quiet
Meshuga	Foolish, mad
Mezomme	Amount of money
Mezuza	A small container with scripture inside, containing a small portion of Deuteronomy handwritten on parchment and put on a door frame
Mishponem	Sullen or cantankerous person

Mokum	Yiddish for Amsterdam
Moshiach	Messiah
Nachas	Satisfaction
Nebbish	Pathetic person
Neshome	Soul
Nigun	Song without words
NIW	New Israeli Weekly
Ongein	Tiresome, unkind
Oświęcim	Place in Poland on the territory of which the destruction camp Auschwitz was located
Parsha	A part from the Torah
Pesach	Passover holiday when the Jews celebrate their redemption from Egypt
Pogrom	Extremely violent act against Jews
Ponem	Face
Rosh Hashanah	Jewish New year
Seder	First evening of Passover
Shalom	Peace
Shalom-aleychem	Lit. Peace be with you, used as a form of greeting
Shalom zakhar	A feast held on the first Friday night after the male child is born
Shana haba a B'Yerushalayim	Next year in Jerusalem
Shecheyonu	A blessing recited giving thanks for having lived to this time, generally recited on a holiday
Sheva Berakhot	Seven blessings
Shikse	Non-Jewish girl
Shul	Synagogue
Shoah	Great destruction (see also: Holocaust)
Smous	German pejorative for Jew
Talmud	Collected rabbinic postulates and discourses

Tenakh	Old Testament
Torah	First five books of the Bible from Moses
Togus	Buttocks, bottom
Treif	Opposite of kosher
Tzaddik	A righteous person
Versjteren	To spoil
Witz	Yiddish for joke

DUTCH-GERMAN GLOSSARY

Ajax	Amsterdam soccer club
Arbeit Macht Frei	Labor liberates
Balg	bellows
Bos	wood
De Bonte Os	The Spotted Ox
De Heerdt	livingroom of a farmhouse
De IJsbreker	The Icebreaker
De Meer	Watergraafsmeer – a district of the city of Amsterdam
De Schim	The Spectre
FC Zwolle	soccer club Zwolle
Feyenoord	Rotterdam soccer club
Kapo	Abbreviation of "kamp polizei"
Kerkstraat	Church street
KNVB	Royal Dutch Soccer League
Kraut	derogatory term for German
Lederhosen	leather pants
Mamma	mom
Manke	limping, crippled
Mavo	advanced elementary education
Nagelhout	smoked beef, thinly sliced
NIW	Netherlands-Israel Weekly
NSB	National Socialist Party

Oma	grandmother
Opa	grandfather
Oude Kerk	Old Church
Oude Kerkhof	cemetery
Papa	dad
PSV	soccer club Eindhoven
Reus	giant
Rode Hert	Red Deer
Rood-Wit	soccer club Putten
SDC	soccer club Putten
Spoor	track, trail, trace
Vlek	patch or mark
Waag	weighing station
Wittekop	blond-haired person

Chapter 1

'Ich bin, Gott sei dank, kein Deutscher…! Ich bin ein Jude, ein "Smous" und dass ich hier noch immer wohne und lebe kommt weil Sie vergessen haben meinen Vater umzubringen…!'
'I am, thank God, not German…! I am a Jew, a "Smous" and that I still live here is because you forgot to kill my father…!'

'Raus…! Raus mit Ihnen und mit den faulen Mörder…!'
'Out… Out with you and the dirty murderer…!'

EXPLANATION AND ACCOUNTABILITY

Prologue
The name Van Zuiden has been chosen at random, although it is an existing Jewish family name.

Chapter 1
For many years the synagogue of Elburg was used – due to its beautiful accoustics – as the rehearsal space for the local musical and choral societies. After the summer of 2006 the synagogue was reverted as much as possible to its original state. Since then the building serves exclusively as a museum, as a memorial to the turbulent history of the Jewish community of Elburg.

The Sabbath starts on Fridays at sunset and finished on Saturday at sunset.

Chapter 3
According to the definition of traditional Judaism whoever is born from Jewish mother is a Jew. Judaism therefore does not recognize half-Jews and considers the children of a Jewish mother and non-Jewish father entirely Jewish. According to this definition children of a Jewish father and a non-Jewish mother are therefore not Jewish.
(Source: *Wegwijs in het Jodendom* – publ. Nederlands Israëlitisch Kerkgenootschap - isbn 90-71727-12-2)

Chapter 6
On November 10th 1933 Germany commemorated the 450th anniversary of Maarten Luther's birthday. That Friday was pronounced an official holiday by the Nazi-regime. From pulpits and platforms

the message was preached that Luther's reformation would now, in Hitler's Third Reich, find its fulfilment nationally. Spiritual and National renewal mingled, as did the faith of the forefathers and the love for "Volk und Reich". Luther's and Hitler's anti-semitism merged on that "Lutherday" into a revolutionary conspiracy.
(Sources: *The Holy Reich. Nazi Conceptions of Christianity, 1919-1945* - Richard Steigmann-Gall – publ. Cambridge University Press - isbn 052/8237/4)
- *Kruis met haken*. Doris L. Bergen. (publ. Callenbach - isbn 90-26606-71-0)
- *Von den Juden und ihren Lügen*. Maarten Luther, publ. 1543. (Dutch translation by René Süss: *Luthers theologisch testament. Over de Joden en hun leugens; inleiding, vertaling, commentaar*. Publ. VU University Press, Amsterdam).

In *Protocols of the Wise Men of Sion* it is stated amongst others that Jews murdered people of different beliefs in order to eat them, and that children of Christians were slaughtered to use their blood in the preparation of *matzos*.

Exodus 4:22	Israel is my firstborn son.
Leviticus 11	Clean and unclean animals.
Leviticus 19:28b	Do not cut your bodies for the dead or put tattoo marks on yourselves.
Leviticus 21:5b	Priests must not … cut their bodies.
Matthew 4:23a	Jesus went throughout Galilee, teaching in their synagogues…
Matthew 5:17a	Do not think that I have come to abolish the Law.
Matthew 5:19a	Whomever breaks one of the least of these commandments and teaches others to do the same will be called least in the kingdom of heaven.
John 5:1	Jesus went up to Jerusalem for a feast of the Jews.

John 7:10 However, after his brothers had left for the Feast, he went also...

Chapter 7
Man's Search for Meaning. Viktor E. Frankl. (publ. Donker isbn 90-6100-173-0)

Chapter 8
Luke 2:21 Circumcision of Jesus.
Leviticus 15:24a If a man lies with her and her monthly flow touches him, he will be unclean for seven days.

Chapter 10
"Remembrance leads to deliverance, forgetting drives us into exile". Ba'al Shem-Tov, founder of the Chassidic movement in Judaism.

Chapter 11
It takes two to three generations to shake off the past. Experience with Jewish children after World War II has revealed that traumas are transmitted, issues one hasn't come to terms with are transferred from parent to child and even to grandchild.
Dr. H.C. Halberstadt-Freud/Psychoanalyst

Genesis 15:16 In the fourth generation your descendants will come back here, for the sin of the Amorites has not yet reached its full measure.
Exodus 34:7b He punishes the children and their children for the sin of the fathers to the third and fourth generation.

Chapter 12
The autobiographic novel of Marijke Spoor *The perfect child* has been published by Van Gennep (isbn 90-5515-292-7)

Chapter 13

Song of songs 2:11-12	See! The winter is past; the rains are over and gone. Flowers appear on the earth
Isaiah 2:2-4 and Micah 4:1-4	Prophecy about the coming of the Messiah and the Kingdom of Peace.

Chapter 14

The *Youth Aliyah* was founded in 1932 in Germany in order to keep as many children as possible out of the reach of the Nazis. Recha Freier, wife of a Berlin rabbi, collected forty teenagers, educated them and took them in the end to what was then Palestine. There they were received by Henriette Szold, who was appointed as the first leader of the *Youth Aliyah*. The children were then "adopted" by a kibbutz. In this way thousands of children were saved. After the war the organisation focussed on saving the children who had survived the Second World War and concentrated on the great problems of thousands of immigrant- and fugitive children that streamed into Israel.

Since its start the *Youth Aliyah* has helped more than 400.000 children find their way in the Israeli society. Just to get an idea about what this means for the country: In the year 2000, 30 of the 120 members of the Knesseth (Israeli unicameral parliament) were former *Youth Aliyah* students! (Source: Jewish Journal)

With thanks to my wife Lucy, on whom the character of Nant is based. Also, to Lub Vonhof for being involved, and to Evert de Graaf as committee member and ex-chairman of the *October 44 Foundation* for reading the manuscript critically. Above all, thanks to Annie and Gert van den Brink for their time and dedication in assessing and correcting the manuscript in the original Dutch version, Marijcke for the English translation, Johanna and Jim for their final editing and good old friend John for restyling and rewriting the poems.